Freedom's Landing

Other books by Anne McCaffrey

RESTOREE

DRAGONFLIGHT

DECISION AT DOONA

ALCHEMY & ACADEME *(Compiled by Anne McCaffrey)*

THE SHIP WHO SANG

MARK OF MERLIN*

DRAGONQUEST

RING OF FEAR*

TO RIDE PEGASUS

OUT OF THIS WORLD COOKBOOK

A TIME WHEN

KILTERNAN LEGACY*

DRAGONSONG

DRAGONSINGER

GET OFF THE UNICORN

THE WHITE DRAGON

DINOSAUR PLANET

DRAGONDRUMS

CRYSTAL SINGER

THE COELURA

MORETA, DRAGONLADY OF PERN

DINOSAUR PLANET SURVIVORS

STITCH IN SNOW*

KILLASHANDRA

THE GIRL WHO HEARD DRAGONS

THE YEAR OF THE LUCY*

NERILKA'S STORY

THE LADY *(aka* THE CARRADYNE TOUCH)*

DRAGONSDAWN

RENEGADES OF PERN

SASSINAK *(with Elizabeth Moon)*

THE DEATH OF SLEEP *(with Jody-Lynn Nye)*

PEGASUS IN FLIGHT

THE ROWAN

ALL THE WEYRS OF PERN

GENERATION/WARRIORS *(with Elizabeth Moon)*

CRISIS ON DOONA *(with Jody-Lynn Nye)*

THE PARTNERED SHIP *(with Margaret Ball)*

DAMIA

DAMIA'S CHILDREN

LYON'S PRIDE

*not science fiction—fantasy

Freedom's Landing

ANNE McCAFFREY

AN ACE/PUTNAM BOOK
Published by G. P. Putnam's Sons
New York

An Ace/Putnam Book
Published by G. P. Putnam's Sons
Publishers Since 1838
200 Madison Avenue
New York, NY 10016

Library of Congress Cataloging-in-Publication
Data

McCaffrey, Anne.
Freedom's landing / by Anne McCaffrey.
p.   cm.
ISBN 0-399-14062-X (acid-free paper)
I. Title.
PS3563.A255F74   1995   94-43820 CIP
813'.54—dc20

Printed in the United States of America

1   2   3   4   5   6   7   8   9   10

Book design by Jennifer Anne Daddio

This book is printed on acid-free paper. ∞

This book is dedicated to the memory
of a special fan/friend,
Judy Voros.
Hope heaven has chocolate (but it must!).

Freedom's
Landing

Chapter One

KRISTIN BJORNSEN WONDERED IF SUMMER on the planet Barevi could possibly be the *only* season. There had been remarkably little variation in temperature in the nine months since she'd arrived there. She'd been four months in what appeared to be the single, sprawling city of the planet during her enslavement and now had racked up five months of comparative freedom—albeit a parlous hand-to-mouth survival—in this jungle, after her escape from the city in the flitter she'd stolen.

Her sleeveless one-piece tunic was made of an indestructible material, but it wouldn't suit cold weather. The scooped neckline was indecently low and the skirt ended midway down her long thighs. It was closely modeled, in fact, after the miniskirted sheath she'd been wearing to class that spring morning when the Catteni ships had descended on Denver, one of fifty cities across the world that had been used as object lessons by the conquerors. One moment she was on her way to the college campus; the next, she was one of thousands of astonished and terrified Denverites being driven by forcewhips up the ramp of a spaceship that made the *Queen Elizabeth* look like a tub toy. Once past the black maw of the ship, Kris, with all the others, swiftly succumbed to the odorless gas. When she and her fellow prisoners had awakened, they were in the slave compounds of Barevi, waiting to be sold.

Kris aimed the avocado-sized pit of the gorupear she had just eaten at the central stalk of a nearby thicket of the purple-branched thornbushes. The bush instantly rained tiny darts in all directions. Kris laughed. She had bet it would take less than five minutes for the young bush to rearm itself. And it had. The larger ones took longer to position new missiles. She'd had reason to find out.

Absently she reached above her head for another gorupear. Nothing from good old Terra rivaled them for taste. She bit appreciatively into the firm reddish flesh of the fruit, and its succulent juices dribbled down her chin onto her tanned breasts. Tugging at the strap of her slip-tight tunic, she brushed the juice away. The outfit was great for tanning, but when winter comes? And should she concentrate on gathering nuts and drying gorupears on the rocks by the river for the cold season? She wrinkled her nose at the half-eaten pear. They were mighty tasty but a steady diet of them left her hungering for other basic dietary requirements. By watching the creatures of the jungle, she'd been able to guess what might be edible for her. Remembering her survival course gave her the clue to superficial testing on her skin. She'd had two violent reactions to stuff the ground animals seemed to devour in quantity but the avians had guided her to other comestibles. Her term in the food preparation unit of her "master" had given her other commodities to look for—though few of those grew wild in this jungle. Still, there were little yellow-scaled fish from the river that had provided her with both protein and exercise.

A low-pitched buzz attracted her attention. She got to her feet, balanced carefully on the high limb of the tree. Parting the branches, she peered up at the cloudless sky. Two of the umpteen moons that circled Barevi were visible in the west. Below them, dots that gave off sparkles of reflected sunlight were swooping and diving.

The boys have called another hunt, she mused to herself and, still smiling, leaned against the tree trunk to take advantage of her grandstand seat. The jungle had quite a few really big, really savage creatures which she had managed to avoid, making like a jungle heroine and taking to the trees and vines. By dint of hard work and sweat, she had used the useful tools from the kit on the flitter to tie vines to trees that led to and from her favorite food-browsing spots and to the river. Her escape routes were all aerial.

Before she had taken absence without leave from her "situation," Kris had done her homework on more than what was edible on Barevi. She had picked up a good bit of the lingua Barevi, a polyglot language, made up from the words of six or seven of the languages spoken by the slaves and used by the "masters" to convey orders to their minions. She had gleaned some information about those who had invaded Earth, the Catteni. They were not, for one thing, indigenous to this world but came from a much heavier planet nearer galactic center. They were one of the mercenary-explorer races employed by a vast federation. They had only recently colonized Barevi, using it as a clearinghouse for spoils acquired looting unsuspecting non-federation planets, and a rest-and-relaxation center for their great ships' crews. After years of the free fall of space and lighter-gravity planets, Catteni found it difficult to return to their heavy, depressing home world. During her brief enslavement, Kris had heard the Catteni boast of dying everywhere in the galaxy except Catten. The way they "played," Kris thought to herself, was rough enough to insure that they died young as well as far from Catten.

Huge predators roamed the unspoiled plains and jungles of Barevi, and the Catteni considered it great sport to stand up to a rhinolike monster with only a single spear. That is, Kris remembered with a grim smile, when they weren't brawling among themselves over imagined slurs and insults. Two slaves, friends of hers, had been crushed under the massive bodies of Catteni during a free-for-all.

Since she had come to the valley, she had witnessed half a dozen encounters between the rhinos and the Catteni. Accustomed to a much heavier gravity than Barevi, the Catteni were able to execute incredible maneuvers as they softened their prey for the kill. The poor creatures had less chance than Spanish bulls and, in all the hunts Kris has seen, only one man had been injured and that had been a slight graze.

As the flitters neared, she realized that they were not acting like a hunting party. For one thing, one dot was considerably ahead of the others. And by God, she saw the light flashes of the trailing flitters' forward guns firing at the "leader."

Hunted and hunters were at the foot of her valley now. Suddenly black smoke erupted from the rear of the pursued flitter. It nosed upward. It hovered reluctantly, then dove, slantingly, to strike the tumble of boulders along the river's edge, not far from her hiding place.

Kris gasped as she saw a figure, half-leaping, half-staggering out of the badly smashed flitter. She could scarcely believe that even a Catteni could survive such a crash. Wide-eyed, she watched as he struggled to his feet, then reeled from boulder to boulder, to get away from the smoldering wreck.

With a stunningly brilliant flare, the craft exploded. Fragments whistled into the underbrush as far up the slope as her retreat, and the idiotic thornbushes she had recently triggered sprayed out their poison-tipped little darts.

The smoke of the burning flitter obscured her view now and Kris lost sight of the man. The other flitters had reached the wreck and were hovering over it, like so many angry King-Kongish bees, swooping, diving, trying to penetrate the smoke.

An afternoon breeze swirled the black clouds about and Kris caught glimpses of the man, lurching still further from the crash site. She saw him stumble and fall, after which he made no move to rise. Above, the bees buzzed angrily, circling the smoke and probably wondering if their prey had gone up in the explosion.

Catteni didn't hunt each other as a rule, she told herself, surprised to find that she was halfway down from her perch. *They fight like Irishmen, sure, but to chase a man so far from the city? What could he have done?*

The crash had been too far away for Kris to distinguish the hunted man's features or build. He might just be an escaped slave, like herself. If not Terran, he might be from one of the half-dozen other subjugated races that lived on Barevi. Someone who had had the guts to steal a flitter didn't deserve to die under Catteni forcewhips.

Kris made her way down the slope, careful to avoid the numerous thorn thickets that dominated these woods. She had once amused herself with the whimsy that the thorn were the gorupears' protectors, for the two plants invariably grew close together.

At the top of the sheer precipice above the falls of the river, she grabbed the vine she had attached there for speedy descent. Once on the riverbank she stuck to the dry flat rocks until she came to the stepping-stones that allowed her to cross the river below the wide pool made by the little falls. Down a gully, across another thornbush-filled clearing, and then she was directly above the spot where she had last seen the man.

Keeping close to the brown rocks so nearly the shade of her own tanned skin, she crossed the remaining distance. She all but tripped over him as the wind puffed black smoke down among the rocks.

"Catteni!" she cried, furious as she bent to examine the unconscious man and recognized the gray and yellow uniform despite its tattered and black-smeared condition.

With a disdainful foot under his shoulder, she tried to turn him over. And couldn't. The man might as well have been a boulder. She knelt and yanked his head around by the thick slate-gray hair which, in a Catteni, did not indicate age: they all had the same color hair. Maybe he was dead?

No such luck. He was breathing. A bruise mark on his temple

showed one reason for his unconscious state. For a Catteni, he was almost good-looking. Most of them tended to have brutish, coarse features but this one had a straight, almost patrician nose, even it there was a lot more of it than an elephant would want to claim, and he had a wide well-shaped mouth. The Catteni to whom she had been sold had had thick, blubbery lips and she'd known that Catteni were developing a sexual appetite for Terran women.

A sizzling crack jerked her head around in the direction of the wreck. The damned fools were shooting at the burning craft now. Kris looked down at the unconscious man, wondering what on earth he had done to provoke such vindictive thoroughness. They sure wanted him good and dead.

The barrage pulverized what was left of the flitter, leaving the fire no fuel. The wind, laden with coarse dust, blew an acrid stench from the wreckage. The man stirred and vainly tried to raise himself, only to sink back to the ground with a groan. Kris saw the flitters circling to land on the plateau below the wreck.

"Going to case the scene of the crime, huh?"

It was completely illogical, Kris told herself, to help a Catteni simply because there were others of his race out to get him. But . . . she backtracked his route, just in case he had left any marks for them to follow. She went as far as she could on the bare rock. Where dirt began, ash had settled in a thick layer, obliterating any tracks he might have made. After all, the Catteni might stumble on her if they did a thorough search, thinking their victim had escaped the crash.

He had got to his feet when she returned to him, dazed, heavy arms hanging by his sides as he tried to get his eyes to focus. She attempted to guide him but it was like trying to direct a mountain to move.

"Come on, Mahomet," she urged softly. "Just walk like a nice little boy to the river and I'll duck you in. Cold water should bring you round."

A sharp distant gabble of voices made her start nervously. God, those Catteni had got up that rock face in a hurry. She'd forgotten they could take prodigious leaps on this light-gravity planet.

"They're coming. Follow me," she said in lingua Barevi.

He groaned again, shaking his head to clear his senses. He turned toward her, his great yellow eyes still dazed with shock. She would never get used to such butter-colored pupils with black irises.

"This way! Quickly!" She urgently tugged at him. If he didn't shake his tree-stump legs, she was going to leave him. Good Samaritans on Barevi had better not get caught by Catteni.

She pulled at his arm and he seemed to make a decision. He lurched forward, one great hand grasping her shoulder in a viselike grip. They reached the riverbank, still ahead of the searchers. But Kris groaned as she realized that the barely conscious man would never be able to navigate the stepping-stones.

The shouts behind them indicated that the others were fanning out to search the rocks. Urgently she grabbed several fingers of his big hand, leading him to the base of the falls.

"If you can't float, it's just too damned bad," she said grimly. She dropped his hand, stepped back, and leaping forward again, shouldered him into the water.

She dove in, right beside him, and when he continued to sink, she grabbed and caught him by the thick hair. Fortunately the water made even a solid Catteni manageable. Exerting all her strength and skill as a swimmer, she got his head above water and held it up with a chin lock.

By sheer good luck, they had surfaced in the space between the arc of the falls and the cliff, the curtain of water shielding them from view. As the Catteni began to struggle in her grasp, the five hunters leapt spectacularly into view in the clearing by the pool. Her "Mahomet" was instantly alert and, instead of struggling, began to tread water beside her.

The Catteni were arguing with each other now and each seemed to be issuing conflicting orders to the others.

Mahomet released himself from her chinhold, his yellow eyes never leaving the party on the bank. They watched, hands making as little movement as possible although the falls would conceal any ripples their motions made.

One Catteni, after a heated debate, crossed the wide pool in a fantastic—to Kris—standing leap. He and another began to move downstream, carefully examining both banks and casually surmounting up-ended barge-sized boulders with no effort. The other three went charging back the way they had come, still arguing.

After an endless interval, during which the icy water chilled Kris to the bone, the refugee touched her shoulder and nodded toward the shore. But when she realized that he was going to head back the way they had come, she shook her head emphatically, pointing to the other side.

"Safe! That way," she shouted at him over the noise of the falls. He frowned. "I've a flitter to hide in." She jabbed her finger in the direction of her hidden vehicle. Stunned as she suddenly realized what she had just said, she stared at him. "Oh, god!"

He raised an eyebrow in surprise, and she hoped for one long moment that he had not understood what she had said. But he had, and now his yellow eyes gleamed at her in the gloom with a different sort of interest.

He's like a great lion, Kris thought and almost choked on fear.

"You have aided a Catteni," he said in a deep rumbling voice in the lingua Barevi. "You shall not suffer for that!"

Kris wasn't so sure when she tried to climb out of the river and found herself numb with cold, and strengthless. He, on the other hand, strode easily out of the water. He looked down at her ineffectual struggles, frowning irritably. Then, with no apparent effort, he curled the long fingers of one hand around her upper arm and simply withdrew her from the water, supporting her until she got her balance.

Shivering, she looked up at him. God, he was big: the tallest Catteni she had yet seen. She had inherited the height of her Swedish father and stood five foot ten in her bare feet. She had topped most of the Catteni she had encountered by several inches, but his eyes tilted downward to regard her. And his shoulders were as broad as the scoop of a roadgrader.

"Where is this flitter?" he demanded curtly.

She pointed, furious that she obeyed him so instantly, and that she couldn't control the chattering of her teeth or the trembling of her body. He reached for her hand, relaxing his grip a little at her involuntary gasp of pain.

Replace "grubby paws" with "high-gravity paws," she told herself in an effort to keep up her spirits as she stepped out in front of him.

"I'll have to lead the way through the thorns," she said. "Or maybe thorns don't bother Catteni hides?" she added pertly.

To her surprise, he grinned at her.

"It is perhaps fortunate for you that they do."

As she turned, she realized that she had never seen a Catteni smile before. She noticed, too, that he was following carefully in her footsteps. It was good to know that he was no more anxious to disturb the thorn-bushes with their vicious little barbs than she was.

They were halfway to the hidden flitter when both heard, off to the right in the valley, the staccato volley of loud Catteni voices.

Mahomet paused, dropping to a half-crouch, instinctively angling his body so that he did not touch the close-growing vegetation. He listened, and although the words were too distorted for Kris to catch, he evidently understood them. A humorless smile touched his lips and his eyes gleamed with a light that frightened Kris.

"They have seen movement here. Hurry!" he said in a low voice.

Kris broke into a jog trot; the twisting path made a faster pace unwise. When they broke into the dell just before the extensive thicket, she paused.

"Where? Are you lost?" he asked.

"Through those bushes. Watch. And when I say move, move!"

He frowned skeptically as she picked up a handful of small stones.

With a practiced ease and careful gauge, she threw in a broad cast to left and right, watching and counting the thorn sprays to be sure she had triggered every bush. To be on the safe side, she scooped up one more handful of pebbles and threw that in a wider arc. No further thorns showered.

"Move!" His reaction time was so much faster than hers that he was halfway across the clearing before she got to the "v." She dashed in front of him. "We have five minutes to cross before they rearm."

An expression that was almost respectful crossed his face. Impatiently, she tugged at him and then began to weave her way among the bushes, following her well-memorized private route through this obstacle. When she made the last turn and he saw the flitter, its nose cushioned in the heavy cluster of thorn-thicket limbs, he gave what Kris assumed was a Catteni chuckle.

She waved open the flitter door and regally gestured for him to enter. He walked straight to the instrument panel, grunting as he activated the main switch.

"Half a tank of fuel," he muttered and cursorily checked the other readings. He glanced up at the transparent top, camouflaged by the intertwining leafy limbs, at the bed she had made herself on the deck, at the utensils she had fashioned from spare parts in the lockers.

"So it was you who stole the commander's personal car," he said, looking intently at her.

Kris jerked her chin up.

"At least I landed it in one piece," she said.

At that he gave one bark of laughter.

"Dropping it in a thicket like this?"

"On purpose!"

"You're one of the new species?"

"I'm a Terran," she said with haughty pride, her stance marred by a convulsive shiver.

"Thin-skinned species," he remarked. He looked at her chest, noticed the slight heave from her recent exertions that made her breasts strain against the all too inadequate covering and slowly started to stroke her shoulder with one finger. His touch was unexpectedly feather-light—and more. "Soft to the touch," he said absently. "I haven't tried a Terran yet . . ."

"And you're not going to start on this one," she said, jumping as far away from him as she could in the confines of the cabin.

His expression altered from bemusement to annoyance.

"I will if I so choose."

"I saved your life!"

"Which is why I intend to reward you suitably . . ."

"By raping me?" She felt for and found a heavy metal tool. Not that such a comparative "toothpick" would do a Catteni much damage but she was determined to try. A Catteni was not her idea of a candidate for the role of lover.

"Raping you?" His surprise was ludicrous.

"Did you think Terran women would faint with joy to be had by the likes of you?" she said, speaking in a low menacing voice and resetting her grip on the tool.

"None have complained . . ." He broke off, ducking with incredible reflexes to a crouch as they both heard harsh cursing.

In the next instant, he had one large hand over her mouth and was pinning her body to his like a fly to sticky paper. The metal tool dangled uselessly in her hand. Neither of them had closed the flitter door and the *vrrh vrrh* as the thornbushes released their darts was plainly audible. There were loud exclamations of disgust and further cursings. Screwing her eyes around, she could just see the Catteni's face and his left eye dancing with malicious amusement.

An authoritative voice uttered a rough command, and even Kris understood that it would probably translate "Get the hell out of here. Nothing came this way."

Mahomet shifted her slightly, looking down at her face as he dropped his hand from her mouth, a gesture that was in part a challenge for her to scream. She glared back at him. He knew perfectly well that she stood to lose more if she did cry out.

They stayed like that until wildlife noises were again to be heard outside the flitter. Then he stood her back on her feet and glanced about him again.

"This car has been gone five months. Why have you stayed so long alone? Are there others of you nearby?" He peered out the one portion of the wrap-around window that had a view of more than branches.

"Just me." She still had the metal tool in her hand and was wondering if she could hit him hard enough to knock him unconscious. "Why were other Catteni so bent on catching you?"

"Oh," and he shrugged negligently, "a tactical error. I was forced to kill their patrol leader. He had insulted a brother Emassi," and now she caught the syllables of the strange word. "As I was without allies, I withdrew."

"He who fights and runs away, lives to fight another day?"

"The next day," he corrected her absently.

"The next day!"

"Certainly. It is the Catteni Law that a quarrel may not be continued past the same hour of the following day. I have only to lie hidden," and he grinned at her, "until tomorrow at sun zenith and then I can return."

"They won't be waiting for you?"

He shook his head violently. "Against the Law. Otherwise, we Catteni would quickly exterminate each other."

"You honestly mean to tell me that, if they can't find you before noon tomorrow, they have to give up?"

He nodded.

"Even when you killed their patrol leader?"

He looked surprised. "It was a fair fight."

"I didn't know you Catteni fought fair."

"We do," and he bridled at her accusation, then his face cleared of irritation and he grinned. "Oh, you think it wasn't fair of us to take over your planet?"

"Precisely."

He straddled the pilot's chair and rested his heavily muscled forearms on the back of it, highly amused by her indignation.

"Your planet had no defenses. It was pathetically easy to subjugate."

"You do that a lot then?"

"A highly profitable business, I assure you. How have you fed yourself?" he asked and she heard the most incredible sound, coming from him, and realized that Catteni stomachs could rumble with hunger just like humans'. Oddly enough that made him seem less menacing.

"There's a lot edible in this forest and I fish from the river."

"You do?"

"I come from an ingenious species," she said. "I've had no trouble at all keeping myself well fed."

He inclined his head respectfully. "Have you any supplies in here?"

Deciding that she did not care to come within grabbing distance, she nodded to the basket on the control panel behind him. "Gorupears and the roots of a white plant that I have found quite edible." As he turned, she caught him wrinkling his nose and heard him sigh. "No diet for a Catteni, I'm sure, accustomed as you are to the best viands in the galaxy, but the simple fare will stop your stomach roaring. The noise of it could give our position away."

He did not, as she had observed some Catteni do, cram the entire pear in his mouth. He also picked up one of the roots, which had a sweetish taste, not unlike a carrot, and switched from one hand to the other, taking polite mouthfuls. Finishing the first pear, he turned to her and raised his eyebrows in a polite query.

"Thank you, no. I had just eaten when I saw the dogfight."

"Dogfight?"

"A Terran term, derived from the aerial combat of fighter planes."

"Fighter planes?"

"We had achieved space flight, too," she added, wondering as pride made her speak out, if any of the SAC units had been launched when the Catteni had invaded Terran space.

"Ah, yes, so you had. Primitive defenses but manned by brave fighters."

Her heart sank. So often lately the answers she discovered were not the ones she wanted to hear. One of the slaves in the compound from the Chicago area had said that surface-to-air missiles had been fired at the Catteni vessels. Terran national leaders had been slow to take a defensive position, not knowing who or what had penetrated so far into the atmosphere. They had dallied too long to make any difference. Bill had been wearing his Walkman and had heard the broadcasts up till the time he had been whipped into the Catteni ship. By talking amongst themselves, the captives had learned that not all big cities had been attacked and looted: just sufficient so that the entire world recognized the superiority of the invaders. Not much consolation for those who had been abducted but enough to restore some pride.

"We disarmed most of them," Mahomet went on in a matter-of-fact voice, "and grounded the airships. Clumsy but showing some signs of developments to come."

"Thanks."

He raised his eyebrows queryingly. "For what?"

"Such praise for the primitive savages!"

Then he threw back his head and indulged in a loud guffaw.

"Ssssh, they'll hear you. You bray like an ass!"

"And you talk like a Catteni female!"

"Do I take that as a compliment?"

"You may," and he inclined his head in her direction, his yellow eyes twinkling in a humorous response she had never seen in other Catteni.

"You're not at all like the others."

"Which others?"

"*All* the other Catteni I've met, and observed."

"Of course I'm not. I'm Emassi," he said with a quiet pride, splaying his great hand across his chest in what she could interpret as a prideful gesture.

"Whatever that is."

"A high rank," he said. With a dismissive flick of fingers sticky with gorupear juice in the general direction of the city she had escaped from, he consigned the local Catteni to an inferior status. "I order. They obey," he added, making certain she understood the distinction.

"And those trying to kill you? They obeyed?"

"Their patrol leader's dying words," he said, with a negligent shrug and a grin, "to make me pay for his death." Then he frowned, looking down at the floor as if reconsidering their import. "Never mind. By noon tomorrow all will revert. Now," and as he began to rise from the chair, intent plain on his face, Kris no longer hesitated.

With a karate-style leap, she flung herself at him, both hands on the metal tool, and brought it down with all the strength in her body on the side of his head. With a groan he collapsed to the floor.

Had she killed him? Horrified at taking a life, even that of an arrogant Catteni, she knelt beside him, noting that red blood flowed from the creased skull, and felt his throat. If he had blood, he had veins: and since he was shaped like most humanoids, he ought to have a pulse in the neck to carry blood to the brain she had just tried to smash. He had! It wasn't even faint but a firm throb against her seeking fingers. Which quickly became sticky with the blood that pulsed from his head wound.

Oh, this would never do, she told herself. The little nasty stingers would smell blood and come searching for the source. The flitter would be unlivable. First she bound up the wound with the absorbent material she had found in the lockers. Then she carefully cleaned up the rest of the blood on his face and rubbed the exposed grayish skin with gorupear juice. That had neutralized the smell for stingers on other occasions: a handy survival tip she had serendipitously discovered on her own.

One of his massive legs had caught on the chair as he fell. It looked uncomfortable that way, and the fabric of his pants were caught against his genitals, outlining the size of them in a way that made her acutely embarrassed for him. And affected her in the oddest way. Well, she told herself, she had no reason, really, to offend the dignity of another living being if she objected to indignities herself. Kris had a strong sense of fair play. She might have conked him to protect her virtue, but that done, she felt obliged to make him as comfortable as possible. How long would the blow keep him unconscious? And, once he regained his senses, what would he do to her? Well, she thought, she could always cite the Catteni rule about reprisals! Quite likely that rule did not apply to slaves or non-Catteni. She looked through the lockers to find something to tie him up with. There was a length of sturdy rope but no chains and that was the only sort of restraint that might prove effective against Catteni strength.

She sat down on the pilot's chair and rethought her circumstances. It had been a tiring day. And nearly at its end. Well, what if she returned him whence he had come? With darkness falling, there'd be a fair amount of traffic back into the city, so this purloined flitter might not be recognized: not after five months. How long did Catteni keep up "wanted" notices? Twenty-four hours? Perhaps for Catteni Emassis but not for escaped slaves—that is, if anyone had even noticed her disappearance. She switched on the controls, reassured that he had said the tank was half full. She couldn't remember how the gauge had stood when she absconded but the little aircraft was supposed to be economical, which was why there were so many in use.

She knew the coordinates of the city, a good two-hour flight from here, but surely there'd be enough fuel for her to get back. No matter. She had to dump Mahomet. She'd get him to the outskirts where a limp ˌbody wouldn't be that uncommon. Well, maybe not the outskirts where the slaves and hangers-on lived in semi-squalor. But there were all those assembly areas where Catteni held drills and public meetings. She'd been to one or two with the cook, who found such displays helpful in maintaining discipline. One view of a miscreant lashed to death with the forcewhips was enough for her. Enough to revive her desire to get as far away from such a discipline as possible.

Powered up, she reversed the flitter out of its concealing thicket. She really had been lucky in that landing, which had by no means been as planned as she inferred to Mahomet. She hadn't been watching the altimeter the night of her escape or realized that the plains surrounding the city had altered to a hilly terrain. She'd felt the scrape of something on the belly of the flitter, panicked, and the nose had dipped. She'd been in the middle of the thicket, and plastered with thorns from the angry bushes, before she could correct the error. It had worked out. Kris had a great and abiding belief that things would work out—if you lived long enough to let them.

She headed the flitter southeast, but not before marking again the coordinates of her retreat. She'd have to come back in daylight or she'd miss the thicket. The branches sprang back up again as soon as the flitter released them.

The lights of the city guided her more surely than the directional equipment. Only the altering position of the needle on one dial face informed her that it was a compass. She supposed there was an autopilot but she hadn't figured which switch for that. She knew as much as she did about flying because she'd had to accompany the cook to the markets for fresh produce every day and had figured out the basics from watching him. Then, when she'd seen the commander's flitter, she couldn't resist the temptation it presented. So she hadn't. Like Oscar Wilde, she could resist anything except temptation. Much good her English Literature was doing her now: it was all the extracurricular stuff, like orienteering, that course in survival skills which her mother had laughed about, and her karate course that were invaluable. Like downing heavy planet denizens. She glanced down at Mahomet but he hadn't so much as twitched a muscle. The bleeding had apparently stopped.

The city looked rather nice lit up, she thought, with floodlights on some of the more unusual architectural styles: not that the huge looming Catteni Headquarters building smack dab in the center of the hub layout of Barevi City would win any prizes. There seemed to be a lot of lights on in the city or maybe it was because she was seeing it on an overview, rather than being in the middle of it. There wasn't enough lighting in the outskirts as she approached them for her to find a good landing spot. Well, she'd go on until she found one of the assembly areas. They were ringed by the stumpy tree forms that had been planted to supply some shade for onlookers of Catteni ceremonies. Plenty of space for her to land the flitter. Strangely enough she didn't see many flitters coming into the city from her direction. Well, she *had* come from open jungle lands. But there seemed to be a great number of the larger army type spreading out from the Catteni HQ.

Something was going on, she realized when she opened the door to the flitter. There was a lot of noise, and it had a menacing sound to it. Of course such distant murmurs often sounded more threatening than they were. She'd just hurry and be out of here in next to no time and on her way back to her hideaway.

She got the rope she'd seen in the locker and tied it around Mahomet's feet. Then she looped that about a stumpy tree trunk. She'd winch his body out. She got his feet and most of his legs, but his butt stuck at the lip of the door frame. She was so busy tugging and pulling his posterior over the obstacle that she didn't notice how much closer all that sound was. And lights. Even the dark assembly area was brighter. Peering down the access lanes that led to the area, she could see lights. Torches? And the rumble was definitely intimidating. What was going on in Barevi City?

The sound made her redouble her efforts to haul Mahomet out of the flitter. The trunk of the man must have weighed half a ton, for she could not budge it. The noise was very definitely heading in this direction and so was the aerial traffic. She stepped over his inert body and tried to lift his torso and shove him out the door. He'd only drop a foot and with his hard head, he was unlikely to hurt himself. Grunting, straining, propping her feet against the column of the pilot's chair, she tried every which way to move Mahomet.

Noise and light were erupting into the far side of the assembly area. She'd better get him back in and *leave!* She skipped over his body, undid the rope from his feet, and was starting to angle his legs back in the flitter when she heard the heavy rumble of big aircraft and felt the compression of air over her. She was panting with her exertions and had no time to cover her nose and mouth as the first sweet, and all too familiar, reek filled the air about her. She collapsed over her victim's feet, wondering why she had been foolish enough to risk her freedom for a Catteni overlord!

Chapter Two

THE INDESCRIBABLE STENCH OF MANY frightened bodies in a close confinement and the unmistakable sssslash of a forcewhip and a scream roused Kris to her recurrent nightmare. She was lodged between two warm and sweating bodies, her cheek against a cold hard surface, her knees up under her chin, in an awkward and uncomfortable position. She wondered she'd remained unconscious so long. Maybe she just didn't want to recognize that she was in a Catteni holding cell. Which was holding far too many right now. It was dark, though not as dark as the hold of the transport vessel had been. She didn't know if that was a blessing or not.

She moved carefully, because she seemed to ache all over and she could feel bruises and scrapes on her uncovered legs, arms, and face. The cold of the wall felt good against a sore cheek.

But there was movement now her eyes were

open and adjusted to the semi-gloom. It was a low-ceilinged chamber of crowd-containment size: she could barely make out the perimeter. The place seethed with bodies but then she saw that there were two openings and bodies were being pushed out into a brighter space beyond.

Catteni whips sssslashed out again and those around her got quickly to their feet, following the example of those in the outer ranks. Rank was right, she thought, breathing shallowly so as not to taste the disgusting air she had to inhale.

She got to her feet by supporting herself against the wall. The person on her right groaned in pain. Kris found herself trying to help the woman, for it was a female, one of the Deski, so slight and spindly-limbed that she was afraid even her helping hand would break a bone. They must be a lot tougher than they looked, she thought, or they'd never survive the usual callous treatment accorded all species by the Catteni.

The whiplash sang dangerously close to her and she ducked. One of the disadvantages of being tall, but she'd got the Deski to her feet and supported her swaying body. Automatic reflexes of the good Samaritan were also a disadvantage, she thought. *I can't help everyone. So help the ones you can.* She put both hands on the Deski's stick-thin shoulders to keep the creature upright as they moved away from the wall, in the general direction the Catteni wanted them to move—the doors.

So she—and Mahomet—had been caught up in the Catteni crowd-control. Well, he was probably out of it since they could scarcely think he was one of the mob that they had quelled with their gas sprays. Her timing was as usual faultless: right back where she'd started. Well, not quite but near enough to make no nevermind. Still, if she'd escaped once, she could do it again. She had to cheer herself up.

They moved close enough to the door now to see that the next room was full of spraying water. One of those mass showers the Catteni used to cleanse captives. There were occasional short pauses as the Catteni guard at the door stripped clothing off. She gritted her teeth. The procedure had overtones she didn't like but she'd been through this sort of line in the slave pens and had come out the other side alive—and breathing fresh air. Anything was better than the stench behind her.

Disrobing her was simple. The Catteni simply ran the cutter down the front of her tunic, pulled at the back, and shoved her forward, naked, into the hot spray. It felt good, battering her from below, above, and all sides. It smelled slightly better than the room she'd just left but the disinfectant was undoubtedly a wise and sensible addition. She walked as quickly as she could, her eyes front and unfocused so she wouldn't *see* anything. The water was hot enough to cause a misting, so there wasn't that much to see but bodies, green, gray, and other shades of pale, moving through it. Then they were in the drying room and assailed by jets of air almost too hot on skin roughened by the disinfectant, but she was dry by the time she had traversed that chamber. A slight pause at the exit and she was handed a bundle and peremptorily gestured to move quickly forward. She found enough space in this dressing room and clambered into the coverall. How her size had been estimated, she didn't know, but the garment fit. The lumps that constituted Catteni-style footwear folded around her feet and took the shape of them in the first few moments. Handy enough if masses of different size and shape feet had to be covered. There was one of the thin thermal blankets which she rolled up and tied over her left shoulder with the strings attached to the ends.

When she was clad, she joined the line going through the next entrance where she was given a cup and a package about a handspan square and about eight centimeters thick. As others did, she tucked the package behind the blanket. She was pushed along to where hairy brindle Rugarians were ladling a steaming liquid into cups and then she was allowed out, thank God, into fresher air and a huge force-field netted assembly area. Catteni marched along a catwalk above it, sending their whips in random directions to remind the prisoners that they were there and *watched.* Having noticed that the perimeter walls were occupied by the early comers, she worked her way deeper in the center: the other area generally safe from forcewhip lengths. And started to sip the soup. It was hot and it was liquid, both of which her belly appreciated, but it was the tasteless sort of filling food that was definitely mass-produced prisoner issue. She noticed that some people had opened their packages which contained the sort of ration bars that had been handed out in the slave quarters. The way the rations were being wolfed down, it was fairly obvious some folks hadn't eaten regularly. And if the Catteni gave them rations in advance, she rather suspected she'd better hang on to hers. They did nothing out of charity: always expediency.

Metallic clangings echoed over the silent throng as the doors through which people had filed were shut. She wondered what was going to happen next but getting clean and being fed was somehow encouraging. Talking was never encouraged in such gatherings and, while Kris had noted that there were representatives of all the common species she'd seen in Barevi City, and she was currently in a group of Terrans, no one had spoken to her. And everyone was avoiding eye contact.

A second series of metal clangings and once again the forcewhips slashed out over the assembled. This time they were driven toward eight apertures which, when she reached the one nearest her, gave access to a ramp. She'd seen such a ramp once before and she started to tremble with apprehension. Where were they being driven this time?

A low terrified murmur arose from those already going up the ramp, and occasional cries of distress, but no one could have backed out: the rampway was narrow and barred. Catteni appeared with the short force sticks that ensured the prisoners would keep moving. The sticks hurt more than the forcewhips and both could be lethal.

As she was pushed toward the ramp by the press of bodies behind her, her height gave her the clearance to see over heads and into a dark place. Closer, she could also smell the combined acrid odors of metal and fuel and realized they were being packed into a transport of some kind that was adjacent to the processing area. She had to give the credit to the

Catteni mind-set that they sure knew how to get the unwilling to do what they wanted them to do and go where they wanted them to go. No Disney World this!

She was halted by a Catteni force stick barring her way. She sucked in her guts so it wouldn't touch her. A hatch slid shut in front of her. The ramp which had been aimed at a lower level now purred softly and moved level with the walkway she stood on. A second hatch slide open, the force stick was lifted, and she ducked into the ship. She, and those emerging from the seven other entrances, moved quickly across the low-ceilinged compartment to the far wall. As she sat down to claim her space, she had a chance to look at the others piling in. A gasp of astonishment escaped her as she saw the unmistakable figure of Mahomet ducking through the low door. She had very little time to be surprised, even less to get comfortable and tuck her food package inside her coverall for safer keeping. Suddenly she was having trouble keeping her eyes open and a strange lassitude spread to her arms and legs. Looking around her, she realized that others were obviously feeling the same way. So the soup had been dosed. Why did she not feel surprised? Some sort of folded as they entered and had to be pushed out of the way of the rest of this consignment. Some crawled a few feet to stretch out in a clear space. *Here we go again* was her last conscious thought.

KRIS WOKE, FEELING AS IF EVERY MUSCLE IN HER BODY HAD been wrenched out of alignment and every bit of soft tissue bruised. She had a headache, a very dry mouth, and her stomach was so empty she was nauseous. Once again she felt the press of warm bodies against her. But the air around her was fresh, free of stench, and her lungs welcomed it. Her eyes felt glued together and she had to fight with her eyelashes to part her lids. What she saw made her close them quickly and speak sternly to herself to recover from the shock. She was lying in a field of bodies, bodies front, left, right and center. And she certainly wasn't anywhere on Barevi. Not with that lavenderish sky.

There was an argument going on somewhere to her right, at least, loud male voices and some odd snorts and grunts. There was also a lot of low moaning and groaning in the background. She wasn't the only one coming round after that damned soup.

Forcing herself to move, she managed to raise herself on one elbow, ignoring the twinges of abused flesh and stiff muscles. Blinking to clear her eyes of grit, she carefully turned her head toward the sounds of dispute. A group of males were evidently contesting the possession of a line of crates. Several were standing atop them and sunlight flashed on knife blades. The ones on the ground were mainly aliens: the goblinesque, squatty Turs, never very pleasant to deal with and given more to grunts than words, some hairy Rugarians, and the green-skinned Ilginish.

Well, knives certainly hadn't been issued before this voyage. Why were they available at the destination? So the prisoners could dispatch enough souls to have more for the victors? That wasn't a likely supposition. Even for a Catteni procedure. Unless there weren't any Catteni around here.

She pushed herself to a sitting position, noting that others were conscious but evidently very unsure of how to proceed now. There were no Catteni anywhere in sight. Not even Mahomet, though he'd have to be here, too, she thought, since he'd also been aboard the transport.

"You only got two hands," the shouted words drifted to her and were repeated in lingua Barevi. Unmistakable gestures emphasized the next words. "You've got three knives now. Go on. Get out of here. Take off. Beat it. Go away!" That last was said in English.

Americans! She grinned with a fatuous pride in her compatriot. She watched until the knot of aliens finally moved off, up the hill and out of sight. That led her to another discovery. Not only was the sky the wrong color, the trees lining this field were of unfamiliar shape. They didn't have leaves, not that she could see, but sort of bottle-brush tufts of a not-quite-green shade.

The desiccated condition of her mouth and throat could not longer be denied, especially when her survey of the area included half a dozen people kneeling down at what must be a stream, for they were dipping their cups in and then drinking. That was when she became conscious that the fingers of her left hand were sore from the death grip she had on her cup, still bearing traces of the drugged soup.

She'd rinse it real good before she did any drinking. And she wouldn't drink too much at first go, she told herself, remembering her survival course again. No one of those drinking seemed to be suffering any ill effects as she watched. And watching them drink became unbearable. She had to moisten her mouth and throat and guts.

She struggled to her feet, still holding the cup and lurching against the person lying sideways to her. She saved herself from falling on her face by propping her free hand on a cocked, bony hip.

"Sorry," she said automatically but the body didn't so much as twitch.

It also felt cold and rigid through the coverall material. Startled, she peered up at the gaunt, odd-cheeked face—a Deski, and from the open mouth and staring eyes, another casualty to Cattenti mass productions.

"You poor devil," she murmured, shaking spasmodically. She got up in the next try, as much to get away from the corpse as to get to the water. That was her first priority.

She started in a direct line to the stream before she noticed what some people were doing in and around the water and veered uphill. As she neared the stream, she saw that it bordered this field, coming from beyond the oddly formed tall vegetation and cascading in almost steps down past the field and beyond the trees on the lower edge. The sound of the water rippling spurred her stumbling steps into a firmer stride. Only the severest self-control kept her from dropping to her belly and burying her face in the clear stream. The water was divinely clear, running over a rocky bottom. Such a stony bed would filter out most impurities. Besides, the Catteni had put them close to water so they'd probably tested it. No one farther down the stream had yet showed ill effects, although the way in which they were contaminating the stream disgusted her. Still, the water before her was clear. She dropped to her haunches and rinsed the cup, doing a bit of polluting herself as a film of the residue in the cup was carried away. She only allowed herself to scoop out enough to cover the bottom of the cup. She sipped once to moisten dry lips. Sipped again and rinsed the cool, sweet water around in her mouth, letting the parched tissues absorb the moisture. Her throat demanded its share. She swallowed slowly, attempting to trickle the water down drop by drop. They landed coldly in the pit of her stomach and her system insisted on more of the same. By then her taste buds had revived enough to appreciate the taste of the water, better by far than any designer water she had ever drunk either at home in Philadelphia or in Colorado. Good, simon-pure, mountain spring water.

A loud altercation started among the people downstream of her. Well, maybe not an unpleasant argument for there seemed to be cupsful of water thrown about. A few people moved away, out of the range, content to watch as they drank from their cups. She watched and sipped. She was not about to get embroiled in any group, not until she had figured out a few details: like where were they? What were they doing here? Were there any Catteni in discreet guard over them? What besides knives were in those crates and who had taken control of them? She intended to get at least one knife. Preferably two—one to hide in her boot. That once-derided survival course had included instructions on how to sharpen, use, and throw a knife. And the guys on the top of the crates *were* humans.

Thirst eased somewhat, her stomach started growling. She reached in her coverall and took out the package, carefully opening it. That was why they'd been given food ahead of time, then. To eat at this destination. Water laid on. As she'd also no idea how long she'd been without eating, or drinking, she broke off a third of the bar and carefully nibbled at that, interspersing it with more judicious sips of water. By the time she'd finished her portion, she felt considerably better.

She rose and looked around her with a keener interest. More bodies were moving among those laid out like disaster victims, row after row. The field must be a couple of acres at least and it was covered. Here and there were empty places where people had roused. There were more empty spaces—she counted—than the number of upright people she could see. How many had been chased off by the guys on the crates?

She dipped her cup for one more draught of cold, pure Adam's Ale and sipped as she hiked slowly around the bodies, toward the crates. When she could see both sides of the crates, she realized that there were quite a few people lounging on the far side: mostly Terrans and some of them female. That was reassuring.

"Whatcha guardin' there, fellas?" she asked when she got close enough, giving a friendly wave with her free hand.

Kris was accustomed to reactions to her tall lanky self. It never hurt to be blonde and moderately attractive. Until the men got past the usual trite remarks and innuendoes, she kept her smile intact and kept sipping her water a few safety lengths from the nearest one.

"Anybody sussed out where we are or what they've done with us?" She directed that query to the men on top of the crates. She could see now that most of the containers had been broken open to discover the contents. She saw other items besides knife blades of which there seemed to a great many.

"Knives, hatchets," the man said. He was a heavyset man in his mid-to-late thirties and had the unmistakable air of the military in his stance. He had two knives tucked in his belt, one in each boot to judge by the way his pants bulged out at his ankles. His thermal blanket was stuffed with other items for it bulged across his chest. "Some medical kits with basic bandages and that orange stuff the Cats poured on anything that bleeds."

"You in charge then?"

He made a gesture with one hand and a second Terran jumped down, a knife on his open palm, the handle toward her. He was as well equipped with extras as the first speaker.

"Can I show you how to use it, beautiful?" the guy asked, leering at her.

"You mean—like this," she said, taking the knife from his hand, hefting it a moment to get its balance before she flicked it into the nearest crate, which it penetrated enough to hold it firm.

"Whoa!" The man jumped back, hands up in front to fend her off. Above her she caught sight of a blade in the military man's hand. "Didn't mean no offense, sister."

"No offense taken," she said airily and retrieved the blade, checking the point to be sure it hadn't been nicked. "Good steel."

"It's not steel," the military man said, hunkering down so he was on a level with her. He held out a weaponless hand. "Nice to see a woman who knows the value of a knife. Chuck Mitford."

"Army?" she asked.

"Marine," he replied firmly and correctingly as marines generally did after such a question.

"Kris Bjornsen. Where'd you get taken?"

"Recently?" He spoke with considerable bitterness. "Or do you mean on good ol' Terra?"

"Both," she said and went back to sipping what water hadn't spilled out of her cup when she'd shown off her knife skill.

"Some damned fools started a riot at one of the discipline assemblies," he said in a growl and in the southernish drawl that had become military standard among American forces. The other man looked about to erupt. "Okay, okay, some of the poor dumbheads they were whipping to death were Terrans, too, but damned stupid to attack Catteni even if there were a helluva lot more of us than them." He made a throat noise of disgust.

"We've taken enough from them, sarge," the other man said, his resentment boiling over.

Mitford acted like a sergeant, too, Kris thought and decided he'd be a good ally.

"And look where it got us," he barked back. "Arnie here's never been against a superior force. Thinks being brave is all there is to overcoming dictators." He ignored Arnie then. "I was on leave from my unit in Lubbock, Texas, when we got pearl-harbored. Haven't found a trace of my family." He shut his mouth tight then.

"Denver," Kris said. She turned to Arnie. "You?"

"DC."

She hadn't encountered anyone from the Philadelphia area so maybe the rest of her family was still safely at home. If that was a safe place to be with Catteni overlords.

"Could I have some of those medical supplies, if they're going begging?"

"Sure," and Mitford walked along the top of the crates while she followed on the ground. Arnie stayed a discreet step behind her. "I figured someone had better take charge of supplies like these," and he pointed down to yet another crate of knives. At the next one he stooped and came up with a hatchet, which he handed to her. "Here. Might as well have one of these, too. There aren't more ration bars so make the ones you got do until we can figure out what's edible on this effing planet."

"I'd planned to," she replied, tucking the hatchet in the belt at her back. She'd hack off a piece of the thermal blanket to make sheaths for knives and hatchet. Mitford handed her a compact kit, already supplied with a broad shoulder strap.

"Hasn't got much medicine. Cats don't use it, seems like. Tough mothers!"

"Hey, sarge," yelled a man, running full tilt toward them, and pointing back over his shoulder. "There's a Catteni! He's waking up. Let's kill the bastard before he does."

Roaring out an order for others to join him, Mitford jumped down, a knife already in his hand.

"Wait a minute," Kris said, holding up her hands. "If a Catteni's here with us, he's as much a prisoner as we are."

"Who cares? He's a Cat and Cats should die," Arnie said, moving around her.

Kris started after them, running to catch up with Mitford, who was the leader.

"Sarge, I saw one Catteni in the same hold as I was. And he's a good guy."

"There're no good Cats!" Mitford said in a snarl, chopping at the air with one flat, finger-braced hand.

"There are," she said just as fiercely. "And if it's the one I think it, don't kill him."

"You're asking too much, girl."

"Not right away at least. Use the sense God gave you, Mitford," she said. "If it's the Catteni I think it is, he'll know a lot we have to find out about this place. Unless there were some guide books in those crates."

Mitford halted so abruptly, the three men right behind him bounced off his back. Narrowing his eyes, he glared at her.

"And how would you know that about him, girl?"

"Because I watched him being hunted by other Catteni. They blasted him out of the sky, and then blew up the crashed plane and searched all around until they were damned sure he'd been blown up in it."

"Then how come he's alive and here?" Arnie wanted to know.

"Because I thought he was an escaped slave like me and hid him under the falls until the hunters left. Only then we got captured together," Kris said, which was true enough. "When I came to in the prison, I assumed he'd been released. Cattenis can't hold grudges past twenty-four hours, you know." Mitford gave a curt nod of acknowledgment. "They must have hated him real bad to dump him in with us.

Besides which, you'd only be doing the Cats' dirty work for them."
Mitford scowled at her and she realized that she'd been clever to bring
that up. "Hell's bells, man, they'd *expect* us to waste him, wouldn't they?
So let's find out—first—what he knows. Then you can kill him." She
said that cheerfully, hoping to God and little green apples that Mahomet
would be able to show himself useful enough so that they wouldn't kill
him. She found it odd in herself to think that way about the Catteni but
he wasn't like the others . . .

"We sure could use some gen about this place," Mitford agreed
reluctantly, glancing around. He gave a convulsive twitch. "Place is too
neat for an unsettled world and I'd rather know what we got to contend
with *now* before we stumble into big kimchee with only knives and
hatchets."

He strode on then, to the man who'd discovered the Catteni. He
pointed in the proper direction and then followed them. It was Mahomet
all right, and she bent down beside him, turning the heavy head to expose
where she'd belted him with the tool. A scar was there but it was well
healed.

"Ohho," she said.

"Ohho, what?" Mitford asked as the other men ranged themselves
around Mahomet. Their expressions were unfriendly and most of them
had knives in their hands.

She pointed to the scar. "I clobbered him there. And it's healed. We
were a long time getting here."

"Kill him now before he wakes," Arnie said in a snarl, leaning over,
knife hand raised.

"*No!*" Mitford's word snapped Arnie erect. "The girl's got something in keeping him alive, and able to talk. Don't tell me he speaks
English?" There was a little more respect for her in Mitford's eyes now
and Kris realized that he'd been thinking she'd been Mahomet's toy.

"Enough lingua Barevi for us to understand him."

She splashed the little water that was left in her cup over the

Catteni's face and he reacted by lifting a hand to his face and moving stiffly from side to side. When his foot connected with someone's leg, she could see him tense. He drew his leg back and, in one quick lithe movement, was on his feet, arms held slightly out from his sides, alert and ready to defend himself despite the knife-carrying odds against him.

"Easy there," Kris said, stepping in front of him. "Remember me?"

He shot a quick glance at her but his eyes went right back to Mitford. Though the Sergeant wasn't holding a knife, Mahomet had immediately taken him as the leader. Kris gave him full marks for quick appraisals.

"Yes. You stole the commander's flitter," he said in lingua Barevi.

"*You* did?" Arnie exclaimed. "You bitch!" And he shoved his face right up at her. His breath was vile but she held her ground and glared down at him, once again glad of the extra inches that had made her adolescence a trial. "I got force-whipped because of *you!*" He jerked his coverall off his shoulder so she could see the weals still purple on his skin. "So did fifty others at the discipline assembly they called because of *you!* She's as bad as he is. No wonder she wasn't for killing him." Arnie glanced at the other hard faces, willing them to join him.

"Stuff it, Arnie," Mitford said, holding his right arm up in a karate-chop position. "We can deal with her later, too, but let's first find out what this mother knows."

Kris' mouth was dry all over again and she was scared cold. But she couldn't have let them just kill Mahomet out-of-hand. She owed him, if only because she'd put him in jeopardy before the twenty-four-hour moratorium had passed. She was sure that was why he was stuck here with the rest of them. She'd inadvertently told the truth. Cattenis had hated him enough to make sure he came to a dead end.

"Hey, sarge," someone yelled across the field and they looked over their shoulders. In the interval quite a few people had roused and were now homing in on the crates. Reinforcements were needed.

"C'mon, you," Mitford said to Mahomet and jerked his head to indicate the Catteni should move with them. "And you," he added coldly to Kris.

Kris briefly considered a belated apology to Arnie and decided not to make the effort. Arnie didn't seem the forgiving type and she might even make matters worse. Mahomet had not moved and when two of the men swiped at him with their knives, he ignored them and gestured for Kris to precede him. Quickly she fell in behind Mitford, hearing the surprised exclamations from the men.

"See how well he knows her," one of them said in a salacious tone of voice.

"She conked him, didn't she?"

"Yeah, but before or after, Murph?"

"Before, Murph," she answered for herself, making her voice as strident as she could. That wasn't too difficult considering how scared she was. The situation had turned very ugly. "And that goes for *any* one with the same dirty ideas." Looking straight ahead, she strode as confidently as she could back to the crates.

Once there, Mitford signed two of the men to take her and Mahomet behind the crates until he was finished with the new arrivals. He jumped up to his vantage point and, arms cocked on his belt, began his spiel. "I'm here to see that these supplies get doled out properly. So one at a time." He repeated the advice in lingua Barvei, speaking with a fluency that Kris hadn't expected.

Arnie was helping Mitford on the crates but some of those who had been lounging on the ground behind the barricade got curious and wandered up to Kris and Mahomet.

"What's with the Cat?"

"Mitford's going to question him," said the lankier of the two, a good head taller than Kris and nearly as tall as Mahomet.

"Okay, Murph, give Arnie a hand with the supplies now," Mitford said, jumping down. "Now, Cat, tell me why we should keep you alive."

"What is needed to know?" Mahomet asked in Barevi, his voice even, his manner diplomatic.

Kris let relief flood through her. Thank God he had sense enough —for a Catteni—to know how dangerous his situation was.

"Where we are. Who lives here. Any bad animals. What can we eat that won't kill us." Mitford tapped the blanket where his ration bars were stashed. "These won't last long."

Mahomet let out a dry rasp, tried to clear his throat to form words. Kris knew he'd be as dry as anyone else but she didn't dare ask for the favor of water for him. She mustn't be seen to favor, much less help, him.

"Here, give me that cup, Bass," Mitford said, snapping his fingers at one of the onlookers who had a cup in his hand.

"Huh? Give a Cat a drink?"

"If that helps him tell us what we need to know. Give it. You've been guzzling water for the past hour."

"I like that!" But Bass handed over the cup. "I want it back."

Mahomet held up his own cup and, with a nod of his head toward Bass, accepted the water Mitford doled out. He took a small sip, rinsing his mouth, and then a longer one.

"I remember some details. This planet surveyed. I did not read all."

"What did you read then?" Mitford demanded.

"Longer day, mild climate, some . . ." He frowned, trying to find the words, "species not other found. Three types deathly." He paused for another sip and then circled the cup to indicate the field. "Better go from here soon. Open field dangerous."

"Then why was we put down here?" Arnie demanded from his vantage on the crates. "So we could all get killed?"

"No." Mahomet shook his head, a rueful grin on his lips. "To live, to fight what is here. This how Catteni settle planets—the not easy ones." He finished the water then, knocking it back in his throat, tapping the cup on his teeth to be sure he had received the last drops. Then he stood there, his eyes going slowly from one face to another and coming back to Mitford's.

"How'd you get sent off with all of us?" the Sergeant asked.

Mahomet gave him a long look, a slight frown on his face. "Say again?" He surprised them by asking in accented English.

"You are here, too," Kris said, rephrasing the question. "Why?"

He didn't look in her direction and shrugged. "I kill. I escape. I am . . . took. Day not over." He shrugged again.

"You killed another Catteni?" Mitford asked and when Mahomet nodded. "And they deported you for that?"

"Day not over."

"That rule you were talking about?" Mitford asked Kris and she nodded. "Why'd you kill a Catteni?"

Mahomet gave a little snort, and the expression on his face suggested that they were not going to believe him. "He insulted Emassi and he kill four strong slaves no reason."

"Slaves? Like we were?" Mitford turned his thumb against his chest. Mahomet nodded.

"Guy's too clever," Arnie said in a growling tone. "Clever enough to lie his way out of being killed."

"I don't happen to think he's lying," Mitford said slowly. "I heard something the day of that riot. Some Cats'd been hunting another Cat captain who'd killed their patrol leader."

"Patrol leader," Mahomet repeated, recognizing the words and nodding his head. "I kill. Not wise . . ." His lips twitched and then he added, "Cat."

Suddenly everyone was aware of a weird noise.

"Down. All down, still!" Mahomet said as he dropped flat to the ground. The urgency in his voice and his tone of command was compelling.

"You heard him," Mitford said and gestured furiously at those on the crate. "Get down, you fools. Lie still."

The noise got louder and louder, piercing eardrums. Some of those in the process of getting up lay back down, covering their ears. The two Deskis who had been issued their knives moaned and cowered against the crates.

A shadow out of the west preceded the shape that overflew the field while the weird sound became an ungodly whistling shriek. Whatever it was was big and it swooped suddenly. Some unfortunate let out a terrified scream which trailed off as the flying monster departed with its prey. Kris saw brief struggles of outflung arms and legs and then all movement ceased. The weird noise cut off as abruptly.

"What the . . . was that?" Arnie cried.

"Deathly," Mahomet said. Then he pointed to the tree shapes at the upper edge of the field. "Watcher?" he both asked and suggested to Mitford. "Alert by call?"

"Many of them things around?" Mitford asked.

"Don't know. One is not enough?" Mahomet asked in a droll tone.

"Yeah, one's enough. Murph, you got a loud voice, you and Taglione, get up there and play sentry. Anyone see who it got?" he called up to those at the far end of the crates who would have had a better view.

"Didn't see. Looked like one of us."

"Would be. We got more meat on our bones than the Deskis," and Mitford looked over to the spindly creatures who were still cowering and moaning against the crates. "Do you Deskis know what those are?" He asked one of them in lingua Barevi. They both shook their heads but lowered their hands from their ears.

"Sound hurt Deski ears," Mahomet said, rising to his feet and dusting himself off. "They hear faster. Send them watch."

"Good idea, Cat," and Mitford issued the orders. The Deskis both tried to slink away until Mitford called Murph and Taglione to escort them.

Mahomet said one brief spate of sounds at them and they instantly obeyed.

"You speak Deski?" Mitford asked the Catteni.

"Deski, Ilginish, Turski, Rugash," Mahomet said. "Ang-leesh not many verds," he added in English. "Unnershtan better talk ssslow."

"Well, now we're cooking," Mitford said. He looked around at his allies, nodding especially at the recalcitrant and dissatisfied Arnie. "I don't think I got across the message to some of the aliens here."

Mahomet nodded. "Easy to say not unnershtan . . . doan like order."

Mitford barked out a laugh. "Damned well told, Cat. I think we keep you alive a while longer."

"Thank you." And Mahomet briefly inclined his upper body toward Mitford.

"Name? Rank?" the Sergeant asked the Catteni, ignoring the mutters of disapproval at that decision. When the mutter grew louder, he turned fiercely around. "Look, you sorry lot asked me to take command. Don't buck me when I make a command decision. Someone's got to. I say this mother is worth more to us alive—until he proves otherwise. Already saved somebody's neck from the flying thing. You don't like it, go it on your own. Get me?"

The human protest subsided and Kris felt her knees wobbling with relief. She was also dry-mouthed again from stress.

"So." Mitford turned back expectantly to Mahomet. "Name. Rank."

"Zainal, Emassi," he said, but Kris knew that wasn't the Catteni word for captain.

"Mitford, sergeant. I outrank you," he added in such a bland-faced lie that Kris coughed to hide her guffaw.

"I'm going for some more water," she told Mitford and walked off without waiting for any permission.

"Water good," Mahomet Zainal remarked in an even tone.

"All right, but I've some more questions for you, Emassi Zainal."

"Zainal now."

Kris grinned as she heard the correction but Zainal kept right on walking to the stream.

"You shouldn't've let him go off like that," Arnie said in a whine of protest.

"Like what? He's only going for a drink. Where else can he go? Now, let's get back on the job. Be glad I didn't ask you to go get water for him." He ignored Arnie's curses and continued. "Here come some more customers. Let's get this done before those flying things strafe us again."

"I dunno why you'd believe anything that Cat says . . ." Arnie said to Mitford. "And you let that bitch away with . . ."

"Stow it, Arnie."

Kris took two slow cupsful of water before she started back to the crates. Zainal, an interesting name, she thought, was ahead of her, but at a tangent, aiming for Mitford, who was looking out over the field of bodies still lying motionless. He'd handled a very difficult situation deftly and gotten her off the hook at the same time. She saw him look out over the body-strewn field. He paused briefly to examine those nearest. Shame-lessly she cocked her ears to hear what he said to Mitford, his rumbling bass carrying easily.

"There are dead."

"Do Catteni expect casualties?"

"Kaz-u-all-tees?"

"Dead ones."

"Long trip here," and Zainal's hand went to the scar on his head. "Some too weak. They feel nothing."

"I guess they didn't."

"Unwise to stay here near dead," Zainal added. "Not only flying danger."

"Just how much *do* you know about this place?" Mitford asked, slightly suspicious.

Zainal gave a long sigh. Kris could see the regret in his expression:

at least he permitted his expressions to show—not many of the Catteni she'd encountered did. Of course, that was one way to communicate when language failed.

"Not enough," he said with visible regret, "now I am here, too."

Mitford gave a short bark of laughter. "Shoe's on the other foot, huh?"

"Say again?"

Mitford waved his hand. "So we should leave the dead here . . . I'd better get a head count, just in case. Most of the goblins have gone and I can't say I'm sorry about that. Those mothers were dangerous all on their own-i-o! If the Deskis got good hearing, I'm for including them. What else are they good for?"

Kris noticed that Zainal had listened very intently to Mitford's words. He nodded once as if he had caught the gist.

"Deski good for much. You name Turs goblins? Ah! Good for hardest works. Hate all but Turs."

"That's the truth," Mitford agreed sourly. "The Rugs at least try to get along," and he gestured to the Rugarians, who had clustered together, drinking water and chewing away at their ration bars. "Don't mind the Ilginish, but they sure stink."

"Stink?"

Mitford held his nose. "We got a mixed bag left. And kids." He pointed to the half-dozen youngsters huddled together behind the crates. Too intent on what was happening to Zainal, Kris only noticed them now. "A rough detail to get organized and moving. And where do we go? D'you know that?"

"Safer in hills," and Zainal pointed to what could be considered the north. The sun of this system had not yet reached its zenith.

"Is it? That flying thing came from there."

"Places in rock to stay best. Creatures in . . ." he reached down and tapped the ground, "come in dark. Very bad." He shook his head from side to side to emphasize that caution. "Don't see."

"Stuff comes out of the earth at night?"

"True." He made the motions of a sinuous track upward with one hand and then pinched his fingers closed to indicate biting. "Day long enough to go. Find rock place."

"D'you know if there are caves—safe rock places—on this planet?"

"Rock right kind," Zainal said, kicking at one that looked like limestone to Kris. "Will make me remember more." He shook his head as if to free up more information.

"I'd rather move into some sort of a defensible position anyhow," Mitford said and jumped to the top of the crate. "Listen up, you hairy lot," Mitford bellowed in a parade-ground voice that made the Deskis clamp hands to their ears and cower to the ground. "This place won't be safe at night. We've got to move to the hills, find caves to shelter in."

"You're taking his word for this?" Arnie demanded, running up to Mitford and tugging at his pant leg. "You gonna listen to a Cat?"

"I'll listen to anyone who talks sense, and as the Cat's the only one knows anything about this planet, I'm not about to ignore any local info I can get, Arnie. No one'll force you to do anything now you don't wanna. Hear me?" He raised his voice again. "First, you lot," and he pointed a thick finger at Bass, Murph, and some of the others who'd been lounging behind the crates, "take a body count. Team up and cart any that are breathing—and I mean *any*—back here and we'll try to rouse 'em. I wouldn't even leave my mother-in-law to what walks at night. Now move it. You, too, Kris, and take the Cat with you."

"If we had a canteen or something to carry water in," Kris started.

Zainal tapped one of the empty crates. They were fashioned out of some sort of plastic and were capacious enough. He tipped it over and shook out some packing debris.

"I carry," he said and nodding at Kris to follow, started down to the stream.

"Good idea," Mitford said and got the two nearest Deskis to start emptying another half-full crate. "Useful."

"Sarge, what do we do with cups and blankets? Leave 'em on the stiffs?" Bass called.

"Strip 'em," Mitford yelled back. "They won't need 'em. We might."

Remarkably everyone, Deskis as well, fell to and by the time Zainal had brought back the filled crate—without so much as puffing from the trek uphill—the count was complete and only the dead remained behind in the field.

By the time the sun had reached its zenith, everyone living had been revived and informed of the current situation. There was one more flying attack, but Deski ears had heard the three creatures approaching long before they were seen and everyone was able to play dead. The creatures, still whistling their unbearable noise, caught nothing on that run.

By tearing strips from spare blankets, crude carrying straps were contrived to make crates easier to transport, for Mitford intended to leave nothing behind that might later come in handy. He even ordered the dead stripped of footwear and coveralls. He got some resistance for that decision but in the end, the unpleasant task was done and garments stored.

When the columns were ready to move off, Kris had acquired considerable respect for Mitford. She was equally glad she'd made the effort to spare Zainal for he had more than talk to use to placate dissenters. The added benefit to his show of strength was that few would have tried to take him on even if they hated his guts for being a Catteni, like Arnie. Some of the more recently revived were weak, so Mitford assigned each a buddy and announced that he intended to take skin off anyone who might happen to "lose" his or her buddy as they moved out.

"How many bought it?" Mitford asked Bass, who had kept a tally.

"Eighty-nine didn't make it," the lanky man said. "Mostly Deski and some older humans and two kids. That'd make about a ten percent loss if you figure a hundred bodies in each of the eight rows. Live head count's five hundred eighty-two: haven't sorted 'em out by race yet."

"Forget race," Mitford said with a snort. "We're all in this together. Operation Fresh Start."

Bass snorted good-naturedly. "You military types with your operations this and that."

Mitford raised his eyebrows in surprise. "It's good for morale."

"So's a fresh start. And being free again," Bass added with a sideways glance at Zainal.

Mitford walked to the top of the field and, fists on his hips, roared for attention.

"Listen up. We're moving out. You lot," and he pointed to a bunch of humans, "form up in a column, four abreast. We got nine water carriers: distribute yourselves along the line of march. You with buddies, sing out if you got trouble but *try* to keep up. Don't be shy asking for help if you need it. Bass, you be rear guard. Take Cumber, Dowdall, Esker, Movi, Tesco, and you three." He held up three fingers at the nearest group of Rugarians and gestured them over to Bass. "We're all in this together, remember!"

"Yeah, sarge, Operation Fresh Start," and Bass, evidently having thought the designation appropriate: "Okay, now move it out."

Mitford motioned for Zainal to join him and they trotted out to where people had begun to form up the column. At the front he swung in his arm the wide gesture that meant advance.

"MOVE OUT OPERATION FRESH START!" His parade-ground voice reached all ears.

Chapter Three

KRIS WAS BUDDIED WITH A FRAIL-LOOKING redheaded girl with the delicate complexion that often accompanies red hair. Patti Sue had been one of the last to rouse. She did a lot of coughing but she didn't feel feverish so Kris decided she must have had some kind of allergic reaction to the drug they'd been given in their soup. Patti Sue spent more time apologizing for being a burden. Such self-effacement bothered the hell out of Kris, who was naturally self-reliant and positive: she tried not to be curt with Patti Sue. The only other information the girl gave was that she'd been taken in Detroit. Every time Kris tried to open a conversation or asked a question, Patti Sue would take a coughing fit. The fifth time that happened Kris got the hint Patti Sue had been giving. She wondered if Patti'd survive until they made it to shelter.

She inserted herself and Patti in column right behind one of the water containers, carried between two Rugarians. There were Rugarians all around Patti and herself and, at first, Patti kept so close to Kris she almost stepped on Kris' feet a couple of times. Rugarians were sturdy, was Kris' reckoning, so if she did need help with Patti, she'd have it at hand. She'd also seen how some of the human males had looked at the redhead. Hope springs eternal, she thought with amusement, but she was reasonably sure Patti would have repelled any offers of male assistance.

She felt the pull uphill in the muscles of her calves and thighs but when they reached the tree shapes, she saw that the next bit of march would be downhill, along another field. The panorama bothered her but it wasn't until she was halfway down the slope that she realized exactly why. This new field was exactly the same size as the one they'd been dropped in. Tree shapes marched along the borders, and in adjacent fields of the same size. It was *too* even. Everything was laid out so neatly, far too neatly for a supposedly unoccupied planet. Only Zainal had not said the planet was unoccupied, had he? He'd definitely said it had indigenous dangers and he couldn't remember what types, only that there were "deathly" creatures. At the bottom of this field was another stream. Brooks created on demand? And another field on the other side, identical to all the others in this area. On the entire planet? Where were the browsers? The ruminants for whom these fields were made? Were they some of the "deathly" creatures?

She looked ahead and saw distant foothills. God, they were a long way away. She looked over her shoulder and saw the four-wide crocodile stretching out behind her. Safety in numbers? It said much for Mitford's leadership ability that he had managed such cohesion from such a diverse group. Well, some of the obedience had originally been inculcated by Catteni forcewhips. A lot of people wouldn't have had time to recover from their enslavement and be able to start thinking for themselves. Mitford was obviously counting on that. Whatever saved as many souls as possible, she thought to herself.

During that long march, she found herself resenting Patti Sue's frailty. She'd've preferred being up front with Mitford and Zainal, able to see where she was going: scouting ahead even. She liked being first, not tamely following others. But she'd accepted the responsibility of buddying with Patti Sue and she'd see it through.

By the time the sun had reached a halfway point down the sky, she was supporting more of Patti Sue on the way up the hills. Downhill was easier except that Patti tended to stumble, always apologizing for the trouble she was making Kris, and telling Kris how good she was to put up with her. Kris had to clench her teeth to keep from telling Patti Sue to shut up and just do her best.

Every hour they got five minutes to rest and get watered, or whatever, although how Mitford knew when an hour was up was beyond her. Maybe his military training gave him a built-in watch or something. Whatever, she welcomed the brief respite.

The Catteni sure had a good footwear design in those shapeless fold-abouts. Body heat had molded hers so faithfully to her long narrow feet that, although her feet were tired, she hadn't raised a single blister or rub. Her leg muscles were complaining about abuse, but after an unknown period of time doing sweet fanny adams, what else could she expect? The spring had gone out of everyone's step, especially the water carriers, although Mitford had seen to it that those were rotated every rest period.

Then the word was passed back that they'd take an hour's break to eat. And if anyone had eaten up all their bars, tough titty. They weren't breaking out any spares today.

Kris had had another third before the trek, so she munched out on the last third and had half another one. She got Patti Sue to eat all of a bar by feeding it to her bit by bit. The girl's fatigue was not put on. Her cheeks were gaunt and her breath was shallow. Kris thought she heard rales in her lungs, but it might have simply been exertion after long idleness. There wasn't much more travel in Patti.

When the call went back to start again, they were on the edge of a fairly dense plantation. And plantation was the appropriate word because the vegetation—trees, whatever—had been set out in rows. There were several different specimens, judging by what went for leaves on this world; different sizes, too, and a soft mulch underfoot that was a welcome relief from the harder surfaces of the fields, despite their grassoid ground cover. While she could approve of forestation, it was real queer to find it on a planet that wasn't supposed to be inhabited. Although Zainal hadn't exactly said it was *uninhabited*, had he, she reminded herself yet again.

Kris got Patti Sue to her feet. The girl was so tired she didn't even have the strength to apologize. Kris draped one lax, thin arm about her waist, holding it to her with her right hand while she tucked her left under the girl as support. Kris gave a half-hip lurch and carried Patti forward step by step.

At the next rest stop, Kris herself was panting and sweaty. She'd draped Patti's blanket, cup, and ration package across her own to free the girl of any burden. Now she rearranged her accoutrements and when the order to move came, she hoisted Patti pickaback as the easier way to deal with the problem. Kris had good strong shoulders and a strong back and it was much easier, in some ways, to carry the girl than try to keep her on her own feet.

She was moving along at a better clip—they had fallen back from the water carriers some time before. She felt someone touch her shoulder and looked a human straight in his blue eyes. He had straight blond hair.

"Hey, there, ma'am, I'll take her. You shouldn't have to pack her."

"Why not? She ain't my brother but she ain't heavy," Kris replied, moving right along, but she smiled gratitude for the offer.

"Naw," the guy said, reaching out to take Patti. "You take my gear and I'll lug her."

Patti felt his hands on her and whimpered fearfully, clinging with what strength she had left in her arms to Kris. Kris moved out of the column.

"Tell you what, you carry my gear and that'll make it easier. But I don't think Patti Sue wants any guy around her. You know what I mean."

The guy looked shocked for a moment, resenting the implication that he might have an ulterior motive to his offer.

"She won't tell *me* more than her name and where she came from," Kris said, "and you must have heard how popular us Terran females were with the Cats."

"Oh, gawd. Didn't think of that." He flushed with embarrassment. "Jay Greene," he identified himself. "Denver."

"I'm Kris Bjornsen and Denver's where I was also caught." She had eased Patti down to the ground. Patti clung to her legs, still whimpering and mumbling unintelligible pleas. "It's okay, honey, it's okay. I'll carry you. You're my buddy, aren't you?" She divested herself of the blanket rolls and her ration bars but kept the cups and Patti's food.

"Hi, Patti Sue," the man said, leaning down to her. "I'm Jay Greene, and I'm just going to lift you to Kris' back. Save her a bit. Is that okay?"

"Just do it, Jay," Kris said and was nearly strangled by Patti, who almost sprang from Jay's hands to Kris' back.

"Wow!" Greene said softly. "Rough."

Kris shifted the girl to a more comfortable position, feeling bones grind in the slender body. "Let's get back in line. We'll be the tail that wags the dog pretty soon."

"Don't fret, ma'am. I won't leave your sight."

"Not while you have my rations, you won't."

The last part of that heroic march was uphill, scrambling on a rock-strewn surface where Greene often had to grab Kris to keep her balanced. She was concentrating so hard on not falling that Kris didn't really see where they were going until they got there. A wide ridge with—when she had a moment to look—a fantastic view of the patchwork of fields and hedging that seemed to stretch out for miles and miles into the twilight. The column also stretched in front of her, and there weren't that many behind, they'd dropped back so far. All along the way, marchers were sitting down where they stood, too tired to move much farther or worry about the hardness of this night's accommodation.

"I don't think much of this as a campsite," Greene said, looking about him. He pushed a spot clear of rocks and pebbles and pointed it out to Kris. "This is as good as any."

This time Patti was too exhausted to even whimper when Greene very gently lifted her off Kris' back. Kris gave a loud sigh of relief. Scuffed a second patch clear for herself and sat down with a "whoof" of relief. Greene handed her the blankets and the food as he swept a place clean.

"Gimme the cups and I'll get us all some water," he said and she handed them over, realizing that she was done! She hadn't the energy to get her own water.

When he came back, they managed to prop Patti Sue to a sitting position while Kris fed her again, and used some of the water to wash her face and then her own.

"Hey, we got a Prometheus in this ragtaggle group," Greene said, pointing toward the front of the column.

Kris cried out in surprise and relief. Somehow the torches bobbing along the ridge in their direction reassured her as nothing else could have. Tears came to her eyes and she bit her lip and averted her face from Greene. She didn't want to spoil the impression that she was a survivor type.

It was a long time, and darkness had fallen, before the torchbearers made it to the rear where she was. Patti was asleep, her head pillowed on Kris' thighs. A few people seemed to have enough energy to talk, or complain: the Deskis were emitting their odd susurruses from the tight little circle they had created. The Rugarians had curled up in hairy balls, blankets hauled over their faces. Kris was too tired to sleep, her back muscles aching from the day's strain and her neck taut. She rotated her shoulders and waggled her shoulder blades, trying to ease things. Then she felt Greene's hands begin a massage for which she was intensely grateful.

She was drowsing when light roused her to attention. Mitford, Zainal, Taglioni, and two others she didn't know were checking on the column.

"You okay, Bjornsen?" Mitford asked, one hand lightly resting on her shoulder.

"She carried her buddy here half the afternoon," Greene spoke up.

"Shut up," Kris said in protest. "She doesn't weigh much."

"And she's your buddy," Mitford said, nodding. "Know this is a lousy campsite. . . ." Beyond him, Zainal was talking to the Deski that had been awakened by the torch. It was a male, his eyes wide with an anxiety which abated when Zainal had finished speaking. "Best we can do. Zainal and a couple are going to scout forward to see if there're any caves near enough. He thinks we'll be safe enough on the open ridge tonight. You're Jay Greene?"

"That's me."

"Can you hang awake awhile?"

"Sure can." Greene got to his feet, stiffly, but made it upright.

"Okay, you keep an eye open here. You'll wake Bass . . . you know him? Good, at second moonset," and now Mitford pointed to the moons just rising, one much larger and ahead of its smaller companion. "This planet has five. Useful for lack of any other markers." He turned his head toward the lanky figure of Bass, who was coming into the torchlight, the rest of the rear guard clustered behind him. "You hear that? Greene here will relieve you. Cumber, Bass'll get you up and you'll be on until the fourth moon goes down, then you wake Movi. Don't cheat and mix up your moonsets, now hear me!"

"We hear and obey," Bass said, according Mitford a fancy eastern salaam.

"I leave you the torch," Mitford said and handed the one he held to Jay Greene. "It won't last all night long 'cause the nights here are long, but it should help."

"Gotcha."

Mitford started to retrace his steps to the front. Zainal favored Kris with a long look and then pivoted to follow the Sergeant and the others.

Kris wrapped herself up good in the blanket, moving Patti until she got as comfortable as she could—after digging up a couple of rocks. The Catteni also did a good line of warm blankets, too. She finally got rested enough to fall asleep.

AS MITFORD, ZAINAL, TAGLIONI, AND THE OTHERS TIREDLY RE-traced their steps to the front of the column, the Sergeant reflected on the wisdom of keeping the Cat alive. For starters, he liked the guy's style when he had to brave it out among folks who had no cause to like his species. Of course, Mitford knew that the psychological moment to waste Zainal had passed back in the field, when the Cat got to his feet. He was one big mother and no one, not even Mitford, would have taken him on single-handed. Guys like Arnie, who'd had too long a taste of Catteni whips, might just organize a lynch party at some auspicious moment. But there were ways of avoiding murder, if you knew who victim and murderer were. Mitford defused a couple of similar situations. Then, too, the big guy kept coming out with damned useful gen: like the five moons. Was he deliberately parceling out these gems or was he putting on an elaborate act? Years in the Army had taught Mitford how to spot liars and malingerers. Zainal was neither but he knew exactly what sort Arnie was. Zainal was neither.

For most of Mitford's life, in particular since he'd enlisted as an enthusiastic, lying sixteen-year-old, the sun had ruled Mitford's days: from boot camp to his one tour in Nam, through his two jaunts to

Kuwait, until he'd been nabbed, by aliens, in a hammock on his dad's veranda.

Idly, his thoughts ranged to wondering if his old unit had seen any action against the Catteni on Earth, but reports from the old world were few and far between. All the more reason for making the one they were stuck on now better. And if keeping the Cat they had alive was one way of doing it, Chuck Mitford would see he lived. He wondered exactly how that tall blonde Bjornsen had met the Cat. She hadn't been lying, but she hadn't told all the facts. Whatever! She'd been clever in handling the situation and keeping the Cat alive. She had class, that one. And she was good people, the way she'd lugged that poor scared kid all day long.

Taglione stumbled again and this time didn't throw off the Cat's hand when it went out to steady him. Maybe they could integrate him, though Mitford doubted it. Too much feeling against Catteni right now. He'd have to figure out some way of using the Cat without keeping him about all the time. That was easy: he'd send Zainal out on reconnaissance: they'd need to know the terrain wherever they finally came to roost. Send Bjornsen with him, and keep two potential problems out of his hair. He'd have enough. Not that he hadn't made a good start but oh, lord, how did he get in this situation in the first place? Mitford, he told himself, don't you know the first rule of Survival? *Don't* volunteer!

"You were telling me you *work* for the Eosi? The Catteni are not the overlords?" he asked Zainal in Barevi.

"No, Eosi. Emassi take orders. Eosi order the galaxy."

That chain of command didn't seem to sit well with the Cat either, Mitford thought, reading the way the guy set his jaw as resistance, if not downright rebellion.

" 'Emassi' is not the word I heard for 'captain,' " Mitford went on in a bland voice.

He caught the gleam of Zainal's eyes in the moonlight as the big Cat glanced down at him.

" 'Emassi' one word for a captain," and Zainal's lips curled up. "Special captain. You have heard 'Tudo' more. And 'Drassi.' "

"Yeah, 'Tudo' for ground and 'Drassi' for space? Right?" So, as Mitford had thought, this Catteni was a couple of cuts above the usual individual the Sergeant had met. "So which was it set us down here? Tudo, Drassi, or Emassi?"

"Drassi by order of Eosi," and that didn't sit well with the Catteni either.

"You killed a Tudo, then . . ."

"As I have told you," Zainal said quietly but with an edge to his words.

"Just checking."

Zainal chuckled. "Know that Emassi have no reason to lie."

The first moon was now well above the hills and shining hard into their faces, lighting the rocky track so that they didn't inadvertently step on sleeping bodies. For a big guy, Zainal was agile. Course he was used to a heavier gravity, but that didn't keep some Cats from being damned clumsy, squashing bystanders in their brawls.

"We'll be left alone now to get on with the job of settling in?"

"That is the way."

"How soon before anyone checks in?"

Zainal paused, walking in silence, then held up two fingers. "Depends. Drop more prisoners if we live. Then check in half a year, year. See how we do."

"You're part of 'we'?" Mitford wasn't sure if he liked that suggestion of solidarity. The Cat hadn't been in the same boat as the humans: figuratively, that is. Or maybe he was.

Zainal snorted. "I drop. I stay. I am not against you. I am *with* you."

"Fine by me," Mitford said, waited a beat, "but you won't find everyone exactly welcoming."

Zainal chuckled. "Emassi are also not welcome everywhere. I will survive."

Somehow Mitford didn't doubt that a moment. And he intended to keep this Catteni alive. Mitford could think of several ways, easy, that this Zainal might be of use to him, especially if he was also discontented with these Eosi overlords who ordered everything. "Then if we can keep alive, they unload more rebels?"

"Rebels?"

"Yeah, rebels," Mitford said, "people like us who protest Catteni rule."

Zainal grinned. "Good word, rebels. I like it."

"You wouldn't be a bit of a rebel yourself, perhaps?"

"Perhaps."

Mitford caught the edge on that mild rejoinder and wondered.

"We must talk about this at a later date," Zainal said. "You speak Barevi lingua well," he added in a louder voice.

"I'm a survivor, Emassi. And learning the local lingo fast is essential to survival. I got enough of five-six languages from Earth to get around the world: Barevi wasn't hard to pick up."

"No, it is not."

"A simple language for simple folk?"

Now Zainal gave a soft chuckle. But that was the last either said because fatigue was getting the better of both as they neared the head of the sleeping column of rebels. *Yeah*, Mitford thought again, *I like that rebel bit.*

After checking that the sentries he had set were still awake, Mitford gratefully spread his blanket on the ground.

"If you think of anything more from that report, Zainal, lemme know," Chuck said as he lay down.

"I will."

Chapter Four

MORNING WAS NOT FUN! ONCE AGAIN KRIS ached in many places and knew that pebbles had moved under her during the night to make tender spots where she didn't need them. Patti was still flaked out when Kris rearranged the girl so she could get up. She had to go. She made her way down the hill to a boulder that had already been used for this purpose although someone had had the courtesy to sprinkle dirt on what they'd done. She did the same. Greene was waiting for her with full cups of water.

"Gawd, what I wouldn't give for a cuppa coffee," he said, grinning at her over the rim of his cup.

"Never said a truer word," and Kris rather liked his grin. Why was it she had to be dropped on this godforsaken planet before she met any decent fellas? She could notice a few more details about him, too. He looked awful thin, and his hands showed lots of healed cuts and nicks and the palms, when he gestured, were heavily calloused.

"Did you really steal the commander's flitter?"

Kris groaned. "I did but I wouldn't have if I'd known the sort of reprisals the Catteni would take."

"Don't distress yourself over that, ma'am," he said, grinning more broadly. "The very idea that one of us could, did, and had gave us all heart."

"Except the ones who had long interviews with forcewhips." She shuddered, her back muscles writhing in sympathetic reaction. The twice she'd felt that sort of nerve-paralyzing lash had been quite enough.

"The Cats looked for any excuse to intimidate us Terrans," Greene said. "We were more than they expected, in case you hadn't heard. Did they recapture you er something?"

"No," Kris said, drawling the negative out to emphasize her chagrin. "My timing was bad. I'd snuck a trip into the city just when the cruisers started spreading gas to quell that riot. And what was that riot about?"

"Oh, we tried to break up another one of their little discipline sessions. One thing led to another and we ended up a mob. No sense, no reason, just rush about breaking up anything to hand!"

She nodded, finishing the last of her bar and licking her fingers.

Word was passed down to get a move on.

Patti Sue managed the morning on her own feet and then collapsed again. She apologized to the point that Kris was grinding her teeth not to snap at her. It was a little difficult to avoid the apologies and self-deprecations when the girl's lips were a few inches from her ear. Greene did what he could, chatting about this and that because his talking silenced Patti. His buddy was a Rugarian who said nothing, stopping and starting when Greene did, and seemingly oblivious to every other stimulus.

"What were you back on good ol' Terra?" Kris asked, to while the time.

"Ahha, computer technician. So, of course, they had me digging, shoveling, and sweeping on Barevi. At least they weren't prejudiced. Anyone big got that duty." He made a muscle in his arm and pulled the coverall tight across it so she could admire the result. "Actually, it beats a sedentary life in front of a screen. I've never been this fit." And he cast a critical eye on Patti's frail body. "You're sure . . ." he began for the third time since lunch.

"I'm sure."

Patti Sue had either fallen asleep or retreated into a comatose state. The only thing that reassured Kris was that her skin was cool, not hot with fever. She soldiered on. However, she told herself that next time buddies were assigned, she was going to choose.

The afternoon became one long struggle to keep upright and put one foot in front of the other. They had to make three climbs up rock faces . . . Kris did hope that Mitford had had accurate reports from his advance scouts, because she sure didn't want to come back *down* the last one. They'd had to rig a blanket sling to get the limp Patti Sue up it. Kris ended up with scraped shins and lost some fingertip skin. The items that hadn't been in the Catteni survival crates were legion. Decent gloves, pitons, rope, pickaxes, backpacks, a bar of chocolate were among those she dreamed of. Needles and thread! Band-Aids.

There were three falls, one broken leg. The Deskis, for all their fragile looks, had almost glided up the rock face. That could be a useful skill, she thought, amazed that she could think of anything other than being able to continue walking.

When her courage was beginning to peter out into utter despair, the word was passed back that their destination had been reached by the first elements.

They'd had one? That amazed and heartened her.

———

WHEN SHE GOT THERE, SHE DIDN'T KNOW IT. ONE, SHE HAD stumbled and had to lean against the cliffside to steady herself. She'd had a terrifying, if brief, look at the drop she'd nearly plummeted down. Two, she was too exhausted even to care that she would now be able to stop walking.

"I'll take her," a male voice said and the burden of Patti was lifted from her back.

Someone put a hand on her arm and led her from the cliff, pushing her head down so she wouldn't crack it on a low entryway. The darkness a few meters inside was suddenly alleviated by—of all things—fires. They didn't *smell* like fires should but the rosy glow *looked* like the real thing. She later found out that Zainal had experimented with various types of wood, for lack of a proper description of the material he gathered from the vegetation, until he found a combustible substance. He found other things, which included dried dung, to augment what "wood" could be gathered as they marched. The dung smelled but it gave off heat and light, which were essential.

Someone took her cup—she protested, but before she could get violent about the matter, the cup was returned to her, full of water.

"Keep moving," she was told and a hand gently guided her in the direction she was supposed to go . . . a narrow path through out-stretched legs and boots. She went left, then right, then left again as guided and had her head pushed down to enter a smaller cave. There was a small fire, one that didn't smell too badly, in a circle of glinting stones in the center. Smoke went straight up and she tilted her head, nearly falling over backward since her balance was as tired as the rest of her senses, and couldn't see the ceiling.

"Over here," and she was guided to one side of the fire where there weren't any legs or boots. "Sit." A gentle hand pressed down on her shoulder and, quite willing to obey, she sat.

When she felt someone fumbling with her blanket, she tried to push the hands away.

"Sleep in blanket."

The odd phrasing caught her attention and she blinked to focus on the face in front of her. Zainal it was who was untying her blanket. No one else was that big. That was all right then. She owed him. Or did he owe her?

"Lie down," he said, an order that she was only too happy to obey.

She worked her way down to a recumbent position and felt the blanket tucked around her. What odd behavior for a Cat . . . no, she must not shorten the name. Catteni. Maybe "Teni" would be less egregious than "Cat"?

That was the last thing she remembered for a very long time.

MITFORD WOKE SUDDENLY, HIS WELL-DEVELOPED INTERNAL clock rousing him after his customary six hours' sleep. It was dark as the inside of a pocket and it took him a moment to establish where he was. He rose cautiously to one elbow, identifying the sleeping forms around him: Taglione, Murphy, Dowdall, and yes, the dark mass of the big-shouldered Catteni.

Fit as Mitford tried to keep himself, apart from that enforced sleep on the prison ship, he felt some twinges of yesterday's exertions. Well, today would be another bitch and he'd better start it, what with all he had to do.

He berated himself once again for setting himself up in command of this chickenshit outfit, but who the hell else in this misassorted herd of humanity, and aliens, would have organized anything? It had made his blood boil to see them quibbling over how many knives they should get, and who'd have the blanket concession. Just chance that he'd known a couple of the looters from being in the same barracks with them on Barevi so he'd been able to inveigle their support with a hint and bit of verbal persuasion. No need for anyone to get greedy over the goodies. There looked to be more than enough to go round. He couldn't stand greed and he hated bullying. Some might not believe that, but it was the truth. So he'd waded in and got the supply situation organized to his satisfaction and doled out the hardware in an orderly fashion. He should have known one thing would lead to another. But no one had contested his authority. Or them that had, had taken themselves off.

And hell's bells, after twenty-seven years in the Marines, he knew how to get a motley crew to act as a unit. He trained up enough raw recruits into good fighting men. Even women. Then he had a couple of advantages, too. For starters, everyone here had been taking orders they couldn't buck so he'd just continue the practice, gradually easing them back into a more democratic government when he had everything suitably organized and independence was feasible. Right now, they'd better stick together, and keep the useful aliens handy. He was glad to be rid of the Turs, sullen argumentative bastards, and the Ilginish had always been difficult to deal with in the barracks at Barevi. They'd taken themselves off, most of them, and that was fine by him. Humans he could handle any day of the week.

So they were in a defensible position, even if he still didn't know what he might have to defend against. They had a good source of underground water in that cave lake his scouts had found. The Cat—Mitford reproved himself—how he treated Zainal, the Catteni, would go a long way to establishing how most of the others would regard the alien. And, if he wanted to make contact with the Catteni at a later date, he'd need someone in his ballpark to hit the homers. Right now the only one available was Zainal. At any rate, Zainal had found time to hunt as he scouted ahead with Tag and Murph and had clubbed some local fauna. He proved it was edible by eating a hunk of it raw. Mitford preferred his meat cooked but, to him, the gob which he had chewed and swallowed had tasted just like raw meat usually did. The critters just squatted on the rocks in droves or herds, didn't move when humans approached—which suggested to Mitford that they hadn't seen any humans to know to fear them—so they were dead easy to bring down.

So there was one source of protein to augment the ration bars. Water, shelter, food. Not bad going for two days on a new world. Mitford was optimistic, even though he rarely allowed himself that option.

He'd had a chance to talk to nearly a hundred or so men and women yesterday on the march and was much encouraged by the fact that quite a few had specialties that would be damned useful. Automatically, his hands went to pockets where he usually kept pencil and pad. Once again he cursed under his breath. A cup, a blanket, a knife, and a hatchet were not much to work with. He'd had less when set loose on a survival course but he was accustomed to privations. This lot weren't. He missed paper and pencil. He was a visual man and committed facts to memory when he could first write them down. Gerry Capstan had been a surveyor in the Colorado Park Service: he was sure they could find something to write with and he'd already seen slate along the rocky way. *Helluva way to write orders of the day*, Mitford thought, *but what the hell?* The old granary foreman in Lubbock still used chalk and a slate as a notice board for his drivers.

Murphy had been a machinist, knew welding, and he'd assured Mitford that all he needed was a decent hot fire to reshape some of those extra knives into a bevy of useful tools.

A woman near Murphy in the line of march perked up a bit when she heard the two men talking.

"I'm a potter . . . Sandy Areson. Yeah, I know what you're thinking," and she grinned at the dubious expression on Mitford's face, "arty-farty stuff you'd call what I used to produce. But I know how to make up pitchers, mugs, plates, and useful things. That is, if this planet has produced clay."

"We'll keep that in mind," Mitford said, knowing that something as simple as pitchers and plates could be a morale booster.

Now, in the cool predawn, Mitford began to plan the day's activities. A good hot meal in everyone's belly would make them optimistic, too. So hunting was the first order of the day. A detailed search of the immediate area and the rest of the cave system was next. And torches to light the corridors that had already been explored.

That herbal guy could see what he could find edible in the vegetable line. There might even be berries.

There were two miners and they could go look for ore deposits.

He'd send out patrols, keep everyone busy, and Arnie could do latrines. That made him smile. And anyone who complained about anything would join Arnie in that duty. With so many people, proper hygiene was of prime necessity.

One of the few pluses was that they were all healthy: the ones who weren't had been left on the field.

He set about waking up men he had tagged the day before as those with some hunting experience back on Earth. He'd have them look out for any wood that could be made into bows, arrows, and spears. And slingshots. Mitford grinned as he pulled on his boots. He'd been a crack shot as a kid: could stun a jackrabbit at forty yards.

And what was the name of that paramedic? Ah, Matt Dargle. Damn, he'd be glad to have writing materials.

Mitford shook Taglione, Murphy, and Zainal awake and started handing out the orders of the day.

IT WAS THE STINK THAT WOKE HER. SHE STARTED COUGHING and couldn't stop. She wasn't the only one coughing, either. Everyone around her was. Then a whiff of cool, clean air wafted across her face and she tried to go back to sleep again. It was much too soon to wake up. It was still dark outside.

Outside of *where?* That question did it: she pushed herself to a sitting position to find out "where" she was.

Inside a cave. The fire in the center was down to embers although someone was trying to revive it by putting lumps—smell-producing lumps—on it.

"I think I'd prefer the dark to the smell," she murmured, realizing that folks were still sleeping around her. In fact, she recognized Patti Sue's frail body next to her. Kris was chagrined. She hadn't even made sure she still had her trek buddy when she'd gone to sleep. Zainal? Zainal. Hmmm. She looked around but she couldn't find his body among those in here with her. She considered going back to sleep and then realized that first she'd better find the latrine.

"Where's the latrine?" she asked the figure feeding the fire.

"From here?" The man paused briefly. "Hmmm. Go left, take the third right-hand opening."

"Can I see where I'm going?"

"Oh, yes."

Although torches had been spaced out along the walls, she found the right cave as much by a certain smell as following the directions. She was amazed at what had been accomplished. Or, how long had she slept? A toothbrush! When she thought of those handy little pouches handed out by airlines if you went Business Class, she wished she'd had one to hand: toothbrush, comb, and nail file, not to mention toothpaste, breath neutralizer, and facecloth would be very comforting right now. And something to eat. She passed by "her" cave on her return because she smelled something scrumptious—well, by comparison with what she'd lately had to eat.

She followed her nose, passing other side passages and peering into caves, filled with sleeping bodies. She took a wrong turning and ended up in a cul-de-sac which smelled not at all appetizing, but nasty, old-moldy, dead.

Her nose led her to the source, and the largest of the caves. It was a-bustle with activity, men, women, and aliens—Kris was glad to see the resurgence of whimsy in herself—coming and going. Though what they were going to and coming from she wasn't sure until she saw a group of men, each triumphantly brandishing their spoils. They'd been hunting and, although the creatures resembled oversized rats without tails, if they were what was being grilled over the fires, she'd forget the resemblance.

She went over to the nearest griller and paused by the rock on which two cooked fragments had been laid.

"How do I get in line?" she asked the dark-skinned cook.

"I wouldn't stand on no ceremony was I you," he said with a grin. "Don't mind what they look like: they taste good and that Cat said they wouldn't kill us."

"He did," and Kris tried to act casual as she reached for the meat? Food? It wasn't too hot to handle and she brought it to her lips, inconspicuously licking the part nearest her to get a taste. The taste confirmed the notion that her stomach needed this no matter what else happened. She took a good bite, inhaling air to cool the morsel, hot against her teeth. But she chewed it good—she had to; the meat was tough. It chewed good and tasted great and fell into a grateful stomach.

"Only one a customer," the dark man said, carefully inserting his knife point to check the state of the portions on the spit.

"Understandable. I've got ration bars to fill in the spaces, but this hot . . ." She paused, not only to take another bite to follow the first one, but also to give what she ate a proper designation.

"We're calling it meat," he said, grinning.

"Well, whatever it's called, it hits the spot. Thanks . . ." And she left her voice on an upnote for him to supply his name.

"Bart," he said. "You're Kris."

"How'd you know that?"

"'Cos you carried that girl fer two days and you know the Cat."

"Oh!" Such glory was unexpected. She looked around, then, rather embarrassed. She saw neither Zainal nor Mitford. "Where's the Sarge and the Cat?"

"Out. Hunting, I think, and seeing if there're more caves." He wrinkled his nose. "This place isn't really big enough for us all. Good idea to spread out anyhow, iffen you asked me. Only nobody did." He spoke amiably.

"Better if we had running water."

"Oh, we do, but the way down to it's no picnic."

"Oh?"

"Underground lake and river. Probably feeding some of the streams we passed."

Kris licked the thick bone that had been covered with meat.

"Crack it open. Marrow makes good eating, too."

Kris scrutinized the bone with reluctance to take his advice.

"Marrow's got a lot of good in it, Kris," Bart said solemnly. "Crunch down quick to break it open and then suck."

Rather than appear squeamish, she did so and the marrow was not at all unpleasant. She made sure she had cleaned both halves and then looked around her.

"In the fire," Bart said. "We burn everything we can find."

"So I'd . . . smelled," she said with a grin.

"Yeah, do get kinda rank, don't it."

Depositing the bones on the fire and hearing them snap as the flame caught, she also got a whiff of the "burned bone" smell. She licked her fingers so she'd remember better the way the meat had tasted. Then she untied her cup from its place on her belt. "Where's drinking water?"

"Over there," and Bart nodded his head toward the side, where she could recognize the symmetry of the water crates, stored against the cave wall.

She had no sooner taken a drink than a woman, with her dark hair roughly chopped to a short length, tapped her on the arm. "You wouldn't know how to skin and clean a dead animal, would you?"

"Yup," she said with considerably more willingness than she actually had for the task. But she'd skinned squirrels and rabbits on her practical for the survival qualification and *now* was a much better time to display her abilities.

"I'm Sandy and I got put in charge without knowing doodly squat. I used to be"—and she gave a droll grin—"a potter."

"I'm Kris . . ."

"Yeah, I know," and the woman grinned at her. "You know the Cat and you carried your buddy for two days."

Did everyone know those two facts about her? Kris wondered as she followed Sandy outside the cave. She hadn't noticed that the hunters had brought their catch outside again. Half a dozen people were busy skinning and gutting, using large stones as worktops. Two men and two women appeared to be dissecting entrails at another and arguing about anatomy.

"Guts are guts and I don't see why we can't use these," said the woman, holding up a long, stringy, gray rope. "Ought to be as tough as any cat's."

"That's what Indians used to use to make bowstrings, wasn't it?"

"Think so. They sure didn't have nylon."

Kris was not squeamish but she didn't want to lose her breakfast. It had tasted so good going down, but coming up? She'd rather not find out.

Finding herself a space, she caught the beastie that Sandy tossed her. Limp, soft, but firmly packed. The hide was unexpectedly pleasant to touch though the muted gray-brown was an unearthly color. It wasn't a furry hide, rather a suedey covering. Turning it around on her slab to examine it closely, she couldn't see what had killed it until she noticed that one half of the "head" had been mashed. Too small to have been done by a club and certainly not a blow from the broad-edged hatchets they'd been issued. It did have four legs, a chunky rounded body, and not much neck before the blunt end that was its "head." She gave a sigh and, giving a quick glance around to see how others were tackling the job, she flipped it to its back and, tipping the head up, began the job of dressing it.

It had more meat on it than either rabbit or squirrel, having heavy haunches and well-developed shoulders. Her knife, while large enough to be a shade unwieldy for precision surgery, was sharp. She made a bit of a hash of stripping the hide off the legs, but hell, you didn't lose much below the "knee." She had just finished when Sandy appeared with another one and thus she spent her morning. There seemed to be endless quantities of that beastie and another, also suede-covered, with membranous wings that felt slimy. No meat on such wings but she was told to save these, too.

"Did you get something to eat?" Sandy asked her at one point.

"Yes, something from one of the squatty things, I think."

"If we had a pot to stew in, we could make everything go further," Sandy said with a rueful smile. "Bob the Herb," and she grinned back at Kris' startled expression, "well, he knew Terran herbs and he found some root sorts of things that oughtn't to poison us. And some rather delicious sharp-tasting berries. At least, the Cat thought they'd be edible. He ate 'em and didn't get the trots but Cats can eat a lot that'd give us the green apple two-step."

Kris paused, another trick coming to mind. She sat back on her heels. "We got any natural holes anywhere? I mean, holes with floors so they wouldn't leak?"

"Why?"

"Well, they'd make a self-contained stew pot. Fill one with water, then drop in clean heated stones. That'd boil the water and whatever else you had in it."

"It would?"

"I haven't done it, but the theory's sound. A pot's only something you can move around."

"What heathen country did you get that from?"

Kris laughed. "The old Irish used to do that. I saw the places in the south of Ireland. Great tourist attractions but the guide swore that was what field workers used when they didn't want to trek all the way back to their homes."

"Well, I never," Sandy said and went off, cocking her head this way and that.

"Hey, gal, you made it up," a cheerful voice said and Kris looked up from the animal she had just eviscerated to see Jay Greene making his way to her. He had a brace of avians in each hand. From the angle of their heads, their necks had been broken.

"Hi, Jay. Say, just how are these things being caught, or killed?"

"Snares work as well on this planet as any other," he said, looking pleased. "Probably better. Fortunately for me, these fowls are stupider'n' turkeys and will eat anything edible, especially ration bar crumbs."

"You knew about snares?"

" 'Semper Paratus,' like the Boy Scouts used to say," he said modestly. "I worked one out and Mitford showed us how to use a slingshot. A crack shot, too." He was properly respectful. "Haven't got any elastic, but with a little practice and the right flick of the wrist, you can aim pretty accurate. The rocksquatters haven't got sense enough to be scared, so they sit there and die young! Hey, you're pretty good with that knife!"

"Yeah, I am," she said blithely. "Yours next?" She reached for his burden while she honed the tip of her knife on the rock of her table.

"Yes, ma'am," he said, and, pretending extreme caution as she sharpened, deposited the bodies on the other side of her table.

The heat of the sun made her stop, mop her sweaty forehead on her sleeve, and realize that she'd been working steadily for long enough to get a crick in her neck and more blood than she liked on her coverall. Blood always attracted insects. At least on Earth and Barevi it had.

She finished the rocksquat she was currently cleaning and stood up, taking the result to the next in the line of preparation.

"I want a wash, a drink, and some time off," she told Sandy.

Sandy gave her directions to find the underground lake. More torches had been installed, so the path was well enough lit to keep Kris from stumbling down the uneven levels of the path. When she reached the end, she saw the viney rope, with knots in it to help you shinny up. Peering over the edge, she saw that there was sand to cushion the shock of the jump, which was roughly two meters down. The torch showed her the perceptible movement of the water flowing past this point. But she remembered the stillish waters could run deep. Sandy hadn't told her not to dunk herself in, but she also hadn't said she could. She bellied down to the edge of the water and took a quick sip: it had a soda-ish aftertaste but it wasn't bad. She buried her face in the water, then, sucking in a longer drink. That was when the desire to be rid of the sweat and dirt of the past few days became irresistible.

Kris was first prudent enough to see if the vine rope reached far enough into the water so she could hang on to it for her bath. It did. She sloughed off the wrap-around boots and the coverall and, keeping the vine rope in one hand, eased herself into the water. It was cold: no doubt about that, but it felt so good. She gave herself as thorough a scrub as she could with one hand—and no soap—in probably the fastest bath she'd ever taken. Using her blanket, she dried herself as well as she could with the nonabsorbent material and rinsed out the bloodied sleeves of her coverall and the front of it where blood had spattered. She was back in her clothes, despite the dampness, and putting on the boots when she heard voices nearing. She hauled herself up to the top and started back, much refreshed by the respite.

She kept close to the right-hand wall as the group descending passed her.

"We gotta keep hold of that rope," one of the men was saying, " 'cos the current's fast according to the Cat."

"God, what I wouldn't give for a razor!"

"Sharpen your knife, buddy," someone else said with a laugh. "That's what pioneers did."

When Kris found her way back to her sleeping place, she saw that Patti Sue was the only one there, and still asleep. She dithered to herself about bringing some food back and making sure the girl ate, but maybe sleep was more important. The way the hunters had been bringing in game there'd be some for her when she did wake up. Only how long would the game remain stupid enough to hang around and die? There were a lot of people to be fed.

That was when she heard a lot of noisy shouting and glad cries. She made her way to the main cave again and tried to figure out what all the shouting was about. Everyone seemed very pleased. Bart was grinning like he'd just drawn a lotto number.

"What's up, Bart?"

"They found food. A mountain of it." Then he recalled himself to his duties and turned the pieces cooking at his fire before they were reduced to char.

"Where? Things we can eat?" Kris found herself regarding the french-browned food hungrily.

"I guess so—or why roar so much?" he said with a shrug.

Kris took herself where she could hear what was being roared.

"Mountains of food!" "Some kinda storage cave. Like a silo." "And other doors we couldn't open . . . yet!" "They'd have to be saving for centuries." "No one near, no footprints, just cracks in the stone like something real big stood there."

She worked her way through the excited people toward the front of the cave, hoping to see someone she could ask for specifics. The "storage" cave bit worried her. It suggested that Zainal's information had been incorrect. You don't store things, especially food, where there's no bodies to eat it.

". . . Scratch tests will give you a quick idea," an Asian was saying in a firm voice. "They worked on some of the game you guys caught as well as the roots and berries."

"Can we use the same method for the Rugarians and the Deskis, Matt?" she heard Mitford's voice ask.

"Gee, I don't know, sarge. I was paramedic for human types."

"Zainal, can you ask 'em?" Mitford switched to Barevi.

"Yes. I will ask," and Kris saw a movement among those crowded around Mitford as Zainal left to make his inquiries.

"Okay, listen up!" Mitford's voice assumed parade-ground volume. "I need some volunteers—you, you, you and you. Roll up your sleeves. We got samples we need to test."

Suddenly the press of bodies thinned out as many decided not to be "volunteered" for any other bright ideas Mitford had in mind.

"Was food all that was found?" Kris asked as she moved toward Mitford.

"Isn't that enough?" a woman asked in an irritable voice.

"It's a help, surely, but we need so *many* things to set up a habitable place . . ."

"Habitable? That's a laugh," the woman said and moved away from Kris.

"All that food could be a laugh, too," Greene said, appearing at her side, "if we can't stomach it."

"Anyone got any idea why there are such stores?" Kris asked him. "And what will happen if the three Bears come home and find Goldilocks?" She gestured to indicate they were cast as Goldilocks.

"Nope. Zainal hadn't any idea either. He insisted that the Catteni survey said the planet was uninhabited . . ."

"With sentient life forms?"

"Mmmm. Yes, he did make that distinction," Greene replied and then grinned. "Scared the hell outa even the Sarge when they came across metal doors, fer God's sake, across the cave entrances."

"How'd they get in, then?" Kris asked.

Greene chuckled again. "We got guys in this outfit with some very interesting skills."

Kris grinned back at him. "Where are these sesame caves?"

"A good half day's trek from here, so don't worry. And no road in or out. How'd they get crops in there without making some kinda tracks is puzzling."

"Stray mechanical things are more nervous-making than some honest-to-god alien creatures," Kris said.

"If you say so. Only the Sarge has sent a detail to scout about and see if they can figure out how and from where the silos get filled. He's calling a meeting this evening anyway, to explain everything. We might even have more to eat this evening, too." Greene licked his lips and Kris found herself doing the same thing as the tantalizing smells were wafted toward them on the breeze. "I could've eaten a whole one by myself."

"You didn't finish off your bars, did you?"

"Hell no, and watch yours, will ya? As I said, we got guys, and gals, with taking ways as well as interesting skills."

"Oh, lord, Patti Sue," Kris said and, ducking around Greene, started back to where the girl still slept. She paused long enough to ask Bart if she could take Patti's share to her.

"I can count on you give it to her and nobody else?" Bart said, fixing her with a stern eye.

"Yes, you can," Kris said solemnly, and found herself a rock on which to carry the hot meat.

Patti Sue was still asleep. Her food packet was gone. Someone had rolled the girl over to get at it. Kris fumed and then decided that Patti Sue would just have to take some responsibility for herself. She leaned over, careful not to tip the hot meat onto the dirty floor of the cave, and shook Patti Sue's shoulder. The girl's reaction—flailing about with hands and kicking out with her feet—was so unexpected that Kris ended up juggling the hot meat from hand to hand, trying to keep it from drop-ping to the floor.

"Hey, Patti. Easy now, gal. Don't make me drop your food. It's hot," she cried, trying to duck away from the girl's windmill of limbs.

"Kris?" Patti's voice broke and she stopped her battering. "Ohhhh, you scared me."

"Didn't mean to. Sit up, will you. This's hot! Use your sleeve . . ."

Patti rolled down the overlong cuff and using it as a pad, took the piece from Kris who set about licking her fingers as Patti regarded her portion suspiciously.

"Don't ask what it is 'cos no one's named the thing yet, but it tastes pretty good and it *is* hot."

"I don't think I could eat anything . . ." Patti said and held it out to Kris.

"No way, gal. You eat it. Think of it as the fried chicken your mother used to make . . ."

"No'm, I won't 'cos she couldn't cook worth doodly," Patti said in the only personal comment yet to pass her lips. Eyes closed, she then pulled her lips from her teeth and took a tiny and tentative bite. "Oh! It isn't bad, is it?" And opened her eyes, eating with more relish. "Or maybe it's 'cos I'm so famished."

"Patti, you didn't think to hide your bars, did you?" Kris asked gently.

Patti looked up at her and her face fell. "No, why should I? No one would . . ." And, with one hand, she felt anxiously beside her and under her blanket, her face falling into tragic lines as she realized that her packet was gone. She started moaning and nearly dropped the meat. Kris propped her drooping hand back in the direction of her mouth.

"So eat that, and we'll share. It's not the end of the world, because they've found a storage cave with food in it."

"Cave? Food?" Patti seemed to shrink in on herself with fear. "There are Catteni living on this world, too?"

"No, not according to our live Catteni expert . . ."

Patti's eyes got wider with her fright. "A Catteni . . ."

"Eat!" Kris said urgently. "There was one Catteni dropped along with us and he's not a bad guy. He won't bother you . . ."

"Oh, oh, oh," and Patti moaned all the time she nibbled at the meat.

Kris had heard about dainty eaters but Patti took the prize.

KRIS STAYED WITH PATTI SUE THEN, AS MUCH BECAUSE THE girl was so preternaturally frightened of every footstep in the corridor outside, every shadow that interrupted the torchlight into their cubby, as because she was also tired. Her hands and arm muscles ached from her stint at dressing meat and she had a couple of little nicks from knife cuts which were annoying. Then she remembered her first-aid kit and dabbed them with the orange liquid. It stung briefly but she knew that the Cat disinfectant would reduce any chance of infection.

She suggested a dip to Patti Sue, but when she had to tell the girl how to get there and the primitive conditions, Patti just curled up, hugging her knees to her chest, and moaned.

"You're going to have to stop moaning, girl," Kris said, driven to it. "I don't mind but there are others who will. We're all in the same condition, smelly, scared, and suspicious. So you're not alone."

"But . . ." Patti Sue began, her eyes wide and distressed as she once again began to either apologize or explain. She shut her mouth for a long moment. "You're right. I am chicken-livered. I always have been and I guess I always will be. And I won't say I'm sorry. I am what I am."

Kris began to regret her outburst. "Honey, we all are. Scared, I mean."

"Are you still my buddy?" And the piteousness of her tone and the beseeching look in her eyes touched Kris the way the constant stream of apologies hadn't.

"You got raped, kid?" Kris asked, hunkering down beside her.

A convulsive shudder swept through Patti Sue's slender frame and she shot Kris an anguished look. "It shows, doesn't it?"

"Not like a birthmark or a scarlet letter," Kris said as kindly as she could. "The giveaway is how you flinch whenever you hear a man's voice or see a shadow or someone, totally harmless, like Jay Greene, who only tries to *help* you. I won't say there aren't guys in this group who wouldn't like to . . . well, you know . . . because you're a very pretty and appealing person. But right now, hon, there isn't anyone with much extra energy. They need it all to stay alive on this crazy world. So why don't you buck up a bit? I'll stick by my ol' trek-buddy as much as I can, but I think I'm going to be getting some work assignments . . ." *or go nutty looking after you,* Kris added to herself, "that'll take me away from you, so let's introduce you to a couple of other people . . . women . . . who keep an eye on you when I'm not here."

Patti Sue had become more and more agitated as Kris explained the situation and Kris could see that the girl visibly fought, and subdued, her immediate reaction to such news.

"Now, c'mon . . . and take your blanket with you. Not that we don't have others but it's wise to keep your things together here."

With nervous hands, Patti managed to roll up her blanket and draped it over her shoulder as Kris had. Still anxious, she followed Kris out of the cave, glancing nervously about when she heard voices issuing from other openings and almost treading on Kris' heels, she was so much her leader's follower. She hesitated, gasping, when they entered the main cave and she saw so many people moving about on errands, or squatting by fires to cook, chatting with those waiting on the hot meats. Others were making their way to the entrance.

Surprised, Kris saw that the exit looked out on a darkness broken by the flickering light of torches and a fire. She was somewhat reassured that Mitford felt illumination was safe.

"We're safe here, Patti," she said, motioning to the opening. "Outside's all lit up like Christmas. Let's go grab some fresh air and get a good seat for the meeting."

Not only did the main cavern reek of cooking odors but others which were not as savory and certainly not appetizing.

"Oh . . ." Patti moaned, cringing.

"You might as well, honey, unless you plan on immuring yourself forever in the stink."

"If you say so . . ." Patti Sue was not going to venture anywhere even with Kris' assurance.

"C'mon, I think I know where we can sit," and Kris hoped that the darkness would be enough to conceal the evidence that part of the ledge had been an abattoir.

She walked, Patti so close behind her that she hoped the girl wouldn't lurch into her and knock them both off the ledge, to a point just above the fire: a fair-sized one, its flames reflecting off the faces seated around it.

"Hey, we'll have a balcony seat to the events," Kris said. "Front and center." Kris sat herself down while Patti Sue edged to Kris' right, with no one beyond her. Yet.

Kris tried to identify the faces in the firelight: she spotted Zainal easily, sitting beside Mitford; Bass, Murphy, a Rugarian, and two Deskis just beyond them and then faces she vaguely recognized from the march but couldn't put names to.

Patti Sue's fearful gasp alerted her to an approach and the girl gripped her arm with surprisingly strong fingers.

"Easy," Kris muttered under her breath for she recognized the newcomer. "It's only Jay Greene and he's decent. Hi, Jay. Don't know if you've met my buddy yet. Patti Sue, this is Jay Greene and he's a veritable Nimrod with Boy Scout snares. Join us. You can be our bodyguard."

Kris regretted that flippancy the moment it was out of her mouth for Patti Sue tried to get inside Kris' skin she sat so close. Kris sternly told herself that she might be as nervous if she'd been raped repeatedly, too. After all, that imminent possibility had prompted her to dare to steal the flitter and secrete herself in the forest, hadn't it?

Greene sat down a couple of good handspans from Kris. She took the moment to turn to Patti Sue.

"You're about choking the circulation off in my arm. Relax!" she murmured and felt the clutching fingers ease their stranglehold. She could almost feel the effort it took Patti Sue to remove her hands from Kris' arm. "What's the scam, Jay? You heard anything?"

"Yeah," and the firelight glinted off his white teeth as he smiled. "I hear that we are not alone!" He spaced the words out so that they sounded like the voice-over of a video trailer.

Patti Sue's hands returned to crush Kris' upper arm.

"I knew that," Kris said and this time just peeled the fingers off, putting the girl's hands back in her lap and giving them a final pat to stay there.

"No, I mean, we're not the only flotsam that got planted on this planet," Greene said.

"Really? Hmm, makes sense, though," Kris said in her most nonchalant tone. Why had she been saddled with such a nerd like Patti Sue! "There were only—what—five-six hundred plonked down in our field. I wouldn't call that an efficient disposition of redundant personnel. That ship they herded us into could handle who knows how many more. I know there were two levels, if not more. Maybe they did a clean sweep of all the holding cells on Barevi. That would make the journey here economically feasible. Any more humans?"

"Well," and Greene shrugged, "I'm not sure anyone could tell."

Patti Sue let out little whimpers.

"Look on the bright side, will you, Patti Sue?" Kris said. "You weren't one of them and you're safe with us. Isn't she, Jay?"

"Safe as houses," he said in a warmly reassuring tone for which Kris gave him a broad smile and a thumbs-up with her left hand which Patti couldn't see. "In fact, the more the merrier. So long as we can exchange information and band together to solve the problems this place poses."

"Any other scuttlebutt?"

"Like what?"

"Did that scouting party Mitford sent out find what brings in the grain harvest?"

"No," Greene said, shaking his head. "They did find other storage caves, all hollowed out of solid rock. And more valleys of fields and stuff. That's where . . ." Kris gave him a quick flash of her hand to stop him saying anything that would set Patti Sue off again. ". . . Where they could see other heavy vehicles had been parked," he finished off.

They all heard the murmur of voices and saw that people were emptying out of the cave now and either making their way down to the bonfire level or finding spaces on the ledge.

"Do we start off with a national anthem, or a prayer?" Kris quipped to Jay.

"I doubt the good sergeant is religiously inclined," Greene remarked.

"For which I am deeply grateful." Kris felt Patti Sue's body stiffen with resentment of her flippancy. "We need a realist."

"I second that!"

Chuck Mitford had now stood up and raised his hands for quiet.

"This is Mitford speaking in case any of you can't see me," he said in his gravelly parade-ground voice that echoed slightly in the ravine. "We've had several teams out on recon—reconnaissance to those of you who don't know military slang."

"We've found storage caves with enough grains—which we humans, at least, can digest—to supply us for years. We don't know who—or what—stored the stuff but they're unlikely to notice what we have taken, and will take, once we get our commissary organized. We're lucky to have some botanists among us who've figured out what we can and cannot eat of the local stuff, berries and roots. As you've all found out, the water tastes pretty good.

"We're also looking for additional quarters so we won't be jammed in like sardines . . ."

"Like those transport ships, maybe?" a man added with droll bitterness and got a laugh.

Mitford's grin was visible in the firelight as he held up his hand. "We've also discovered that there were other parties . . . landed here. We haven't made contact but if anyone does, send your buddy back here for assistance. *Don't* lead anybody here. Even other Terrans." He paused to let that warning sink in. "We'll be safe sticking together with folks we've already got to know on the trek here. We'll integrate anyone who wants to, but I think they ought to be vetted first."

There were murmurs of agreement there.

"No more aliens . . ." a voice said.

"That's a no-go," Mitford said sternly, glaring in the direction of the comment. "I make that plain right here and now. I don't know where you were on Barevi, but I learned that some of the aliens got just as many smarts as I do." He jerked his thumb against his chest. "And some have skills I don't. We get to make a fresh start on this planet so let's leave that sort of crap behind us. Huh?" He had a wide murmur of support for that suggestion. "For those of you who didn't know, it was the Deskis who found the caves for us. I doubt we could have. They climb like the spiders they resemble, only they're humanoid like us. I don't want to hear them called spiders anymore. Hear me? Well, hear me good. They were ripped away from their planet same as we were. So we treat them the same as we treat one of us—because they are one of us. Have I made that point clear enough?"

The response he got was vociferous from most, which reassured Kris. She tried to spot those who were reluctant to grasp that announcement.

"A Deski carried May Framble's kid on the trek and never made a single complaint." The look on Mitford's face chided those who had bitched. "So remember, they're in this, too, and pulling their own weight . . . what weight there is of them. The Rugarians are part of us, too, by the same principle. They accounted for more of our catch than human hunters did." He grinned. "Crack slingshoters!

"Another thing we gotta get straight like right now!" He pointed downward to emphasize the immediacy. "Any nasty individual caught stealing someone else's ration bars—*or* in the possession of more than a fair share—loses any he or she has on him or her and does latrine duty for a month. Understand?" He glared around the fire and up at the ledges. "We don't have much *to* steal, but this colony isn't going to tolerate any pilfering. Not no how, no way!" He sliced both hands across his body to indicate the finality of that statement. "You all got that straight?"

"Who made you boss, Mitford?" a male voice demanded irritably.

"You did!" Mitford jerked out his chin and glared in the direction.

Kris thought the voice sounded like the same one that had protested including aliens. She wondered if it was Arnie the weasel-faced, but on second thought, Arnie wouldn't have the guts to speak up about anything. He was the kind to go behind your back. And steal a sleeping girl's ration.

"You want the job? Have it!" He made as if to leave the bonfire.

There was immediate loud and vehement protest from human voices and, Kris was glad to hear, a waving of arms and hands from the Deskis and Rugarians.

"I've had years of knowing how to get even more ill-assorted bunches of bods working together than you possibly could, buddy . . ." and Mitford's tone made that noun a dirty epithet, "so unless you can beat my twenty-seven years—fifteen of them as a master sergeant—close your mouth hole. Anybody else got some complaints about how I run this chickenshit outfit? No? Well, that shows you've some sense upstairs. I don't like the assignment any more than you do. But I took it on and I'll see it through until we know what's what on this planet. So listen up now.

"We've got a base camp but we need to check out the area so we don't get any surprises. We weren't the only ones dropped, you know, and some might like to move into our own choice piece of suburban development." That provoked some laughter. "Not much, right now," and his pause suggested that he had many improvements in mind so there were a few groans. "But we'll do well—if we're let alone. So, two points . . ." And he held up his fingers. "First, we have sentries—with their eyes open —round the clock, even if we weren't issued one. Second, when you hear me or a sentry bawling *red alert*." And he cupped his hands around his mouth and roared the phrase, the sounds reverberating even as the people nearest him flinched back, with sheepish grins. "You come running as fast as you can, knives ready for action. Eternal vigilance is the price of liberty, my friends," and his expression became very solemn. "We lost out back on Earth but you may be damned sure I don't intend to lose out here. When we were dropped on that field, we got liberated again and I intend to stay free and make a great start! So anytime you hear *Red Alert*, whaddya do?" He cocked his head, hand to his ear.

"We come running, daddy," the wit from the shadows beyond the fire yelled.

"You better believe it! We also got to stay healthy, so that means latrines and they need digging where we haven't found long-drop holes. And throw in some sand every time you go. Keeps the smell down. We need hunters out every morning and we need volunteers to try foods and others to cook 'em. I talked to a lot of you on the way here but now I need to know which of you have specialist training like medics or chemistry or even survival courses. Everyone's going to work at something here to make this go. And I don't want any bitching about taking your turn at the dirty jobs. You'll be rotated. Now, you individuals with special train-ing that I haven't had a chance to talk to, come to this side of the fire when this meeting's over. You hunters, get your assignments from this Rugarian—he calls himself Slav—and he's got the best throwing arm I've seen since Lou Gehrig."

"Sarge, you weren't born when Lou Gehrig played," some wit yelled.

"Nope, but I sure saw enough footage on him in his prime. So hunters with Slav. I'll need more scouting parties tomorrow, so if you want some exercise"—and there were guffaws at that—"see Zainal here."

"You trusting that Cat?"

"Until hell freezes over," Mitford said in a tone that brooked abso-lutely no argument. "He got dumped here just like the rest of us and I'm not brave enough to ask him why."

Again a ripple of surprise but Mitford went on. "I want twenty individuals to make another run to get more grain . . . lemme see a few hands before I volunteer you." The hands were raised, far more than twenty. "Now, one last thing. There're more males than females. Some of our women got raped by the Catteni. We're humans! No one bothers a woman in this camp."

At the first mention of rape, Patti Sue moaned and tried to burrow into Kris. She was trembling all over as Kris put a protective and reassur-ing arm about her.

"What about a gal raping one of us?" the same wit called, and got snarling reactions from the women nearest him.

"If that kinda rape's inevitable, relax and enjoy it . . . buddy," a woman's voice called out, a distinctly bitter and contemptuous edge to her words.

"I'll personally stake out any *man* forcing a woman," Mitford said, holding up his big and capable hands. "The same goes for any female dick-teasing." He paused a beat and then gave a wry grin. "That is, if anyone has any energy for anything after a long day here."

"You see, Patti Sue," Kris murmured soothingly, patting the nervous hands clenching and unclenching on her arm, "and he means it."

"He can mean it, but what if . . ."

"No what-ifs, Patti Sue," Kris said as firmly as she could. But Mitford's call for explorers would give her the freedom to leave this clinging vine tomorrow and do something more noteworthy than gutting squatters. "You heard and he means it."

Patti continued to moan, despite her earlier promise not to.

"Now, I'll listen to *intelligent* questions, preferably ones I can answer," Mitford said. "I'll keep an open office but if I'm busy, talk to Bass here. Zainal, you just got appointed our alien liaison man, only because you speak better Barevi than I do. Dowdell—stand up there, and you, too, Murphy. They're acting as corporals. Got any complaints? Bring 'em to them. I assure you they'll be looked into and remedied . . . if humanly possible."

"Sergeant Mitford?" A man called, standing up so he could be seen, "Any ideas *why* we got dumped here?"

"Zainal says Cattenis do this to settle some planets. They come back at intervals to see if anyone's still alive and breathing."

"Then we won't get off?"

"I didn't say that," and Mitford's voice was grim. "But they have to land to take a look-see, don't they? There's no guarantee it's them'll take off in the ship, is there?"

That comment brought a lot of hopeful murmurs and muffled remarks.

"And one good reason to be friendly to the one Catteni we got on our side," Mitford went on. "Any other questions?"

"Then who's farming this planet?"

"Good question and I don't know the answer."

"Does the Cat?"

"Our Catteni ally," and Mitford paused to be sure everyone caught his use of the full name, "does not, as his knowledge of this planet is almost as spotty as ours . . . except he'd heard that some of the indigenous specimens are dangerous. Outside of this camp, you keep your eyes and ears open. Or live long enough to tell us what you saw or heard."

"Gee thanks, sarge," and a ripple of laughter ran through the crowd.

"Everyone's in remarkably good spirits," Kris said to Greene.

"Amazing how a full belly improves your outlook."

"Some bastard stole Patti Sue's rations," she added.

"Doesn't surprise me," Greene replied in a low voice. "We can get her more. Or should you keep them safe for her?"

"After what Mitford said about having more than my fair share? Thank you, no."

"Ooops! Hmmm. Well, I don't think she'll lose 'em again. Maybe you should trade buddies with Sandy."

"A thought," Kris replied, knowing even as she spoke that she'd be conscience-stricken if she did. "Why should I saddle her with Patti?"

"She's one tough lady and will watch out for the girl," Jay said. "And someone's going to have to watch for her because she's sure one nervous kid."

Kris sighed. *Decisions, decisions.* But she wasn't going to be tied by Patti Sue to the cave and not get some "exercise." *And* she'd survived on her own on Barevi so she was confident she could be useful as a scout or food hunter here on . . . wherever they were.

She cupped her hands to her mouth before she could think twice. "Hey, sarge, does this planet have a name?"

Mitford looked up, trying to see her in the darkness beyond the firelight.

"Bjornsen? Zainal, you guys name your planets?"

Zainal stepped into the firelight. "Only numbers," he said in Barevi, shrugging.

"What about 'Bounty'? Like in *Mutiny on the* . . . ." a woman called.

"Alcatraz?" "Be positive—El Dorado."

The exchange of names and opinions stirred an uproar which Mitford let go on for a while before he held up his hand.

"Murphy found some sort of chalk. He'll put it by the cave entrance and those of you who can write"—there were laughs—"can put up your choice of name. We'll settle the matter tomorrow right here," and he pointed to the fire, "when we issue tomorrow's progress report. Got me?"

"Gotcha!" was bellowed back at Mitford from every corner and the word bounced about the ravine.

"Okay, then. Sentries, take your positions. You'll be relieved at first moonrise. Dis-MISSED!"

Despite the military order, Mitford was grinning as he stepped back from the fire and into the darkness beyond it.

"C'mon, Patti Sue," Kris said, rising to her feet. "I want to find Sandy and see where she's sleeping. That way you'll know who to go to tomorrow."

Patti Sue was clutching her arm again. "Tomorrow? You'll be going? Where? You can't leave me!"

"Honey, I can and I will," Kris said. "You'll be all right. You heard Mitford. No one's going to mess with you."

"But supposing . . ."

"Shut up, Patti Sue," Kris said firmly, giving the girl a shake. "I can't baby-sit you every minute of the day."

"Oh," and Patti sank back in on herself.

"Now, Miss Patti," Greene said in a soothing voice, making no move toward the frightened girl, "you *will* be safe. Sandy and I are supposed to inventory the supplies we've got and what's been brought in. We may have to use the walls for our records but I got some of the chalk Murphy found and you can be our secretary. Is that what you did on Earth?"

"Secretary?" Patti's voice took on a little substance. "Yes, I was secretary. A good one, but . . ."

"You've just been promoted to the job here," said Greene so kindly that Kris could have kissed him.

"You heard Mitford, we all have skills that he can use, Patti Sue," she said and, with one hand around the girl's waist, eased her along the ledge to the entrance. "We'll just find Sandy. We'd better move along now or we might miss her. She's good people."

"But *you're* my *buddy*," Patti Sue said in a quavering tone.

"Yes, I was," Kris' conscience forced her to say, "for the trek, but that's over and we're here. Besides, Sandy's a good cook and it's a smart idea to be on the right side of the cooks, you know. Now let's find her."

They did, grilling the last of the day's catch.

"Sentries get what's left over," she said, taking in Patti Sue's terror-stricken face and smiling reassuringly. "Patti Sue, you just sit here, right by me." And she physically manhandled Patti Sue into the space she wanted her in. "You go on now, Kris, so Patti Sue and I can get acquainted."

Give the woman her due, Kris thought, she didn't even blanch at the idea of having Patti Sue hanging on to her. As Kris hastily departed, Greene on her heels, she heard Sandy telling the girl that she had a daughter about Patti's age and where had she come from on Earth.

"You can't be saddled with that one any longer," Jay said as they made their way down to the bonfire.

" 'And there's no discharge in the war,' " Kris chanted out, resorting to Kipling.

"Huh?"

"Nemmind. Can you see Sarge or Zainal?"

"Beyond the fire, I think."

It was an easier climb down than up, so she realized that wider, better steps had been carved out of the cliffside at some point during that day.

They had to wait their turn to speak to Mitford as there was no lack of volunteers for the scouting and hunting parties. Maybe another day Kris could go to the caves to see the stores with her own eyes.

"Got room for me on a scouting party tomorrow, sarge?" Kris asked when he looked around and saw her. When he spotted Greene behind her, he scowled. "Oh, I left Patti Sue with Sandy but I've got survival skills."

"Yeah, you did well on Barevi," Mitford said, but she thought, for a moment, that he had other plans for her.

"The skills're good anywhere . . . in the universe . . ." And she grinned. " 'Sides, I had a good rest today, gutting beasties."

Mitford hesitated until he saw Zainal watching him. "Go with our ally. You're safer with him."

"I am?"

"You better believe it." That came out as a growl. "Rendezvous at last moonset. Same cave? Good, Zainal'll know where to find you." He started to turn to those waiting behind her.

"Sarge, someone stole Patti's rations while she slept."

Mitford nodded to Jay Greene. "Mark a package with her name then, Greene, and keep it in stores. At best, she'll get used to dealing with a male again. Next?"

And he looked beyond them to others waiting patiently for his attention. Kris and Jay moved off.

"I don't know if that was an insult or not," Jay murmured drolly.

"Well, I'll know it's safer in your care and she'll get fed."

"Patti Sue'll always get fed," Jay said cryptically.

KRIS COLLECTED PATTI SUE FROM SANDY, TRYING TO IGNORE the look in the girl's eyes which suggested she had doubted that Kris *would* return for her. Sandy asked which cave they were stashed in and she'd just change her bedroll into it.

Kris escorted Patti to the water containers for a drink, and then to the latrine cave and showed her how to take care of that basic problem before they retired. There was one woman fast asleep and snoring along the inside wall. So Kris directed Patti Sue to lie next to her, then she stretched out and there was space left for Sandy, at least, and probably someone else. Because her noise would keep everyone awake, Kris leaned over and, shaking the woman, suggested that she turn on her side. Sleepily the woman complied and then Patti sighed deeply in appreciation as she made herself as comfortable as possible.

Not that Kris needed any help getting to sleep. She didn't even turn once—that she remembered.

Chapter Five

THE PANORAMA FROM THE TOP OF THE cliff was breathtaking—and Kris needed to get her breath back after the climb Zainal had led his squad on. Before them stretched in a westerly direction—as far as the eye could see—the large neat fields, punctuated by streams that glistened as sparkling ribbons in the morning sun. Some of the fields were occupied by graziers whose form was difficult to decipher at this distance. Off to the south there was a huge body of water, but whether it was an ocean or a lake could not be ascertained.

This party was also told to hunt and Zainal had said tersely that it was best to hunt farther from the camp. To this all the experienced hunters agreed. There was little grumbling from the humans about the Catteni—or none after they'd been on the way an hour, for he set them a bruising pace and sheer human perversity required the eight members of her species to keep up with Slav, the

Rugarian, and the two Deskis, Zewe and Kuskus—or that was what their names sounded like.

Mitford's claim that the Deskis were useful was borne out when the spindly creatures seemed to ooze up cliffs. They didn't have suckers on their feet, but that was the impression you got, Kris thought. They stood firm behind the ropes they let down for others. So did Zainal, who was the first humanoid to follow. Some way or other, in the five ascents made, Kris always seemed to get hauled up by Zainal, who grinned each time he handed her safely onto the next level. She felt oddly pleased by his continued attention . . . considering the fact that it was all her fault he was on this planet anyhow.

A day on Botany, which was what Kris privately decided to call the planet, was longer than Earth and Barevi, so they'd been going quite a long time before the sun was at zenith, which was when Zainal called a meal-break halt on the summit. The ration bars would have gone more easily with some water to soften them though they'd all had a good drink at the last stream. Kris, dangling her legs over the edge of their vantage point, munched away and looked at the view, trying to figure out what crops were being grown, and for whom. As far as she could see, the land was cultivated or used as pasture, yet Zainal had repeatedly said the planet was not inhabited. So who was nurturing it and why? Considering that the harvestings were stored in caves, could the consumers be cave dwellers, residing deep within the planet? That would explain why there were no cities or visible occupants. Not that Kris was eager to meet troglodytes.

The range of hills, of which this was an outcropping, loomed behind and around them, spreading to the east. Mitford had marched them northward from the field on which they had been dropped by the Catteni, up the ravines until the caves had been found. But those had showed no sides of occupation, past or present, even by the local wildlife, which apparently favored forested and vegetated areas. Curiouser and curiouser, Kris thought.

Just then the Rugarian, Slav, uttered an odd cry and pointed, his oddly jointed furry arm directing everyone's attention to the northwest. Kris could see nothing but more rolling fields in their neat patchwork arrangements.

Shielding his eyes, Zainal peered out and jabbered something to the Rugarian, who gave his head a sharp affirmative nod.

Zainal turned to the others. "Slav has seen what is different . . . not animal." He made a cube shape with swift gestures.

"Any people?" Kris asked, thinking that the presence of geometrical objects might indicate another drop point and more castaways. Not that she really wanted more people whose needs had to be considered.

The field was a fair distance away, though there were two little forests to traverse and in each the guys with slingshots brought down some of the alien birdy-like things and enough rocksquats to make the hunt worthy of the name. Kris had coaxed one of the hunters into letting her try her hand with the sling when he didn't need it. By the time they had reached the second woods, she was getting closer to the target she aimed at.

"Wait'll you see a covey of the critters," Cumber suggested, "and then, if you miss what you're aiming at, you might hit something else."

"You're encouraging," Kris replied.

"Are you?" and Cumber cocked his head at her, his eyes bright with suggestion.

"Well, on that score, no, buddy, not encouraging," she said bluntly but with a smile.

She would have liked to stride forward, right up on top of Zainal's heels, but that didn't seem a good idea either so she shortened her stride and dropped back with the Deskis, who were ambling along, both festooned with necklaces of the rocksquats which their unerring aim had downed. They were as good as hunters as they were as climbers.

The cubes were indeed Catteni-issue: one was even unopened and contained blankets which Zainal parceled out among the hunters to be carried back. There were dried brown puddles in an irregular pattern across the field but little else. Kris felt a wave of regret for those who had lost their lives here from "unknown assailants," as a news bulletin might say.

Reassembling her clutch of blankets, Kris saw the Rugarians quartering the field while Zainal had several others spread out and searching the borders.

"Think those flying things got 'em?" Cumber asked, returning to her.

"Could be. But all of them? When the crates have been opened?"

"Or what comes out of the ground in the dark and sucks corpses dry," Cumber went on, waiting to see the effect his words had on her.

"This world does its own recycling," she replied. "No waste, no debris, no Coke bottles or dead aerosol cans."

"Huh?" Cumber was plainly a literal-minded man and her facetious remark did not register with him.

Then one of the border patrol let out a shout and everyone, of course, had to go see what he'd found: a clear trace that some large objects had pushed their way through the bushy hedge.

"Looks like something stampeded through there," Cumber told Kris.

She could see the line of retreat, or flight, through the foot-high crops in the next patch. At that point one of Rugarians shouted.

"Quiet, he says," Zainal said in his deep-voiced Barevian that carried just loudly enough so that the entire group heard him.

Slav was gesturing with his knife and then Kris clearly heard the Barevian word "hot."

"Hot metal?" she asked, making her voice carry as she strode toward the knot of people clustering about Slav.

"Hot metal?" he was asked. Someone else pulled out their knife, pantomiming a hot blade.

"Yissss," and the Rugarian pointed downhill and inhaled deeply.

"He smells hot metal," Kris said.

Zainal took charge, directing everyone to hide behind the hedges and for Slav and a human male to go investigate.

"Hot metal? The people who farm this planet coming to see who's messing up their fields?" Kris asked of no one in particular.

" 'Bout time someone came to have a look-see, if ya ask me," Cumber said in a pessimistic tone.

"And all we got is knives!"

The returning scouts were not much ahead of the "thing" that lumbered after them. Only it wasn't *after* them: it was following a course to the fields above. It was gliding along on an air cushion, for it negotiated the hedges in a smooth hop and, while Kris and everyone else watched in fascination, it reached one of the crop-bearing fields and immediately went into a different mode: spraying the field.

"Willya looka that!" The speaker rose to full height in his surprise. Immediately those on either side of him pulled him back down behind the screening hedges. "Ah, it ain't got no eyes. It's just a farm machine. An' I think I saw another one down below, spraying another field."

He was correct, as everyone immediately discovered by the simple expedient of taking a careful look.

"Close look now," Zainal said in Barevi and pointed at not only Cumber but Kris and Slav to take the detail. "Stay down. Stay quiet. Don't know what these machines can do."

"Wal, I doan mind restin' my dawgs," was someone's response. "That Cat can sure trot the klicks."

Kris was rather pleased to be singled out as someone whose opinion on the machine might be useful. Crouching low—and indeed Zainal moved as close to being on all fours as she'd ever seen a man move, even in Rambo pictures—they traversed the field where another group of whilom settlers had been deposited. They could see the top third of the machine, diligently switching back and forth, spraying evenly.

"That's why the fields are so damned regular," Cumber muttered beside her. "So the machines don't have to do corners or nothin'."

"Work-efficient," Kris replied in a whisper.

Zainal's hand flagged at them, and they saw him put his finger to his lips for silence. Kris grimaced at having to be reminded. Machines who came all on their own to do even methodical tasks might be programmed for other actions.

When they got closer to the farther hedge, Zainal motioned them to get even flatter to the ground. Kris suppressed a groan as she fell to her belly and inched along like the rest of them.

They found gaps at the base of the hedges, between the thick trunks of the vegetation, and peered out at the machine, which was now on the far side of the field. It was still balanced on its air cushions, still spraying, and the only mechanism that it reminded Kris of was a Dalek from old *Doctor Who* videos.

"Exterminate. Exterminate." The Dalekian cry echoed through her head and she wondered just how apt it was. Was the thing spraying fertilizer or insect killer? It was nearly finished, whatever. When it got to the last corner, however, it turned and came toward them.

Zainal signaled for them to make themselves as unnoticeable as possible by squinching up against, under if possible, the thick hedge. Kris heard the thing nearing just as she also damned near gutted herself on a pointy root. Grimacing, she endured the discomfort for what seemed to be hours.

She heard a clicking, whirring, and other such noises that were so much like the sounds of that old *Doctor Who* series that she was also close to laughter. Except this wasn't a laughing matter.

Then the machine "jumped" the hedge and they all got a blast of hot, smelly, metallic air before it swept across the field, not touching any of the debris but certainly, Kris felt sure, checking it over.

Another hopscotch leap and it left, fortunately never getting into the field where the rest of the hunters were, hopefully, making themselves as scarce as possible.

"That thing's dangerous," Cumber told Zainal, who merely nodded.

"We get the others and leave," he said, emphasizing the last word significantly.

Slav, who had been listening carefully to the Catteni, now raised his hands to his lips and emitted a shrill sound that wasn't birdcall or dog call or anything.

It was answered by a similar call from Zewe.

"Tell. Go," and Slav pointed uphill, the way they had come.

"Good!" And so they started on the way back, joining the rest of the hunters by the time they reached the next field.

The Deski then gave one of their warnings, quick gestures indicating flying things, and everyone froze in their tracks. A formation of five fliers came gliding in from the east, swooping down over the field and then quartering it. As nothing moved, the predators were balked of their reward and, with squawks of complaint drifting back to the breathless waiting hunters, they proceeded on down the slope.

"Wow!" Cumber said in a low and respectful voice. "That damned machine called in an alarm."

"We weren't seen by it," Kris said thoughtfully, "so it must have some sort of sensors, because it sure knew we were there. Like a Dalek."

"A what?" Cumber clearly had never watched the old s-f serials.

"A robot with deadly intentions."

One of the other men grinned and said in a nasal falsetto. "Exterminate! Exterminate!"

"Hey, mac, keep it down!" someone else ordered in a nervous whisper.

"What is said?" Zainal quietly asked in English.

"The machine reported our presence," Kris said, pantomiming the actions of her words. "It may be heat-sensitive. Knew we were in the hedge because of body heat."

Zainal nodded. "Take good care. We go to caves now. Hunt. But watch always." He tapped Slav and Zewe and gave them some rapid orders. "They hear best," he added to Kris.

The two Rugarians moved to the sides of the main group and then, on Zainal's signal, everyone moved out again.

The return home was even rougher, with all the descents to be made while they were laden with the rewards of their hunting. No unusual hazards were encountered. On the plus side, the six-legged graziers which they had spotted in the field bled red blood when nicked. Two were slaughtered and dressed right there in the field so that their meat could be portioned out among the hunters to carry home. The additional blankets were put to good use. And very helpful later when the insects began to rise after the sun went down.

Deskis evidently had a sharp homing instinct because they led the way back in the semidarkness. Kris had never been so glad to see the campfires of home!

There was certainly applause for the hunters when they returned so well laden. No sooner had she divested herself of her burden than Zainal touched her arm and gestured for her to join him in reporting to Mitford. Cumber and Slav were there, too.

"Cumber said you identified these machines, Kris," Mitford said. He looked very tired.

"Me? No, not really, only that they're some sort of robots."

"Cumber said they didn't even touch the ground."

"Air-cushion propulsion?"

"Hmmm. High-tech. And heat-seekers?"

"Well, the machine must have called in those flying predators," Kris said. "And there were five of 'em so I'm extrapolating that the machine sensed our five bodies hidden in the hedge. But anyone's guess is as good as mine," she ended modestly.

"But yours is a tad more educated from watching all those kidvids. I'll buy it, Bjornsen, I'll buy it. G'wan now, and you as well, Cumber. We've got a sort of bread tonight, soda bread." He grinned. "One of the chemists found a deposit of sodium bicarbonate. Bread doesn't taste half bad—if you're hungry enough and you ignore occasional grits from the grinding."

No sooner had Kris reached the main cave, to stand in line for her hunk of bread, than Patti Sue discovered her. The girl threw her arms about Kris' neck and howled with tears of relief.

"Hey, now, Patti Sue, I was perfectly all right," Kris told the girl, trying to calm her down to mere hysterics.

Sandy came to her rescue. "There now, Patti, I told you Kris can take care of herself."

Patti Sue was persuaded to release her death hold on Kris. As she stood back, she looked down at her front, now smeared with what also covered Kris' garment.

"Oh, my gawd, what's that?"

"Probably blood," Kris said, for the meat she had lugged back had dribbled down her, attracting the insects.

"Oh, my gawd!" And Patti Sue backed away from Kris as if she had turned leprous.

"Guess I need a bath," Kris said cheerfully and, taking her portion of bread, ate it on the way down to the underground lake to make herself more presentable.

She wasn't the only one to want to get clean. There were quite a few white bodies splashing in the water. Someone had added more ropes. Pausing only to add her wrap-on boots, food packet, and blanket to the row of similar belongings awaiting the return of their owners, she grabbed a spare tether and plunged into the water. Twisting the rope about one wrist, she then winkled herself out of the garment and rinsed it thoroughly. The water was invigoratingly cool and somewhat restored her energy level. She got out, drying herself on her blanket and then wrapping it sarong fashion. She squeezed the water from her coverall and then made her way back out of the lake cavern. She was sure she'd sleep that night.

She did. Until Zainal roused her. It had to be the middle of the long Botany night because everyone around her was fast asleep, especially Patti Sue, who would have had a knicker attack if she'd awakened to see the Catteni so close by.

There was just enough light supplied by the flickering torch in the passageway for her to see Zainal touch his lips for silence. Groaning involuntarily because she was stiff from yesterday's exertions, she had trouble rising. Zainal put out a helping hand and—zip—she was on her feet. She grinned up at him as she followed him out. He didn't release her hand and she was content to let it stay in his strong mitt. She had to entertain the thought that she was definitely attracted to the Catteni, and not just because he was taller than she was. He had conducted himself with such dignity and tact during the past few days that surely even those who hated the Catteni violently couldn't fault him. Certainly Mitford had made it plain to the motley crew that Zainal was a large and useful entity in their continued survival. Once the euphoria of the past few days settled into boring routine and less exciting uncertainty, she suspected there would be problems.

"Trouble?" she whispered in Barevian once outside the room. "Don't you ever sleep?"

"Not in danger," he murmured back and led her.

It was third moonset when they got outside. Kris could see faces lit by the campfire in the ravine; one of them was Mitford's.

"Sorry to rouse you, Bjornsen," he said with a grin and gestured for her to hold up her cup. She didn't realize until that moment that she had unconsciously gathered up her accoutrements—her blanket, the cup, and her ration bars. "As far as my internal clock is concerned, this is well past dawn."

"And you're a creature of habit?" She grinned at him, accepting the warm liquid. It was some sort of herbal tea, which was an improvement on bare, naked hot water.

"Pull up a stone," he added and she sat on the one just to his right. "I want you to go with Zainal, here, and Slav and the Deski Coo, and suss out what other surprises this place has in store for us. No sense in thinking we're safe in this ravine. One of the eggheads mentioned that there are indications this," and he waved about the walls of the ravine, "may get flooded in spring. High-water marks and scrapings of trees on the sides, higher up than we can stand, and I ain't that good at treading water."

With a start Kris wondered if he was quoting an old Bill Cosby routine.

"I want you to circle around," and he gestured, "as far as you can go in a day's march, and map. Zainal here says he knows how to map. He's picking up English real good. Officer material for sure." This last Mitford said in a lower voice and with a grin meant for Kris alone. "Seeing as how you know him, and seem to be able to charade things to Slav and Coo, you'd be the human in the team. Unless you got any real objections to the duty."

"Is there going to be trouble for the . . . ah . . . aliens, sarge?"

"Ain't there always?" Mitford said in a cynical tone. "I can trust you, Bjornsen," he added in a dark low tone. "You've proved you can hack it, too."

"Thanks, sarge," and Kris felt a good deal taller for that unexpected praise.

"And with the Catteni along he'll see you don't come to harm."

"Thanks, sarge," she said, this time wryly. Build 'em up to knock 'em down, but she grinned to show she had no ill feelings. It was enough that the Sergeant wasn't as misogynistic as some career soldiers she'd heard about.

"I want you to draw additional rations from Greene for all of you. Seems like the Deski can't stomach the red meat and they need somethin' in their diet, though what it is I haven't been able to figure out." He sighed. "That's another reason I'm sending one along with you. And you're to eat!" He shot one thick index finger at her so suddenly that she rocked back. "We've got enough to supply patrols away from camp. That stuff may be less tasty than field rations even, but it's got all the nutrional crap you need to march on. Get another issue of blankets and an extra coverall. Got it?"

"Got it, sarge," she said, her hand halfway to her brow to salute when she realized that might not be appropriate even if it was an instinctive reaction to his manner.

"Good," and he grinned in the firelight, having caught that abortive gesture. "Zainal, get the rations and supplies and move out at your leisure."

"Leisure" in army parlance meant right smart. So in next to no time they were making their way in dawn's early light up the ravine, and into undiscovered country.

Zainal led at a spanking pace that didn't seem to alter whatever the terrain they had to traverse. But, like Mitford, he did call a halt when full daylight lit the skies.

The first thing Zainal did was tie a knot in a thin strip of blanket, of which he had quite a few tucked inside a thigh pocket. A tally rope? Well, they had no writing materials and Zainal, strong as he was, couldn't exactly carry a sheet of rock with him to chalk up the miles. Or should she say "klicks" since she was on a military operation?

"What are you counting, Zainal?" she asked.

"Steps, so I know distance," he said in Barevi.

"Oh . . ." And that steady pace now made sense. "What's the Catteni word for miles, or kilometers? How do you measure distance?"

"My . . . step . . ." he said tentatively in English.

" 'Stride' is the better term," she said.

"Stride is one Catteni *pleg*."

"*Pleg* for the leg," she said, using her own brand of *aide-mémoire.* "Make a stride for me, please?"

"Hmmm," and he complied.

Stretching her own long legs to their limit, she could just about make the same length. "Hmmm. Over a meter then. Hmmm. Well, I could almost spell you on a level surface so you could have a break."

"Hmmm," he said again, blinking rapidly as he sifted the meaning of her words.

So she "charaded" what she'd said and then he understood with a grin.

"One *pleg* is almost dead-on a meter. One *pleg,* one meter," she said.

Slav and the Deski were watching, too, their expressions keen enough to show they were interested in the demonstrations. So she pointed to the Rugarian, gestured for him to take a stride. His was the same length as hers but the Deski's was much longer since he had spiderlike, long leg bones. Although Kris tried to get Slav to tell her what a *pleg* was in his language, and attempted to extract the same information from the Deski, she had no success. Both kept saying stolidly, "*Pleg, pleg.*"

A plague on it, she thought but smiled and patted each in turn before she sat down again to get the good of the rest period. She wasn't sure if they didn't care to have a language lesson or if they had some obscure reason for sticking so perversely to the Barevi words. Both Rugarian and Deski had rather flat, inflectionless voices, but then what she knew of Catteni was flat and inflectionless, too. The lingua Barevi had had more rhythm and tone to it than the languages in which Zainal had spoken to both Slav and Coo.

As they hiked on, they reached another plateau, where a second break was called: another knot in the tally string. When Zainal told her how many *pleg* each knot represented, she realized they were traveling at slightly better than four miles an hour . . . that is, if Zainal was stopping every hour. So, in the next onward push, she counted the minutes while he counted his paces. She thought she might have lost a few minutes because she got sidetracked watching the Deski check the vegetation on the plateau—what there was of it because there were no fields or hedges or much of anything. But just when she felt they had been marching for an hour, Zainal called a halt.

"Gee, man, you got a clock in your head?" she asked as he made a third knot.

He raised a querying eyebrow at her. It made his face seem more humanish, less Cattenish.

"Lordee, how do Catteni tell time?" she muttered to herself, trying to remember if he'd had some sort of digital device on his wrist, like good spacefarers should, when she'd first encountered him.

"Time." He picked up on that word and tapped his skull. "Time kept here. Good time."

"Now don't tell me your home world has long days and nights like Botany?"

The two spent the rest period explaining and understanding that concept.

"Full turn of planet is not as long as here," he said in the best English sentence he had so far made.

"Boy, you sure learn fast."

"Is 'boy' a good thing to say of me?" Again that quizzical expression.

"Well, yes," Kris replied, grinning, delighted with his sense of humor: something she hadn't thought Catteni possessed. "But you are a man, I am a woman. Boy is a young man. I'm using it in the context of a slang expression, so it doesn't mean the same thing as the word should."

He grinned in such a polite way that she wasn't sure if he understood her explanation at all before he gestured them to take up their journey again.

The day grew warm on the plateau, which had no shade at all on its sandy and gritty surface, only the wiry plants with their odd-shaped leaves that didn't look like anything on any Earth deserts—and Kris had been in the Las Vegas and Salt Lake City scrubland areas. Coo kept tasting plants, and even different-colored patches of soil as they went: usually spitting the samples out so that Kris wasn't sure what verdict was being rendered. She was becoming so thirsty that her tongue felt swollen, so on what was the midday rest stop she didn't have the desire to banter with Zainal. The others took out "lunch," chewing off good hunks from their bars, but she didn't think she had enough saliva in her mouth to chew, much less swallow.

"You bite, you chew, be better," Zainal said kindly and rolled his mouthful about to show that he wasn't swallowing either.

She tried a small piece and discovered that something in the bar helped generate some moisture. She didn't eat as much as the other three but felt better for what she did put in her stomach.

They traveled on, then; the plateau was gradually sloping down to a lusher sort of terrain. And a stream. She had to restrain herself not to prostrate herself *in* the stream but carefully reeducate her mouth and throat to wetness.

"God, what I'd give for a canteen."

"What is this 'god' so many call on?" Zainal asked. "Another 'boy'?"

Coming as the question did in Zainal's rich guttural voice, it sent Kris into a fit of the giggles. She'd often been told that she had an infectious laugh—and had proved it from time to time by setting a whole classroom off—but it pleased her no end that the effect extended to another species. The Catteni's chuckle sounded very human. Slav cocked his head at her and frowned while Coo merely looked at her in consternation, as if the Deski thought Kris was having a fit or convulsion.

"I won't answer that question now, Zainal," she said when she had reduced giggle to grin. " 'God' was never a boy! I will explain another time when we have several years at our disposal."

Zainal frowned, not having understood all she said. Which was about par for the course, she thought. And just as well.

Having drunk sufficient water to revive her, Kris now pulled out the rest of her lunchtime bar and finished it. She was ready to go then, but Zainal did not urge them away from this pleasant spot: as much because there were new varieties of plants along the stream bank which Coo was sampling with great eagerness. He came back with something which he showed to Kris, the first time he had done that.

"Looks like a kind of watercress to me," she said, testing one of the stems and a leaf. "Can you eat it?" she asked, gesturing to her mouth with the sample.

The Deski nodded and popped a stalk into his mouth and chewed with every indication of pleasure. Kris nibbled carefully and, feeling her lips and gums go slightly numb, buried her face in the water and gargled vigorously. She felt Zainal's hands on her shoulders supporting her. She rinsed and gargled, being careful not to swallow, and rinsed and rinsed until the sensation was washed away.

"Thanks, Zainal," she said and then saw how concerned all three of her companions were. "Oh, I'm fine. I didn't swallow any of it. All yours, Coo, all yours."

The Deski nodded vigorously and made a show of clutching the rest of the sample plant to his chest.

"No more try," Zainal told her sternly.

"You bet!"

His concern altered to a glare of frustration. "More 'boy' words?"

"Well," and Kris rocked one hand back and forth to indicate neither one nor another. Oh, lord, but she'd never appreciated how complex English was. Or did she mean "idiomatic American"?

They went on then, until Kris wondered how much longer she could ignore the swelling of her feet which the wrap-around boots were not compensating for. And she thought she'd been fit! Ha! She had dropped behind the two aliens . . . two of her companions, she amended quickly . . . and found herself watching the rippling of the hairs on the Rugarian's legs. His feet did look funny in the wrap-around Catteni footware and he didn't seem to have "muscles" where humans did: but depressions came and went with each stride sort of laterally instead of up and down the way calf muscles did. And in front of him, Coo seemed only to have leg bones, no muscular movement at all, only the tendons—or what passed for tendons on a Deski—on either side of the one leg bone, lifting and lowering it, like the shaft of a crane. She tried to imagine the anatomy of her companions, sans their skins, and failed utterly. Biology had not been one of her stronger subjects. Oh, the gaps in her education. *Well, there's nothing like on-the-job training,* she thought, or whatever it was they were now doing.

Some place and time later, she was able to stop moving her legs and sat down on a rock. There was a small fire enclosed in a circle of rocks and around a cairn of rocks. *Odd formation,* she thought bemusedly. Then, as the buzz of fatigue allowed it, Kris could hear the babbling of a brook nearby. Water! She half rose and then was pushed back onto the rock and a big leaf presented her.

"Drink!"

She grasped the leaf, feeling the thickness of it, and found a "lip" from which to drink. The water was ever so cold and tasted ambrosial. Real Adam's Ale!

"More?" asked Zainal, looming over her.

She struggled to rise. "I can get my own water . . . Ohhh, no," and her voice came out just this side of a wail. Zainal's big hand pushed her back onto the stone just as she realized how weak she was.

She sipped this time and was able to take in more of her surroundings. Someone was chipping rocks?

She looked around and saw Slav and Coo hammering a hole out of the slab of rock not far from the fire. They were on a slab of rock, an outcropping that edged yet another of the fields, a meter above ground level. Large-leaved plants formed a bit of a canopy over the portion of the cliff, affording them some shade. Beyond this small campsite she saw the spray from a little cataract that spilled off the rock and into a pool, then on down across the field. A crop field, she noticed.

Looking back, she realized with a start of amazement, the men were making a rock caldron. On the far side of the campfire were the limp carcasses of rocksquatters and some other smallish beasties she hadn't seen before: six-legged which, she thought idly, would make skinning them tedious. Then Zainal knelt to perform that task. Rather deliberately, she thought, he gathered up the entrails and threw them off, onto the field below.

"Zainal," said Slav, and pointed to the now sizable hole they had chipped into the rock.

"Water," Zainal said, and Slav and Coo, reaching up to pluck more big leaves from the trees shading them, made several trips each.

When the hole had been filled to within a handspan of the top, Zainal threw in the dissected joints of the animals and Coo added some roots, similar to the ones already in use at the cave. Then Zainal, deftly using a forked stick, started transferring hot rocks into the improvised stew pot.

Kris was delighted and clapped her hands that someone was making use of her suggestion. She reached about her and gathered up more stones, which she piled in the center of the fire. They'd probably need a lot to get the stew cooked enough.

Full dark and first moonrise had occurred before they were able to eat, using twigs like chopsticks to get the pieces from pot to leaf. A little salt would have made it even more palatable, but hot food in the stomach was enough of an improvement in itself over dry, hard rations no matter how nutritious.

When they had eaten as much as they could, Coo covered the "pot" with a flat rock, wiping his hands as any human would, for the finish of a good job.

"Slav, first moonset," Zainal said. "Then Kris, to second moonset. I third, Coo, final."

No one argued but Kris was just as glad to have a long enough sleep to restore her energy. She visited the waterfall, drank, and then, unfastening the boots, presented her swollen, tired feet to the cascade. She had to set her teeth against the pain but shortly enough the abused flesh was too cold to send any other messages to her brain. She stood the cold as long as she could before she minced her way back to the fire. She thought her feet's flesh had been reduced but she couldn't be sure, they were so numb. Coo and Slav had been off on a necessary absence, too, so they all arrived back to settle down for the night.

She unrolled her blankets, spread them, and settled herself on the rocky surface, her cooling feet toward the fire. A good pile of dead material had been piled near at hand to feed the fire all night. What primeval holdover made her feel better for having a fire?

It also didn't matter that there was no way to cushion her hips and shoulders on the hard rock: she was too tired to care. Briefly her mind dwelt on the distance they would have traveled that day, but she hadn't really noticed how many tally knots were on Zainal's string. Well, a good night's sleep mended many aches.

Slav woke her and the first thing she noticed was that the first moon was still visible in the sky. But it gave enough light for her to see that Slav was agitated . . . all the fur on his head stood up. He had also roused Zainal. He pointed down, to the field, and gestured for them to come. Whatever it was did not require either stealth or quiet.

Slav just pointed and looked at them for their reaction.

Kris wanted to throw up. Zainal simply watched the . . . things: things with long tentacles and writhing hairs, and seemingly no body unless the body was still underground: the things were crawling over the intestines that he had discarded onto the field. There wasn't that much left of the entrails, for whatever was feeding on them absorbed the matter quickly, and before many minutes had passed, there was only the grassy covering left, no trace of the refuse. Maybe she had just imagined the squirmy, wriggling roundnesses that had feasted.

Zainal was nodding his head as if this was what he had expected. Kris swallowed. Was that what had happened to those who had bled on the other field? And bodies that had been left on the one she had awakened on?

"Neat," she said softly. "An internal garbage collection! Sure keeps the neighborhood clean. And those are not 'boy' words."

In the moonlight his teeth showed whitely.

"You knew?" she asked him.

"A thinking."

"Thought, you mean."

"Think, thought?"

"Right."

"Sleep now. Show's over."

Now where had Zainal picked up that one? Kris wondered as she returned to the warmth of her blankets. She sighed; maybe she should stay awake and give Slav just that much more uninterrupted rest. But she was asleep again so quickly—and without a single dream—until Slav roused her to a moonless sky.

She stood her watch, walking the perimeters of their rocky outcropping. Was that why Zainal had picked this camp? Or was it because they could make a stew pot in rock? Not that she didn't put it past this planet to have rockdwellers of horrific abilities, too. There was no sign of any further activity on the ground, however. And she was a little tempted to throw another piece of garbage down there to see what happened: the sort of compulsion one has to be sure that what one saw was just as horrible the second time as the first.

Nighttime and silence were great aids to imagination and she had to keep her mind firmly on the positive things: she *was* alive, her stomach *was* full, she was as safe as anyone else in the camp, even if this planet had too many anomalies and mysteries to give anyone peace of mind. So, to keep from thinking of the wrong things, she reviewed all the camping trips she'd ever made—the stone pot was a good notion—to see if she could remember any other "doables." A knife, a hatchet, a cup, and a blanket were not much to survive on, with, by. Not that they hadn't been doing pretty well with just that basic equipment. But there were so many "things" they lacked. A pail to carry water in, a frying pan to cook food in, a fork or two would be right handy. Why, when she needed it the most, did she not have her Swiss Army knife? Boy, that item would be worth its weight in platinum!

Of course, there were spare blades back at the main caves. Wasn't there someone at the camp who thought he could manipulate blades into other useful tools? Her stomach began to rumble. Damn this planet! Even mealtimes were skewed. She slowly ate half a ration bar. Nowhere near as tasty as that stew.

Despite such a positive bout of thinking, she was glad enough to rouse Coo to take over sentinel duty.

THE NEXT MORNING ZAINAL HAD ALREADY HOTTED UP THE remainder of last night's stew for breakfast and a hearty one it was to fill night-empty stomachs. They cleaned up the leftovers, sopping up the last of the juices with another ration bar. Kris was stuffed but she'd work it off soon enough.

She asked Zainal how far they had traveled the day before and he showed her the tally string. She whistled appreciatively: they'd made forty klicks, no mean feat when you considered the ups and downs they'd had to negotiate. Her feet, which she had bathed again in cold water, certainly knew they'd walked that far. Maybe she shouldn't have asked. It made her feel tired to think she'd trekked that far.

Zainal kicked out the fire and used the stew-pot rocks to make a cairn before he signaled them all to move out.

"Where are we heading for today?"

"Circle," he said, gesturing a wide arc, and ending with his finger pointing to the cairn. "Find what is find."

"What we can discover, find, see, know." Kris had never thought of herself as a pedagogue but she had this intense itch to correct Zainal and improve his language skills. Thank goodness he was amenable to learn-as-you-go.

They jumped down off the outcropping and made their way across the field. Zainal moderated his pace from yesterday's stride but not by much. Maybe his feet hurt, too? How much walking did a space trooper get to do?

Coo found some green globes in one of the hedges that he gobbled juicily, humming happily to himself, but Slav curled his upper lip in distaste, a process which fascinated Kris as Slav really did *curl* his lip up and into a fold above his uneven set of teeth. She wondered again how Rugarians kept from seriously biting the insides of their lips with such dental equipment.

Everyone kept their eyes open, surveying behind them and above them, especially when they were out in the open. A rearview mirror would have been right handy, Kris thought. Dead things got sucked into the ground at night but clearly the avian critters patrolled daily for their sustenance on things that moved.

The fields were endless on this gently rolling terrain. Streams were laid on at such intervals that Kris' earlier wish for a canteen was redundant. There were no roads, no bridges, no overpasses, nothing more serious than rather abrupt little hillocks of stone that seemed to rise straight up out of the ground. She'd seen something similar somewhere on Earth, but it took her time to dredge up Ethiopia from her memory. Most of the hillocks were bare, but a few seemed to have caught enough soil to support bushes and one or two were crowned with the almost-trees that baby bushes became, if they had a chance to live long enough.

Then they came to a whole series of fields that had recently been harvested. No track to tell them in what direction the harvesters had come from or gone to. Although the direction would take them out of the circular loop Zainal had proposed they make, they followed the harvesting signs.

They heard it before they saw it and only had time to take cover before the mechanical gadget floated over the intervening hedge in the very next field.

"Do we stand or run?" Kris whispered hoarsely to Zainal. He shrugged, but he was stuck as far into the hedge as he could get, and stock-still. She imitated him, wincing as branches dug into the softer parts of her.

They could smell hot metal, combined with odder smells that must have been fuel—only that begged the question in Kris' mind: *Who manufactured the fuel, not to mention the machinery?* They waited in this position until she got a knotting cramp in one side and grimaced, trying without moving much to relieve the spasm.

When is that mechanical going to move on? Or, and the thought pierced her with a good deal of fright, *is it waiting for reinforcements? Does the machinery on this planet learn?* Very carefully craning her neck up, she could see through the funny-shaped foliage of the hedge material that the Dalek hadn't moved a smidgeon: it just hovered there, on the other side of the hedge.

She poked Zainal, who was also watching for movement, and when he carefully turned his head to her, she raised her eyebrows in query. Just then Coo came alert: not that the Deski hadn't been tense with the waiting. He turned his glance down the field and very carefully pointed out a direction. Something was coming for them? The fliers always seemed to come out of the sun at them. What would be coming up the hill? And should they leave? If they could, with the mechanical monster an arm's length away. And if they did make a run for it, where would they go? There wasn't even a hillock close enough that they could scramble up.

Kris didn't like this at all.

She liked it even less when Coo let out a whimper and pointed with more agitation down the hill.

The things moved so fast that Kris barely saw the glint of them in the sun when they were upon them . . . and shooting their little darts. She felt the prick and she lost consciousness from one moment to the next.

Chapter Six

A HAND ROCKING HER SHOULDER ROUSED her from the stupor caused by the drugged dart.

"Kris, wake up." Zainal's voice.

"Lemme sleep." She ached and she was soooo tired.

"No, we go now or not."

That brought recent events back and she shot up so fast she nearly cracked her head on Zainal's as he knelt beside her.

It was dark all around but she could make out both Slav and Coo, and then the odd stamping and heavy breathing, as well as animal smells, gave her another clue. They'd been dumped in a barn? Classified as animals by the mechanical? She didn't know whether she was amused or indignant.

"Water?" And Zainal handed her a full cup, which she sipped to revive her parched mouth and throat.

"Thanks." She got up as she finished and,

when she would have handed him back the cup, he pointed to the empty loop on her belt. "Oh! Yes. Thanks again." Then she felt for the important parcel of ration bars and her blankets. All in place and accounted for. She breathed a sigh of relief. "So how do we get out of here?" she asked, sensorily aware of the size, as well as the darkness, of the building.

"This way," and Zainal cupped one big hand under her right elbow and turned her in the proper direction. "Care . . ."

She just avoided tripping over a sleeping beastie of some kind: one of the creatures that made a liquid looing sound. She blinked furiously to accustom her eyes to the gloom and took a couple of quick and careful steps to catch up to Zainal, Coo, and Slav.

"The main door, of course," she murmured when she realized that that was their destination. A very large set of doors. And how they were to open them, when there was no apparent handle or lock or knob. . . .

She heard a little snick, a click, and a pleased mutter from Zainal and heard the rumble of a door moving on a track as he replaced his boot knife.

"Come," Zainal said and she and the others wasted no time in slipping out. Zainal carefully closed the door behind him and it snicked once more when shut.

They were by no means clear yet, for their temporary prison seemed to be only one of many such buildings, set in a long line, visible as a greater darkness against the lesser one of the sky. For she could see stars above but none of the moons.

"Hold," and Zainal took her hand in his and then she felt Coo's dry fingers closing around her left hand.

Slav, with better night sight, was their leader.

They must have completed a full circuit of the immense yard before they halted again.

"Place to hide?" Zainal asked Slav. The Rugarian shook his head.

Coo said softly, "Up?" and pointed in the direction of the stack of crates that had been halfway around their exploratory circuit.

"Maybe we can see more when a moon comes up," Kris suggested.

Zainal nodded and they made their way back to the tall crates. Once again, Zainal's height and heft made the difference as he boosted each of his team up onto the first level of the container stack. It took the three of them to haul him to their level. The process was repeated until Zainal decided they were high enough up not to be immediately visible from the ground.

Visible to what? was Kris' question but she didn't voice it. They had at least reached enough space for all of them to lie down, which is what seemed the best idea although Zainal just sat, propped against the crate, obviously intending to stand the watch.

"Wake me to spell you," Kris told Zainal and made to lie down on the hard surface. *How odd*, she thought, *that a simple convenience like a mattress was a distant memory.*

Then she felt hands pulling at her and, quelling her immediate resistance because the only hands that were that strong were Zainal's, she allowed herself to be pulled around, her head resting on his thigh. Not quite as hard as the crate, and warm, so she made herself comfortable. He shifted her briefly and gave her a sort of a pat before he crossed his arms. She was obscurely glad that there were only Slav and Coo to witness this coziness. Well, hell, she didn't care. She rubbed her head into his leg, wishing the muscles were not quite so firmly packed. There was rather a lot of Zainal that was commendable. *Slow down, girl*, she warned herself. *Why, then, do I feel more comfortable with him than with anyone else, even Jay Greene?*

THE SUN SUDDENLY BLAZING RIGHT IN HER EYES WOKE HER more speedily than any alarm. She was facing into it, unlike Coo and Slav, who had carefully put their feet in that direction. Zainal's head had dropped to his crossed arms and he was breathing heavily enough for it to be called snoring.

She was about to wake him when sudden activity below startled her. Machines were whirring, grinding, revving, and there were all kinds of noises, except those of intelligible speech of any kind. She eased away from Zainal . . . *Has he moved at all since he volunteered himself as my pillow?* . . . and crept to the edge and looked down: shuddered and then took a grip on herself. They had climbed considerably higher than she'd realized last night: there was only one more tier of crates above them. And the crates looked fairly well used, scraped along the sides and dented in places: the usual result of careless packing and unpacking. Only what packed and unpacked them? Where did they get emptied? With what were they now filled?

One building now gushed forth smoke and another stench that was unmistakable. Kris had only encountered it once before when she passed a meat-packing company on a detour through a grotty area of Denver. The abattoir? And it was opposite buildings that resembled the barn they'd been in that night. To confirm her hideous surmise, the double doors of one of the barns now opened and its inhabitants, comprised of the six-legged graziers and some other smaller and different types, were being herded to the abattoir by a curious mechanical which had long extendable "arms" and which spat electrical sparks at laggard beasts. All unconscious of their imminent demise, the beasts jogged into the building. Kris steeled herself but heard nothing and saw only the animals entering the building. The doors slid closed and noises she didn't want to describe issued forth, making her clamp her hands to her ears.

"They gather meat, too," Zainal said right beside her. Instinctively and desperately wanting some comfort for the harrowing so near by, she burrowed against him. He was warm, alive, and nearly human. To her surprise, he embraced her, soothing her with his hands and thus restoring her courage. It struck her as very odd that a Catteni could be comforting.

It was when the doors of the next barn opened and its occupants driven out that matters changed abruptly. For there were recognizable humans staggering out into the light, shielding their eyes from the bright sun that poured, almost obscenely, down the passage between the buildings. They, too, were being herded by a long-armed, spark-spitting machine. They were not, as the beasts had, amenable to such herding.

Even as Zainal reacted, rousing Slav and Coo, some humans were trying to evade the machine's extensions. Which was obviously unaccustomed to any sort of protest. In fact, all the humans seemed to be trying to escape, as if they had figured out the fate which awaited them.

"THIS WAY! HERE!" Zainal yelled, waving furiously and glanced toward Kris to shout directions.

One human spotted them, pointing upward and calling to the others. Although Kris couldn't imagine how they could manage to help others escape when they didn't even know how to themselves, that was not as important as getting humans out of the clutches of the mechanicals.

The four scrambled down the big crates they had so laboriously climbed the night before. At least, *down* was easier than up. But it was *up* they'd need to do again.

The humans pelted down the alleyway to be met by Zainal, who had halted his three companions on top of the ground tier with an imperious hand. He gave Kris the unmistakable order to stay where she was. But, as she saw him link his hands, she realized what he was going to do: throw the people up onto the first crate. Kris, Coo, and Slav then pushed them to the next level, urging them to get higher up, out of any possible range of the mechanical's extendibles. So they formed a human "lift" system for the escapees, humans, Deskis, and Rugarians, three green Ilginish and two Turs, the goblins who were so short that Zainal was slinging them up.

In the panic of the effort to get everybody off the ground and started up the crates, Kris got bruised, cut, and had her right wrist wrenched so badly that she had to rely on her left hand. Then there was Zainal to get up to safety because the mechanos were now aware that something was distinctly out of order. Kris wondered if they had counted bodies coming out of the barn and had now discovered that the appropriate number were not being processed. A shame to put their production figures out. But they'd rescued more than twenty from slaughter.

Zainal had to jump to reach the helping hands that would take him off the ground. A funny little clicking machine was now quartering the passageway.

"Climb!" Zainal said to those on his level. "Seek heat. We go to cold."

They climbed and climbed until they reached the top with the others and then they all stopped in awe. As far as they could see, there were crates stacked to the same height. Acres of them to the horizon.

"Now this is one mother of a stockpile," a human muttered with an understandably hysterical edge to his voice.

"And we damned near joined it," someone else said.

"More down there?" Zainal asked and Kris noted him breathing heavily for the first time since they'd started this reconnaissance.

"Hell, all we saw was that one stinking barn after those flying turrets darted us. Are we going to hang about to see?" Clearly that was not his preference.

"Hey, you're a Cat!" the first speaker said accusingly.

"Cat or not, he just saved our lives. Thanks, pal," the second man said to Zainal, holding out his hand. He was filthy and the slight breeze on the top of this incredible stockpile wafted a stench off him that nearly gagged Kris.

Most of the escapees now sank to their butts to rest after their scrambling retreat.

"Zainal is my name. These three and I explore. You are?"

"Speaks good English for a Cat," the second man said.

"Kris Bjornsen, Slav, and Coo are us," Zainal continued the introductions. Then he paused for the others to identify themselves.

Their stories were similar to the experiences of Kris' group except that they hadn't had the benefit of a Sergeant Chuck Mitford to marshal them out of danger. The field they had been dumped on had been attacked by the fliers in spite of Deski attempts to warn of incoming danger. Everyone had scattered in twos and threes and small groups, only to be rounded up when they were spotted the second morning by a harvester unit. They'd been in the barn for several days but had survived on their food parcels, which were now almost gone. Several of their number had been trampled to death in the barn when the animals had, for some reason, panicked the second night of their incarceration.

"That's why we all smell like this," said Lenny Doyle, a slightly-built, dark-haired man with a pleasant, open face and a nice smile. Dick Aarens had been the first speaker and still regarded Zainal with frowning suspicion. He was taller than Kris, but he had a dreadful slouch and a mean slant to his mouth as well as deep scowl lines.

"Zainal got dumped down here along with the rest of us," Kris said with an indifferent shrug to relieve the sudden tension among the newcomers, "and I don't know why he's here, but he is and he was ready to risk his neck to get you out, so cool it, mac."

Dick Aarens reluctantly subsided but Kris caught him more than once glaring at either her or Zainal.

"So do we go back and see if anyone else's stuck in those barns?" Lenny asked Zainal.

"Why should he risk his neck for us humans?" a stocky man of apparent Italianate origin demanded in a surly voice.

Zainal had his head down in what Kris was beginning to know as his "thinking" pose. He looked up at the sun and then did a slow circle, squinting against the glare of the sun. He said a few brief words to Slav, who nodded.

"Slav leads to camp," Zainal said. "The machines learn . . ."

"Yeah, but do they have something that climbs crates like a spider?" Aarens demanded.

"You have food?" Zainal asked.

"What's it to ya?" Aarens wanted to know.

"Oh, cool it, Aarens," Lenny said. "The machines didn't search us. We got cups, knives, and bars."

"No water," and again Zainal glanced sunward.

"I take the point," Lenny said. "Look, I'll volunteer to go back to the edge and see what's up with the mechanicals." He grinned at Kris for his description of their captors. "They must've . . . processed . . . another group yesterday. We heard screaming a coupla times." He shook himself convulsively. "So we figured we might have to make a break for it."

"There're a lot of barns down there," Aarens said, shaking his head.

"We go back," Zainal said. "See."

"Now, wait a minute . . ." Aarens said, holding up one hand in protest.

Protesting to the idea as well as the spokesman, Kris thought, marking Aarens as troublesome.

"Then go with Slav," Zainal said, shrugging his indifference. "There is much to see and know." This time his gesture meant learning as much as possible about the machines and their operation.

"Can you open barn doors from outside?" Kris asked.

Zainal nodded. "Easy," and now he grinned. "Animals do not unlock doors. Humans, and Cats, do."

Lenny laughed out loud at that and nudged the hostile Aarens. "Sense of humor, too. Shall I go back for a look-see? I had a long drink just before we got ejected from our happy home."

Zainal nodded and Lenny trotted back the way he had come.

"Hey, bro, I'm coming, too," and a second man followed.

"The Doyle brothers stick together. I'm Joe Lattore," the stocky

Italian said with a grin, nodding at both Kris and Zainal. "So what do we do if there are a lot of other humans, and aliens, stuck in with the cattle?"

"We get them out," Zainal said, and hunkering down, unrolled one of his spare blankets and, taking out his knife, began to rend the blanket into strips. To make ropes, Kris immediately realized.

"Yeah, a rope would be real handy," Lattore said and took a blanket as Zainal handed them around.

It wasn't easy to do, given the sort of indestructible fabric it was. Kris had to stop: her wrist ached and was next to useless. But hauling folks to the top of the crates with the help of a rope would be a lot easier. That is, if the mechanicals hadn't figured out where the escapees had gone—which was possible. By the time they had acquired several lengths of sturdy rope, the Doyles returned. They had seen no more except smoke from the processing plant.

"Yeah, machines operate on logic, and our escape—since they classified us as 'meat animals'—would be inconsistent," Kris said, as she worked. "Somehow I don't think their programming would extend to coping with inconsistencies. We came up as heat sources where heat sources shouldn't be, in there messing up their crop fields. That was easy for them. So they dumped us in with the other animals they were collecting."

"I don't think I like that," Joe said, shuddering. "Bad enough to be mistaken as food. How come they don't recognize people?"

"Does sort of beg the question, doesn't it?" Lenny said. "I dunno how they figure it all out. We were there four-five days without anyone taking a blind bit of notice of us, or even opening the main door. When they did, we couldn't get out for those six-legged things being crammed in. And suddenly there was only standing space. Then—whammy! We're scheduled for the chop. They must have started . . . well, processing . . . yesterday if what we heard were human cries. . . ." Lenny gave another shiver.

Kris watched Zainal thinking over this information. She wondered how in heaven's name the Catteni scouts hadn't noticed such installations on their exploratory pass of this planet. Surely they would have spotted such a vast number of crates? Unless, and she thought of the evidences of scrapes and bad handling, these were new, and the last lot had been collected? By what? For whom?

"We see if there are . . . more people," Zainal said, having reached a decision. "You help?" He looked around at the recently rescued.

Ten decided to remain and help, including the two Doyle brothers and, oddly enough in Kris' estimation, Aarens. The others were led off by Slav, who once again assured Zainal that he could find the cave campsite. He kept pointing to the north and east. The two Deskis went with him, to keep a listen-out for the fliers and any roving mechanicals that would need to be avoided at all costs. If nothing else, this recon had taught Kris, and the others, the sorts of hazards that had to be avoided: sleeping on bare ground, avoiding the harvesters, and freezing when fliers were spotted. Simple, homey rules, Kris told herself facetiously. She was glad she'd had a good drink of water before they'd set out. Still, maybe they could sneak back down to the vacant barns.

Which is what they did when Zainal and his stalwarts reached the yard. The fact that no one had been searched, much less stripped, was discussed.

"They didn't search the six-legged critters," Lenny said. "Why would they search us?"

"But we're . . . we're humans," Aarens said and Lenny's brother, Ninety, snorted.

"Did you introduce yourself? Well, then, how would the machine know we're different?"

"You mean they thought we were animals?" Aarens was outraged.

"Not very flattering, is it?" Lenny said drolly.

"Just another warm body, bro," Ninety quipped back with a grin. "Any warm body'll do. If it registers."

"That is how the machines know," Zainal said. "Heat."

"I'll buy that," Lenny said. "And movement."

"There are no . . . people . . . on this planet," Zainal added.

"Yeah," Lenny said thoughtfully. "Think you're right. I thought robots were supposed to protect humans." He glanced slyly at Kris.

"Not if they're not programmed to."

"So who, or what, programmed 'em?" Lenny wanted to know. Kris could only shrug her ignorance.

Having made their way across the crates and to the nearest barn, they had climbed the roof and now looked down through one of the ventilator slats into the nearest barn. It was empty. Empty and smelling of some kind of a disinfectant which had its own unmistakable stink.

"What a stink," Lenny said, wrinkling his nose.

"Could there be such a thing as a totally mechanized farm planet?" Kris said, wondering out loud. Then she turned to Zainal, who was lying on the roof beside her, still looking about the empty space below. "How many continents are there on this world, Zainal?"

"Four. Two large, one not so large, one small."

"Which are we on?"

Zainal shrugged.

"How come he knows so much?" Ninety asked, jerking his thumb at Zainal and addressing Kris.

"He once saw a report on the place. He just didn't look hard enough to remember everything we're dying to know," she said, grimacing. "What he has recalled has already saved us a couple of times."

"Who's us?"

Kris told them, and Lenny grinned at his brother when she described Chuck Mitford.

"They never quit, those old soldiers, do they?"

"Mitford's not old," she said defensively, "and we were very lucky indeed he was there, because we stayed free."

Lenny gave her an odd look. "Can you be sure of that?"

"No surer than I am of anything else on this planet."

Zainal rose. "We look at all."

As soon as a quick peek proved that there was nothing moving in the yard below them and the smoke was no longer coming out of the abattoir building, they checked the other barns: twenty in all, half of which reeked of the disinfectant. Three of the other ten they examined held nothing but animals. They would call down the vent, tentatively at first, but then with more vigor until they were sure there was no one there to answer. The graziers kept making their stupid "looooing" sound in response to all questions.

"All the same," said Lenny in disgust, "never did like cows."

"These aren't cows," Aarens said. "Nothing like cows."

"So? They're loo-cows instead of moo-cows," Kris said, a comment which brought chortles from Lenny and Ninety.

"They're still not cows," Aarens said. "Cows give milk. Those things don't have any equipment beyond two extra legs."

The next barn produced astonished and glad cries and a jumping about of obvious people-shapes in among the loo-cow forms.

"Keep it down, will you?" Aarens called urgently, glancing nervously around.

Lenny Doyle crept to the edge of the barn, looking up and down the quiet avenue and gestured an "okay."

"What do we tell 'em?" Aarens asked, not looking at Zainal.

"We come at night. They keep quiet now," Zainal said, ignoring being ignored.

"Night's a long way away," Aarens said.

"We watch."

"We could let down those ropes we made and haul 'em up?" Aarens suggested.

"It's much easier to open the door at night and let them out," Kris said firmly, knowing that she wasn't up to hoisting who knew how many heavy bodies. "Like we did."

"Night best," Zainal said, nodding.

"Why? Machines don't care if it's night or day. Machines don't need to sleep." Aarens was persistent.

Zainal muttered something under his breath. "Do not run at night. Can't."

"Why not?" Aarens was getting belligerent, deliberately, Kris thought, trying to find fault with Zainal.

"I think the machines are solar-powered," Kris said, grasping at an explanation that fit. "Sun power?" she asked Zainal who nodded, smiling that she had grasped the correct explanation.

"Yeah," and Ninety's eyes widened. "Yeah, they got those funny panels. At least the harvester did. Makes sense. There hasn't been any rain yet."

Zainal grinned. "Rain very bad here. In places. We see who is where," and he gestured toward the other barns waiting to be searched.

Four more contained humans and the message of imminent release was repeated, caution urged, and the prisoners were told to get as much rest as they could because the escape route was a rough one. There was some protest, but Kris, speaking for Zainal—as that seemed diplomatic —assured them there were reasons for the delay.

They returned then to the roof of one of the empty barns. Prying open one ventilator slot, Lenny Doyle, as the slimmest of the men, crawled through. He was going to check to be sure there were no interior sensors. They let him down far enough so that he could peer around, swinging on the end of the rope.

"Looks clean to me. Sensor eyes can't be all that different," he said in a loud whisper to those waiting on the roof. "Lemme down. I need a bath as bad as I need a pee. Begging your pardon, Kris."

She chuckled and watched as he was lowered to the floor. She was sent down next and heard them ripping away enough of the slot to permit the heavy frame of Zainal to pass. The thin blanket rope was rough on the hands and she slipped a couple of times because her wrist wasn't functioning, but all of them made it safely to the floor.

There were a dozen or more watering troughs to service the animals the barn usually held, so a few on one side were designated as baths. Piles of some sort of dried fodder had been placed in wall mangers, and Kris looked forward to sleeping a tad more comfortably on a hay bed until moonrise.

Zainal, with Aarens and the Doyles, did a circuit of the empty building, checking for any other sort of sensors that might tell the mechanicals one of the barns was inhabited again.

While most of the men decided to bathe, Kris was more interested in piling up enough fodder to make a decent sleeping surface. She hadn't liked the leer on Aarens' face when he looked at her. He struck her as the sort of devious personality who'd peep if given the chance. She wasn't going to give him one. . . .

At that, he sought her out, his longish hair still dripping. She couldn't really hold that against him, but she disliked the proprietary way he made as if to join her on her pile of hay.

"You find your own, buddy," she said as discouragingly as she could.

"Hey, lady, just thought you'd like some quality company. Can't say I approve a nice girl like you having to be paired with a Cat. Or is it voluntary?"

"I volunteered for the patrol, if that's what you mean." And her tone implied that had better be.

"Are there more like you back at this camp of yours?"

"Aarens, get lost. I'm tired and I want to sleep . . . by . . . myself," she said, emphasizing her wish for solitude. "Git!"

"The fresh stuff is over there, Aarens," Lenny said, pointing to the manger, his expression pleasant. But there was no doubt that he wouldn't move until Aarens had.

When she was left alone, she lay down on her pile, so comfortable that she fell asleep despite the muted voices of the men.

MITFORD SURVEYED THE CAMP, WELL PLEASED WITH THE IM-provements the last two days. They had plenty of game and some of the women had thought of sun-drying the overage into a sort of jerky.

"Waste not, want not," was the theme for the day.

Scouting parties kept coming in with little treasures throughout the long day: fine sand that could be used for a timer.

"Like you use to time your boiled egg."

"No glass."

"Well, there're these nut husks. Cut a teeny tiny hole in one, let the sands run through. Turn it over. Couldn't be simpler."

"You lose a couple seconds turning the damned thing over."

"Complaints, complaints."

"Hey, what about a sundial? There's that flat place at the top of the rock just below the sentry post."

"Yeah, and how do we time it?"

"Hell, you're the mechanical engineer. You figure it out. One one-hundred, two one-hundred, three one-hundred is still a second even here."

A commotion midafternoon brought fifteen angry women and one bloody-nosed Arnie to Mitford's office. Noticing that all the women had wet hair, it didn't take him more than a minute to figure out that Arnie had been peeping again.

"He didn't stay warned off, Mitford," an irate Sandy Areson said, pinching the man again. "He's a dirty pervert, is what he is. And with him doing latrine duty only makes it easier for him to know when we're going to bathe. Chain him to a rock or by God, I'll sharpen my knife and . . ."

Mitford had begun to chuckle, as he'd had a sudden inspiration. "I think we can provide restraints for our little Arnold Sherman. And provide an object lesson at the same time. Jack Lemass, front and center," the Sergeant added in a bellow.

"Yo!" And a man who had been carving at various types of the woods available in the nearby copse loped over. "You rang?"

Most people were in good spirits, Mitford decided, and proving ingenious in what they could contrive. They didn't have nails, but Jack Lemass, who'd been out early in the morning on a hunting party, was sure they could fashion chairs and tables and other useful items from the larger trees.

"Yeah, d'you think you could construct me a pair of stocks?"

"Stocks?" Jack poked his head forward on his neck in surprise.

"Stocks?" Sandy exclaimed and then burst out laughing. "Hey, that'd be great. And we could belt him with rotten eggs—if we could find any rotten eggs." She gave the cowering Arnie another swat but she, and the other women, began to grin in happy anticipation of his future discomfort. "Make 'em as uncomfortable as possible, will ya, Jack?"

Jack went through a little routine of pretending to measure the quivering Arnie so that he moaned in apprehension.

"Okay, ladies, as you were," Mitford said. "Sorry you've been pestered."

"Thanks, sarge," Sandy said and took his hint, shooing the women out of the "office." "We've got work to do, too, ladies."

"Better yet, Jack," Mitford said, "take him with you to cut the wood, Jack, and make him help you build it. To fit him because I think he'll be in the stocks a lot. Won't you, Arnie?"

"I was only looking," Arnie whined in self-defense. "I wasn't doing more than that."

"That's enough. Shut your face and be damned glad I don't get Jack to put a stake and whip you at it."

"You wouldn't *whip* me?" His voice cracked in terror and his whole body trembled. "You're human, you're American. You can't," and Arnie ended on a note of pure panic.

"Be grateful then, because the next step for someone like you, Arnie," Mitford said, raising his voice loud enough for everyone working the area to hear, "is being staked out on a field for the scavengers. And don't think it can't happen. It can!"

Jack's eyebrows were raised almost to his nonexistent hairline and he whistled softly.

"Okay, Arnie, we go walkies now."

Old-fashioned stocks wouldn't really hurt a man, or a woman, Mitford thought as he picked up another slate to record their construction as a deterrent. But it would prove his administration had teeth and wasn't afraid to bite. So far, people were far more interested in how they could turn their skills to improving their living quarters. And that was what settling was all about. Living off the land you were on and getting the best you could.

Late that evening, long after the second serving of the evening meal, two more patrols reported in: one had found rock salt, which could only improve the taste of food, and the other—geology and mining types— had located deposits of iron and copper and had brought back samples. Murph had bent his ear about all they could do with iron and copper. So Mitford said that he'd organize a squad to help Murph mine and refine. Murph went off, muttering happily to himself.

"Every day in every way, we are getting better and better," Mitford muttered to himself, able to see one more step in their adaptation. Another few months and no one would recognize themselves as the dispirited dregs they'd been waking up less than a week ago.

———

WHEN NIGHT CAME, KRIS WAS ROUSED WITH THE OTHERS WHO had rested. Zainal showed the Doyles and Aarens how he had manipulated the lock with his knife blade.

"The ol' credit card trick, huh?" Lenny remarked, then added when he saw the confusion on Zainal's face. "I'll explain later."

"More boy?" Zainal asked Kris, his teeth white in the dark as he grinned.

"More what?" Lenny asked.

"I'll explain later," Kris replied, chuckling. She wondered what Aarens would say if he knew she'd prefer the Catteni to his company any day of the week. Or any night, come to think of it. *Down, girl,* she told herself, but having said that, the notion came back often enough to tease her.

They slipped out of the barn, Zainal closing the door carefully until they heard the lock snick. Then they went to the first of the inhabited barns and Zainal opened it, too.

"Oh, my god, I thought you'd gone and left us," cried the man, his voice sounding loudly in the quiet night. He was only one of many crowded close to the door.

"Sssssh," said the relief team as a chorus.

"Damn mechanicals might hear ya," Aarens said. "Follow me and fer gawssake, be quiet."

While Kris was asleep, the rescue had been organized. Two men would lead each rescued group down the road to the crates and start them up the ropes hanging in readiness. Zainal and Kris took the last group since Zainal was the only one who knew the exact trick to open the doors.

In the group she and Zainal released, there were two women, one of them heavily pregnant and awkward in movement, and the other one older and limping badly. The pregnant woman was also slightly hysterical with the relief of being rescued.

"It's bad enough my Jack got killed on Barevi, but I thought I'd at least have my baby to cherish," she said weepingly. Not that Kris blamed her, but this was neither the time nor place for true confessions. "Then that awful discipline meeting and I wasn't doing a thing but standing where I was told to stand and then I get gassed. I prayed that, somehow, God was with us still and we'd be rescued. And we are, and I simply can't believe it. Oh, you're so good to risk your lives to save ours."

Kris couldn't seem to stem her flow of talk. At least Patti Sue would shut up when told to.

"How're we going to get her up the crates?" she asked Zainal in a tense whisper as they started the people down the road.

"I carry. Not heavy. Big."

"Just don't let her see you're Catteni," Kris said, glad that the poor light hid the telltale gray of his skin tone.

The pregnant woman, Anna Bollinger, presented less of a difficulty getting up on the crates than some of the others. Fumble-footed and -fingered, some of them, and four, besides Anna, had to be hauled up because their shoulder muscles gave out on the third "lift."

Eventually, all thirty-five were on the top and moving off north by east as Slav had. Not moving very quickly either as if the release and climb had about taken all the physical energy they had left in them.

Sometimes, Kris thought as she trudged along beside Zainal, *you can do the right thing for the wrong reason.* Her hands were stinging, her wrist ached despite the strip of blanket she had wrapped about it as a brace, her shins were scraped and raw, her toes hurt, and she was sure her arm and shoulder muscles would never recover. She would have loved to have a trough to wallow in.

By the time the first moon came up, they had not yet made it to the end of the crates. Again she wondered what was in them, if it wasn't halves of loo-cows, and for whom the machines gathered the supplies.

———

THEY HAD TO CALL A BREAK THEN, TO REST THE LESS ABLE OF their number. Anna, in particular, and Janet, the older woman, were totally unequal to a steady march. When it was discovered that most of them had eaten the last of their ration bars in preparation for escape, Zainal immediately gestured for the patrol to share out the extras they had brought along. Chewing the dry bars without water to soften them made eating a chore. One of the Turs gobbled his down as if he hadn't eaten in days.

"He didn't know the Cats had packed us rations," Lenny said. "Ninety and I have been sharing with him."

"That was damned good of you," Kris said, "considering you wouldn't have known where your next meals were coming from."

"Oh, I figured something would turn up," and Lenny grinned impishly at her.

"Why, may I ask, is your brother 'Ninety'?"

"Aw, now, we're Irish, you see . . ."

"I had noticed."

Another grin. "And we've this saying in Ireland—that the crack, the fun, is ninety."

"And we don't mean the cost of the stuff," Ninety said in an irritated voice. "I like the crack . . . pubs and all—god, wouldn't a Guinness taste good about now."

"I told ya, don't, Ninety. I can stand anything but your mentioning Guinness," Lenny said, an edge on his usually cheerful voice for the first time in a very trying night. "Sorry, Kris."

"So I'm Ninety because I look for a good crack," Ninety finished up and gave the final bite of his ration bar a wistful look.

"Damned micks," Aarens muttered. He had positioned himself near Kris, she noticed, on her other side, away from the Doyle brothers.

"Let me straighten you out on one detail, Aarens," Kris said, not that she cared if she saved him some knocks for his attitude, but his comments grated against her sense of rightness. "We're *all* in this together: humans, Deskis, Rugarians, Ilginish, and Turs. And especially the lone representative of our former captors. He got dumped on this godforsaken place just like the rest of us and he's in command of the patrol that just saved your skin, bones, and meat. So cut the bigotry out. Understand?"

"You know him *well?*" and the man's tone was lewd and his suggestion unmistakable.

Lenny and Ninety both reacted, but Lenny was nearer. He leaned forward until his face was right up to Aarens'.

"If Kris here says the Cat's a good guy, we'll take *her* word for it, Aarens. Now cut your bellyachin'. He got you free and, if you want to slope off now and do your own thing, we'll never mention we ever met ya."

Aarens subsided as Kris inched closer to the Doyle brothers.

"Where's the Cat . . ." Ninety began, looking about him.

"His name is Zainal," Kris said, as ready to insist on that point with Ninety as everyone else.

"Okay, where's this Zainal leading us?"

"To the camp our clever Sergeant Mitford established. A series of good-sized caves with an underground lake. It's a pretty good place. Hunting's great. How good are you with slingshots?"

Lenny chuckled. "You see before you one of the great rabbit hunters of the Blasket Islands."

Ninety snorted. "You used a two-two," and then he leaned toward Kris, grinning from ear to ear, "with a telescopic lens and a silencer."

"That was so I could get in a second shot without the little scuts hearing me on the odd time or two I missed my first shot. Once I got my eye in, I didn't need either silencer or 'scope."

"We've also found a huge grain store," Kris went on, "so we should even have bread when we get back."

"How far is it?" and Lenny glanced over at Anna and Janet.

"I don't know . . . Wait a minute. . . ." Out of the corner of her eye, she noticed Zainal suddenly rise to his feet, looking pointedly in one direction. Peering in that area, she made out several figures moving in the moonlight down the slope above the crates. "That's Slav come back. He either made damned good time or our camp's not far away."

Slav had brought two other Rugarians and four humans with him—and cold roast rocksquat, some unleavened bread, and earthern water bottles that were leaking slowly but still contained enough for everyone to have a drink. They also carried ropes and more blankets.

"Sarge says go. We come," Slav said in Barevi, grinning his jagged toothy smile which included Coo and Kris.

They had to split the meat portions further to give everyone a piece, but Lenny and Ninety were definitely impressed.

Anna had to be coaxed to eat—mainly because she was exhausted, Kris decided, but Janet said she would have eaten anything on six legs. They were both given two cups of water as a special concession.

That was when Zainal noticed Kris' bandaged wrist.

"You hurt?"

"Just a sprain. Nothing to worry about," she said, feeling a little foolish at having strapped her wrist.

"You go with Pess. Lead walkers. Report to Sarge."

"I'll bet he's full of questions," Kris said, glad that Slav had arrived with humans to give Mitford a verbal report. "But I should stay to help the women."

"No," Zainal said firmly. "Much help. *You,*" and he cocked his finger at her, "better to report."

"All right," and she conceded as gracefully as possible. There were more than enough men to assist the two women, and Deskis and Rugarians to help with portages.

Although Lenny and Ninety protested that they were more than willing to help, Zainal ticked them off to go with Kris. She wasn't surprised that he sent Aarens back with her as well as Joe Lattore and some of the other men who were all too eager to see this great camp that had been contrived.

Revitalized by the meat and the water, Kris went to reassure Anna and Janet that they weren't all that far from the safety of the caves.

"We've got medical personnel, too," she reassured Anna.

"Medicines?" Anna asked hopefully.

"If they've found bread, they've got the start of penicillin, now don't they?" Kris said jokingly, but she had the feeling Anna was hoping for analgesics to take the edge off her imminent delivery. She left quickly then, not wanting to have to face any further unanswerable questions.

As there wasn't a damned thing wrong with her feet and ankles, Kris set the pace, right behind Pess. Aarens started out beside her but she didn't fancy him for company and she gave him grunts for answers to his conversational gambits until he got her message. Muttering curses about ungrateful bitches and butchy women, he dropped back to the rear of the group.

Kris wondered if she had been wise in discouraging him. But he was the sort who'd need a lot of discouragement and his attitudes irritated her. Better discouragement than an all-out brawl.

A couple of good long climbs were successfully negotiated in the light of the second moon, Aarens bitching about night maneuvers. By third moonset, even Pess was slowing up. But, when the Rugarian hit the beginning of the ravine, he brightened and so did Kris, surprised to recognize the terrain she had first walked in a semi-stupor, carrying Patti Sue. But a landmark that led you home—to any home—was always heartening.

"We're nearly there, guys. Home stretch now," she called over her shoulder and worked her shoulders out of a tired slump.

By sunrise they were back in a camp amazingly altered in the four days of her absence. As she turned the final curve, she stopped short, noting all the improvements. And the sight of Sergeant Chuck Mitford more or less where she had last seen him, at his "command" post.

That, too, had improved. The hearth had been enlarged, obviously to be used as a barbecue site, and a fire burned cheerfully in the center. Blocks of stone had been moved to form a semicircle around Mitford's central "desk," which had also been enlarged. On one side he had a pile of thin slates, bearing chalk marks, but he was working on something thin, like paper, with a sturdy wooden affair that near as nevermind looked like a pencil.

Sentries topped the higher points around the camp ravine: the stairs to the main cavern now boasted wider risers and a handrail. On the opposite side of the ravine, she couldn't fail to notice what looked like medieval stocks. Two of them, one occupied, though she couldn't see the face of the stockee since his head was hanging. The thin frame looked like Arnie's. She wondered what he'd done to rate that sort of incarceration. And what a novel idea for discipline!

The ravine floor had been swept clean and she really couldn't take in all the other improvements because Mitford had seen her. He grinned as he beckoned her to join him.

As she did, she saw him lean to one side and lift a creditable pottery pitcher. It seemed to be clad in some sort of odd matting, and a little steam escaped its lid.

"Pull up a rock, Kris, and tell me what you and that Catteni have been up to," he said, gesturing for her to present her cup so he could fill it. "It's hot, at least, and doesn't taste too bad. I've been in places with worse coffee."

"Didn't the first group tell you?" Kris asked, blowing on her drink.

"I'm debriefing everyone, Bjornsen," was his reply, emphasized by a slight frown at her objection.

She covered her embarrassment at questioning his methods by taking a sip from her cup.

The heat of the beverage was not its only recommendation, for it had an oddly minty flavor that knocked the dryness out of her mouth. If she hadn't had the cup in her hand, though, Kris would have been tempted to salute Mitford.

Ignoring the fatigue that made it difficult to find the words she needed, she gave what she felt was a concise report of the patrol. She emphasized the dangers of nighttime scavengers, of crop-filled fields, and the notion that the mechanicals were solar powered. Mitford nodded at that, making a short notation on the thin stuff.

"You've a source of paper, sarge?" she asked, interrupting herself.

"Bark, don't know how long it'll hold the lead . . . even got a pencil. . . ." And, grinning, he held up the thick shaft. "One of the geologist types found some carbon lead. The bark's a lot easier to handle than those slates. Doesn't break and flake. Tell me more about this solar-power notion?"

"You've heard it before?"

"Patrols at the granary mentioned 'em on the machines garaged there. Nothing moves at night so it's safe to haul in supplies then. Go on. Tell me more about the rescue. That first contingent were too damned wiped out to do more than say they got rescued." He poured her more of the hot drink.

"Remind me to tell you how glad I am to be in the same outfit with you, sarge," Kris said with a grateful smile.

"Ah!" and he dismissed her remark with a flick of his hand, turning his head briefly away in modesty. Then he grinned at her. "Wait'll you hear what I got in mind for you tomorrow."

"So long as it's tomorrow, sarge," she said, managing to produce a cocky grin despite her present fatigue. The drink was helping but the stimulation it provided wouldn't last very long.

"We got thirty-five more refugees." She looked about the camp. "Can we handle them?"

"Handle as many as we can find. Picked up a few more coming south from another dropoff. They either picked the right sort of fields or were plain lucky. They were right glad to find our camp. We'll need all the reinforcements we can get to start our offensive."

"Our what?" She peered numbly at Mitford.

"You don't think I intend spending the rest of my life on this mudball," Mitford said with a growl.

Kris shook her head. Mitford seemed so sane. And he was planning to get off this world?

"But that's for later. Any new useful recruits?" he asked, bringing her back to her report.

"Well, I suppose so, but I didn't think to quiz 'em. We've got one very pregnant woman and an older one who's not too spry. Zainal made me come on ahead." Mitford nodded and Kris looked back over her shoulder to see the rest of her group straggling in.

"The two guys in front are good people, Irish, the Doyle brothers. Right behind them is Joe Lattore and he's okay." She paused, seeing Aarens stumping in behind the Italian.

"And the tall individual?"

Kris hesitated long enough for Mitford to raise his eyebrows. "Name's Dick Aarens," she said as noncommittally as she could.

"I'll debrief him myself," Mitford said with a grin for her reluctance. "You go get yourself some rest, gal. You're off duty for the next twenty-eight." He pointed above his head at what she then recognized as a sundial. "Took the team three days! All the way from counting sand particles by the second to hourly divisions. Rough still, they say, and Greenwich mean time it ain't, but it's an improvement." His tone was prideful.

"All the comforts of home and time, too," she said, grinning at such a clever device.

"Not that a twenty-eight-hour planetary revolution is an improvement on what we're used to."

"And the stocks? Your idea?"

Mitford chuckled, without even looking up from the notes he was jotting down. "We got too many indi-vid-u-als," and by separating the word into syllables, he made it sound like an epithet, "to deal with who won't make life easier by disappearing when they don't like the way this outfit is run. Get some rest, gal." He gave her a good-natured buffet to her arm and jerked his head toward the cave.

She was halfway to the steps when he called the newcomers over, the Doyles startled to hear their names and Aarens giving her an accusatory glare.

At the top of the steps, she noted other signs of organization—workstations along the ledge and the legend "Home Sweet Cavehome" scrawled in chalk across the entrance. On the space where people had written their choice of name for the planet, "Botany" was underscored and all the others erased. She grinned. Home now had a name.

Inside, the early-morning crew were busy stoking fires, putting earthenware pots on trivets to heat, setting out slightly misshapen bowls for cereal. She noticed bowls of what looked like coarse salt by the hearths. On the ledges were other pots and pitchers: Sandy Areson had been very busy.

"Kris!" a voice shrieked and she was enveloped in Patti Sue's arms before she had a chance to evade the girl, who proceeded to weep all over her.

"I told you she'd be back safe, Patti," said Sandy, coming over and prying the girl off. "Now she's tired, and dirty, and you don't go moaning all over her. She's been just fine, Kris," Sandy added. "She was certain Mitford had put you in danger."

"No, we got people out of danger, Patti," Kris said, "and there's a woman who's going to need your help especially: Anna Bollinger. She's very pregnant. Sandy, who's the medic to see to her when she gets in? They're a couple of hours behind us."

"I'll see to that. You hungry, Kris?"

"Had a bar not long ago but I'd sure love a bath."

"I'll get a clean coverall, and do yours while you're sleeping," Patti said, gushing with her efforts to be helpful.

"Now, Patti, you're on breakfast detail."

"I know, I know," the girl said on her way to a pile of material stacked on one side of the cavern. "I'll just be sure she knows the latest improvements."

Sandy raised both hands, grinned reassuringly at Kris, and went back to stirring the pot. Leakage sizzled into the fire, but even that primitive attempt at a pot was an improvement over no cooking vessels at all.

"No chance at building a kiln for you, is there?" Kris said, realizing that the pottery must only be sun-dried.

Sandy's grin was beatific. "Mitford knows his priorities. Got the 'specialists' "—and she grinned—"working on a beehive type. Murph made bellows for me as well as for his own forge. Jack the Nail found a nice hard wood that ought to burn hot. So we're cooking. And I am until I get that kiln up and firing." She gave Kris a humorous grin as she waved smoke away from her face. "Go bathe."

Patti danced about Kris all the way down to the lake, telling about finding the clay and that she'd managed a cup or two that had been fired, and they needed a proper kiln for best results, and they had discovered a nearby crop field of some very tasty root vegetables that were almost like potatoes only the Deskis couldn't eat them at all without getting violently ill. Kris grimaced as she hadn't remembered to tell Mitford that Coo had found a plant that was Deski-edible. The tunnel to the lake was now well lit. When she and Patti reached it, there were also wooden steps down, a well-lit area, and a rack of pegs to hang clothing on and a rough reed basket of cattail-like seed pods.

"Where'd you find reeds?" Kris asked, noting the construction of the basket.

"Oh, Bob the Herb did. He finds all sorts of good stuff. Has two patrols under his command."

"And what're these?" Kris picked up one of the pods.

"You'll see," and Patti Sue giggled with anticipation of her surprise.

Then Kris saw that a raft had been anchored securely for safer bathing and there were even steps fastened to the side of the lake. So Kris stripped off the smelly, grimy coverall and slipped into the water.

"Here," and Patti handed her an oval pod. "It's not exactly soap and it'll ruin your complexion but it gets the dirt and . . . smells . . . off your skin."

Kris would have welcomed a Brillo pad, which was what the pod felt like. There was an odd herbal—almost astringent—smell off it and that was quite welcome after what she had been smelling like. She rinsed well and then clambered out of the water.

Patti, with an air of great accomplishment, then broke open one of the cattails, which puffed up into a white fiber.

"Your towel, madam?" She grinned at Kris' surprise. "It works, too, soaks up all the water. Then we put the used ones over there, in the other basket, and once they're dry, they're good fire-starting material. Clever, aren't we?" And she giggled as she handed Kris the fresh coverall.

"I think we need the twenty-eight-hour day to get everything done," Kris murmured.

Considerably refreshed and cleaner, Kris was quite ready now to get the rest her body urgently desired. She yawned all the way to the cave. That had improved, too. With beds made of mounds of branches and, she thought, filled in with more of the cattails.

She stretched herself out, turned to her right side, sighed with relief to have her sore hips cushioned, and never even felt the blanket which Patti lovingly spread over her.

Chapter Seven

THE AROMA OF ROASTING MEAT ROUSED Kris, although her stomach was probably sending the message. It was empty. She could hear muted voices, pleasant voices; and, encouraged, she angled herself up out of the flattened bed. One other sleeping accommodation in her cave room was occupied by a sleeper and she slipped into her footwear as quietly as possible and left.

Neither Sandy nor Patti Sue were in the main cave, but she spotted Bart and approached to see if she could scrounge a meal off him.

"Hey, Kris," the man said, smiling a welcome, "you did great!" and he dished up some of the food he was cooking onto a nearly round clay plate.

"Me? At what?" she asked with a cautious grin. When he also handed her a wooden fork, she exclaimed in surprise, "All the comforts of home."

"We're improving. And I mean the rescue of all those folks trapped by the mechanicals."

"Oh, that. That was Zainal. He knew how to open the doors."

"Yeah, but I ask myself, *how* did he know how to open them?"

"Aw, c'mon now . . . Bart!" And Kris quickly donned her public relations hat. "He knew how, so what? Maybe I could have opened it, given a hairpin or a credit card which I didn't have. Door catches are door catches: there are only so many ways to lock one. He figured out the mechanism and opened it. The important thing is that he *did* know how and we could get all the others out before they got slaughtered."

"I heard . . ." Bart began uncertainly.

"What you *heard* and what happened could be two different things entirely. Who did you *hear from?*"

Bart shifted uneasily. "One of the guys that came in with you."

"Wouldn't be named Aarens, would he?" Kris asked, letting her tone drip with scorn. "Next thing you *hear*, he'll be saying we oughtn't to listen to Mitford 'cos he's a slave driver, a martinet, endangering us, who does he think he is, when he was only a sergeant at that, and what does he know?" Kris waved her arm around, at the well-organized kitchen area, the pots and pottery, the water crates, people moving about at assigned tasks. "Well, Mitford knows enough to organize us to an amazing degree of self-sufficiency, I'd say. Aarens is a troublemaker and he started almost the moment we hauled him out of that barn."

Bart glared at Kris, resenting her tirade, so she smiled at him.

"You're too smart to fall for that kind of drivel, Bart, and this smells too good for me to let it get cold." She sat herself down on a convenient rock and started to eat. "Now, can I give you the facts, nothing but the facts, about the great slaughterhouse rescue? I'd hate for you to have a bad opinion of me because I stuck up for the guy responsible for saving forty-five people, forty-six if Anna has her baby."

The expression on his face told her it wasn't her he had a bad opinion of, which meant she really needed to put the record straight.

"Well, maybe what I heard was a bit garbled . . ."

"Scariest moment in my life was waking up in that barn," she said, giving a shudder, and was still answering his questions when Jay Greene spotted her.

"Sarge needs you, Kris," he said.

"Great meal, Bart," Kris said, standing up and then looking about her for the proper place to dispose of her plate and fork.

Bart grinned as he pointed. "Outside, to your left. Aarens himself is on kp."

"No better man," she said and left the hearth with Jay.

"I'll take that," Jay said, removing the plate from her hands. "You don't need to meet Aarens."

"Why? Is he bad-mouthing me? Or Zainal?"

Jay snorted. "Don't worry. Mitford has his measure."

"Does everyone else?" Kris asked urgently. "Hell, he'd've been better off—*we'd* be better off—with him as sausage meat after all," she added callously.

"He'll spend some time in the stocks if he keeps up."

"Which will only confirm his opinion of this chickenshit outfit."

"Who cares?"

"Speaking of caring," and they were now outside in the bright sunlight. Mitford was precisely where she had left him a good—she checked the sundial—nine hours ago. "Does he never rest?" Her question was hypothetical, for she went on, "How's Anna Bollinger, our pregnant lady?"

"Doc says she'll be fine. Although she's grieving for her husband." He paused to click his tongue over that tragedy. "Janet's making her her special assignment . . . Janet and Patti Sue. Was that girl raped?"

"I suspect so."

"She never said anything?"

"It'll take a long while before she's able to talk about whatever it was happened to her."

"Oh?"

"You like her?"

"She's a sweet kid," Jay said, shaking his head, with a "gone" smile on his face.

"Go as slow as slow."

"I figured that."

Kris went down the steps while Jay turned left toward the crates where Aarens was clumsily drying cups with cattail fibers. They must have found a humongous supply of the things for them to be used in so many different ways.

The man in the stocks was gone and Kris wished she'd thought to ask Jay what his offense had been. Was that why he'd asked had Patti Sue been raped? Mitford had meant what he said about punishing harassers.

Kris heard steps on the stone behind her and, looking over her shoulder, saw Zainal with Slav and Coo right behind him. She wondered if they shared a cave. All of them looked clean and rested.

"What are you guys doing up so early?" she demanded.

"I slept much," Zainal said, grinning back at her, his marvelously weird yellow eyes echoing his good humor. "Slav and Coo well rested. Lot to do."

"Lots to do," she corrected him absently, then hastily added, "but you're real quick to learn."

"Need to learn," he replied, his smile broadened.

"Ve all learn," Slav said in his liquid voice. "Hi, Krissss," he added, emphasizing the sibilant.

Just then the Deskis on the heights let out the whistling alarm and slid, as suddenly, down out of sight.

"Fliers?" someone cried anxiously.

All activity in the camp was suspended. A beat later, everyone out in the open made for caves. Kris looked skyward, pivoting as Zainal, Coo, and Slav were, to scan the horizon. So was Mitford, in his exposed position on the floor of the ravine.

Coo gave an odd and earsplitting cry, which was echoed from above.

"Large thing," the Deski said, spreading his arms to their farthest extension, indicating great size. He rolled his eyes. "Baaaaaaad. Bad, bad, bad, bad," he repeated, shaking his head and then covering his ears tightly. But that was as much to mask the noise, which was becoming very, very loud—like half a dozen subway trains converging on you and every one of them clanking and grinding and needing full servicing—as to stress the approaching danger. Kris thought the intensity of the sound was comparable to standing in a continuous sonic boom. Her bones began to vibrate right up to her teeth. Even the stone under her feet reverberated.

She wanted to ask where was the noise coming from and what made it, but she wouldn't be heard above that racket.

The shadow of it came first . . . longer and wider by far than the ravine: even the hill the ravine dissected. The shadow came on and on, and then they saw the blunt prow of the leviathan that growled and rumbled and still made the very stones shake.

It was coming in, prow definitely aiming downward, on a descending slant: several thousand feet above them, Kris estimated, blotting out the sun like an island-sized umbrella. A big island, with all kinds of protuberances, long and thin, squat, rounded disks, with all kinds of sticklike rods planted here and there, even on the massive belly doors that were acres long and wide. It seemed to take hours to pass overhead. By then, inured to the noise it made, people were outside again, peering up at the monstrosity. Their curiosity was stronger than their initial panic.

By then Kris had followed others to the nearest height—Mitford, Zainal, Jay Greene, Slav, Coo, the Doyles led the way, joined by half a dozen other men and women who wanted to get a good long look at this vessel.

"It's heading in the direction of the slaughterhouse," Kris yelled above a slightly diminished noise.

"Yeah," Mitford said thoughtfully, rubbing his hand over his mouth, his expression very thoughtful indeed. "Recognize it, Zainal?"

Zainal shook his head slowly, never once dropping his eyes to look at Mitford.

"Catteni have no ship that big." He seemed as impressed by the size of it as everyone else. "Strange . . ." He rolled his hand, trying to find the appropriate word.

"Configuration?" Jay asked.

Zainal shook his head, made shapes with his hands that looked like the protuberances and spokes jutting out of the ship.

"Oh, those things. Yeah, the ships you took Earth with weren't anything like that one."

"No," and Zainal grinned down at Jay. "Too big, no good."

"Well, there's that aspect of big, I suppose," Jay replied amiably.

They watched until it was out of sight but not out of earshot. On the noon air, they could hear it changing gears . . . or whatever it did, causing the sound to alter.

"Hovering?" Mitford said, disbelieving what his ears reported. Then he shook his head. "I sure wouldn't want to have to *lift* that dead mass from the ground." He sighed. "How can they?" He looked queryingly at Zainal, who only shrugged again and shook his head. Kris saw anxiety for the first time in Zainal's expression.

Kris swallowed. "If we hadn't got those folks out yesterday . . ."

Mitford nodded. "You did great, Bjornsen."

"Zainal did all the work, sarge," she said quickly.

Mitford's chuckle was audible to her and he patted her shoulder in approval.

No one moved from the uncomfortable height, human or alien. Then, to their listening ears, came a second change of engine sounds. They also heard the powerful blast of rockets, or whatever powered the great ship, as it headed skyward again. It burst into view, nose angled up now. Kris was awed by the technology that could produce such power. It wasn't a beautiful craft, the way the *Discovery* and *Challenger* had been, delta-winged and shingle-clad. But it did have a triangular shape to it, blunt-nosed as it was.

"You guys willing to take a quick run back down there?" Mitford asked. He was looking at Zainal, Coo, and Slav.

"We sure are," Kris said, and then gulped because she hadn't intended to volunteer.

"Not you, Kris, you're off duty."

"If I am, they are. Only I'm going. I got just as much curiosity as the next one. I can't believe that ship just gulped up *all* that was there and then calmly took off again."

Mitford put his hands around his mouth to shout down to those on the ground. "Dowdall, send a team out to the granary. See if that got emptied."

"Oh, lordee," Kris said in a groan. She felt vulnerable again. And she'd brought in more mouths to be fed, too.

"Don't worry," Mitford said, "we're stocked up, all things considered."

So the two teams set off. Kris thought their return to the abattoir didn't take half as long going back as it had coming in. When they got there, the acres of crates were all gone. In their place were stacks of what looked like collapsed units. *That would account for some of the dents and scratches, she thought,* still rather numb at the sheer volume that ship had lifted. Did they have matter transporters? *Beam it up, Scotty,* was the facetious thought that bounced in Kris' mind until she gave a slightly hysterical laugh to stop it.

"It's all right, Kris," said Zainal, his accent improving all the time. He must have a terrific ear for language. Somehow that reassured her more than his words or the arm he laid briefly across her shoulders. "We check the barns."

"How?" And Kris gestured broadly at the empty space that had once been conveniently bridged by a pyramid of crates. There was a drop of six or seven meters to the first of the piles of collapsed crates. She suddenly felt oddly disoriented by the alteration.

Zainal pointed to the rocky terrain. That was when Kris first realized that the mechanicals had sliced the crate storage out of the cliff side: the barns as well. From what she'd been told, the granary was also stored in natural rock. No arable land was taken up by even such essential facilities. If this was the condition of the entire planet, it was a remarkable achievement in its own right. *And here come humans,* she thought dourly, *to mess it up.*

The barns were empty, disinfected and ready for the next batch of occupants. Had the prisoners been dumped down on this planet at harvest and culling time? How often did that monster arrive to collect? Monthly, bimonthly? Semiannually? What season of this planet were they currently in? The weather was mild enough to be spring, but the crops in the fields were more mature than springtime growth. And she'd heard that grain had kept pouring into the storage caves, which suggested fall harvests.

The other salient fact was that the machines' masters were probably as omnivorous as humanoids. And needed so much food that they went to the expense of developing highly specialized machinery to nurture and cultivate food crops and meat animals: and had sufficient planets available for their use so that they could devote all?—most?—of this one to food production. The collection vehicle as well as the mechanicals meant an extremely high technological level. And yet Zainal, for all the Catteni were well traveled and doing a lot of exploration on their own—did not recognize the type of craft used, and his exploratory service had registered the planet as uninhabited. Of course, if there were nothing but machines on the planet, that figured. Only why hadn't the Catteni seen the machines on their appointed rounds? The Catteni hadn't surveyed the planet in the night only, had they? Or maybe during an infrequent downtime during the "winter" months. Kris' knowledge of farming suggested there were few "down" times on a farm: something or other had to be tended all year round. And what would winter on Botany be like?

Then Zainal blithely insisted that they have a look at the "garages" where curious vehicles with a variety of strange attachments awaited recall to duty.

"They do not recognize humans. No problem!" he told Kris and she was so flabbergasted that he had acquired the "no problem" slang that he was in the garage before she could protest.

One machine, standing inside, was hooked up to a framework which blinked and blipped. A servicing mechanism? Kris wished that they had someone with engineering training along. But then, who'd've thought they'd have a chance to inspect so thoroughly? Oh, for some of that bark and a pencil so she could make diagrams of the various types of mechanicals parked in the several garages. The last of the big barns contained sacks and sacks of what? Logic told her seeds or possibly fertilizers, more than likely. Had they been brought by the leviathan that had collected the meat? She used her knife to get into some of the bags and got samples of everything. Seeds, definitely, over half the shipment and, by the smell of it, fertilizer in the others.

The patrol got back to the camp by first moonrise. She didn't feel quite so wimpy when Coo and Slav showed signs of wanting to rest, but she and Zainal first had to report to Mitford.

"They didn't take the grain, Bjornsen," was Mitford's first comment, but she thought he seemed depressed. "What did you find?"

While Kris told him, including her surmises as she passed over the samples she had secured, Zainal had taken several large sheets of the papery bark and was quickly sketching on them. A couple of times Kris lost the thread of her report when she saw his accurate depictions of the various types of machinery they had seen in the garages. Mitford stole the odd glance, his eyes switching to Zainal's face as the Catteni's pencil flew over the surface, but his sketches looked remarkably accurate to her eyes. Zainal regarded his handiwork and then calmly made necessary emendations, correcting occasional lines. They'd had an engineer along all the time, hadn't they, thought Kris. Zainal had rather more talents than anyone had realized.

"These," Zainal said, handing over the sheaf to Mitford.

"Hey, Bob the Herb, Mack Su, Capstan, Macy, front and center and bring those granary sketches," Mitford roared in his parade-ground voice, then grinned approvingly at both Zainal and Kris. "There's quite a range of these things. Now we got to figure how to disable them."

"Why?" Kris blurted out the question.

"Like you, Bjornsen, I think there are humanoids bound to be involved in this kind of food production, seeing as how they seem to need the same sort of foods we do. However," and he went on briskly, "we're obviously dealing with a very high-tech race." Kris nodded her head vehemently. "That ship confirms some sort of periodic check. So there's got to be some sort of ongoing monitoring, even if we haven't found a central control point."

Kris wondered just how much of this Zainal understood, but he was *listening* with every ounce in his big frame. She could feel the tension in the thigh next to hers on the wide rock they were sitting on. Odd that she didn't mind tactile contact with Zainal, but he was so subtle about it, unlike some guys with impudent, wandering paws she'd encountered.

"So, if we start lousing up the machines, someone will come look," Mitford concluded.

"And we just overpower them?" Kris asked, aghast at the mere thought of invading a ship the size of the collector. Especially since the only weapons they had were knives, hatchets, spears, and bows and arrows. She let out a burst of laughter.

"Don't laugh, Bjornsen. There's more than one way of infiltrating a spacecraft. And I'm more or less counting on the fact that the investigatory ship would be smaller and have a live, not a mechanical crew.

Machines are good enough for routine jobs but evaluation requires brains."

"Then what?"

"First things first. Get the investigator here."

Those Mitford had called for arrived and then he roared for a cook to bring two plates of food. He must have heard Kris' stomach rumbling.

"We've been tossing ideas around while you guys were investigating, so I'll bring you up to speed, Zainal, Bjornsen," he said and nodded at them both before turning to the other patrol members. "Coo, Slav, get some grub. Go eat." He pointed to the main cave. "And thanks. Oh, Coo, Bob the Herb harvested more of that green stuff you like."

Coo nodded and, with the Rugarian, made a beeline for the main cave. Mitford's eyes followed him.

"Ration bars are now reserved for Deskis, Ilginish, and Turs, folks. The rest of us can live off the land. They can't."

"Really?"

"Not until we find something their stomachs don't reject." Mitford gave the sort of resigned sigh that meant he was worried about the problem. He was leader enough to want to preserve all his troops, especially those with abilities like the Deskis'. "The cooks are busy whipping up a sort of pemmican for patrols to eat so you don't upset the mechanicals by reducing their herds." He grinned. "What did you call those critters, Kris? Loo-cows." He chuckled.

"Sarge, I thought you *wanted* us to upset the mechanicals," Kris said, wanting clarification on that point.

"We *plan* the upsetting"—he grinned again—"but I don't want any of our guys to get darted out in the fields. So we disable the mechanism. Okay, fellas," he said to the newcomers. Capstan and Macy were new faces and names for Kris, but they seemed to know who she and Zainal were. Mitford passed Zainal's sketches around. "Zainal's drawn the sort of mechanicals that are housed at the slaughterhouse. Seem to me to be different from the ones at the granary."

"Highly specialized equipment," Su said, leafing through the drawings, pausing briefly to scowl at several before he switched his lot with Capstan. Kris found out later that the older man had been a designer of highly specialized production-line equipment.

"Look, all of 'em are solar powered!" Su said, flicking his fingers at various flat surfaces on the individual machines. "Like I said, they had to be. Ecologically sound, using renewable energy. Small wonder the Catteni scouts thought the planet was unoccupied. They'd probably been scanning, or whatever they do, for life forms and those mechanicals aren't alive. Now, they have to have collectors and storage batteries, too, and where'd they . . . ah, yes, possibly these units. Hmmm."

"And if there's no sun? Do they all just go down when it's overcast or rainy?" Kris asked, making a mental note of the solar panels on each variety of machine.

"Hasn't rained yet and we've been here ten days," Mitford said with a sigh, his glance going up and down the ravine that had experienced floods which had left visible high-water traces on the walls.

Zainal also looked around the camp and smiled. "Much done in ten days."

"Good for morale," was Mitford's terse reply, but he added a brief smile at the compliment. "Now, we got individuals who've got real expert with slingshots. Can take out a rocksquat at twenty-five meters. Stones'd take out those solar panels, wouldn't they?"

Su thought about that but Capstan shook his head.

"We'd have to know what sort of material they use in the mechanicals' panels. But it would follow that, if enough of the surface was marred, it might not collect sufficient solar energy to perform efficiently."

"Perhaps," and Kris adopted an ingenuous look and tone to her voice, "we should practice some creative mudslinging? I didn't see a carwash in that Dalek barn."

Zainal flicked her a quick glance because he didn't understand her allusion so she charaded it and then he smiled, nodding. Su seemed to like the idea and even Capstan gave a droll little smile.

"There're sure enough brooks where we'd need 'em to make mud," Su went on with enthusiasm. "And if we got enough on the panels, the sun would dry it hard in place."

"Mud at night. No machine runs in day," Zainal suggested with a shrug of his shoulders.

"Good idea, Zainal," Mitford said, grinning. "Decommission them at source."

"Well, now, hold on a moment," Capstan said. "There would have to be storage batteries to keep them ticking over and start them off in the morning. Or there should be something like that. We'd have to disable those as well, you know."

"So we do," Mitford said cheerfully. "I wonder how many we would have to knock out for someone to come check the situation?"

That question was tossed around but they all agreed that they would first have to locate more installations for the plan to be effective. Kris, Zainal, and the two aliens had not been the only patrol which Mitford had sent out and one group, Mitford told them, was still missing. He wasn't worried about them—yet—because they'd gone north, away from the slaughterhouse. He admitted that there would need to be a lot more such facilities to service all the land they could see cultivated and grazed. Enough hills could be seen from the sentry posts: each range could hide more mechanicals, farming nearby arable land.

"Zainal," Kris said after a brief pause in the exchange of ideas, "how many would the prison ship have dropped in one journey?"

Zainal's shrug was almost apologetic. "Don't know. No need for me to know."

"Well, they landed more than us and those you just freed up," Mitford said in sudden anger. The others nodded solemnly. With a sigh, the Sergeant went on. "One of the recon patrols tangled with a savage bunch of individuals: only two of our guys got away and one was badly sliced up. Estimated there were close to thirty in the lot that jumped them. So it'll be more important than ever for any patrols to post sentries at night. Esher was smart enough to hide himself, and Barrett, who was injured, until they could be sure they weren't followed back here. And that," Mitford's thick index finger pointed at each one in the circle to emphasize his warning, "is what no one does! I'll tell you one thing: they really hopped to it next time I called a Red Alert. And Murph made us a triangle out of metal that would wake the dead."

"But we could hold off hundreds here, sarge," Kris said, startled. The mere thought that the camp was vulnerable, and to renegade humans, depressed her. As it must have depressed Mitford.

"You better believe it," Mitford said so resolutely and with such a knowing grin on his face that Kris relaxed. Mitford had obviously been busy placing safeguards as well as amenities. "Do they ever check up on the job lots they drop down?" he asked Zainal who nodded.

"Not soon," he said. "In half a year," he added, dropping into Barevi to express the time.

"Half a year," Kris murmured in English and he nodded again as he accepted that new word.

"Would they bring in more prisoners?" Mitford asked Zainal, who nodded.

"Drop people many places," and he made a spreading gesture with his hands. "Many times to seed planet."

Kris wasn't the only one who received that information with a sinking heart. How many did the Catteni expect would survive? And if none did, was the planet written off? What a way to colonize! While she hadn't even thought to estimate how many prisoners had been in that holding area prior to being forced aboard the transport, there had been a lot more than the few hundreds ending up in this camp. They knew of at least four other deposits now. How many had there been in the initial load? At that, they might be better off making first contact with the Mechano Makers.

"Well, we deal with what we can," Mitford said staunchly. "And we'll explore as thoroughly as possible under the circumstances. Zainal, any more information on how they seed the planet?"

"I was in space more," he said, spreading his hands wide open to express his ignorance.

"Huh, so the Catteni operate just like any other army?" Mitford said in a droll tone. "Left hand doesn't know what the right hand does."

Kris had a time explaining that remark to the puzzled Zainal, who grinned when he did understand.

When Mitford finally dismissed them, Kris made her way down the ravine and over to the stairs. The kitchen cavern walls were now decorated with outlines of vegetations. These were divided into several sections: one marked "Human," with those plants to avoid and those to gather; another had "Deski" in elaborate Gothic lettering as a caption and the enscription "potassium? calcium?"

"Hi, there," a cheerful voice said, and Dick Aarens moved to intercept her.

"Not now, Aarens," she said, altering her direction to avoid him.

"Hey, gal, I'm only trying to be friendly." He stepped in front of her.

"So am I, but right now all I want is my bed."

His eyes, a pleasing shade of blue for all she didn't like the man who wore them, widened. "Why, so do I!" And he attempted to put his arm around her as if to lead her off.

She ducked out from under. "By myself, Aarens."

"Kris . . ."

She was both relieved and concerned to hear Zainal's voice behind her. She turned, took a step toward the Catteni.

"Yes?" She hoped her response conveyed her relief at his timely arrival.

"We talk tomorrow's patrol now?" he asked.

Behind her, she heard Aarens mutter something and then the crunch of his feet on the sandy floor as he moved away.

"Thanks, Zainal. You saved my life."

Zainal regarded her with a thoughtful expression. "You do not like him?"

"No," she said, shaking her head for emphasis.

"I think so."

"Watch him, though, Zainal. He's dangerous."

"How?" Zainal was amused at her response.

"He doesn't like you."

"Because you do?"

She shook her head. "Because first you're Catteni and second he fancies himself better than you. And irresistible to me."

Zainal shook his head, lightly gripping her on the arms, a tacit request for explanation.

"I'm not sure I can explain the nuances," she said, grinning up at him. Yellow eyes were much nicer than plain old blue. And she liked Zainal's hands on her whereas Dick Aarens' touch made her skin crawl.

"Nu-an-ces?"

She put her hand on his chest, felt the faint pulse of his heartbeat—Catteni had hearts after all. "I'll explain later, Zainal. Right now, I'm so tired I can't."

"Go," and he turned her toward the corridor. But when he gave her a little push, she grabbed his hand.

"You come, too. I don't mean to have Aarens jump out at me."

"I like to come," Zainal said and there was a decided glint in his eyes that made Kris wonder how she was going to dismiss this courtier. And, if she hadn't been so tired, she might—just now—have considered . . . She shook her head. The timing was wrong. She was so tired.

So, her hand tucked into his large one, they walked to her cave.

"Sleep well, Kris."

"Don't you just know I will," she said fervently.

To her utter surprise, he cupped her head briefly, tousling her hair before he let go. But he was off down the corridor before she could react.

"Too damned tired even for a goodnight kiss," she said ruefully and gratefully sank onto her bed of boughs.

THE NEXT DAY, HER PATROL CONSISTED OF ZAINAL, COO, Slav, and the Doyle brothers. Their main objective: to find and disable as many mechanicals as they could, starting with those at the abattoir. The optimum, according to Capstan, would be to dismantle the solar panels if they could do so. Smashing the panels or smearing them with mud were equally viable, so long as the mechanicals were disabled. The secondary aim was to continue the interrupted reconnaissance of their immediate vicinity. They started out better equipped than ever, with ropes braided of vines which didn't burn the skin as the tough synthetic material of the blankets did. They each had slingshots, a pouch of suitable small rocks— that was one of the duties for the few youngsters in the camp—a flint-tipped lance, and bags of the new trail food. Kris had sampled it when Jay handed over the ration and it was definitely an improvement over the dry compressed Catteni bar as far as taste was concerned. Coo and Slav were given ration bars, Patti Sue doling them out with thoughtful care. The girl evidently had no trouble serving the alien males, though she never once looked at Zainal.

"We don't know if the pemmican supplies all your daily nutritional needs," Jay said, "but you can hunt to augment protein."

The Doyle brothers made cheerful companions, asking questions of both Kris and Zainal. Kris wondered if they had been chosen because, being Irish, they seemed to get along with anyone.

THEY MADE GOOD TIME, ZAINAL SETTING A COURSE DIAGO-
nally west of the patrol's earlier trek, the one which had resulted in
their capture. They found a hillock and made their evening camp on its
crest . . . until the rain came. It wasn't a soft rain: Kris figured that it
was comparable to standing under the waterfall in her Barevian refuge.
They huddled under an improvised tent made from their blankets, which
gave them some protection from the driving force of the torrent. It rained
hard for what Kris and the Doyles decided was probably an hour, though
battered as they were, it seemed an endless period. Then, as abruptly as it
started, it stopped.

"Like someone turned the shower off," Lenny said, peering out of
the damp shelter. "And hey, not a cloud in the sky and it's only the first
moon. I'd recognize her anytime by her craters."

They shook the blankets out: the synthetic seemed to shed the
water—the outside a trifle damp to the hand but the underside dry.

"Amazing fabric," Ninety said, crushing the edge of his blanket in
his hand. "Give credit where it's due. Those Catteni make good survival
gear."

"Durable," Kris agreed and looked over at Zainal, who was staring
about the land below their retreat. "What d'you see?"

"Nothing."

"That bothers you?"

"Yes," the Catteni said and then lowered himself to the ground.
"You take this watch, Kris. Wake Slav. Slav, you wake Coo. Coo, wake
Doyles. You wake me." Feeling which was the dry side of his blanket, he
then pulled it around him and pillowed his head on his arm. "I sleep,
then think better."

Whatever he had feared at least kept them all alert on their separate
watches. Maybe, Kris thought as she woke Slav to take his turn, that was
what Zainal had had in mind: sneaky so-and-so.

They were all awake before the sun came up, still not yet adjusted to the longer days and nights. They had saved enough dry droppings to make a fire to heat water from a nearby stream in their cups, adding the dried herbs that became a fragant tea to sip while eating their pemmican. There were worse ways to break a fast.

When they came to the next ridge, Zainal climbed to the highest point and surveyed the distances before pointing to their right.

"Hills," he said cryptically.

"Can the mechanicals have built into every hillside?" Kris asked, half running to keep up with his long stride as he marched downhill again.

"We see," Zainal said, grinning at her, his yellow eyes twinkling.

They made the new destination by noontime, striding along the crest of that hill complex until they came to the bare rock and another silent, but full, garage.

"D'you think they take a lunch break and oil and grease themselves?" Lenny asked as they all looked down at the closed doors of the anonymous facility. "Another granary?" He gestured toward nearby fields, straw brown and shorn of whatever crops they might have sprouted.

"We look."

"And smear?" Ninety asked, mopping his perspiring forehead, for the last several klicks had included considerable climbing. "I could moisten a hill or two with the sweat I've raised."

The storage barns were empty, not so much as a grain of whatever they had held.

"That was one busy mother of a ship," Lenny said, "if it cleared this, too."

"Long time," Zainal said, showing dust on the finger he had drawn across the floor.

"Oh? Cutting back the farmers' subsidies here, too, huh?" Ninety asked facetiously.

Zainal gestured for the patrol to check out each building of the fifteen in this complex. The last one was the garage where the mechanicals were standing in motionless lines. They didn't look dusty, but just as Ninety started to enter the building, Zainal held up his arm and then pointed to the long rectangles on the eastern overhang of the garage.

"Sun power."

"Yeah," Ninety said, gulping. "D'you think they'd registered us as thieves?"

"Doubt it," Lenny said. "What've they got to guard against on this planet? They don't even know we're here. And dangerous!"

Zainal chuckled. "We are. To them." Then he gestured to Ninety, made a cup of his two hands, and waited. Ninety, shrugging at the thought of his not inconsiderable bulk being hoisted by the Catteni, put his foot in the hand and climbed to Zainal's shoulders where he was now high enough to examine the panels.

"Hey," he said after a moment's scrutiny, "I think they come off." He grabbed one, rocking a bit on Zainal's shoulders, but the Catteni compensated easily and Ninety unclipped the panel from brackets. "Easy to install, replacements in stock, no waiting, no problem!"

He handed each of the four panels down, then examined the links to wherever the power was collected. "Wish I'd seen the specs of the solar-power stuff they were bringing into Dublin before we left."

"You weren't taken in Ireland?" Kris asked, somehow having assumed that they had.

"Naw, we were working on a construction site in Detroit. Pay wasn't great but better'n getting only fifty quid a week on the dole."

Then he jumped neatly down from Zainal's shoulders and joined his brother, Slav, and Coo, who were peering suspiciously at the units. Zainal seemed to be waiting, his attention on the unmoving machines.

"How much power would these things store up?" Ninety asked him. "Do we have to wait until dark? We wouldn't be able to see then."

"Maybe they're on standby anyhow," Lenny suggested. "They're not armed er anything."

"Darts," Zainal said and peered into the garage to see if he could locate the little aerial menaces.

"I don't see anything set in the frame," Lenny said, running a hand down the side of the opening. "No sign of security devices. Not as if I'd recognize any if I saw 'em. There has to be some . . ."

Coo broke the thoughtful silence by walking right in and straight to the back of the dim garage. Turning around, he raised his long, spider-fingered hands in a "so there" gesture.

"Okay," said Ninety, brushing his hands together. "Let's see if we can't disable these fecking mechanicals."

He jumped to the flange of the nearest big farm machine and, finding toeholds, climbed high enough to reach the canted solar panel surfaces. "And these come off with a twist of the wrist, too," he said, after yanking first one, then the next panel out of their brackets. There were seven in all. Having done that, he looked down at Zainal.

"Okay, boss man, whaddawe do next?"

Zainal stepped up on the flange and then on tiptoe to look into the opening left by the removal of the panels. Kris held her breath, hoping nothing would turn on and knock him out, or off. She couldn't remember, from her brief glimpses of them, what sections of the machinery lit up when in use.

Zainal began tugging at a section which came away in his hands. He grunted, handed this down to Kris, and he and Ninety began dismantling the exterior sheets. Even Slav looked pleased as he, Coo, and Lenny handled the pieces.

"Simple," Zainal remarked after a good look at the innards. "This" —and he touched a cube the length of his spread hand—"is the power collector." He pulled it loose.

"Hmmm, a regular pop-tool," Ninety said, grinning. "Handy dandy mechano set."

"Well, if other machines had to service it, it might as well be easy to disassemble," Lenny said, changing his voice on the last word to sound more like Short Circuit Number Five.

The wires and connectors plugged into the power cube also came away easily, and Zainal, with yet another grunt, removed the cube.

"Could we use that back at the camp?" Kris asked.

"For what?" Ninety said with a snort. "We haven't anything to power up."

"We could if we had power . . . and maybe some of the engineer types could rearrange all those parts into something useful for us."

"For what?" Ninety asked.

"What's the matter with you? Don't you like technology?" Lenny wanted to know, dismissing his brother's attitude.

"Mitford will want," Zainal said. "We bring on later back to camp." He looked around again, his eyes narrowed.

"What's wrong?"

"No dart thing."

Coo suddenly pointed up, chattering in the way of Deski laughter. Craning their necks, they finally saw the aerial unit, high up in the ceiling.

"No wonder we didn't see one in the slaughterhouse garage. We never looked *up*," Kris said. "Well, now we know where it hangs out, we can get that one, too.

"Already half-launched like that, isn't it?" Lenny said. "That thing has to be programmed by a machine, doesn't it? I mean, it can't go off in here, can it?"

"I hope not," Ninety said.

They had to do a circus act: Ninety on Zainal's shoulders, with Coo on Ninety's, to get enough height to reach the thing. In trying to remove it from the brackets that held it in place, the human ladder swayed alarmingly back and forth, with Lenny and Kris doing a dance around Zainal, ready to cushion any faller with their own bodies.

Coo ended up swinging on the thing, to break it loose from its mooring. So it and he fell, Coo uttering amazing cackles as he plummeted, clutching the mechanism to his thin chest. Lenny and Kris smacked into each other as they reached out to catch his spider body. But they did break his fall even if Kris got clouted across the nose by one wing extension of the flying device. She saw stars but managed to hang on to the frail Deski body until they could ease him to the ground.

When they separated, Kris gasped, for the wicked points of the anesthetic darts were visible along the leading edges of both wings, pointing right at her. She could so easily have been pricked. She sat down and then had to tip her head back to stem the nosebleed.

The men were all for breaking up the evil device.

"No way," she said with muffled urgency because she only had her sleeve to use to stanch the blood on her face. "Let's find out if there's a reservoir or well of that anesthetic they use," she said.

"Why?" Lenny demanded. "I'm not a vindictive sort, but when I think about what happened to some bodies who got darted . . ."

"I'm thinking of a medical use for the anesthesia, Lenny. It put us to sleep. And that could be useful."

"Oh, yeah."

So they were even more careful as they disassembled the unit.

Then they disabled all the other machines in the garage, making neat piles of the various components.

"Don't fancy lugging all this back," Lenny said, eyeing the lot thoughtfully.

"We get more people to carry. Aarens is strong," Zainal said, grinning maliciously in Kris' direction.

"He'll love you for that," she said with a snort and a laugh.

"Lugging's about all that gobshite's good for," Ninety said as he regarded the piles dubiously. "But, hey, is it safe to just leave the stuff lying here?"

Zainal shrugged. "No machine has power!"

"That's true enough," Ninety said, still worried.

"No power in the garage either," Kris reminded him.

"Suppose they have got some sort of security patrol that comes around checking to be sure they're on duty er something?" Ninety wanted to know.

After a moment, Zainal grinned. "That is what is wanted."

"Yeah, I guess you're right," and Ninety scratched his head. "So, shouldn't we break all this up so it can't put them all back together?"

"We hide," Zainal said decisively after a moment's thought.

They had to haul the panels and cubes quite a distance to find someplace that would be secure from an aerial or surface inspection and that task took the rest of the day. That night they camped inside the inoperative garage, safe from the torrential rains that once again pummeled the ground. The rocksquats they'd hunted—Kris had surprised herself by stunning one in her first attempt to hunt with a slingshot—were roasted over the fire they made. The patrol ate, watching the rain sheeting down.

IN THE COURSE OF THEIR SEVEN-DAY PATROL, FOR THAT WAS the time given them by Mitford for this tour, they found and rendered useless four more installations, including another empty abattoir. They camped there that night, more comfortably on fodder bedding, while outside the hour-long rain pelted down. It rained every evening, hard, for approximately an hour and they preferred to be undercover during such onslaughts.

"This sort of rain can't be natural," Kris said the fourth night. "Not rain at night, when all the machines would be safely back in their garages."

"They got the farming so well organized here, I wouldn't put it past 'em to organize the weather, too," Ninety said. Then added thoughtfully: "Sure would be nice not to have the soccer games rained out."

"You would think of soccer," his brother said with amiable asperity.

"Then there'd have to be a central control facility somewhere on this planet," Kris said, turning to Zainal. He nodded. "Only where? We aren't going to be able to cover a great deal of distance on foot and we don't even know which continent we're on. Do we?" she asked Zainal.

He shook his head, sighing again and indicating his own frustration over insufficient data.

"Well, if we keep on the way we're going, disabling garages, we may meet our landlord soon. Maybe sooner than we'd like," and unconsciously her hand went to the knife at her belt. "Comforting a knife may be, but it's not really sufficient to combat the kind of technology we've seen."

"No intelligence on this planet," Zainal said with a shrug.

"D'you mean anything that comes after us would be a machine?" Kris wasn't at all happy with that notion. "Or more flying darts?"

"We were trapped in that place," Zainal said, but he was obviously turning over the possibilities in his head and then gave a convulsive shrug. "We are careful. We keep watch." He delivered a short series of guttural barks to the Deski, who was chewing a mouthful. Coo nodded and pointed to his ear flaps. Then, to Kris' surprise, he held up one of his two opposal digits in the "gotcha" gesture.

"They catch on quick, don't they?" Lenny murmured as he beamed at the Deski and made the thumbs-up with both of his hands. Coo nodded enthusiastically but kept right on chewing.

Kris, watching the Catteni's face during this exchange, decided that he had also noted the alteration in the Deski. Though the alien kept up with the patrol, climbing was no longer as effortless for him and, to Kris, he seemed even more spidery and insubstantial than ever. And he was constantly trying out some new greenery, root, or the nutlike objects he found in the forested areas. Some of the vegetation sprouted sort of nuts, or fungi, on the trunks. Coo tried everything and, when the others chowed down on rocksquat, he ate slowly of his ration bars. Twice Zainal had evidently told him not to save the bars: there would be more back at the camp. At least that's what Kris *thought* Zainal was telling him.

On the morning of the sixth day, Slav pointed out their homeward direction. Kris was suitably awed by the confidence he displayed, since they'd done so much up- and downhill travel, so many detours around impassable rock faces, that she had no idea where the home camp was.

Chapter Eight

AT FOURTH MOONRISE THREE DAYS AFTER
Mitford had sent out five teams to search and disable, the Sergeant was reviewing plans: renovations
made by the three architects among them for the
abattoir barns. The processing equipment in the
slaughterhouse had been completely dismantled although they'd have to have serious overcrowding
before anyone who knew what had happened in
that plant would live in it. However, there'd be
more folks who hadn't a clue.

He heard one of the sentries hiss at him.

"Sarge, something's coming."

"Well, don't tell me. Challenge them," but
Mitford reached for his spear with one hand and
eased the knife out of its sheath with the other.

"Who goes there?" the sentry yelled.

Yells answered him but not the passwords.
He ducked.

"Shit, sarge, they ain't ours," and he ducked

behind the prominence on his height. "RED ALERT!" He clanged fiercely on the metal alarm triangle set on the height.

"WHICH WAY ARE THEY COMING, GODDAMMIT, RAINEY!" Mitford roared. "ATTACK! ATTACK! TAKE YOUR STATIONS!"

It was fortunate that, even with many out on exploratory patrols, there was usually a handful of people awake at any hour of the twenty-eight.

"COMING DOWN THE RAVINE, SARGE! Omigod," and Rainey ducked as a spear clattered on the rock beyond him. "They're shooting at *me!*"

More spears came spinning out of the darkness. Aimed at the source of light which was the "office" fire. Crouching to make a smaller target, Mitford dashed forward. In the stocks, Aarens was shouting to be released as two spent arrows and another spear fell close to him.

"C'MON," Mitford roared at the men and women rushing out of the main caves, spears and knives ready, just as they'd been drilled. With grim satisfaction, Mitford knew there'd be no complaints about his drilling them after this. Only how many were attacking? he wondered as he pounded up the ravine and grinned as he saw the first attackers appear on the edge of the lighted areas. A good fight, that's what was he'd been missing. Seeing a target, he paused long enough to launch his spear at an oncoming body. It pierced the chest of the leader, who dropped like a stone. Now the sentries on the heights were using their weapons, firing arrows and launching their spears into the crowd. Then the next of the attackers was howling as he charged at Mitford.

The Sergeant met the frenzied attack: the man had a knife in each hand but he hadn't the first clue about effective fighting, slashing the air in the hopes that one knife would connect. Mitford ducked, sidestepped, and then plunged his knife into the attacker's ribs. The man screamed, an awful wailing desperate sound, knives falling from strengthless hands as he fell back. Mitford remained in the crouching position as he quickly jerked his knife free and then tackled the next attacker. He was peripherally aware that his force was pressing in behind him. Then a stone, thrown from the heights, bounced off his shoulder, and he staggered against the wall of the ravine.

"HEY, WATCH WHERE YOU'RE AIMING," he roared as he saw Bart, Taglione, and quite likely Sandy Areson swarming past him.

It was over quickly: the attackers had obviously had no real plan in mind. They'd seen lights and smelled cooking, then attacked at a time when they thought everyone would be asleep.

There were fourteen bodies to be buried and three whose wounds could be sewn up. They were starving, and even their Catteni-issue clothing was torn and incredibly filthy. When the sun came up, three women crept in, begging for help. They were in dreadful condition, not only starved but beaten and repeatedly abused. Mitford approvingly watched Patti Sue gently leading one of them, little more than a child, into the kitchen for probably the first real food she'd eaten since being dropped.

Only five of the defenders had been wounded: two of those by "friendly fire" from stones thrown down into the ravine. Mitford's shoulder was sore but he didn't mention it to Matt Dargle, who was busy sewing up knife cuts. Another man had tripped in the dark and broken his leg and was cursing his clumsiness while the bone was set.

"Sorry about that, sarge," he said when Mitford walked around the infirmary to check the damages.

"Weren't you right behind me up that ravine, Bart?" Mitford asked as he watched Matt Dargle sewing up the nasty slice on the dark man's arm. "Teach you to keep your guard up."

"Naw, they was aiming at you," Bart said, grinning.

"Saving my skin, were you? Good man!" Mitford gave his uninjured shoulder a quick squeeze of appreciation.

The battle had roused the entire camp, so the cooks made an early breakfast for everyone. Mitford took advantage of the meal to drive home the lesson that they had to maintain vigilance.

"Good reaction, quick response time, folks, but they never should have got as far as the ravine at all. I think we'll move the guard perimeter out a bit."

"What about traps, sarge? Maybe we could rig some on the approaches?"

"Draw me a plan," Mitford said, nodding approval.

"You know, with so many out on patrol, didn't we leave ourselves a bit thin of fighting men here?" Sandy asked.

"Not when you were right in the vanguard yourself," Mitford said in blunt approval.

"It's my home, too," Sandy said with a shrug. "Besides, you drilled all of us!"

"Didn't I just?" Mitford said with a grin.

"All right, all right, we bitched," she said, flapping her hand at his inference. "You knew what you were doing. I guess we've got a bit cocky."

"We all know better now, don't we?" Mitford said, glancing around him. "Hell, they didn't even get as far as my office, did they? Now I need a disposal patrol."

"You mean burial party?" Dowdall asked, looking up from honing his blade.

"No, disposal. I want those bodies dumped four fields over at least, Dowdall."

"Aw, sarge," Dowdall groaned in protest to being tacitly assigned the duty.

"Don't want that carrion stinking up our camp, do we? You, you, you, you, and you," and he ended up with a full squad. "Take care of it before the sun warms 'em too much."

As soon as he got back to his "office" to write up the incident, Aarens began his complaint.

"You'd've let me die here, unable to defend myself! And you call yourself civilized! Think you're such a big leader."

Mitford walked straight up to Aarens, jerking him by the hair of his head so Aarens couldn't evade his eyes.

"Look, you sorry piece of shit. You keep on this way and I'll stake your living body out right beside the others."

Aarens gasped. "You wouldn't dare?"

"Oh, wouldn't I? Just give me an excuse. Just give me one!"

Mitford knew that his rage was fueled more by a reaction to the stress of the surprise attack and the runoff of adrenaline in his system. He oughtn't to lose control by taking it out on Aarens but better him than anyone else.

"Hey, sarge, take it easy. Take it easy," and though there was a quaver in the man's voice, his conciliatory manner caused Mitford to let his hair go. "You don't want to waste me, sarge. Not now. Not when you're going to need me."

"Need . . . *you?*"

"Yeah, me, sarge," and Aarens actually grinned. "Like I told you when I got here, I'm a mechanical genius. I can make machinery work when no one else can. I don't even need manuals to tell me how things work. It's a knack I've got. I used to make big money back in the States, just telling executives how to improve the efficiency of their production lines. Look, I heard what you were discussing with Mack Su, Capstan, and the others. They're all desk jockeys. Me, I'm guy on the floor who carries out their notions. And makes 'em work. You don't want to waste the one real talent you've got who can give you lights for the caves? Hot water! Distant early-warning devices."

"DEWs? How could you do that?" Mitford was suspicious but certainly willing to use Aarens—if the waste-of-space could produce the goods.

"You could mount solar panels—and their collectors, of course—

all around the camp," and Aarens gestured with his stocked hands, "with a circuit, say of a lighter wire. Anything breaking that wire and the alarm sounds. Simple."

"At night?"

Aarens shook his head, denying that qualification. "Collectors should save enough of a charge to be functional all night long. Or how do those mechanicals start up? I mean, it's simple enough."

Mitford thought there was no harm in running the idea past Mack and Spiller.

"Yeah, simple enough. Now shut up for a while."

"Yeah, but I'm supposed to be out of this contraption today," Aarens complained.

Mitford gave him a long look and then pointed to the sundial. "Not until the sun's on the first division. That makes it exactly a day since you got sentenced for harassing the little Chinese kid." Mitford gave the man one more long stare before he turned to pick up a sheet and his pencil.

He almost regretted the fact that Mack, Spiller, and Jack the Nail thought Aarens' idea had enough merit to make a prototype from materials that had been brought back to camp from the abattoir buildings.

Zainal's team made it back to camp, just before the evening rains, by jogging whenever the terrain permitted, and were met with a stern demand from the sentries for the password.

"Password?" Kris yelled back. "What password? You know who we are: hell, it's Kris Bjornsen, Zainal, the Doyle brothers, Coo and Slav. Damn it all, Tesco, don't be so hostile."

"Well, it's my duty, Kris. We got attacked while you was all gone." His grin gave her the immediate good news that the attack had failed and no one in the camp had evidently been killed or badly hurt.

They passed Tesco's post by and hurried down to the caves, eager for more details about the incident.

When Kris saw that the Sergeant wasn't in his office, she grabbed the first person by the arm, a youngster she remembered rescuing from the barns.

"Pete, where's Mitford?"

"Inside," the boy said. "Didja hear about us being attacked?"

"Yes, but we could do with some details."

"Who? What?" Lenny demanded.

"Aw, just some starving renegades. Sarge led the counterattack—he was something else." The boy's eyes shone with admiration. "Bart and Sandy Areson right behind 'im. I missed most of it," and Pete's face fell in disappointment. "The sentries rained down arrows and stones and clipped a few of our guys." Pete grinned irrepressibly. "Friendly fire, the Sarge called it. And they had fourteen bodies to dump—over that way," and Pete made a wild gesture that indicated a considerable distance, "to keep the scavengers happy." He gave an expressive shudder. "So you see, you missed a lot!"

"Were any of our guys hurt?" Kris asked urgently, glancing at the empty "office."

"Aw, a broken leg and a couple of cuts is all. And the Sarge took in the ladies the bad guys had messed up bad."

Inadvertently, Kris' glance went to the stocks. They were empty. Could both Aarens and Arnie be on good behavior? Had the attack scared manners into them?

"Death to all invaders of our Camp Ayres Rock!" And Pete shot his arm up in a clenched-fist salute.

"Camp Ayres Rock?" Kris repeated, stunned.

"Sure, why not? The rock that protects us."

"Well, you *are* named Peter."

"Huh?" The kid screwed his face up.

" 'Peter' means 'rock,' honey."

"Oh, I never knew that."

"D'you know where the Sergeant is right now, Peter?" Kris asked.

"Sure. Follow me," and he gestured them after him. "He's rigging distant early-warning devices."

"He is?"

"Yeah, that Aarens guy did 'em. Not bad. And they work."

"Aarens?" and Kris turned in amazement to Zainal.

"Wonders will never cease," Lenny said, grinning at her, appreciating her surprise. "So he isn't a total waste."

"Takes all kinds to make a world," was all Mitford said when they met up with him on his way back from the perimeter.

"But Aarens?"

"Surprised me, too," Mitford said, leading them to a small cave that was his "inside office"—since the rains came, he said. "Did Pete there tell you all about the raid?"

"Can we debrief you, sarge?" Kris asked, laughing.

"Later. Give me the report on your findings, first. You do all right?" He glanced around at the others.

"Fine, sarge, we did great," Lenny answered him.

"Coo's gotten much weaker though, sarge," Kris said quietly, not glancing in the Deski's direction. Mitford grimaced. "Has anybody else found something to help?"

"Matt Dargle has narrowed it down to the lack of vitamin C, potassium, or calcium, and we're looking for sources of those two," and Mitford looked dour. "Right now there're only three Deskis strong enough to go out with foragers to search." He turned to Zainal. "You got any good ideas?"

"Deskis always need special foods. Bring in to Barevi. I do not know what." And Zainal sighed. "Good guys, Deskis!"

"S'more'n I can say for some," Mitford said in a low disgusted growl. He went on in a more positive tone. "Believe it or not but Aarens is the mechanical genius he told me he was!"

"So we heard."

"Well, he cobbled together some perimeter circuit warning devices in case some other individuals think they can raid Camp Rock . . ." He grinned when he realized they'd heard the location had received a name. "He and Spiller believe we can even get adapt the panels to make water hot and maybe even internal lighting and heat. D'you remember anything in that report about the winters here, Zainal?" There was a hint of deep concern in Mitford's eyes. "Like snow or floods or what?"

Zainal looked down at his big hands as if they might hold the answers. Then, with a sad sigh, he shook his head. "My people did not explore well. They did not see a lot we have now seen. But this planet has air to breathe and food for most to eat." His voice held a tacit apology for the shortcomings of that exploration team. "The basic are here. Air, water, food needed to survive. And we survive well now, thanks to you."

Mitford nodded in acceptance at that approval.

"Well, then, since the farm machinery seems to be shutting down after harvesting everything, and the farmers among us say that those loo-cows of yours, Kris, haven't been rounded up in a wintering environment, looks like we all can expect to survive whatever the winter season brings."

"Say, sarge, if the machines are all shut down, either by us or their programming, couldn't we move into the buildings? We've found enough to accommodate all of us," Kris said.

"That's being considered as an alternative," Mitford said. "Some folks are scared of the possibility of more marauders and feel safer here in Camp Rock. They'd resist leaving. However, those barns would be equally as defensible. Now lemme talk to the Doyles, will ya, and you two get some rest."

The rain was still pelting down when Kris and Zainal stopped in the main cavern for the hot soup and the rather tasty form of soda bread that was available. It was so good that she didn't even spit out the hard bits.

No one she knew was on duty there so she ate with Zainal. She tried not to, but she couldn't help notice the sideways looks directed at them: some quite speculative and unfriendly. Well, it didn't surprise her that there would still be animosity leveled at Zainal. Maybe that was why Mitford kept sending them out of the camp on patrol. Out of sight, out of mind. She sighed, a little sound, but Zainal caught it and looked inquiringly at her. She smiled dismissively and broke off a piece of her bread to scrap the last of the thick, tasty soup out of the rather lopsided pottery bowl. Zainal followed her example, grinning back at her.

They washed out their utensils and returned them to the storage racks.

"I go see Coo," Zainal said.

"I'll come . . ." But when Zainal shook his head, she decided that a dip was the next order of business for her. "Give him my regards."

"Regards?"

"Warm greetings."

"Oh! Not a 'boy' saying."

"Nope!" She grinned at him.

"One day you explain the 'boy' thing?"

"Any day now, m'friend," Kris said with a laugh. "Your English improves in leaps and bounds."

"Leaps and bounds?" He frowned as he tried to figure out the meaning of what she had said.

"I'll explain that, too. Me for a bath," she said in farewell.

The water in the underground lake was cold enough to curtail any lengthy wallowing. She was out and blotting herself dry beyond the main lights when she heard voices.

"Aarens had a point. How do we know that Cat isn't a spy? How do we know he doesn't have a comunit of some kind? How do we know he hasn't left messages with those machine-things in the garages?"

"Come off it, Barker," and Kris, hurriedly dressing, recognized Joe Lattore's thick voice. "What would the Cats need to spy on us *for*, for God's sake? And he's no ordinary Cat anyway. I saw enough of the upper-class dudes and he's one of them."

"Then why's he here with us?"

"That Bjornsen chick told me he'd killed a patrol leader and they caught him before the day was up."

"Yeah, and who goes everywhere with that Cat? Huh?"

"You also heard the Doyle brothers same as I did, and they said there's nothing doing between 'em."

"They was careful, is all."

"Oh, stow it. The Cat's risked his neck to save us and I'm going to be grateful to him until I find a damned good reason not to be. And Aarens isn't good enough. I know *his* type and I tell you what, was I hiring, I wouldn't hire Aarens no way no how."

Kris stepped as far back in the shadows as she could, a frisson of fear for Zainal running up her back. Did Mitford have any idea that such feelings were running against the Catteni? Probably, and that's exactly why Zainal was sent out on constant reconnaissance—to reduce the possibility of reprisals against him.

"When's Mitford going to ax him, then? Said he would when he found out all the bastard knows. Seems to me he'd've done that by now."

"Maybe that's why he keeps sending him out of the camp? Get something else to waste him?"

"Next time he might just not come back," a new voice said with a malicious chuckle. "We don't need no Cats here."

"Ah, you guys make me sick. He's one man, and he's been useful. You don't have to like useful people but you *can* use them. That's what Mitford's doing."

Conversation altered when the first man got in the water.

"Keeee-rist, but that's cold! Freeze m'balls off, it will."

"You have 'em?"

Kris grimaced and stopped listening as the comments became more personal and derogatory. Men were worse gossips than women. She hunkered down in the shadows, her back against the cold stone, and waited. Fortunately the group was not any more inclined to stay in the cold water than she had been and they were shortly out of it and dressing. She waited another long moment until she figured they had reached the upper corridors of the cave and then she left the lake.

She stopped by Mitford's "office" but he had a crowd, all talking and pushing diagrams at each other, so she went to her own cave. Sleep was the next order of her day.

DURING HER LATEST TREK, SOMEONE HAD TAKEN ADVANTAGE of her absence and stolen some of the brush which formed her mattress, so she didn't have quite as comfortable a night's rest as she'd hoped for. Still, she woke rested before dawn. When she got to the main cavern, hunters were grabbing a cup of the hot herbal tea before setting off to check snares or to hunt. With her cup in hand, she wandered hoping to find Jay or Sandy. They'd level with her about Zainal. At this point in time, Kris couldn't really see Mitford executing the Catteni for any reason. And there was no way Zainal had been "planted" among the prisoners. He was here because other Catteni wanted to get even with him. Sandy was absent, as was anyone else with whom she had some acquaintance.

Finding an unoccupied rock near the front of the cavern, she seated herself and kept watch of those coming into the cavern for their breakfast, waiting for Zainal's appearance. She wondered how Coo was doing. They really shouldn't have let him fuss with that flying thing: that fall had not been good for him, even with Lenny and Kris cushioning his landing.

She heard the rumble and the warning yell from the sentinels at the same instant. And darting to the outside ledge, tried to see what was making the noise. Whatever it was, it was still some distance, but it sounded awfully like the harvester vessel: big! Only everything had been harvested. Hadn't it?

"Where's Mitford?" was the cry and several of the hunters took off to locate him. Kris went for Zainal.

She met him, head-on, bouncing off his hard body and cracking her head against the rock on the rebound. His hand grabbed her upper arm to steady her.

"Another big ship, Zainal," she said, pointing outside. Still holding her arm, the Catteni drew her along with him, and others who had been roused by the general furor.

Once again, this time in the dark, everyone who could clambered to the nearest height and peered in the direction of the oncoming airborne vessel.

"Think they've come on reprisals?" someone asked. "With us messing up their mechanicals?"

"Zainal?" Mitford called.

"Here."

"Any ideas?"

Kris could see that Zainal had cocked his head, listening intently to the sound.

"That is Catteni engine sound," he said. Then pointed as a bulk, outlined by running lights, materialized out of the dawn gloom. Even Kris could see the basic difference in design between the first enormous vessel and this one, which was not as large, if the lights indicated its perimeter. Zainal watched a moment more and then pointed in the direction of the abattoir. "That way."

"Jaysus . . . what're they doing?"

"Any chance they're landing more prisoners, Zainal?" Mitford asked.

"Yes. Good chance." And he began to climb down. "Who comes with me?"

"I didn't say you should go, buddy," Mitford said in a tense voice.

"Only fast runners," Zainal said, ignoring Mitford. "They must unload."

"Yeah, but *you'd* get there fast enough to take off with them, wouldn't you?" Mitford said in a hard tone, coming out of the darkness to grab Zainal by the arm.

Kris caught her breath. Maybe, after all, Mitford wouldn't object to a summary execution of the Catteni, and Kris did not, definitely did not want to see Zainal killed. She *liked* him too much!

"Don't do anything foolish, sarge," she said. "I'll go with him."

"Of course you will," Mitford said cryptically. They had to pause now because the noise of the overflying craft drowned out any conversation. Zainal kept his eyes on the vessel, then nodded.

"Transport. More people. We must *try*. It is night still," Zainal said and, pulling Kris by the hand, hauled her with him down from the height.

"Try what?" Mitford called out in the same breath that Kris echoed his question but Zainal was already sprinting down the ravine in the direction the long ship above them was headed, dragging Kris along with him.

She was aware of some conflicting and confused orders behind them as Zainal ran onward. In the first few strides, she wondered why he was so keen on having her along, but then she had to concentrate on her footing to keep up with him. The fact that she could was a plus. She was sure fitter on this crazy planet than she'd ever been. She could hear others following, cursing at the dark and the bad footing, but she concentrated on watching Zainal's movements and the track in front of them.

They were well ahead of those pursuing when Zainal allowed her to pause for a few moments. They were on the downside of the ridge, the lights of the vessel obscured by the lay of the land. She quickly recovered her breath enough to speak.

"Will they stop the same place they dropped us off?" she asked.

"That would be good," he said. "Nothing there."

She took that to mean that the field would be empty and thus a good spot to dump more unconscious bodies. She wondered how long it would take, or did the Catteni have some way of just rolling bodies out of the ship's hold that didn't require individual handling? Then she remembered, all too vividly, what happened to living creatures lying on fields on this fecking world. No wonder Zainal was in such a hurry. Dawn was still far away. Would they get there soon enough to prevent slaughter?

He started off again and she followed, all too aware that it had taken them two days to reach the caverns from that site. Even at the pace Zainal had set, would they make it to the field before the ship took off again? Well, they *had* to try. Or maybe he was hoping to attract attention from one of the hill points overlooking the field? They clambered up a slope now, and Zainal stopped, so abruptly that she ran into him.

"Hey, warn me, will . . ." Her voice trailed off as she realized that the running lights were higher than they should be for a ship that might be landing. They hadn't seen its gradual ascent. Zainal cursed, whirled, and looked back the way they had come, running his hand and arm along the line the ship had traveled as if trying to impress the direction in his mind. He started back up the slope they had just slid down, digging his toes in and slipping in the urgency of his passage.

Shaking her head, Kris followed him, pausing only briefly when the roar of engines told her that the ship was boosting out of planetary gravity. The flame of its propellant was as vivid as she remembered launches from Cape Kennedy. She would have liked to watch but had to keep up with Zainal.

They met up with the others in moments, due to the pace that Zainal was setting.

"The ship's already dumped its load," she told them, clinging to someone as support as she gasped out an explanation. "Back that way. We gotta get there before the scavengers murder 'em all."

"Was that why the Cat was in such a flaming hurry?"

"Hell, he wanted to catch up with them and get off this bleeding planet," another man managed to gasp out.

"Think what you will, but are you going to help?" Kris cried, shouting the last of her challenge over her shoulder as she took off after Zainal.

They did gather more help as they went back through the ravine again. Dawn was brightening the sky, so it was easier to see where to put your feet. Where the track split, right down into the ravine, or left to continue on the upper ridge, Zainal signaled for Kris to report to Mitford, who was standing in his "office," fists on his belt as he saw them emerge on the height.

"Need Slav badly," Zainal added and then charged off again.

"What'n'ell's going on?"

Kris stopped, hands on knees, catching enough breath to speak. "We need Slav. Ship took off. It's already dropped its load. We gotta get there or the scavengers will."

"Right on!" And Mitford snapped into action, yelling for Slav, Pess, Tesco, Su, Dowdell as she took up her chase of Zainal.

She finally caught up with him when he stopped by one of the many streams to rinse out his mouth. The sun wasn't up yet and the air was cool, but she was hot from her exertions and wondering if she would last the distance.

"Mitford's organized more help. Is it far?"

He shook his head. "Ship climbing." He looked up at the lightening sky. "Lucky."

She hoped so, but how long did those creatures scavenge? Would this half-light be sufficient to send them wherever they spent the daylight hours? She had her breath back and now dropped to her belly, burying her hot face in the cool water, intaking a mouthful to moisten her throat and letting only a little trickle down to her stomach. She was on her feet when he was.

And they ran on.

Actually this wasn't a bad pace, she thought, now she had her second wind. She tried to keep her mind off what scavengers could do to a field full of nice juicy warm live bodies. Now that wasn't productive thought! At least it should now be clear to everyone at the camp that Zainal had been motivated to "save" people, not get himself off this planet. Though she wouldn't blame him if that had been his goal. Would he have taken her with him? That, too, was not a productive thought, but she was beginning to appreciate how much the big man meant to her. She'd never found anyone else who treated her as a competent equal, had never once tried to come on since the day she had floored him in the flitter. She knew from comments made back in the kitchens at Barevi that, while the Catteni were equipped, to put it discreetly, much the same way as human males were, only more so as one woman had said dryly, the two species were incompatible as far as propagation was concerned. No Catteni-Human offspring would be forthcoming. But, since the day she had clobbered him in the flyer back on Barevi, Zainal had never visibly lusted after her. And she was quite familiar with that sort of look. Zainal treated her not quite as he treated the male members of their patrols, but with a courtesy she found unusual and maybe even special to her. Even when he knew that it was her fault he was stuck with this bunch of suspicious, unappreciative, and sometimes intolerant mixed bag of humanoids. Oddly enough, though the Catteni were the "subjugating" race, the Deskis and Rugarians didn't seem to feel any animosity toward Zainal . . . certainly not as much as the Terrans did.

This was not terrain she was familiar with and Kris was relieved to see the sun coming up and clearing off the shadows, so there was less danger of her stumbling on the rough ground. That was the one thing she did fear—an injury that their meager first aid supplies could not remedy. Or unfamiliar infections that were life-threatening. The Catteni antiseptic lotion was not a specific cure for everything that could happen to the unwary. And the anesthesia from the darts could be a boon.

Zainal was bounding up the hill in front of them now, then switching to a zigzag on the steeper parts. He waited on the height for her and pointed. Two fields over she could see the cubes of Catteni supply crates and the fringes of space occupied by inert bodies. At this distance, she couldn't tell if they were being beset by scavengers yet.

Zainal cupped his mouth and hollered a weird cry. It was answered, she thought, by one of the aliens following. He nodded satisfaction and began the descent. This hillside was covered with some sort of thorny growth that clung to the fabric of their coveralls with a tenacity which made her glad it wasn't her flesh that was bared. Zainal, caught on a thick limb, hauled out his hatchet and hewed the limb. Even separated from the mother bush, it still clung.

"Careful," Zainal said, holding up his free hand to warn her back. "Chop first," he added, pointing to the bushes in her way.

"Can I help you?"

"Go down. Hurry," he said, gesturing emphatically to the field, now out of sight behind the next rise. "Stamp, yell."

She hesitated a brief moment more but the flash of his eyes when he glanced up from disentangling the thicket branch from his coverall was enough to send her on her way. She used her hatchet to slash and bash a way in front of her and succeeded in reaching clear ground, covered by a stubble of harvested crops, with no delays. Glancing over her shoulder, she saw him finally free of the branch. So she ran on, across the field, neatly leaping the low hedge on the far side and down into the next. She thought she heard cries rising from the drop field. That made her run faster, shouting, giving the cowboy yells she had practiced as a tomboy. She paused long enough at the separating hedge to pick up handsful of stones. Then she leaped that hedge and almost landed on someone's face. A human. In fact, every body near her was human. Some had already been attacked by the scavengers.

First she threw her rocks in as wide an arc as she could, shouting as she did so. Then she stomped her way up the long side of the field, sometimes running and jumping down as hard as she could on landing, yelling and yodeling as she stamped until she reached the upper boundary. There were no signs of the scavengers in the center of the field, so she continued her progress around the outer edge, stamping, yelling, pausing only when she had to get her breath and try to moisten the dry tissues of her mouth. She'd completed two sides of the big field when she saw others arriving and yelled and gestured at them to square the field in the other direction.

Then she spotted several people rousing from their drugged sleep and went to assist them. Once again the Catteni had dropped people comfortably near water and she borrowed cups from belts to give people that much comfort in recovering from their ordeal.

Dowdall was opening the crates, going first for the first-aid kits and blankets while the others did what they could for those the scavengers had attacked. She was so busy she didn't at first realize that Zainal was not among the rescuers.

"Tesco, where's Zainal?" she asked when she did notice his absence.

"Saw him back there," and Tesco pointed vaguely over his shoulder before kneeling to give water to a groggy woman.

Reassured, Kris moved to the next group, who happened to be Deskis. A glance around the field gave her the irritating information that none of the rescuers were doing doodly to help the aliens, so she concentrated on them. Not that she found herself kindly disposed toward the Turs, who regarded the water with great suspicion until she took a sip herself and deposited the cup on the ground beside them. They could do as they chose. Three Ilginish had been badly chewed and before any one could stop them, they suicided, evidently by swallowing their own tongues and suffocating. Their face skin turned from a normal dark green to almost black. Other Ilginish came to view the dead, then piled the bodies to one side under the hedges. Ilginish "faces" did not register any expression, so Kris didn't know if they were upset or not, but as quickly as she could, she doled blankets and knives out to them, and indicated the first-aid kits.

More people arrived from the camp, including Mitford. She was surprised to see him away from his "office" but glad of his presence. That's when she realized she still had not seen Zainal.

"Sarge, you seen Zainal?"

"No, I haven't," Mitford said, frowning as he looked about the field where more and more of the latest arrivals were regaining consciousness.

"Did you come down the thorny hill?"

"No, Su was there to warn us away from it. Why?"

Kris didn't answer but, grabbing up a first-aid kit and a handful of blankets from the nearby crates, she started off at a fast trot, dodging around groups and leaping over still-sleeping bodies. She flew across the intervening field, now entirely visible in the full morning light, hurdling the low hedge without losing her stride, and pelted to the thornbushy hill. They weren't like Barevian thornbushes but, where she was damned sure she had hacked her way through was now as solid a vegetation patch as if she hadn't cut it back. There was no sign of Zainal.

Scared now for him, because Zainal of all people should have been able to free himself unscathed, she looked anxiously around. Since he wasn't up at the field, he had to still be around here, somewhere. And, if the thorns had been toxic enough to slow down a Catteni, he'd have sought water. The thornbushes were not tall enough to have hidden his big frame, and anyway his browny-gray coverall would have made him visible even in the dense undergrowth. Water!

There was always water on these damned mechanically cultivated fields. While this field had been harvested, there had to be water nearby. She listened hard. Her ears finally caught the unmistakable sound of running water. Downhill there was a small copse of some of the dia-mond-leaved bushes. Those seemed to grow near the streams.

She heard a low groan, the sort that would reluctantly escape tightly closed lips. With a new awareness that the bushes on Botany could be dangerous, she parted the branches of the diamond-leaf and saw Zainal, half-in, half-out of a little brook which welled up from the rocks around which the diamond-leaves clustered. A boot had been cast aside and his right pant leg was rolled up over his knee, exposing the injury.

"Oh, lord," she breathed, seeing the massive inflammation on the outside of his wide muscular calf. The thorns of Barevi had been danger-ous in a nuisancy way, but this injury looked serious. Bending over him, she checked first for any signs of blood poisoning. Not that gray Catteni flesh might exhibit such a trauma. He had blood, as red as any human's, and it had clotted almost black where it had run down his leg. That was when she realized by the size of the wound that he had evidently carved the thorn out of his own flesh.

"Ouch!" she murmured, shuddering convulsively. She sorted through the first-aid supplies for the Catteni antiseptic. *That* was defi-nitely in order. And it would sting like billy-be-damned when she poured it in that open wound but what other choice had she? She took a deep breath and *emptied* the entire vial of the solution into the crater he had made in his leg.

"Rorrrrrgh!" Zainal shot to sitting position in protest to the treat-ment, his right hand cocked back to strike, his left arm up in guard.

Kris lurched backward, away from him.

"It's Kris, Zainal. I'm trying to help!"

His eyes focused on her face, wild in reaction to the pain and alarm, but, in that brief instant, he recognized her.

"You came," he said in a barely audible voice before he seemed to collapse inward and fell back on the ground. His eyes rolled upward, the lids fluttering as well as any southern belle flirt could have done under different circumstances, and then he passed out again.

"Did I do the right thing, Zainal?" She shook, or rather tried to shake, the massive shoulder to rouse him. She retrieved the first-aid bag, which had fallen off her lap, and tried to think what else she could *do* to help him. Swollen tissue could respond to cold compresses. With all the antiseptic in the wound, there wouldn't be much in the water that could exacerbate the wound.

There were sheets of some sort of material in the kit, so she soaked those until they were cold and placed them on the wound. He moaned a little but didn't writhe in pain so she felt it was safe to continue with that treatment. She made a pillow of one of the blankets she'd brought, brushing the leaves and pebbles off his surprisingly fine, soft gray hair, and covered his big frame with another.

It was Mitford himself who came looking for her. She emerged from the brush in response to his calling. Beyond him she saw the lines of the newest immigrants starting the trek back to the camp. He hadn't lost any time deciding to take them in, even if another four or five hundred souls to tend must be the lowest option on his agenda.

"What's the matter, Kris?" he said, trotting up to her in an effortless lope. How he kept so fit with all the sedentary work he was now saddled with, she didn't know, but he rose another notch in her estimation.

"Warn people off those thornbushes," she said first, pointing urgently to the slope. But the line seemed to be taking the less direct route, around the inhospitable-looking incline. "Zainal's down, with a thorn wound. He carved the thorn out of his own leg but it was toxic enough to knock him out. We'll need to make a litter to carry him back."

Mitford winced and scratched his head, half-turning in the direction of his new charges.

"I know, you gotta get them back first, but considering how much Zainal has done . . ." And she was surprised at the bitterness in her voice.

"Now, now, easy does it, Bjornsen, I'm not about to abandon him. He *is* too damned useful." In the Sergeant's voice, she caught the nuance that Zainal might be useful, but not popular, and knew that some of the gossip about him was true. "We're all in the same boat or," and Mitford gave her a wry grin, "on the same planet, but this new dump isn't going to help!" He sighed deeply.

"Don't mean to add to your problems, sarge," she said apologetically.

"Dammitall, Bjornsen," and now he was angry at her apology, "*you're* not a problem and I won't *let* him be. Can you hang on until I see this bunch installed?" With one hand, he gripped Kris' right arm, emphasizing his intent while he hauled his blanket over his head and dropped it beside her. Then he handed over the other sack he carried. "Food, firing, and other stuff. Now, where is he?"

She led him to where Zainal sprawled. When Mitford lifted off the temporary dressing, he curled his lip and recoiled slightly at the look of the puncture, then carefully replaced the bandage.

"Nasty, all right. Hope he got all the thorn out, but probably he did," and there was approval in the Sergeant's tone for the measure of the man he knew Zainal to be. "Hell's bells, he can't be comfortable like that," Mitford added, so the two of them pulled the big body out of the water. Then, when Kris had hurriedly cleared a space and spread two more blankets, they managed to roll him into a more level, comfortable position.

Mitford stood then, surveying the area, kicking at the roots of the bushes. "How'd they find enough soil to grow in?" he muttered. "Rocky enough so those scavengers can't come at you."

"They come out at night," Kris began and then realized that it might indeed be nighttime before help for a Catteni arrived.

"Firing's in there and some of those matches Cumber made. We found sulfur, y'know."

"No, I didn't," and she wondered if sulfur had any medicinal qualities.

"Look, I'll send a litter back for him as soon as possible. Get some more firing when you can." He surveyed the massive Catteni's prone body. "Hope he doesn't get delirious on you or something."

"I'll manage, sarge," she said, gritting her teeth.

" 'Luck, Bjornsen, but you're the kind who can handle things."

As Kris watched him make his way out of the little copse, she was somewhat heartened by his confidence in her. Mitford didn't often praise, and while that might be a bit backhanded, she appreciated being thought capable.

She went back to her patient, resigned to a long wait, knowing that Zainal's welfare would be low on the list of everyone else's priorities. She wet the compresses again, glad of the almost indestructible quality of Catteni materials, and then she moistened Zainal's lips.

You had to keep people from getting dehydrated if they'd been poisoned, didn't you? His lips parted as if the moisture was what he needed, so she managed to dribble water down his throat and he swallowed eagerly. A good sign. His forehead and cheeks felt warm, but not hot-hot. She couldn't remember from her previous contacts with him just what a normal body temperature for a Catteni would be. She also couldn't tell if his skin had altered as a human's would with fever. While one part of her was glad that Catteni were not totally impervious to natural hazards, she was damned sorry Zainal was laid low by as silly a thing as a thorn.

Chapter Nine

JAY GREENE, SLAV, THE DOYLE BROTHERS, A man she didn't recognize and, surprisingly, Coo, returned by second moonrise. By then Zainal was sweating copiously and she tried to cool him off with the compresses. There was such a lot of him to cool! He was restless but not so energetically that she'd had any trouble keeping him prone. But she was getting more and more worried. Faint slithers had caused her to fear that the scavengers might be bold enough to penetrate the rocky dell. She'd taken to periodic stampings about the small clearing, hoping to scare them away. It was only quiet victims they went after, cowardly as they were.

She nearly cried with relief, though, when she heard her name called. She heaped firing on the little campfire to show the way to them.

"This is Dr. Dane, Kris," Jay said, urging the

medical man through the thicket. "He's even treated Catteni back on Earth."

"Thank God!" Kris breathed, anxiously urging the doctor to his patient and whipping off the latest compress to show the ugly wound. It looked even worse in the flickering firelight.

"G'day," Dane said in an unmistakably Australian accent, giving her a keen look before he knelt by the patient. "Did a proper job on himself, didn't he?" With deft fingers he pressed the sides of the gaping wound mouth. "Got it all, I'd say. Tough bastards, these Catteni. Pour the whole bottle in, did you?" and now he grinned at her. "Fair do."

"It was all I had and it *is* Catteni issue," she said, noticing that she was wringing her hands.

"Did the right thing, all right." He felt Zainal's skin, placed a hand over the chest and then to the large neck vein. "Not so ragged after all. Right then, let's get him back. Hey, what?" He had straightened up after his examination and saw Coo coming to crouch in the firelight, something in his hand which he wanted to inspect.

The Deski's hand was trembling—with fatigue, Kris wondered, deeply grateful to the alien, in his own debilitated state, for wanting to help an injured Catteni. What Coo was examining was the lighter gray crown of a thornbush, the new growth, since vegetation even on this godforsaken planet seemed to follow certain botanical precedents. Then, before she could say anything, Coo had popped it in his mouth and was masticating with every evidence of enthusiasm and relief. In the act of springing upright, the Deski also turned and, with more energy than he had shown in days, plunged toward the hillside.

"What was that all about?" the doctor asked, in surprise.

"I think Coo's located something to take care of his dietary deficiency," Kris said drolly.

"One man's meat's another's poison," the man replied philosophically. "Now let's get this poisoned boyo back to civilization. Quite a setup Mitford's organized," he added with approval.

"Good ol' Yankee know-how," Jay said with a grin.

"What about Irish improvisation?" Lenny Doyle said, pretending offense as he unlashed the ties on stretcher poles.

"Ya think this is strong enough to hold 'im?" Ninety asked, measuring Zainal's bulk against the litter design.

"Those blankets are indestructible," Jay said.

It took all of them, with Kris holding up heavy Catteni feet, to get the unconscious Zainal onto the litter. Strips of torn blanket secured him for the arduous journey back to camp.

Kris kicked out the fire and stored the remaining firing into the sack Mitford had given her and followed them. In the bright light of the big rising moon, Coo was busily, and carefully, plucking the very tops of the thornbushes and stuffing them into the open blouse of his coverall.

"Is that what you need, Coo?" Kris called. "Can I pick, too?"

"Noooo," Coo said, shaking his head emphatically. "Baaaad for oomans." With one hand he kept fanning the air to reinforce his warning for her to keep back while he kept nipping the crowns with the other.

She tried to recall how many of the newest "immigrants" were Deski but, suddenly, thinking was beyond her strained and tired mind. She fell in step behind the litter bearers, relieved that her long and anxious watch had concluded.

WHEN SHE TOOK HER TURN AS A LITTER BEARER, FOR SHE insisted on that, Leon Dane gave her some interesting and oddly welcome news: Earth was fighting back against the Catteni invaders—an evidently unprecedented reaction.

The Catteni method of subduing a planet by swooping down and carrying off whole cities of people generally cowed a species totally. Not so with Terrans. Despite the invasion, resistance began almost as soon as the great Catteni transport ships began loading hostages. Leon Dane had remained in Sydney, using his position as a physician to relay important information to a very active unit in the Blue Mountains. On orders, he had volunteered to treat Catteni for, despite thick hides, they broke bones and had "accidents" that would have killed humans.

"If you know your invader's weaknesses, you have a better chance of striking back." He turned a grin on Kris as they moved across the second field. "That was my job. Unfortunately there isn't much that gets a Catteni down and they seem impervious to any of the Terran toxic materials I tried on 'em. To see the clinical reactions, of course. But, oh my word, they can mess each other up on their little twenty-four-hour vendettas!" He whistled appreciatively. "I spent a lot of time sewing 'em up. They don't break easy but they sure do lacerate a treat."

"I guess I'm glad you were willing to help Zainal. He was a victim of one of those twenty-four-hour vendettas."

"Was he? And they dumped him in with you lot?"

Kris nodded, finding that talking and keeping up her corner of the heavily loaded litter was tiring.

"How'd you get caught?" she asked the doctor.

"Ha! We had orders to riot at a certain time and place and I was sent from my hospital to officiate. I got gassed along with everyone else. The Cats don't ever ask questions. They're effective that way. But sending one of theirs to colonize . . ." He shook his head in surprise. "Whad-did he do?"

"He killed a patrol leader," Kris said. "I watched the pursuit from where I was hiding."

"You were hiding?"

Kris grinned. "On Barevi."

"Barevi?" He shot her a quirky smile. "Sounds Aborigine."

"Does, doesn't it—Catteni Aborigine, at least. Barevi's one of their big distribution and R and R planets. Only one big city and spaceports. Slave trading's the biggest industry there. And resupply of Catteni ships. I figured out, from watching the guy who owned me, how to drive one of those little flitters of theirs and appropriated it one evening." She grinned at Leon. "Managed quite handily in the jungle there until he," and she jerked her head back at Zainal, "dropped in on me. I was taking him back to where he belongs when I got caught in a riot-gassing, too."

"Hmmm."

"He knew a bit about this planet, enough to save a lot of us from getting eaten by those scavengers or caught by the avians."

"The Cats didn't leave much for us to go on with," he said in a gloomy tone.

"Zainal says that's how they've colonized a lot of places." She shot a look at him and wondered if she'd offend with her next comment. "Sort of like you Aussies were. We voted to call the planet Botany."

"Did you now?" And Leon Dane shot her a startled look, but he grinned. "Well, it fits. Australia—well, the Sydney area at least—was settled by convicts."

"Made a good job of it, too, didn't they?"

"I take the point, Kris Bjornsen. And they had as little as we have. Maybe less. We at least have a lot of specialists."

"Many aliens? Deskis, Turs, Ilginish, Rugarians?"

Leon shrugged. "I was working more on the human injuries. But I noticed some strange-looking creatures in the hospital cave. Stick-thin, like the one that came with us to fetch you."

"The Deskis. They're not doing well here. Missing some essential ingredient in their diet."

"Is that why that bloke was picking the thornbushes?"

"Hope so."

Then Lenny and Ninety declared they were rested enough to take over. Kris was quite willing to give up her end of the litter, guilty though it made her feel for the rest of the way back to the camp.

———

LIT BY MANY TORCHES, MITFORD, MURPH, GREENE, AND Dowdall were still interviewing new arrivals when the rescuers arrived by third moonrise. In spite of the late hour—or was it early?—there was a great deal of activity and the smell of freshly roasted meats.

Instead of going into the main cavern, however, the bearers swerved to one of the lesser caves.

"Hospital," Lenny said when Kris wanted to know. "Quite a setup now." But there was something about the way he wouldn't meet her eyes that bothered Kris.

"I'll stay with him," she said firmly. "He'll need . . ."

"You"—and Leon Dane prodded her chest with a firm finger—"need rest." In the better light of the torches, she realized that he was a good-looking man in his mid-thirties, spare as so many Australians seemed to be.

"I'll rest better with . . . my buddy," and she added that designation with defensive pride. Dane was looking at her now in a way that made her refer to him in that fashion.

"That way, is it?"

"NO! Not *that* way," she said, fiercely now. "But I got him into this mess and I'll stand by him."

"Good on you, sheila," Dane said, and squeezed her arm in approval. "But he'll be tended while you"—and he prodded her chest with one finger—"sleep."

It was a small cave and anyone entering had to stoop or risk a crack on the skull. Inside there was more headroom, sufficient even for Zainal when he recovered. She said "when" as positively as she could to herself though he lay far too still to suit her when his litter was placed on the waiting mound of blanket-covered boughs. There was another bed on the other side of the den and she looked longingly at it. Then turned back to see Dane checking the wound again and Zainal's pulse.

"He'll do. Tough bastard," he said. "You," and he pointed at Kris and then the bed, "get some rest. I'll check in during the night." He gave her a grin. "Haven't lost a Catteni patient yet." Then, when she did not immediately obey his injunction, he hauled her the step to the bed and pushed her down on the boughs, spreading the blanket over her. "Sleep."

She did, rousing once or twice when she heard movement, but it was always caused by Dane, checking on his patient.

When she finally woke up, she stretched luxuriously, knowing that she had slept herself out. But a low moan brought her alert instantly and scrambling to Zainal's side. His injured leg, bare of covering apart from the compress, was twice its normal size well up into the thigh. The flesh when she gingerly touched it was almost burning to the touch. The compress was dry and clung to the suppurating flesh when she tried to check the wound.

"Oh, lordee," she murmured and then banged her forehead on leaving the den. "Ouch!"

"Gotcha, did it?" said Lenny sympathetically, rising from a stool by the entrance.

"What are you doing here?" she said, inhaling against the pain of her scraped forehead. Her hand came away with dots of blood.

"Being careful not to bang my skull open like you just did," he said, grinning. There was that in his quickly averted glance that told her he was there for another reason entirely.

"Was I supposed to leave him out there to die?" she demanded.

"Don't jump on me, Kris, I like the big guy," Lenny said. "Mitford just doesn't need any trouble."

"Mutiny on Botany, huh?"

"Huh?" Lenny echoed, totally nonplussed by her cryptic remark. "Look," he added hurriedly, "Dane'll be around again soon. Go get some breakfast. I'll be here till you get back."

"It's ridiculous with all Zainal has done for the camp that he has to have a guard."

"Now, look, Kris, I'm not so much a guard as I am a sort of orderly," and Lenny looked embarrassed, "in case he needs help. You know what I mean?"

"I'm paranoid, I guess," she said, relaxing a little. "Dane said anything about his chances?"

Lenny shrugged. "Didn't ask. I just volunteered. I'm on duty for them, too," he said and gestured to the opening obliquely across the tunnel. "We got a lot of patients. Oh, and that Missus Bollinger had a baby boy while we were gone. Fine big lad."

Kris smiled through her sigh of relief. "That kind of good news is very welcome."

"Don't worry. Mitford's got everyone organized already," and Lenny's grin was mischievous. Then he gave her a little push toward the tunnel entrance. "G'wan. Eat. You're off duty today, anyway, with your buddy on the sick list."

Kris didn't hear any nuance in his use of "buddy" so she relaxed. She could safely leave Zainal in Lenny's charge.

"G'wan," he said, smiling kindly, and gave her a half turn toward the entrance. "Eat. Bread's getting better now the chemist lads've got a good yeast going."

She took her time, peering in at the various units in this "hospital," noticing a lot of unfamiliar faces, some obviously in a good deal of discomfort, to judge by their expressions.

She saw Anna Bollinger, sitting up in her "bed," nursing her infant, and would have passed by but Annie saw her and waved her in.

"How's the Catteni? I heard he was badly hurt," she said. Then added in a hard voice and with a scowl, "How?"

From the "doorway," Kris answered, wondering about the change in her voice. Anna had good reason to be grateful to Zainal. In a neutral voice she said: "On his way to keep people from getting scavengered in the dark, he got a thorn in the calf of his leg and had to carve it out."

Anna shuddered. "Ooo, nasty. Give him my regards," and she

looked lovingly down at the swaddled mite in her arms. "I'd never have had my baby if he hadn't helped me get here." She sighed. "I'm just glad it was . . . I mean . . . He'll be all right?"

"Yes, Anna, and thanks for your good wishes. I'll tell him. And thanks," Kris said and strode the rest of the way to the outer ledge feeling that perhaps, after all, she'd been imagining things.

The sundial indicated the time as near Botany's noon and, for a wonder, Mitford was absent from his "office," though there were others, busily bending over the desk-stones at their tasks. There were other people, the newest arrivals since she didn't recognize any of the faces, evidently revived enough to take part in the business of the camp. There was also a handful, just sitting in the sun, eyes closed: a mixed bag because she could spot some Asians as well as the dusky skin of the East Indians. Above their heads, tacked to the south-facing wall of the ravine, was displayed a veritable mural of rocksquat hides, indicating the continued prowess of the camp's hunters. How much farther were the hunters having to go to catch enough to feed the multitude now here?

She shivered and not so much because the air felt cool to her despite the sunshine but because she worried about the tactical problems of supply. For instance, would there be enough hides to give everyone a warm coat this winter?

And, if a Botany day was twenty-eight hours long, how long were their months? Years? How long till spring? How many more loads would the Catteni drop down on this unsuspecting planet? How would they cope with this influx, much less *more?* She was hungry and that always made her attitude negative.

Sandy hailed her as she came into the cook cavern.

"Hi there, gal, got something just out of the oven for the likes of you."

"The likes of me?" Kris said in a low voice as she hunkered down by Sandy. She'd glanced quickly about the cavern and saw welcoming grins on other faces: people she did recognize.

"Yeah, you're a heroine, didn't you know?" Sandy winked as she held up the pitcher, waiting until Kris hurriedly undid her cup from its belt loop. "Right up there with Mitford, charging down the ravine like a berserker." She put a pottery plate, almost a perfect circle, on the rock nearest Kris: it held a browned piece of rocksquat, a slice of nicely toasted bread, and some fried circles. "Not quite potatoes but as near as nevermind," Sandy told her, passing over a gracefully carved fork.

Kris grinned, looking down at the utensil and turning it over in her hand.

"Chantilly silverware it isn't, but better than risking sharp knife points in your mouth." Sandy poured herself a fresh cup and settled close to Kris. "How's the Cat—'cuse me, Zainal—this morning?"

"I don't know. His leg is swollen awful big."

"The medics are trying a bread poultice. Penicillin it isn't, but my grannie was big on a bread poultice for boils and things." Sandy patted Kris' knee encouragingly. "They're tough, Catteni. Imagine him, cutting the thorn out of his own leg!" She clicked her tongue at such courage. "And we got quite a board of medical men now." She chuckled. "And other specialists. Most of 'em seem to have been taken from Sydney. From Botany Bay to Botany," and she chuckled again.

"Hey, this is good," Kris said, having tried a fried tuber. It was not unlike a sweet potato in texture and taste. "Say, are those thornbush leaves doing the Deskis any good?"

Sandy nodded. "Made a tea when Coo explained what he wanted and we've dosed even the sickest." Her expression altered. "We lost three, you know, while you were out on that last patrol."

"No, I didn't." Kris stopped chewing. "They look so frail . . ."

"They are if they don't have the right food." Sandy remained grim. "Their bones break if you so much as touch them hard. You know who helped nurse 'em? Patti Sue!"

That did surprise Kris.

"She's not much heavier than they are and has a light touch. She volunteered." Sandy grimaced. "She feels safe with the Deskis and even the Rugarians, you know."

"Jay Greene?"

Now Sandy chuckled. "He's going slow but it was him who suggested she'd be good at tending the Deskis. She has been, but it damned near kills her to lose one."

"Look, they got the same rations we all did back on Barevi. I thought the ration bars were enough," Kris said.

"Ah, Coo says they were allowed 'plursaw,' too, and that's what they have to have in their diet to keep their bones from going soft. A kind of calcium additive, I guess. There isn't an equivalent here . . . unless that thornbush junk fills the gap. He looks better, I know, but he's a young one."

"I didn't know," and Kris was remorseful. "I never asked either."

"There now, Kris, don't take on about it. It isn't as if you've had *time* to be social, you know, in and out of camp as you are." Sandy reached over for a covered pot set to one side of her hearth. "Made this special for Zainal. It's sort of a broth and the nearest thing to chicken soup I can put together here. It is nourishing and it doesn't taste too bad. Maybe you can get some down him. Leon says injured Catteni sometimes have a problem with dehydration. 'Bout the only thing that can debilitate them."

Kris thanked Sandy, deeply touched and much reassured.

"Would you know Aarens?"

"Yeah," and there was no joy in Sandy's reply.

"Is he around?"

Sandy gave a malicious chuckle. "Him! Boy, didn't he luck out. Seems there's some good to him after all. He's a genius with gadgets. Don't worry about him."

"I don't worry about *him.* I worry about his mouth."

"Don't."

Kris thanked Sandy again and then made her way back to the

hospital. She paused briefly when she saw the line of laden hunters returning to camp. She grinned to see the loaves and fishes that were being supplied to the multitude. She should have asked Sandy how many had been on the latest drop. And her patrol had found yet another nest of empty barns.

Lenny was gone from his post and the small room was crowded by those attending Zainal: Leon among others she identified as medical personnel. She made herself small and inched in, carefully ducking under the lintel and looking for someplace safe to put the pot of broth, which was hot. Leon rose to his feet just then.

"Certainly unsophisticated but the best we have to hand. Ah, Kris," and she could see how tired he was, though his hazel eyes were very much alive and keen in his saturnine face. "We're using a bread poultice to draw the infection. Now that providentially you lot have rediscovered bread on this godforsaken planet." He grinned. "Great bunch of improvisors here. She's the one found that anesthesia . . . if we could only figure out how to dilute it without losing its effectiveness." His grin extended to his colleagues, who acknowledged her appearance with smiles or nods. "Are you available to watch him? Lenny's off duty."

"I am," she said. "Sandy gave me broth for him."

"I'll be right with you," Leon said as the others moved out of the den, all being careful to duck on their way out. "Good-o on the broth. When I was treating Catteni in Sydney for wounds, dehydration was the big danger. See you get as much in him as he'll swallow, even if it's only water," and he pointed to a condensation-beaded covered pitcher on the floor out of Zainal's immediate reach. "But he'll need the nourishment in the broth, too. Catteni are big, strong, and tough but they need to keep their internal economy turning over."

"I'll see to him."

"Good," and Leon glanced down at a slip of the bark paper. "Who's next?"

"That leg fracture," one of the men said, also consulting a slip.

They all left and Kris got a good look at Zainal's now poulticed leg. She could smell the yeast of the hot bread as she bent over him. He was motionless, his breath slow and steady, but his skin, when she touched one broad flat cheek, was as hot as ever.

She rinsed out the fluff that was being used as a compress and cooled his face. Then, taking a spoon—the bowl of this utensil was deep enough to hold a respectable quantity of liquid and the rim was smoothly polished—she dribbled water onto his lips. Automatically he licked and swallowed. She got maybe half a cup down him with patience and then bathed his hot face, moving down to his chest and arms. His coverall had been removed at some point and a decorous and swift peek of curiosity showed that he'd been given some sort of a modesty cloth to cover his private parts, relieving her of embarrassment. He wasn't quite as heavily muscled as she'd thought, with the bulky coverall disguising a body that, by any standards, was beautiful. She shook her head at that wayward thought. *What the hell's wrong with admiring a beautiful bod on a guy? Nothing, unless you also think of that body next to your own! Whoops, girl. Down!* she told herself sternly. She allowed herself to stroke his skin, softer than its grayness looked. And exhaled, trying to shake off a sensation in her gut. *Lusting after a Catteni, girl? You are the pits!*

Nevertheless, the opportunity to touch him in more than a nurse-patient relationship was too much to resist. She smoothed back his silky gray hair, as fine as a baby's. In repose his features were even more patrician, when she compared him to some of the other Catteni she remembered. Yes, decidedly he was several castes above the average male mercenary. She was so accustomed to the look of him now that he didn't even seem alien anymore. Hmmm. Well, that attitude was better than rampant xenophobia!

Between her sessions of watering him—she also got him to take some of the broth, which had cooled enough to be dripped into his mouth—she rested on her bed, drowsing occasionally. She wondered if he knew they were trying their best to help him, because he lay stolidly unmoving, even when the poultice was still hot. The only response he gave was to swallow when moisture was offered.

Time to water him again.

MORE NOISE OUTSIDE, MUTED THOUGH IT WAS, WARNED HER of increased activity in the hospital. Lenny popped his head in.

"He may not be eating but you should."

Until he mentioned it, she hadn't realized how empty her stomach was.

"So, what's for din-dins?" she asked facetiously.

He grinned and brought a plate from behind his back, complete with pottery-domed lid.

"We're getting quite fawncy, this weather," he said. Then he lifted the top.

"My god, it looks human," she said in pleased surprise. For the meal consisted of more tubers, boiled by the look of them, a section of avian, to judge by the configuration of the wing, and two portions of greens.

"Just what the doctor ordered! Leave you to it! Oh," and he reappeared in the doorway, "mass meeting this evening at the sound of the gong!"

"Gong?" she asked but he was out of earshot.

She ate with good appetite and the food was delicious. The ration bars and the travel meal had doubtless been nutritious, but real food of differing texture, now *that* was civilized.

Leon came bustling in when she had finished, and he was looking rested.

"Got some sleep, did you? Report?"

"He's been taking both water and broth whenever I offer them and

I've cooled him down in between. But he doesn't move much," she ended lamely, looking expectantly at Leon Dane.

"Hmmm. They don't. Real adherents of the grin-and-bear-it brigade. They suffer in silence. I suspect he's more conscious of what's going on than you realize. Zainal?"

Leon leaned over the Catteni, hand on his brow and then on the main artery on the left of his neck. He proceeded downward, checking the temperature of the skin and then palpating the thigh tissues. "Hmmmm."

"Your 'hmmms' are getting longer," Kris remarked sardonically.

"When in doubt a thoughtful 'hmmm' is reassuring."

"To whom?"

"Whommmm does it as well, y' know," and Leon was now delicately prodding the wound area, having lifted the poultice. It had turned an obnoxious shade of gray/orange/green. "Yes, indeed. I think that's doing it."

"You do?" and Kris leaned over to see what he could possibly have taken as encouragement. The ghastly hole did look . . . healthier was the only word she could find. Nicely red instead of raw red, and the swelling had noticeably subsided so that the kneecap was once again visible. "I think I agree."

"Keep on with watering him. Ah, you're with us," Leon added suddenly when Zainal startled them both by opening his eyes.

"I need to lose water," Zainal said clearly.

Laughing, Leon collected a cleverly shaped pottery utensil at the end of the bough bed which Kris hadn't actually noticed before and she beat a hasty retreat while Leon attended the patient.

He came out with the utensil in his hand, chuckling to himself. "He'll do fine. Just fine. Don't forget the meeting tonight, will you?"

"How long have you been awake, Zainal?" Kris asked in a diffident tone of voice.

"Off and on," he said, his eyes closed, but he held out his hand and when she took it, his eyes opened. They held a look which made her chest swell with some unidentifiable emotion, so strong that her eyes began to water. His grip was very delicate and his skin still more than warm. "I knew you were here. You were there, by the water, too. Good of you, very good of you."

"Not at all," and she covered his hand with her free one. "You're . . . we're buddies. We look out for each other."

His eyes flicked open. "Buddies?"

"For lack of a better term, yes. I won't let you down."

"That I know." Then he released her hand and dropped his arm to his side, closing his eyes again. "Water? I am no longer full." And his lips lengthened in a slight smile. "The tasty water."

"We call it broth."

"Good."

She fed him and felt good about it.

THE MEETING WAS VERY WELL ATTENDED THOUGH KRIS MISSED some of Mitford's usual satellites, the Rugarians, as well as the Doyles. Even patients who could be moved out to the ledge in front of the hospital were present: Anna and her baby, the fracture cases—everyone except Zainal.

Kris was obliquely offended by that but talked herself out of indignation: plainly Zainal was too ill to be moved and she could report to him—and defend him if necessary. Now why was she feeling so defensive about the Catteni?

Jay Greene had Patti Sue on one side of him. She joined them, leaning against the rock face on Jay's left side.

"What's up?"

"Oh, a Mitford morale-building session and the latest news." Jay grinned.

"What latest news?" Kris demanded, knowing he was baiting her and giving him an ingenuous grin.

"The batch you and Zainal discovered weren't the only drops that night. Mitford sent off an exploratory patrol to see how many fields got seeded in what we believe is the typical Catteni drop pattern."

"More people?" Kris gave a frantic glance around the cave system, certainly overcrowded by the latest group of refugees. How *were* they going to cope? Then a rattle of the alarm triangle brought a wave of hush over the congregation. Mitford stood up, waiting until he had complete silence.

"Okay, folks, listen up. There're more drop-ins . . ." He paused until the mutter—Kris thought she heard resentment as well as surprise and concern—had subsided. "I take it as a good omen, considering what debriefing I've had." He chuckled. "The Catteni aren't finding it as easy to subdue good ol' Earth as they expected." A cheer went up. "And they've just increased our specialist department by four doctors, eighteen nurses, nine computer specialists, fourteen engineers, some good ol' hunter types from Australia, and a bunch of other real useful individuals, including some professional cooks, so we oughta be eating even better in the near future."

"Even with so many mouths to feed, sarge?" a woman shouted.

He waved off that concern. "We got a whole planet to hunt and plenty of grain stored where we can get it."

"Winter's coming . . ."

"So's Christmas and we'll have heating units from those solar panels long before. Now settle down. What we're going to do to relieve the housing shortage here is move into the buildings we know are empty and already plumbed for our benefit."

"But all those machines . . ."

"Have been decommissioned," Mitford said, raising his voice to parade-ground volume. "The Botany Hilton or Sheraton or whatever, is safe, sound, and has," he paused, "space available. Our local home decorators have been busy designing alterations, so I think you'll be surprised at how comfortable you're going to be."

"I'm not so sure I wanna live near *machines*. . . ."

"Quietest neighbors you ever had, I'll betcha," Mitford said and got another ripple of laughter. "Good chance of us having an intercom system, too, now we got more technicians. All that machinery's going to be recycled for *our* benefit!"

"Yeah, and what happens when their owners find out?"

The man spoke with a slight accent but Kris couldn't locate the speaker.

"As I understand it, Doctor Who always managed to evade the mechanicals and so can we," Mitford said with great good humor and got more laughs. "Seriously, though, folks, our population's growing and," once again he paused, "everyone's welcome. This is an equal opportunity situation. Let me make *that* plain. D'you get me?" He waited for the response and, to Kris' relief, got a fairly hearty cheer. "For one thing, there's safety in numbers, especially when you can recruit a lot of specialists who can improve our conditions. And we do. Hell, sixteen days since we got dropped to freedom on that field, we've even got decent spoons and forks, and better rations than we landed with. Furthermore, we've sorted out some basic problems our allies were having since Zainal and Kris Bjornsen found the nutrient plant that seems to be helping the Deskis. Even if Zainal found it . . . the hard way."

Applause and good-natured laughter acknowledged that announcement and Kris was well pleased by both elements: that Zainal was getting the credit and that the Deskis were stabilizing.

"We Yanks have a reputation for making something out of nothing, and now that the Aussies have joined us, we'll do even better. There'll be duty and housing rosters up on the bulletin board," and he pointed to the location on the main cave wall opposite him, "in the morning, so be sure to check. We're going to try and make space here in the headquarters to process incomers and as general hospital. Tesco's in charge of quarters, Dowdall'll take work assignments. You need to see me, check with Cumber. That's all for now, folks. Dissss-MISSED!"

There was good-natured laughter at his military salutation and he disappeared into the darkness beyond the main campfire.

"Hi, Patti Sue," and Kris leaned around Jay to speak to her. "Heard you've been a real Nightingale to the Deskis."

Patti Sue linked her arm through Jay's in such a proprietary fashion that the gesture indicated her improvement from terrified refugee to self-confident young woman.

"Do what I can," she said, her drawl more pronounced than ever.

"You've done marvels, and you know it," Jay said, stroking her hand.

"D'you know if you're moving from the Rock?" Kris asked Patti Sue and then looked at Jay.

He shrugged. "Dunno yet. COQ'll be up tomorrow morning. We'll all know then."

IN THE MIDDLE OF THE NIGHT, KRIS WAS ROUSED BY CONSID-erable noise in the corridor. Even Zainal was awakened, propping himself up on one elbow and trying to see out.

"Don't you dare put a foot on the ground," she said, pressing him back down. She felt his cheek and he was considerably cooler than he had been when she had last checked him. "You're better. Don't mess up. I'll go see."

She'd told him about the meeting and also that Mitford had given him credit for finding the remedy for the Deskis.

"Even if you had to do it the hardest way possible," she'd said with some acrimony. He'd only snorted. "At least they know one Catteni's a good guy." Maybe others wouldn't. She didn't add that, but that sentiment naggingly lingered at the back of her mind.

She folded on her shoes, the only thing she took off before going to bed, and went out into the corridor.

"Good!" One of the new Aussie medics grabbed her by the arm. "We need all the help we can get."

The newest arrivals had not had a Zainal or Kris to stamp the ground and dispatch the scavengers, and there were many with mangled arms and legs. Most of the victims spoke languages she didn't understand but which sounded Slavic or Scandinavian. Only a few had some English.

When she was sent by Leon to get more supplies and rouse additional helpers, she saw that the ravine was crammed with bodies, draped wherever they had stopped, too tired to move another step. But the cook cavern was ablaze with lights. Sandy, Bart, and half a dozen others were busy at their hearths, and the "store" was busy with Jay and Patti Sue doling out supplies. Jay instantly filled the hospital order and she returned.

The third moon had set before she was released, and when she got back into the tiny den she shared with Zainal, she had to step carefully over the three other bodies bunked in there during her absence. Fortunately they were fast asleep, though she thought she saw Zainal's eyes glimmer in the corridor light as he checked out her arrival.

So no one was able to follow the carefully detailed rosters that were up on the camp's main bulletin board. More parties were sent out to help stragglers, to hunt, to collect additional supplies of grain from that supply depot. Jay complained that folks had to search fairly far from Camp Rock to find firing and brush for bedding.

By high noon, all the new arrivals had been fed a decent meal and had someplace to lay their blanket.

The Rugarians, led by Slav, finally returned, bearing the crates with the basic supplies that had been left with this new group. Class C was what Mitford decided to call them. All morning had to be spent extracting information from those who could speak English among the Russians, Norwegians, Swedes, Danes, Bulgarians, Romanians, and some Greeks who comprised this drop. The fact that so many different nationalities were resisting the Catteni on Earth gave the entire camp a morale boost.

"But why'd they have to dump 'em here when they don't even speak English?" one man complained in a wail.

"Who asked?" a wit demanded. "We'll manage. Hell, I know five Deski phrases and nine in Rugs. I'll manage another few lingos. Well, at least, until they learn English."

By evening the population had increased by a thousand and fifty-two: far more than the camp could accommodate even by crowding into all available cavern space.

Of Class C, those that could speak English and had not been injured or had suffered only minor hurts were sent off with Sandy, Joe Lattore, and Tesco to organize quarters in the abattoir buildings.

"They don't know *what* happened there, and I don't plan to tell 'em," Sandy remarked to Kris when Kris came upon the woman, packing her pots and utensils. "I'll organize the cooking there. Twenty barns, are there?" When Kris nodded, "Ah, we'll probably be able to accommodate a lot more than we're taking with us right now, but it'll sure ease the crush."

There was no longer sitting room in the cook cavern and every single hearth was going full-out all the time. The smell from unwashed bodies exuding fear as well as sweat quite masked the more appetizing odors of grilled meats and fresh bread.

When Sandy and her contingent had left, Kris couldn't see where space had been gained and went back to the hospital with the broth she'd gone to collect. Zainal was more eager for any news she had than the food she brought him but he ate that hungrily enough. His leg was nearly back to its normal sturdy size and the wound was healing cleanly. But it was still crater-sized and Leon had made it clear that Zainal was not to move about much.

Zainal did, though, helping with patients who had to be lifted when their dressings were changed or were being moved to new accommodations. He did more than he should, but she couldn't keep her eyes on him all the time and there was a lot to be done to make the injured as comfortable as possible with no pain relief or more anti-infection medication than the harsh Catteni fluid. The merest drop of the powerful anesthesia tended to render a patient unconscious for a full day. Medically that was imprudent, however much relief it afforded the injured party.

"Whatever those critters are that scavenge, at least they bite clean," Leon said later that day when Kris helped him bandage an arm wound. Flesh had been excised as cleanly as a scalpel would cut, but the patient had lost muscle as well as flesh and, from the extent of the injury, Kris rather thought the man would lose the use of his arm entirely.

"They bite big, too," she murmured under her breath, after looking to be sure the victim was unconscious.

Leon only sighed and continued his repair. Kris was rather surprised at her ability to regard hideous tears of flesh and muscle with an objectivity she didn't know she possessed. She hadn't been nauseous once, though others on the temporary nursing staff were.

The dressing complete, both she and Leon finished the current round and walked toward the front of the "hospital." A breeze was blowing in and freshening the air of the "emergency room," which, for the first time in several days, was empty of patients.

"You," and she took Leon by the arm, "need food and rest, not necessarily in that order, but I can see to it that you eat!" She gave a deep sniff of the incoming breeze. "Smells good, too." Hauling him by the arm, she marched him out and down the ledge to the cook cavern.

"I hate managing females," Leon protested, but weakly, as she maneuvered him past those busy with chores on the ledge.

Below, in his "office," Mitford was still debriefing the able-bodied of the last batch though, from the expressions on his face and Esker's, he was making slow work of it with two blond Scandinavian types sitting there.

"Most Scandinavians speak English," Leon remarked.

"The ones you've met in Sydney, or the ones in Oslo, Bergen, or Copenhagen?"

Leon laughed wearily. "I always wanted to take a travel year."

"Well, guess what? You're on it."

Already Kris missed the presence of Sandy at her hearth, but Bart was present, and evidently in charge of the catering.

"Never been in a job that was so damned constant," Bart said when they presented themselves at his hearth. He rolled his eyes and then mopped the sweat off his forehead with a pad of fluff which he then dropped into the fire. It hissed. "I'm cooking all the hours the good Lord put in this crazy day. What's your pleasure? We got soup for starters, soup, and then, for the main course, soup. We even got crackers," and he offered a square of unleavened stuff, " 'cos we ran outta bread and the new baking hasn't risen yet."

"Why, I think I'll have soup," Kris said, getting herself a clean bowl from the stack at the hearth.

"I'll have a taste adventure, then, and try the soup," Leon said and Bart grinned as he ladled out their portions.

"Don't ask what's in it, will ya," he said as a final caution when they moved out to the ledge to enjoy their meal.

"That's a promise," Kris said with a laugh.

The soup was tasty, with a tangy bite to it, as well as unidentifiable shreds of meat. The satisfying warmth in the stomach revived her. That was, until she saw Zainal carefully making his way down the steps to Mitford's office.

"What the hell does he think he's doing?" Dane demanded.

"Something other than lying in bed doing nothing," Kris answered

Leon's complaint. She nervously shifted her feet, knowing she shouldn't follow the big man, but wanting to be sure he didn't open that leg wound. He very carefully negotiated his descent, so she made herself relax. The question was: what urgent business could Zainal have with Mitford that he'd risk opening that wound? Something he couldn't trust her to do for him? *Down girl,* she told herself firmly. She might be his keeper but she was not his conscience. Whatever he was saying to Mitford, the Sergeant was listening very hard. Zainal was still there in the "office" when she and Leon had finished eating and had to go back on duty.

THAT EVENING ESKER FOUND HER, SETTLING THE OTHER PA-tients—none of whom had any English—in her den.

"Mitford needs to speak to you, Kris. And you, too, Zainal."

He was gone before Kris could question him but, thinking over the tone in which the summons was delivered, she felt no apprehension. After all, Zainal had had that intense discussion with Mitford. Had the Sergeant reached a decision? If one was needed?

Mitford was, as usual this time of his long workday, sitting by the fire, the pottery pitcher of beverage by the side of his rock, the half-full cup in one hand. In the other, he had a stick and was prodding a chunk of wood to a better position in the fire.

"Zainal has some cockamamy notion of sending a mayday to his people next time they overfly us," Mitford said, narrowing his eyes as he looked up at Kris. "He feels we haven't had the last of these drops." Mitford gave a little sigh for the problems yet another influx of people would provide. "Now, fer starters, I don't know as how I want to appeal to them for any help, but it's the truth we need some sort of medical supplies as well as the proper nutrients for the Deskis. That thornbush junk is not quite enough, not for the older Deskis, though it's helping

Coo. I just don't like to lose anyone, human or alien." He scowled as he delivered that remark.

"How could we possibly contact them?" Kris said, turning to Zainal.

"Make this message on field," Zainal said, and unfolded a slip of bark on which were written, or maybe drawn was the proper term for the four complex hieroglyphics Zainal had inscribed.

"How? We haven't rediscovered paint yet here."

He gave her a brief smile. "Ground is dark under . . ." and he waggled his hand to try to find the appropriate word.

"Stubble? Grass?" she supplied.

"Whatever. Take off covering, leave ground bare."

That was a good idea, only somehow Kris shared Mitford's obvious reluctance to make any contact with the Catteni.

"We put message many fields off," and Zainal gestured to the north. "They know we live. They bring more they don't want."

"They know we're here?" Kris asked, more disturbed by that than she liked, though a quick look at Mitford showed him more sanguine.

Zainal nodded. "Heat sensors." Then he stretched his lip in a humorous grin. "That's why they fly over."

"Humph, thought that might be it," Mitford said. "Bastards!"

Then Zainal's grin altered to one of amusement at the Sergeant's acceptance and once again Kris was amazed at how that smile transformed his alien cast of countenance. He looked almost human, except for the white of his teeth contrasting with the gray of his skin. "Know we live so send more."

"Yeah, but they still don't know about the existence of the Mech Makers!"

Zainal shook his head. "Sensors find warm bodies, not machinery."

"Hmmm," Mitford said, stirring the fire with his branch.

"Coo still weak but young. Older ones worse and get worser," Zainal said urgently in English, then, in his concern, resorted to Barevi.

"Catteni take captives everywhere, but they take good care of them. Of Rugarians, Deskis, Turs and Ilginish, and Terrans. Healthy bodies work better. Asking for proper food is acceptable."

"Won't they find it strange that we ask in Catteni symbols?" Kris asked, pointing to his bark message.

Zainal grinned broadly again. "They know humans are smart," he said in English. "Too damned smart so they drop them here. No trouble here. Coo and Pess good folks. Can't lose." Now he turned his earnest expression on Mitford. "I work with Deskis and Rugarians before. Good folks. We save them?"

"You sure have learned English quick, Zainal," Mitford said in a drawl, temporizing, Kris thought. Then he regarded Zainal for a long moment. "And the Deskis deserve saving. Your guys'd just drop the supplies?" Zainal nodded. "They wouldn't come down to find out?" Zainal shook his head. "Why not?"

Zainal now laughed. "You make trouble. They . . ." He paused and Kris could almost see him trying to sort through his head to find the right words. "Play it safe. I play it safe, too."

"You mean, you wouldn't take the opportunity to get off Botany?" Mitford asked that in such a mild tone that Kris hoped Zainal would see he was being deftly interrogated.

"They don't take back what they put down," he said with a philosophical shrug.

Mitford grimaced. "So there's no chance we *could* commandeer one of their transports?"

Zainal considered this and finally shook his head. "They be careful where they drop." He grinned. "Especially near you Terrans."

"How do you know that?"

Zainal's teeth gleamed in the firelight when he smiled. "Know it before, back on Barevi. Lots of talk. Hear it now from the new ones. Believe it, too. I see how you work."

"Thanks, buddy," Mitford replied sardonically but amused by Zainal's approval. "Why would they do us a favor then?"

"I tell you why." Now Zainal seemed to tense and Kris felt Mitford was pushing him too much, as if he didn't quite believe Zainal was on the level. "Keep healthy to . . . improve this planet."

Suddenly Zainal held out the slip of bark with its symbols and, with one thick fingertip, explained them.

"This says 'drop,'" and he pointed to the intricate hook in the center of the first glyph. "This says 'food,'" and he ran his finger halfway around the next curlecue. "This Deski creatures. This means"—and he moved to next glyph—"'danger to the death surrounded by urgent.' Fourth one says 'medicines for infection.' Four only. Easy to make, easy to read from distance." His tone was cold and firm.

"Okay, okay, man, I believe you," Mitford said. "Just had to ask."

"These my people, too, now," Zainal added, straightening his wide shoulders as if he, too, would assume some of that burden from Mitford.

"We are one people now, or by god I'll know why!" Mitford said so fiercely that Kris almost recoiled. The Sergeant saw her reaction and gave her a quick grin. "I could even get to like being in charge of this motley crew. So when will you be able to travel, Zainal?"

"Sunrise . . ."

Kris started to protest but Mitford held up a hand to silence her. "If he thinks he can, he can. Those Deskis need the right food. And we can use the Deskis' abilities. You go with him, Kris. How many will you need to carve the message, Zainal?"

The Catteni waved his hand to indicate he'd go alone.

"Stuff it, buddy, man," Mitford said irritably. "You'll need help making those figures large enough to be seen from that altitude. I know. Had to do it in Nam once. Even SOS takes time to make." He turned to Kris, an almost wistful expression on his face. "You don't happen to speak any Scandinavian language, do you?" And when she shook her head, he sighed. "New guys are all I have to send with you, but you can break 'em in to our new ways at the same time. And I'll pick you one that speaks English and the rest'll be told what to do. Got it?"

"Got it, sarge," and she rose, recognizing a dismissal when she heard it. Zainal extended one hand to Mitford, which the Sergeant took readily enough and shook.

"You will not be sorry," Zainal said as he rose.

"I sincerely hope not," Mitford replied. "Esker will have a patrol ready at first light."

Chapter Ten

THE NEXT MORNING, THOUGH ZAINAL walked slowly, he did not appear to favor the injured leg. But, as they left Camp Rock, Kris realized that last night both men—maybe unintentionally—had avoided discussing what would happen if the Mecho Makers appeared first. Of course, with winter approaching . . . but it struck her as unrealistic to think that everything mechanical went down with the close of the growing season. Surely there was some sort of supervisor, or superintendant or overseer on the planet? Maybe on one of the other continents? Nevertheless, some *thing* must be in overall charge. When there was no response from the garages now that the solar panels were disconnected, some *thing* must register the lack of response. And check up.

And response was what they hoped to get. Or

had Mitford's objectives changed now he was getting accustomed to being the top man here on Botany?

Well, as her grandmother used to say, why borrow trouble? It finds you soon enough.

DESPITE A BROKEN NIGHT'S SLEEP—SINCE TWO OF THEIR roommates were so restless that any long period of sleep was impossible —Kris and Zainal were up well before dawn on Botany. They'd eaten— Bart was absent, asleep, one of the other cooks said, yawning—and were getting their travel rations when Esker came in with six people, five men and a woman who was nearly as tall as Kris. She seemed relieved to see that Kris was in the party.

"I speak English," she announced. "I am named Astrid. These are Ole, Jan, Oskar, Bjorn, and Peter. We lived near Oslo. Esker has told us we go with you to dig?"

"Yes, dig," Kris said, with a reassuring smile because she obviously thought it an odd job. She shook hands all round. "This is Zainal, our leader."

"You have Catteni as leader?" Astrid asked in a startled whisper.

"Good one, too, or you'd all been eaten."

"Pardon?"

"The scavengers? The things that go bump in the night on this planet?" And Kris made a mouth of one hand and bit her other arm. Astrid reacted to that, jerking back and away from the demonstration.

"I do not always understand," Astrid said apologetically. "We are still alive. We keep others alive?"

"Exactly! To help the Deskis keep alive we send a message."

"Someone will read?" Astrid was clearly amazed. One of the men shot her a quick sentence in the oddly liquid Norwegian language. She answered him as quickly and turned back to Kris. "I don't believe."

"Believe. We will carve the symbols on the ground to be seen in the air," and she pantomimed the actions.

"Oh," Astrid said and explained to her compatriots, who nodded in vigorous understanding.

"Kris?" and Kris recognized one of the Australian nurses, hurrying into the cavern, waving a sack made from part of a blanket, the ubiquitous material used for anything from aprons to tents. "More fluff dressings for Zainal's leg." Then she shot an accusing look at the Catteni. "I knew you'd go off without them—and that leg still needs support and dressings every day. I don't care if you are some kind of superman, you bleed red like the rest of us. Here!" And she jammed the sack into Zainal's hand and whirled about and ran out again.

With a half-grin, Zainal managed to look slightly embarrassed as he stowed the sack into the larger one he was carrying.

"*Now* we go," he said. Whether he had seen Mitford's gestures on their first trek or not, he raised his arm above his head and brought it down in the direction they were to travel.

Reassured by his manner, Kris motioned for the rest of the patrol to follow her and they left, as a good team, she thought.

While Zainal was not setting the pace he had on the first patrol Kris had done with him, he certainly didn't amble. By the first rest stop, Kris knew that the Norwegians weren't going to slow them down. Probably skied all winter in Norway. She kept her eyes on Zainal, though, to watch for any signs of an unconscious favoring of his injured leg. Then she became aware that he was watching her watch him.

"You tell us names of things?" Astrid asked during the break.

"I don't know as we've named much, Astrid," Kris admitted, taking a swig of water from her pottery bottle. Sandy's kiln worked and she'd found a glaze, so the canteen, while still breakable, didn't leak. She even had a proper pouch for it, now attached to her belt. "There're botanists going about checking plants to see if they're edible and stuff like that, but I can't say as I've kept up with what they're doing."

"You are out on patrol?"

"Most of the time."

"What are these machineries?" She looked puzzled.

"Ah, yes, well," and Kris explained, pausing while Astrid made quick translations to her compatriots until Zainal gestured for them to take the road again.

"You have done most well," Astrid said when Kris finished her brief history of Botany. "We are glad we drop here."

"Got dropped here," Kris corrected automatically. "Ooops, sorry, Zainal has me helping his English."

"Oh, help my English, too."

"You . . . teach . . . us?" one of the other men, Ole, Kris thought, asked her. She hadn't quite sorted the guys out yet.

"Might as well. English lessons on the march."

"We have no Deskis to hear flying danger," Astrid said, her eyes wide with apprehension now. "We were told that there is danger that flies," she added when Kris regarded her with astonishment at her knowledge.

"The nearby garages are all disabled, so I don't think we're in danger of any avians swooping down on us."

"Pardon?" Astrid's English was not up to Kris' comment.

"My pardon," and she rephrased the remark in better English.

"Explain 'boy' now," Zainal suddenly said, dropping back so that he was abreast of the two women.

"Oh, yes. Well," and Kris floundered briefly. " 'Boy' can mean several things. No, I guess many. A boy," and she held up one finger, "is a young male person: too old to be a baby and too young to be considered a man yet. Okay?"

" 'Boy'? Is only that?" Zainal twisted his face into a perplexed expression.

"We have what we call slang in English: patois, idiom, in other languages," Kris continued determinedly. " 'Boy' used as slang is an expression of amazement, amusement, pleasure, and it's usually said as 'oh, boy!' or 'oooo, booooy!' 'Oh, boy!' " And she emphasized the different emotions with exaggerated gestures and tones.

"All boy?" asked Zainal. "I don't understand how a boy, a young male person, can be surprise, funny, good times."

"I think you do, Zainal," Kris said, suddenly realizing that he was teasing her. "G'wan with ye now, m'boyo!"

Astrid translated to the others, grinning and laughing and saying "oh, boy" in different tones of voice.

"Oh, boy, and isn't this getting out of hand," Kris said, shaking her head at her predicament.

"Oh boy, oh boy, oh boy," Zainal said and, to nonplus her further, he put one arm around her shoulders and gave her a hug.

"You've been talking to other people," she said, throwing off his arm and stalking ahead of him. Then she realized she was overreacting. Why on earth, when she really wanted to get close to him, had she repudiated his friendly gesture? Regretting her behavior, she slowed up and caught his hand, holding it while they walked.

At the second rest stop, Zainal struck off northerly, pointing to broad fields of golden stubble that spread upward to a rocky summit. If, as Zainal had suggested, the Catteni kept to the same line to make their drops, those fields would be visible if they were going to buzz Camp Rock again.

They reached their objective by midafternoon. Zainal sent Kris and two of the men off to hunt for for rocksquats sunning themselves. Oskar and Bjorn were proficient with the bows and arrows they had been supplied with, while both were congratulatory when she brought down four creatures with well-placed slingshots. Of course, she'd missed six so she didn't think that much of her accomplishment.

The men were obviously accustomed to good hunting practices because, as soon as they found the next stream, they skinned and dressed down the meat without directions from her. They washed all the carcasses and pelts well before going back to Zainal's field. They were setting about to bury the entrails when she indicated they should leave them.

Kris spotted some nourishing types of greens in the hedgerows and harvested them. She kept her eyes out for the tubers, which also grew wild at the edges of fields. Fried, they'd be a good addition to the roast meat and the travel rations.

Zainal had had the others helping him outline with rocks the glyphs that they would have to hack out of the soil. He was pacing out the second huge pattern, putting down the bordering rocks while the others gathered more. Kris could also see, at the top of the field, a circle of stones with a nice fire burning in it, fueled by the loo-cow droppings collected on the way. They'd be only a step away from the safety of the rocky height, which was just fine by Kris. The scavengers foraged in crop fields as well as pastures, and only the stomp-stomp of the loo-cows' six legs kept them from being fair game. Was that why the loo-cows had six legs? More to stomp with? But the scavengers were no doubt the reason why Kris had noticed that the loo-cows seemed to sleep during the daylight hours. Those loo-cows probably had to do an all-night stomp to stay alive.

The hunters displayed their spoils, and Kris set about finding the right size of flat rock to cook them on. She'd been warned to be careful about overheating her newly issued cooking pot, since it was after all only glazed clay, but she'd been assured by Jay Greene that it would bring water close to the boil . . . and that would mean she could cook the greens. She took them to the ubiquitous stream to wash and fill the pot, and very shortly the stones were hot enough to start cooking rocksquat.

By then, Zainal had outlined all four huge glyphs. After a good dinner, he suggested that they start hacking out the soil to bare the dark ground.

That was tougher work than they had anticipated, for the ground cover had deep, tough root systems and Kris found these had to be cut out: the roots wouldn't just pull away like any well-behaved Terran weed would. Her arms and shoulders ached from her labors and she was quite glad to break off to heat water for the nighttime beverage.

The medics had come to the decision that the herbal-type tea that had been concocted contained useful trace elements, so a bedtime cup was standard issue. A nice homey touch and no reason not to continue it out in the rocky wilds of Botany. With warmth in the belly, it was easier to sleep.

The turf-cutters made themselves as comfortable as they could on the rocks and those who had later watches had no trouble falling asleep.

IT TOOK THEM FIVE DAYS TO COMPLETE THE GLYPHS: FIVE days of fingernail- and back-breaking, arm-bruising and blister-making toil, since the only tools they had were hatchets and knives. They'd been issued with spares of each tool and had needed them to complete their task, resharpening the dulled edges every night. Then, determined that his message would be seen, Zainal had them outline the cuts with the sparkling white stone that comprised this rock outcrop. The full sunlight that fell on the glyphs caused the mica in the rock to glint. Almost as good as neon. Exhausted as she was, Kris had to admire the final result.

"Do all Catteni read?" she asked Zainal.

"Those on watch do," he assured her.

His leg was a bit swollen from his unremitting labors, but the flesh was gradually filling in and he took a brook-shower night and morning. Cold as the water was, Kris liked the new type of ablution. She and Astrid bathed upstream of the fellows, but the rivulet was deep enough for a person to lie down on the sands and let the water cascade over her in a horizontal shower. The sand was very fine and provided a rough but effective cleanser. Besides, you were so cold you didn't feel the abrasions. Or so Kris told herself.

The rocky height was home—or had been home—to a huge colony

of rocksquats. The patrol took some time out each day to hunt and cut the excess meat into strips to dry on the hot rocks the next day. Kris was very pleased to be so productive—especially since there were so many more mouths to feed.

Each night, however, reminded them that a colder season was approaching and Kris did worry about how cold that would be! Fortunately the Catteni-issue thermal blankets were efficient in containing body heat inside them. The evening showers blessed them on schedule but those were no longer as violent as they had been: more like a gentle watering than torrential rains.

On the sixth day they started back to camp, hunting when they could, for additional protein was always welcome. Zainal set a faster pace this time, to allow for interludes of hunting, and they reached the caverns to find them still crammed with people. Bart took their offerings with profuse thanks and then asked Kris if she'd take a hearth and cook what they'd brought in. As she certainly couldn't refuse the man when he looked so harried, and the cook cave was obviously pushed to the limit, she obeyed. Astrid lingered, as much because she didn't know where to go as anything else, and Kris was a familiar face. Until a messenger came for Kris to report to Mitford.

"I watch you. I now know to cook," Astrid said, taking the long-handled fork Kris had been using and pushing her on her way.

Zainal and Ole, who did have some English, were in Mitford's "office." The pile of bark sheets was higher than the stone he used as a desk and was weighted down by what looked like a gold nugget, a lump of iron, and a greeny mess that had to be copper.

"Gold in them-thar hills?" Kris asked when he motioned her to a seat.

"That and more. We've been busy while you've been carving that mayday."

"You're never not busy, sarge."

"Patrol found the remnants of another drop and nine survivors.

Eight Deski and a guy from Atlanta, Georgia, who had the sense to stick with the aliens. Damn it," and Mitford's face was suffused with anger, "I shoulda had you put a PS on that message: make the drops in daylight. I hate it when I lose people like that."

"But they weren't *ours*, yet, sarge," Kris said, trying to be conciliating. Mitford gave her a dirty look. *Hey*, she thought, *he's really into this Leader bit. Well, it's not as if anyone else had volunteered for the responsibilities—and the headaches. And look at all that Mitford had gone and done.*

"They could've been. And another garage was found and deactivated. Twenty more barns to be made into domiciles."

"Now that's good. And the supplies?"

"We put them in the barns. Easier that way, but I'd rather have the people to go with them."

Zainal had been constructing another glyph and now held it off to inspect the result. He made a few more strokes as adjustments, then turned it to Mitford and Kris. "That should do it," he said.

Mitford reacted to that almost unaccented remark. "You learn quick, doncha?"

"I have to," Zainal replied. "Take two three days there and back." He rose, glancing up at the sundial. "Have enough light to travel."

"How's your leg?" Mitford frowned at it as he could see nothing past the bulky pantleg. Then he caught Kris' surreptitious headshake. "No, better start fresh tomorrow. The others are only Terrans, not as tough as you Catteni." His little snort took the sting out of that remark as he looked up at Zainal towering above him. "You think your guys'll listen?"

Zainal nodded solemnly. "They don't know the dangers here. They don't know scavengers. They wish this planet . . . col-on-nized. We have survived," and he shrugged, "so they think all can."

"But even the report you saw said there were dangerous animals down here." Mitford's scowl deepened.

Zainal shrugged and grinned broadly. "We have survived. Water, air, animals, light gravity, better than Catten!" As if that answered the necessary criteria.

Mitford snorted, shuffling several pieces of scribbled bark about on his worktop. "As far as we know, they made three drops this time. We were one of four. And three weeks between trips. That right?"

Zainal cocked his head thoughtfully. "Could be. I was space, not col-on-y." And he spread his hands in a very contemporary human gesture of ignorance. "You know the problem: one group does not know what other does."

"Yeah," and Mitford's drawl spoke of much experience with such inequities.

A woman, face red, hair messed, coverall opened halfway to her waist, came stamping her way up the steps to Mitford's office.

"Mitford, either you cut his libido off at the root or I'll do it myself with a dull knife."

"Arnie?" and Mitford rose, gesturing authoritatively at two men lounging to one side, playing some sort of game involving pebbles. "No questions, no answers. Bring 'im. Put 'im back in the stocks. And he'll stay there till he rots or we can think of something else to do with him."

"Tie him out in a field for scavengers—and even that's too good," the woman said, closing the fastenings on her coverall and then smoothing her hair. "Horny pervert! I'll give you a full report of this latest trick of his when you're done here," she muttered as she politely took herself to one side so Mitford could finish with his current interview.

"At least the ratio between male and female evened up a little in the last drop. But I don't need guys like Arnie," Mitford said when the woman had settled out of earshot. "He's been in the stocks four times for peeping and twice for stealing."

"Stealing what?"

"Food! Extra blankets, a sharper knife because he's too lazy to hone his own." Mitford made a noise of disgust. "I need him like a boil on my ass. Don't ever feel sorry, Kris, that he got force-whipped. He just got his in advance."

"Tie him out for the scavengers," Zainal said blandly. "Good idea."

Mitford grimaced, showing his teeth and expelling air through them. "Can't, but I may yet. . . . You get food and rest, ya hear, Kris?" When she dutifully nodded, he added: "And make sure Dane sees his leg."

Over Zainal's protests that's exactly what Kris did, roundly scolding the Catteni because he hadn't reported in to Leon Dane when they reached camp. He was at first amused by her tirade and then frowned as she grabbed him by the arm, to lead him to the hospital end of the caverns, when he did not turn in that direction immediately.

"Now listen here, Lord Emassi Zainal," she said, "you were given an order by Mitford and, if you plan to go out tomorrow, you'll obey it or you won't go. And no one will go with you to help dig that message."

"Then no message." He shrugged as if it were all the same to him.

"Ohhh, you make me so mad . . ." Kris tried to keep her voice down because she knew she sounded shrewish. But he was being so unreasonable. "Just because you're a Catteni doesn't mean you don't bleed like us frail Terrans, and that you didn't damned near die from that thorn toxin, and I don't want to go through *that* again. You're too important to me to be stupid about your health."

He grabbed her by the finger she was shaking at him, looking around because he had noticed just how much attention her accusation had focused on them.

"I go. I see Dane," he said far too docilely and she watched to make sure he did.

Lordee, you'd think a man as old as Zainal would have the sense to take care of himself. And she didn't like it when he got all compliant. *That* wasn't Catteni of him.

———

THE FIFTH GLYPH TOOK THEM MOST OF THE CLEAR DAY BUT went more smoothly since they all knew how to do it. They immediately started cutting sod at the top as Zainal laid it out and they were well started when he finished the design. They didn't even have to find more mica rocks since there was a still a pile left over from their first job.

"Shropshire Man this isn't," Kris said when they retired to the next field to get an overall view of their labors.

"Man? Another 'boy' thing?" Zainal asked, one eyebrow quirking upward in amusement.

"Yeah, you can if you wish substitute man oh man oh man, for boy oh boy oh boy. It's how you feel."

"Young or old? Small or large?" Zainal asked, his eyes twinkling down at her.

"I think," she said in a severe tone, "that you're kidding me."

"Ah, kid, a small goat," Astrid said with an unexpected display of humor. "Oh, in slang a 'boy'!"

"Right!"

Ole asked her a question and she replied, laughing when he grinned in comprehension. "Baby, kid, boy, man," he said with just a hint of the liquid Norwegian in his tone.

"Kidding? Can one having boying, too?" asked Zainal.

"Yes, actually," Kris said. "But it's spelled differently and means a floating object in the water to warn seamen off underwater dangers."

"See men?" Zainal asked, gathering his brows slightly, which made him look quite ominous.

"We have a lot of words in English that sound the same but mean different things."

"How do you know then what each means?"

"Context—how the word is used in the sentence. Hey, is this a language patrol?"

"Why not?" and Zainal grinned. "Work is done. Now we . . . play?"

"Ha! You wouldn't know how to play," Kris retorted.

"Wanna bet?" he replied.

"You've listened too much to the Doyle brothers," she said, waggling a finger at him.

He grabbed her finger and she tried to pull away, which resulted in a tugging match, then turned into him chasing her, trying to recapture the finger while the Norwegians watched this juvenile display with unsmiling dignity.

Kris was quicker on her feet than the heavier Catteni, so she eluded him, ducking under his grasping arms and hands and taunting him to catch her. When he did, he held her tightly against him. She could barely move, but she scrunched her hands behind her back so he couldn't recapture the finger. It was all very silly, since inevitably his superior strength would win out, but she found she enjoyed Zainal's surprising playful side. Inexorably, he recaptured the right hand, and, with amazing gentleness considering the strength he applied to the task, he drew her hand up and, recapturing the finger, kissed it. Then the palm of her hand.

A spurt of something ran through her at the touch of his lips on the softer, if blistered, skin of her hand. Startled, she caught his eyes. The twinkle was there, for the success of his recapture, but some other emotion darkened his odd-colored eyes and made her catch her breath.

"Happy now?" she asked with some asperity.

"Yes," he said simply and immediately let her go.

ON THE WAY BACK TO CAMP, IN BETWEEN FORAGING, ASTRID and her compatriots kept up quite a lively discussion until Kris finally asked them what was so interesting.

"The land," Astrid said with a sweeping hand. "It is beautiful country for growing and for animals who eat grass. Very well done, too. Oskar and Peter are raised on farms. They say very well done."

"It is, and wait till they see what the farmers are," Kris said.
"Pardon?"

There was a brief delay in the conversation while rocksquats were added to the day's bag. Throughout the rest of the day, Kris heard about the ecologically—the word was the same in Norwegian but sounded different—sound fashion in which Botany's agriculture was done. Proper drainage, available water, copses of vegetation where land was not arable used as windbreaks, even the hedging that separated the fields was approved. For what it was worth. Kris did not want to be the ones to tell them what farmed the land here. But she began to have more respect for the acumen of the absentee landlords: whatever they were besides omnivorous.

GREAT EXCITEMENT BUZZED ABOUT THE CAMP WHEN THEY RE-turned and she didn't report that observation to Mitford. The Sergeant was sitting with what looked to Kris very much like a hand-held phone. He was talking into it, so unless Chuck Mitford had flipped his wig, and she wouldn't have blamed him if he had, he was talking to another unit of the Botany Colonial Establishment.

"Great, huh?" Bart said when Kris, Bjorn, and Oskar brought the results of their hunting into the cook cavern.

"We've got a phone?"

"Yeah, but more importantly, now the technies know what chips do what in the mechanicals' circuitry. Real breakthrough."

Kris allowed as how it must be since everyone was so happy about it and she supposed she should be as elated, because it was one more step back toward sophisticated living. She was oddly disturbed by the breakthrough. And certainly couldn't figure out why. She'd probably been enjoying this atavistic hunter-explorer life more than she should—consid-

ering it also involved lots of discomfort and uncertainty: as well as
enough hazard to get the ol' adrenaline flowing freely most of the time.
Camp Rock would really benefit by some modern conveniences. On the
other hand, was instant communication *really* a benefit?

"Put another toggle on my belt," she muttered under her breath,
"for the hand-held!" Then she added: "Say, Bart, where do I find out
where I'm bunking tonight?"

Bart pointed to the irregular opening that led to most of the
dormitory facilities as well as the lake. "List right there."

Her name had a big fat P beside it: so did Zainal's, and, as she
looked down the list for the Norwegians, they were P's, too. P for Patrol?

"Bjornsen?" someone sang out at the front of the cave.

"Yo!"

"Sarge wants you."

Muttering about being homeless, Kris made her way to the "office."
There were three handsets on Mitford's "desk."

"Latest in recycling mechanicals," Mitford said in great good humor. "We can keep in touch with our outposts and our scouts. You gotta
get some height to boost the signal . . ." and he jerked his thumb over
his shoulder to the top of the cliff behind him where, of all things, an
aerial now swayed in the evening breeze. "But don't seem to have any
trouble with range. Anyway we'll know soonest when the Catteni make
another drop. We've got a network of lookouts—and not just for the
Cattenis' next move." He rummaged briefly through the sheets on his
worktop and flipped free a large one—no, it was quite a few sheets neatly
glued (?) together. Well, the loo-cows had hooves, so someone had remembered to boil 'em up for glue. A map had been drawn on the big
sheet—or, the beginnings of one, for only the center showed contour
lines, streams, fields, forestry. The map gave Kris a much better idea of
the terrain in and around the main camp, and the siting of the various
mechanical facilities.

"Neat," she said.

"We got a bona fide surveyor," Mitford said proudly, tapping the map. "Pretty good, huh? Even got relative distances."

"Nat Geo Soc would be proud to claim it," she agreed, grinning at Mitford. "You don't waste time civilizing us, do you, sarge."

"Not much," he agreed amiably, "but then we got lots of Yankee know-how—and Aussie." He noticed her jaundiced expression and cocked eyebrow so he cleared his throat as if he'd had to do that before continuing. "Alien allies, too," he added. Then he surprised her by hefting one of the units and plonking it down in front of her, all businesslike again. "I want your patrol to start examining this area," and his thick index finger wandered down to easterly uncharted areas. "I'll need to keep in touch with you in case we want Zainal."

"Sarge?

"Yah?"

"Are you keeping Zainal out of camp for a reason?"

Mitford regarded her steadily, his gray eyes not avoiding hers.

"You might, at that, think I am, and I am. He's too valuable a resource to be wasted . . ."

"Then I haven't been wrong—there's feeling against him."

"Can you honestly blame people for resenting him as Catteni?"

"Even if he was dumped down like everyone else?" Kris asked plaintively.

"Even then, because he's still Catteni and no weapons but a knife, and alone."

"He's *not* alone," Kris said staunchly.

"I know, Bjornsen. But there's this thinking that there must have been a good reason he got dumped, other than killing another Cat . . . Catteni," Mitford said and, when she started to protest, he held up a hand. "I've seen and heard all about Catteni one-day vendettas, Bjornsen, and if it was only for killing a patrol leader, he'd've been released from the slammer the next day. He sure the hell isn't like any other Catteni *I ever* met or heard about."

"What about the latest drop? If it hadn't been for Zainal . . ."

"Kris!" Mitford's hand on her arm and sharp tone stopped her. He didn't look around to see who might be near enough to hear their discussion, but there was something about his manner now that suggested to Kris that he didn't want her blowing her top right now. "There are a lot of folk who should be grateful to Zainal. But they aren't. And that's the long and short of it. I can't change human nature, you know." And he sounded sincerely regretful. "And I *won't* run him out of the camp." He blinked and then said softly, "He's too useful a resource. Now, girl," and carefully he began to fold the map. He put it into a flat envelope made out of the ubiquitous blanket, complete with shoulder strap. He laid that alongside the comunit, then added a thick carbon "pencil" and fidgeted until he had them aligned to his satisfaction. "I want you and Zainal to go walk about with Astrid. She's chosen Oskar to go with. Zainal says she's competent and can keep up. I've a pair of Australians who swore blind they could keep up with Aborigines, so they oughta be able to keep up with you two. They were in the last drop and are grateful to Zainal. Though half the time they act like this was some great joke. Possibly it is." He paused, musing on that theory. "One of 'em has medical training and did botany in the Outback Down Under. With this hand-held, you can keep in touch with me. Esker, Dowdall, and a new guy, ex-Anzac major by name of Worrell who did some military governing so he knows more than I do . . ." He waved off Kris' immediate disclaimer. "I'm glad to have him aboard. They call him 'Worry,' and he does, so I don't have to anymore. He'll be at the other end if I'm not. That clear?"

"In a way, yes," she replied as civilly as she could, for she was seething with indignation that Zainal should be exiled and with relief that she was going with him. "Your friendly roving reporter!" She rose.

"Good girl, Bjornsen, I like your style," Mitford said, peering up at her. "I gotta defuse the situation, you understand."

"Yeah, I guess you do. Only why," and she nodded her head in the direction of the stocks where Arnie was constrained, "can *he* be tolerated and not Zainal?"

Mitford snorted. "Takes all kinds and he's . . . supposedly . . . human. One more complaint lodged against him, though, and we take punitive measures he won't like at all. Especially as we wouldn't use anesthesia." Then he looked over toward the main cavern. "That's your patrol, Bjornsen. I told Zainal, too. Report in every day, will ya? So we know the equipment's still working. The code here is 369," and he grinned.

"Sir!" she said, stamping her feet up and down, coming to attention and saluting him in the manner of a British soldier.

He waved her away and three people vied to take her place, eyeing her map case and handset. She strode off, head high, looking neither to right nor left.

Zainal was leaning against the wall, arms folded across his chest, watching her progress. The other four members of the patrol were talking quietly. She nodded to Astrid and Oskar, then looked at the two new folks. She held her hand out to the woman, whom she liked on sight: almost spare in build but wiry, with a complexion that had been roughened by hot Australian summers, and faded, short, curly hair of a ginger shade. But she exuded an air of competence, a characteristic of so many Aussies. At her feet, beside her travel gear, were a first-aid kit and a light bow with a sheaf of arrows.

"M'name's Sarah McDouall," she said, giving Kris' hand a firm, hard shake before letting it go. "This here's Francis Marley. We made a good team in the resistance 'fore we got caught. I'm your medic."

"Call me Joe. Anything's better than Francis," he said, giving Sarah a mock glare for her introduction. He spoke in a slightly nasal tenor voice which seemed to have a lilt of quiet laughter to it. He was tall and lean, with sun-creased eyes, an open face and smile, and dark hair growing gray at the temples. One hand kept going to his head as if to adjust a missing hat. The gesture developed into a scratch of his skull. "Stockman—I know a bit about plants." He had a sling tucked in his belt, a blanket pouch that bulged with pebbles. He sort of leaned against the three light lances he was armed with. They had, Kris noticed, metal tips. *My,* she thought, *the Arsenal is improving, too!*

"Anyone know where we're bunked?" Kris asked.

"Zainal knows."

"I lead, you follow," Zainal said, pushing himself off the wall and moving off, past the hospital cave.

Kris wondered if he was annoyed that Mitford had given her the comunit. His expression did not give her any clues.

It was more a dugout than a cave, but it would shelter them from the evening shower and the colder winds that now blew during the night. There was just room enough for six bodies, but there were hooks for hanging and even a ledge.

"Rather snazzy," Kris said. "Did Zainal tell you our mission?"

"More or less," Joe said with a grin.

"You don't mind a Catteni patrol leader?"

Joe's eyebrows raised slightly and Sarah gave her a sharp look.

"Well, now . . ."

"Zainal here leads," Kris said firmly. "I'm signals," and she tapped the comunit.

"Gotcha!"

"I need a bath," Kris added, carefully stowing the map case and the hand-held on the ledge. She turned to Astrid. "You coming?"

"Wash?"

"That's what we call it," Kris said with a grin, easier now she'd made her point, and turned to Sarah.

"Had one. I'll get our grub. Smells good. C'mon, Joe, Oskar. Don't take too long," Sarah said to the bathers.

"You better believe it," Kris replied, and then, with Astrid on her heels, retraced her steps to the cook cavern and then down to the lake.

Astrid had no problem with cold-water bathing but then, if she was accustomed to saunas in Norway, she wouldn't be. But the temperature did not encourage one to dawdle and they were washed, dried, dressed, and on their way back to their quarters about the time their evening meal was ready.

"I do miss a beer," Joe said plaintively, sopping up the last of the gravy from his bowl with his bread.

"I miss a cigarette," Sarah said.

"I, too," Astrid said with a smile, and translated to Oskar. He raised both hands skyward in longing. "You know plants?" Astrid asked Joe. "Find us one like tobacco."

"Now there's a right good idea," Joe replied. "Do my damnedest, I will."

Chapter Eleven

EACH MORNING KRIS CHECKED IN AND usually spoke to Mitford, giving him an all-clear. Each evening, around the fire, she got the others to help her add the terrain to the map they had covered that day. The fourth day they came upon another mechanical garage and spent the day dismantling it. Kris added that detail to the map with a certain amount of pleasure.

Joe Marley pushed back his nonexistent hat, scratched his scalp as he viewed his first mechanicals. Oskar, examining the first large harvester (Kris thought last out, last in) rattled off a long sentence to Astrid.

"He want to see it work," she said, eyeing the large mechano dubiously.

"Maybe next year," Kris said airily, "if we decide to put 'em all back in operation. If there're any with full parts by then."

Zainal had already unfastened the solar

panels on the top of the garage. Then he went after the flying-dart dispenser. Leon had asked particularly for them to collect any they found, for the anesthetic.

"Oskar asks how machine go with no wheels," Astrid said, peering under the skirt of the biggest farm machine to check on that lack.

"On an air cushion," and Kris mimicked the sound and the method.

Oskar nodded approvingly, still walking about the mechanical-beast. He also examined the flying device, carefully, since Kris warned him about the darts peeking out from the leading edge. Oskar seemed to approve most of the harvester design. Then made a roller-coaster motion with one hand and said something to Astrid.

"His farm is on hill. This thing," and she kicked at its flange, "fall over," and Astrid demonstrated something losing its balance and tumbling downhill.

Joe had moved to the storage areas, hunting for something.

"They left no tools behind them. These things self-repair?"

"We saw some working on others," Zainal said and stepped up to the face of the harvester to start removing its solar panels.

"Oh, my word, this planet's odd," Sarah said.

"You can say that several times," Kris agreed. "They'll want panels and storage batteries back at the camp, or wherever. There's quite a herd of them here." She peered into the shadows of the garage to the dimly seen forms parked there.

"Could we bed down here tonight?" Sarah asked with such a lack of expression that Kris almost grinned.

"I think so," she said. "I wouldn't mind being out of that wind for a night, myself."

"There're rocksquats back aways . . ." Sarah said, picking up her weapons.

"Kris, go with her," Zainal said when the woman started off on her own.

"I can handle myself," Sarah said indignantly.

"You go *with*," Zainal said. "This planet has dangers. Kris knows dangers."

"Yeah, but I don't hear as well as Coo," Kris said, carefully setting down the comunit and the map case.

"Is he always like that?" Sarah asked Kris when they were out of earshot.

"Like what?"

"Don't bristle," Sarah said with a grin. "He's not half-bad for a Catteni. Not that I've met that many. But I heard . . ." and she let her tone rise up, a subtle prompting for Kris to expatiate.

"As Catteni go, he's pretty good," Kris said noncommittally. "And he's saved a lot of folks. . . ."

"Oh, my word! You don't need to defend him to me. I came to on the outside of that bloody field and the guy next to me was being chewed up. I would have been next but for you stomping about like a brumby. Anyway, it's only good sense to go out *with* someone. Believe me, you do where I come from!"

They came back with rocksquats and some of the tender-fleshed little avians, brushwood, and a pile of droppings from the next field over. They had spotted only distant fliers but Kris pointed them out and told Sarah how to avoid becoming a meal.

"Are they after one now?" Sarah asked, squinting at the aerial menaces.

"Who knows?" Kris didn't particularly want to find out. "Now, if you were back on Earth, you'd probably jump into your four-by-four and go investigate."

"Probably, but we're not on Earth now, are we?" and there was a world of regret in her tone.

"Sorry," Kris said in a rueful voice. She hauled her gaze away from the distant avians and they walked on in silence for a while.

They reached high ground, where Sarah stopped and looked out over the vista of neatly squared, hedged fields and sighed. "Oh, my word! My da would go spare. And no one is in residence?"

"Haven't found any *one* yet. And that's why we're dismantling the garages, to sort of give notice."

Sarah's eyes bulged. "You mean you *want* to find out who made those . . . machines?"

"Did anyone tell you about the ship that collected the harvest?" Kris grinned down at the slighter woman, the braces of rocksquats swinging from the stick she carried over her shoulder.

"I heard something—a ship as big as a city?"

"Small city," Kris said with a laugh.

"You *want* to go on it?" Sarah's eyes went wide again but from respect.

"Not me, personally," Kris replied, though if Zainal were involved in the adventure, she'd probably be right there with him. And he probably *would* be in the boarding party. "It'd be interesting to see what species set up this planet, made it self-sufficient, self-repairing, yielding so much *food* . . ."

"*Food?*" Sarah gulped and a brief panic almost made her drop her stick.

"That's what this planet does—makes food—and we don't know for whom. Or what. Except that they're probably omnivores like us."

Sarah gulped again. "I hadn't thought about that aspect of it."

"Well, it's easier to concentrate on making out day-by-day at the moment," Kris agreed.

"Yeah, there's that all right," she said as they came around the bend of the smooth-domed rock that housed this garage.

The others had dismantled what could be taken back to the camp for recycling. Oskar had shown himself particularly adept with the disassembly and the others had started to defer to him. As he worked, he asked for English words for various items and cheerfully muttered them under his breath, committing them to memory. Joe was almost his equal but then, he said, from the time he was old enough to lift a screwdriver, he'd been taught how to do repairs on his father's sheep station.

"You're looking at a heap of future hand-helds and other useful gadgets," Joe said, gesturing to the neatly stacked things, including wires, connectors, linkages, and all kinds of curious gadgetry that had been inside the mechs. "A DIY's treasure trove."

"Would you know how to make something out of this?" Kris asked.

"Depends," Joe said cheerfully, "on what's needed."

Zainal came up then, Kris' comunit in his hand. "You are asked to call home."

"E.T.?" Kris asked with a grin but only Sarah and Joe caught the reference. She shrugged and tapped out 369 and a strange voice answered.

"Worry here."

"Worry?"

"Ah, I'd be speaking to Kris?"

"You are, and you'd be Worrell."

"Since I landed here, it's been worry, miss, so 'elp me. Report?"

She gave it to him and he expressed pleasure in the discovery of yet another garage and its reusables.

"Mitford's all right, isn't he?" she asked before she signed off.

"Never better," Worry said and even over the line his voice sounded sardonic. "A truly amazing man."

"No sign of any fly-bys?"

"You'd be recalled on the double if there were!"

"I can believe that!"

There was a laugh at the other end and then Worrell signed off with a reminder to register the approximate location of the new garage on the map. Zainal assisted her, as he was able to give her the relative distances from their previous camp and what he called a good guess as to the contours of the day's travel. Although Kris knew her legs could testify that they'd traveled far that day, her legs only knew they'd traveled, not how far uphill and down.

THE NEXT NOON THEY REACHED THE TOP OF A HIGH RIDGE and saw the unmistakable shine of sun glinting off a large body of water. Large enough so that a farther shore was not discernible even from their vantage point. Then, to their right on the shoreline, the obvious square outlines of an unnatural formation bulked large.

"A place for boats? They fish, too?" Astrid asked, shielding her eyes with one hand.

"Could be. They'd hardly let the wealth of a sea just sit there without harvesting it," Kris said.

"Too right," Sarah murmured, also peering ahead. "Would it be a salt sea?"

"We'll find out," Joe said.

"Zainal?" Kris asked, since the Catteni had said nothing but was staring hard at the building.

"We go careful. Fishing year long."

"True, but how could a machine fish? I mean, the sea doesn't follow any program, does it? Storms and stuff . . . unless they can control tides as well as the rain. Not that I wouldn't put it past them," Kris said, mildly bitter.

"They do not control us," Zainal surprised her by saying. "Tell the others."

"About the flying darts and stuff?" She did and then turned back to Zainal. "However, if there are machines, surely they'd be specialized for use in the water. That building seems to be right on the edge. I don't think we have much to worry about them charging inland at us."

"Famous last words?" Joe said, nudging her with an elbow and grinning.

"I hope not. One trip to an abattoir is quite enough."

"Canning factory is what this'd be," Joe said, still teasing.

"Hmmm." Then Kris giggled. "Imagine him in a sardine can," and she tilted her head irreverently at their patrol leader, still looking intently at the building.

"We go slow. We do not approach until second moonrise. . . ."

"If you say so, boss," Kris said flippantly.

THERE WERE TIDES ON THIS WORLD, JUDGING BY THE HIGH-water marks and the flotsam deposited along the beach.

"With so many moons, tides would be complex," Joe remarked.

"Swim?" Astrid wistfully asked Kris, though she peered at Zainal for permission.

They approached the beach a kilometer or so from the building. Hiking through the white sands had been hot work, for the shifting surface made the going difficult even where it was somewhat held in place by tufts of a sturdy grassoid and, in one place, a plantation of reeds. Joe took samples of each plant in case one or more of these supplied trace elements that would help the Deskis. The sea might be several days' journey from the main camp, but not inaccessible. Another stumpy-branched growth which reminded Kris of wind-stunted cedars bore a hard fruit of some sort. Joe stuffed the harvest from two bushes in his pack.

Zainal swung his glance right to the building, which now seemed to be hovering above the sandy ground, an optical illusion, Kris was sure. Then, for a long moment, he watched the sea itself and finally shrugged.

It'd be ironic, Kris thought, to have survived all the dangers the land was providing to get drowned by some sea creature, but she couldn't see any disturbance on the lightly rippled sea: certainly nothing that would indicate underwater denizens. Then Zainal strode down to the edge of the water, and scooped up a handful from the next incoming ripple. He smelled it, then stuck his tongue into the liquid. "Salt. You swim first," and his finger pointed from Sarah to Astrid to Kris. "We watch."

"Us?" Sarah piped up impishly but she was already walking down to the water's edge, opening her coverall.

Kris had lost a great deal of her conditioned notions of modesty over the last few weeks so she followed Sarah, Astrid trotting ahead of both of them, shedding her coverall with haste and nearly tripping as she removed the right pant leg. She threw the coverall away from her, where the sand was still dry, and then ran the rest of the way into the water.

"Don't go too far out," Joe called, and then he and Oskar hunkered down on the sand. Zainal remained standing, scanning the sea constantly.

The sea wasn't as salty as Kris remembered the Atlantic on her eastern seaside vacations, though there was sufficient to make it quite buoyant as she settled into a crawl. Sarah was whooping and splashing.

"Hey, I like this. A sea I can swim in without worrying about sharks."

"Don't go so far out," Kris called, all too aware that Botany was quite likely to put up a few seaborne surprises. She was a bit surprised that Zainal had let them swim at all. "Let's keep close enough to shore to get there before anything out there," and she waved at the innocuous spread of water, "can get us."

"Good thinking, mate," Sarah said and paddled back toward her.

Astrid swam with studied economy of stroke, Kris noticed, while Sarah thrashed about with little expertise. They didn't stay in long, out of deference to the men who were keeping watch and who probably wanted the refreshment of a swim as much as they did. But Kris felt better for the bath and waved to the men that they were coming out now. Zainal was still watching, but not the three nude women emerging from the ocean. Joe and Oskar had politely turned their heads as the girls came out.

"Okay, guys," Kris called when they were dressed again. "Your turn." She went up to Zainal. "I'll keep watch."

He shook his head. Then, with a wide sweep of his arm, gestured Joe and Oskar to go in without him.

"Don't you swim?" Kris asked, amused.

"Too quiet," he said cryptically and continued his scanning, not just the horizon but the beach on both sides of them.

"On Earth—Terra—fishermen usually go out at dawn, or on the tide," she said conversationally. "So the machines, if there are some, *would* be quiet this time of day, I think."

"I have never been to sea before," Zainal replied in the same tone.

"You look a bit like a lighthouse, though," and Kris giggled, "standing like that."

"Light house?" He frowned but didn't pause in his vigilant and careful scrutiny.

"Hey, I think this planet has clams," Sarah cried. She went down to her knees and starting digging with her hatchet. The next little wave ripple flooded over her legs.

"Didn't know you had clams in Australia," Kris said as she strode down to Sarah.

"Biggest clam beds ever outside of Sydney. And oysters."

Kris' one seaside vacation had included hunting for quahogs on a Cape Cod beach, so she recognized the little holes left where mollusks had opened an air passage. She began to dig, too.

"What you do?" Astrid asked, joining them.

"Dig and . . . oh . . ." Sarah closed her fingers around something and hauled it out of the wet sand. "What on earth?" She rinsed the rest of the sandy mud off the shelled creature and showed it to the others. It was oblong with a shell obviously "built" around it, rough like an oyster, not smooth like a clam.

"Well, it's like both clam and oyster," Kris said. "And with no claws it's not a crab. Oysters are good for you, and so for that matter are clams.

Might even have the trace elements the Deskis need. Sea stuff is full of minerals and junk."

"Yeah, I know," Sarah said, rolling her eyes. "I drank enough cod liver oil as a kid. Hey, Joe, c'mere a minute, will ya?"

Joe, totally unselfconscious about his nudity, joined them and took the "clam" from Sarah.

"We will have to go the empiric route, I suppose," he said without real enthusiasm. "At least it won't eat us first."

He took Sarah's hatchet, held out his hand for Kris' and, using one as a counter, hit the shell with the other.

"Oops, hit it too hard," he said, looking down at the mashed stuff that oozed off the side of the blade. "Get me another one."

After the capture and dissection of three more mollusks, Joe decided the "flesh" might indeed be edible. He dressed and they all went to find something burnable. No one quite had the courage to try the mollusk raw, though they all thought it smelled as seafood should. Joe was game enough to be the guinea pig when the first one turned brown and a prod with the knife point went easily into the meat.

"A bit chewy but rather tasty, chums. Rather tasty."

Sampling another morsel, Oskar agreed and immediately went out to gather more shells. Zainal only smiled and, although he put a piece in his mouth, did not swallow it, shaking his head.

"You don't have things like this on Catten?" Kris asked him, teasing.

He shook his head. "Eat land animals only."

"Fish has better protein content and less fat," Kris said, enjoying his reaction.

Zainal went back to watching.

Making a camp in the dunes, out of sight of the building and shielded from the light breeze that had sprung up, they ate a meal that began with clams broiled on the half shell and then cold rocksquat. Joe suggested that they wait and see if any of them had a reaction to the mollusks before they went on a binge of them. Oddly enough, they all wanted to eat more.

"Probably they contain some trace elements our present diet is not supplying," Joe suggested. "Sometimes our bodies know better than our heads what is required. But let's give it the overnight test. If no one's had diarrhea, vomiting, nausea, or dies on us, the clams should be fairly safe to eat."

"Fresh," Kris added.

"By the seaside, by the beautiful sea," Joe warbled.

Then the talk shifted to the point of whether or not scavengers lived in the sand dunes.

"Maybe something even worse," Sarah suggested, shuddering.

"I'd kinda looked forward to making a sandy bed," Kris said wistfully. "At least you can get it to conform to your bumps and lumps, which rock won't."

Joe whistled. "Yeah, great contours!" and he made a show of leering at her. Sarah pinched his thigh, calling him to order.

"I do miss mattresses," Kris said, sighing. "I honestly don't miss much else. Most of the time, that is. But I'd really, truly, deeply give my eyeteeth for even a pneumatic camping mattress," she said, hugging her knees to her. She caught Zainal's amused glance where he sat opposite her, his eyes twinkling in the firelight.

"Eyeteeth?" he asked.

She bared her lips and showed him.

"What good are your eyeteeth to anyone else?"

"They aren't. It's just a saying."

The remainder of the evening was spent in language lessons. Oskar was picking up more and more English and Astrid's was becoming more fluent. She was also picking up some of Kris' pet phrases though such flattery made Kris just a little uncomfortable.

When fatigue made longer and longer pauses between conversations, Zainal announced the watch roster. He suggested that the sentinel stomp, and that was the word he used with a grin at Kris, around the perimeter from time to time, just in case the sand did harbor a species of underground scavengers. The others were to bed down in the sand around the fire, which the sentry would keep going.

"In between stompings?" asked Sarah irrepressibly.

"As you say," Zainal agreed, nodding.

The long night passed with no alarms and Kris, comfortably positioned on the sand, slept deeply and well. As usual everyone roused well before the Botany dawn. Since no one had suffered any alimentary reaction to the clams, a beach party was organized. In the dim predawn light, they dug clams and when they decided they had enough for a good feed, they took a quick dip in the sea to wash off the clinging shore mud.

Rather a festive breakfast ensued. Then Zainal suggested they use the last of the night to approach the building and scout it out. No one had yet figured out how long a day's charge of solar power lasted in the collectors since the mechs were usually inactive during darkness.

The building was bigger than they'd originally thought and seemed to expand as they approached it. Zainal, whose night vision was superior to the rest of the patrol's, discerned some curious superstructures on the front of the building and a railed runway leading down into the water.

"A launch site?" Joe suggested.

"On Terra, fishing is done in the old ways," Astrid said. Joe and Sarah agreed.

"Do they have an automated boat, then?" Kris asked.

"Maybe they whistle the fish into their nets," Joe murmured.

"Haven't heard a mechanical make any noise apart from 'clank-whir,'" Kris said facetiously.

Machinery did not need windows, either, and the building had none. It looked as if the entire front of the building opened to permit the exit of whatever machinery was stored inside. The largest solar panels they had yet seen occupied the roof, held up by a heavy stem, which implied the panels altered direction to accumulate as much of the sun's rays as possible. That was a new wrinkle in the mechanicals' technology.

Zainal could find no exterior slit or lock or anything that would give them access within. He even had Joe up on his shoulders, searching the seaward walls as high as he could reach.

So they waited at a discreet distance to see if the building would open itself up once daylight had arrived. They waited until the sun was at its zenith, and occupied themselves by trying to fish, using the thinnest possible strips of blanket attached to a pole, and a piece of thin wire bent into a hook with a portion of clam attached as bait. When they caught nothing from the shore, they waded out as far as they could without losing their balance and finally caught some flatfishes. These they grilled for lunch, taking cautious bites.

"What I'd give for a testing kit!" Joe sighed wistfully. "You miss mattresses, Kris, I'd give my eyeteeth for just a magnifying glass." He paused. "And a few odd chemicals to test for toxicity. I'll not even dream of having a microscope. . . ."

"Don't!" Sarah said.

"Look, why put such tools past our panel of talented DIYs," Kris said, "considering what they've managed to produce so far," and she tapped the comunit.

At high noon, when no activity emanated from the building, Zainal said they would take measurements of this, the biggest facility they'd yet seen.

"Maybe it only goes after certain types of fish that aren't running right now," Joe suggested.

"Or maybe there's a satellite up there," and Sarah pointed skyward, "that tells it when to go fishing."

Zainal shook his head. "No satellite or Catteni do not explore."

"Are you *aware* then," Kris asked, startled by the concept, "that there *are* other sentient space-traveling species?"

Zainal gave her a slightly patronizing look. "Space is very big. Many planets can be settled," and he added with one of his engagingly broad grins, "not always this way." Then he added. "It is a mark of honor, not unhonor. . . ."

"Dishonor," Kris interposed.

"To be transported."

"I could have done without the honor," Sarah said drolly, then added quickly, giving Zainal's arm the briefest touch: "But then I wouldn't have met you, or learned that we Terrans are pretty damned good!"

"You are!" Zainal gave his head one of his quick affirmative nods. "Honor to me to be here."

"Well," Joe remarked, obviously gratified.

"Now we go search more," he said, and raising his arm over his head, gave the move-out signal.

Kris was gratified, too, by that little exchange. She was even pleased that Sarah had touched Zainal: up until that gesture of conciliation, no one had made any physical contact with Zainal—except herself. And Leon, medically, but not socially. *Touch him, he's real live flesh and bleeds red blood,* she thought sourly as they moved out, matching his easy jog pace: a disciplined squad, fit and able to cope with anything Botany had so far meted out.

Joe paused a couple of time to collect samples of berries or hard-shelled tree and shrub fruits. The soft ones he sampled or had someone else sample; judiciously, of course. Some of the soft berries were so bitter the merest morsel caused the mouth to pucker. A good rinse with water helped dissipate the effect. One, a dark green, was sweet enough to encourage the taster to try more. The green fruit was gathered but not eaten until the samplings proved there would be no ill effects.

They spent the rest of the day on the shoreline, noticing the flotsam pushed up by high tides, mainly seaweeds. These Joe thought might have nutritional value so he gathered specimens. They also noted the abundance of mollusks along the coast by the frequency of the blowholes.

Toward evening they dug out a quantity and, along with a plump rock-squat, tuber roots, and greens that grew in abundance, made an appetizing stew, to which the seawater was added to provide the salt they were all beginning to crave.

They found another sandy camping spot on a height above the shore, which stretched out in both directions as far as anyone could see. Just visible in the dim light were the lavender blobs of a spattering of islands which made them wonder, around the evening campfire, if this was an inland sea and there might be a distant shore. They considered continuing along the coast as far as they could go.

"We come again. Mitford will evaluate the situation first," Zainal said.

"Hey, now, listen to him," Sarah said, grinning. " 'Evaluate,' huh? That's a fifty-dollar word, mate."

"I listen, I learn," Zainal said, grinning back at her.

MITFORD HIMSELF GOT IN TOUCH WITH THE PATROL THE NEXT morning to call them in.

"Getting too close to the time the Catteni might come back," he said. "Swing wide but start back now."

Zainal had them strike obliquely back to camp and they came across two more agricultural garages and an abattoir, empty and waiting. They disabled everything, stacking the various useful parts for later pickup. Scratching his head, Joe regarded the piles.

"I wonder has anyone reinvented the wheel yet," he said. "Sure save packing that stuff out on our backs."

"If you have air cushions which hop over obstacles, a wheel is backward step," Kris said. "Hence no need for roads . . . a waste of good arable land, if you ask me."

"Too right, mate."

Oskar nodded approval. He was having to rely less and less on Astrid for translation.

"Just so long as I'm not around to carry the can when the bosses discover what we've done to all their facilities," Joe said, washing his hands and flicking his responsibility away.

"What if it's only more machines?" Kris asked, for she had considered that possibility. "At least machines don't get angry."

"Machines also don't eat meat or make bread," Sarah said staunchly. "The bosses have to be humanoid or why all of this?"

"Yeah, but I'll bet they use machines for all their dirty, boring chores," Joe replied thoughtfully. "I mean, the technology level that went into the design and manufacture of these mechs is phenomenal. We don't have anything its equal. Not even you Yanks with those great combine harvesters you have in your midwest."

"But machines have to be designed by . . . something else. They might be able to repair themselves—but design?" She shook her head. "There are intelligent sentient beings somewhere at the end of the line of machines."

Sarah and Joe snorted in chorus. Joe, with a grin, added: "So long as they're friendly."

"They are earth-friendly," Astrid said, speaking brightly.

"Are they human-friendly? That's the big question," Joe said.

"I like this planet," Oskar said. "Now we run it, not machines. Not bureaus or men who do not understand the land."

"Anything different in this lot?" Zainal asked Oskar as he added a coil of wire and a handful of connectors to the pile in front of the young Norwegian.

He shook his head but looked at Joe for confirmation. Joe shook his head.

"Nope, Zainal. Nothing that can't wait, as far as I can see. And I've got the anesthesia darts wrapped up in my pack."

"Good!"

They settled down for the night in one of the barns.

"So Kris can cushion her bones on straw," Zainal said with a grin.

"Too right," she said, having picked up that Australian phrase from Sarah.

First the girls retired to second barn for the privacy of their evening baths in watering troughs. When they returned, straw was piled in outrageously high beds.

"Deep enough for you, Kris?" Zainal asked, sweeping a sort of bow toward her accommodation.

She made a big show of spreading her blanket and then hesitated, not sure how she would get *on* to it. Zainal picked her up and, with a deftly controlled throw, deposited her, squealing in surprise, in the exact center of her "mattress."

"Ohhhh," and she drawled the exclamation as she wiggled her shoulders and hips deep into the soft mass. "Heavenly."

"And I do not ask for your eyeteeth," Zainal said, stepping back to take a brief run to launch himself onto his bedpile.

"I wonder," Kris said as she settled down to sleep, "what the mechos will say when they find six piles of battered fodder in these barns."

"Probably check the programming of their mechs," Sarah said sleepily. She was the last to speak that night.

THEY MADE IT BACK TO CAMP ROCK LATE THE NEXT AFTER-noon. Kris and Zainal made their report to Worrell, who said Mitford was out inspecting the latest gadget to be put together from "all those spare parts you blokes keep finding." Worrell was a balding chunky man, more barrel than leg, with a flushed complexion and many small red veins on his cheeks and chin. He had a habit of hitching his coverall, and the leather belt of worked rocksquat hide that circled it, as if he were afraid it would slip around his hips. Kris wondered if he had once had a beer belly, though he was thin enough now: an effect of being long aboard a Catteni transport ship.

"Anyone with any claim to mechanical skills has been drafted," he said, grinning, and then, losing his grin, pointed to the empty stocks. "That Aarens fellow's organized quite a production line at Slaughterhouse Five." Worry blinked at their exclamations. "Publicly we're calling it Camp Narrow for the narrow escape I hear some of your blokes had from a processing plant. So," and Worry gave another hitch to his pants before he motioned her, and just as politely, Zainal, to take a stone seat.

These had been improved by a reed-woven cushion, probably filled with fluff seed: much more comfortable than plain stone. *My, but I've become soft,* Kris thought, *wanting mattresses and cushions to put my sit-upon upon.*

Although Worrell looked first at Kris, it was Zainal who gave the report in an English that was almost as unaccented as Kris'. He even managed the tinge of a drawl she was in the habit of using. She drew out her map and showed Worrell the distance they'd covered—which drew an appreciative whistle from him—and the new garage locations.

He was particularly interested in the shoreline building.

"Think Mitford'll want that inspected and entered."

"Anything else exciting happen around here?" Kris asked, noting that the main camp did not seem as crowded as it had been when they left.

"Well, we've set up two more camps besides Camp Rock," and he grinned broadly at Kris, who chuckled. "Camp Shutdown's one of the garages you lot found on your last walkabout, and Camp BellaVista's the other side, which Cumber's patrol found," and he waved his hand to the east. "The miners've got living quarters in their adit, Ironclad."

"How many patrols have gone out?" Kris asked.

"At the moment, four others." Worry pulled a sheet from under a pretty agate used as a paperweight, checked that it was the one he wanted before he showed Kris the small-scale map with its lines indicating patrol directions. "We'll know this place as well as the mechos do."

"Is something burning?" Kris asked, aware of an acrid metallic stink in the breeze that was blowing across them in the "office."

"Ah, yes, we got us a forge here, too. There's another one at Iron-clad. Found us a real top grade of iron ore, plus copper, zinc, tin, gold, and bauxite." He winked at Kris with a grin on his face. "You'll note how far down the list gold is. Any road, mines, are over thataway," and he waved a hand northward and then northeasterly. "Got us two farriers, a wrought-iron fabricator, and nine welders. We've screwdrivers, now, and screws, all kinds of other tools, nails and hooks; soon maybe even needles and pins and I dunno what all else. Skillets, kettles, and pots are being turned out of the sandpit daily. Pretty good stuff considering we're back to reinventing essential equipment."

Kris grinned back at him, amused. "The mechs didn't mine any metals on the planet?"

"Nary a nugget, as far as we can see, and some of the ore was just lying around like they couldn't be bothered shoveling it up."

"So they bring in all their equipment," Zainal said thoughtfully, fingering his lower lip.

"Looks like. Leastwise we haven't found any garage or building or mine adit or anything suggesting the alloys they use in the mechos were indigenous. And oh my word, some of our engineers would give their eyeteeth" (Zainal shot Kris a quick amused look) "to know the composition of the alloys used for the chassis of those mechos." Worry whistled again.

Kris was wondering if this was an Antipodean habit—whistling for emphasis. Joe Marley was prone to whistle, too. Well, it made a nice change from swearing.

"And the computer guys are right beside 'em, wanting to know where the crystals used in the motherboards came from."

"So no one reinvents the wheel here?" Zainal asked, astounding Worrell again.

"I thought you didn't speak much English, Zainal," he said, giving Kris a suspicious glance.

"I learn languages easily," Zainal said. "I learn"—and he paused briefly, touching his fingers in his counting—"fifteen with English."

"Some people got a real talent for it, that's the truth. I still have trouble with the Queen's English." Then Worry gave a big grin. "You mentioned the wheel, well, I want to tell you, we have gone beyond the need for something as primitive as a mere wheel."

"We did?" Kris asked.

"One of the engineer blokes got one of the air-cushion mechos working. Only *now* they gotta reprogram it to work when *they* want it to."

"Boy oh boy oh boy." Zainal startled Worrell into an open-mouthed stare. "Then we don't have to carry all those parts back here."

"You bet!" Worry's smile was prideful as he shuffled to find another sheet of paper. "Ah, here we are. Your patrol's bunked in Mitchelstown. You got tomorrow off and I think they'll want you hanging about here a bit."

"Mitchelstown?" Kris asked.

"Yeah, we started naming the caves. Makes it more homey. So the main cook cavern's now Cheddar. We even got name plates so you'll know when you get to the right one. Mitchelstown's quite roomy. Second turn on the left past Cheddar. Near the johns, too."

"Where is the Deski, Coo?" Zainal asked and Kris was annoyed with herself that she hadn't thought to ask after their comrade.

Worry looked his nickname. "Not good. Leon says he's holding his own but the thorn greens are not enough. Something, but not enough. Sure hope that message gets read soon."

"We found a lot of stuff on our patrol: maybe edibles that might be good for the Deskis," Kris said. "Clams, berries, nuts."

"Clams? No oysters?"

Kris shook her head.

"I *liked* oysters," Worry said emphatically. Then he slapped both hands on his knees, rose, and shook hands first with Kris and then Zainal before turning to Joe and calling him over. "So, Marley, pull up a stone and show me what you brought in." His gesture included not only Joe but Sarah and the two Norwegians.

CHEDDAR HAD IMPROVED ALMOST BEYOND RECOGNITION—NOT the least of which were the solar panels, like chevrons, above the entrance. There were tables and stools, and brick hearths replacing circles of stones, and ovens ranged on one wall. Bread racks showed the day's produce, which was not limited to large, economy loaves, but featured small ones as well. The supply area now had a front counter and shelving behind on the wall to display goods, which proved ingenuity was rampant. A neatly curved doorway gave into a storage area beyond the main cavern but the door was closed. Store shut!

Someone had also been successful in blowing glass, Kris realized, noticing that the corridor lighting had glass shades: sort of lumpy and blurred but glass nonetheless. Mitchelstown not only boasted a carved name plate, the letters outlined in black against the lighter stone, but also some rough bedsteads and mattresses, covered by the ubiquitous thermal blankets and probably filled by the fluff. At least it wasn't raw dirt or stone. Little alcoves had been cut into the wall for shelf space and there were thick wooden pegs hammered into the wall for hanging things. As if they had something to hang. But Kris did now—the map case which Worry had told her to hang on to for their next patrol and the comunit, which she carefully put on the pegs.

"Well," Kris said, settling tentatively down on the nearest bed, "all the comforts of home. What?"

Anne McCaffrey

"You did not give eyeteeth, Kris," Zainal said, his eyes twinkling at her.

"Didn't have to," she said, lying down fully but starting upright so quickly that Zainal looked around anxiously to see what had startled her. "Muddy boots," she said and unfastened hers, kicking them off. "Definitely the comforts of home." She lay back again.

"What was your home on Terra like, Kris?" Zainal asked, removing the accoutrements from his belt and neatly bestowing them on the shelf above the bed next to hers.

"It wasn't a cave, that's for sure," she said, unexpectedly irked to be asked such a question. Suddenly she had a glimpse of why others could dislike Zainal simply because he was Catteni: his presence reminded *them* of what they had been taken from. She pushed down that irritation and, as civilly as she could manage, described the split-level ranch-style house she, her parents, and her brother and two sisters had lived in: her neighborhood, her friends. She rattled on, unable to stop talking about her black-and-white cat, about the dormitory she'd lived in at college, until Joe and Sarah appeared in the opening, Astrid and Oskar just behind them.

"Is this our home from home?" Joe asked in a bright voice.

"Yes, it is," Kris said and was suddenly impelled to *leave*. Rising from the bed, she stamped back into the boots she had removed, left the room, and half-ran across the cook cavern and out, taking the steps as fast as she could without any caution, and across the ravine and campfire site, beyond the stocks and up onto the heights, down behind them and off up the next rise, where she was away from anyone.

There she sat herself down and, burying her hands in her face, cried. She didn't know why she'd react in such a childish way unless it was just that "loss" had finally caught up to her. Up until the moment Zainal had asked her, she hadn't *allowed* herself to *think* about home, her family, and all the things that were dear and familiar. She had forced herself to concentrate on first surviving, and then on the challenge of patrolling with Zainal, of proving herself useful on this crazy world. She'd kept up, she'd done all that was asked of her, but that didn't make up—at this moment—for the future she had once planned for herself.

She sensed, rather than heard or felt, someone near by. Whirling around on her bottom, she saw Zainal.

"It was all your fault . . ." The moment the words were out of her mouth, she cried out, *"No!* I didn't mean that, Zainal. I didn't mean it! Don't go."

He stood where he was, rock solid and unsmiling, but apparently concerned enough to make sure she did herself no harm.

"Sarah says to cry is good."

"How did she know I'd cry?"

A twitch of one huge shoulder. "She is woman, Terran like you. She was right, wasn't she? You cry."

"Don't blab it all over the mountain, damn it," she said, blotting her cheeks so she had a reason for keeping her head down. She didn't want Zainal to see her crying: she really didn't. "Do Catteni women cry?"

"Yes," he said so stoutly that she knew he was lying.

"You're lying in your teeth." The knowledge that he would prevaricate made her feel better.

"My *eye*teeth?" And the rumble of his voice under her ear was tinged with laughter.

"You're laughing at me . . ." she said in an ominous tone.

"I am laughing at the thought of teeth with eyes as if teeth can see."

"Yes, that is a bizarre concept, isn't it?"

Zainal had eased himself closer to her and his proximity was comforting. He had a different body odor than human males, she realized. It wasn't an offensive stink, not oniony like most guys, but she couldn't identify what it did smell like, except that she liked it.

"I rarely get silly," she said briskly. She didn't want a sentry to come by and see her: this meeting could be misconstrued and she didn't want any more rumors about Zainal scooting about the camp. "What is your home like—or will that make you sad enough to cry?"

The notion of a Catteni in tears made her giggle.

"You are better now," Zainal said and, putting a hand under her chin, tilted her face up.

Kris was nearly unbalanced by the unexpected tenderness in his warm yellow eyes. Why had she ever thought them an odd color?

Then he slid an arm around her shoulders. "Are you better now? Food is ready. Are you not hungry? Hungry brings tears, too."

She shot him a keen look. "I won't blame tears on hunger. I got homesick."

"Home sick?" He was puzzled.

"Yes, sick for the sight of familiar things and people you love."

"I don't think Catteni understand 'homesick,'" he said at his drollest. Now he eased her toward the cavern. "Why do they call this Camp Ayres Rock? Joe laughed."

Kris grinned again. "That's a big landmark in Australia." She glanced about her. "Much bigger than this, but I guess the outline might be similar. The Aussies must have padded the vote . . . if they even took one."

"That does not make them home sick?"

"*That* wouldn't," she said. "Do you never miss home?"

"Not my home world," he said so emphatically that she wondered if it was the planet itself or the people on it. "We go see Coo and Pess. Tell them about the new foods."

"Yes, we should," she said, now ashamed of her weakness when good friends were in desperate case.

Coo and Pess, and the other ill members of their species, were all together in one hospital cave. Weakness lay on them like a palpable cloak, turning their skin a pale, sickly green. They were lying on plump pallets, but to Kris it seemed as if it was an effort for them even to breathe. Pess looked nearly transparent: he was the oldest of the Deskis. It was their bones, wasn't it, that were weakening? Not their lungs.

All the Deskis seemed happy to have visitors and they all gabbled in their own language to each other when Zainal and Kris told them about the foodstuffs that they had found on their latest patrol.

"You think good, you do good," Coo said, looking from Kris to Zainal and nodding. "Coo walk with you soon."

"Learning more English, too," Kris said, shifting her feet and slightly uneasy in the face of such a wasting illness. She remembered how indefatigable Coo and Pess had been on their first patrols together. To see them in such poor condition really disheartened her. If she wasn't careful, she'd start weeping again.

"Do you have seas on your planet?" she asked Coo.

"See?"

"Large waters, salty."

Comments were exchanged and Coo, as spokesman, shook his head sadly. Then Kris tapped the water jug. "Big water, you can't see across it."

"Oh." Both Pess and Coo responded to that and vigorously nodded. "Big water good."

"Good for Deskis?" and again Kris was rewarded by a nod. "Maybe the clam things will help."

Then Leon put his head around the doorframe. "Don't overtire them, but I hear you found some possible nutrient sources on your latest trek."

All too relieved to have an excuse to leave the Deskis, Kris was happy enough to describe what Joe had found.

"I'll catch him later."

"How are they, Leon?" Kris asked in a low voice.

"Holding their own and the female's pregnant."

Kris glanced over her shoulder. "Which is she?"

"The one next to Pess. Her mate. We're hoping he can last until she gives birth but it's doubtful. His age is against him. He's not as resilient as the others. If they were humans, I'd say they had rickets and they'd need vitamin C. I've ordered a microscope," and he gave a brief grin, "from those engineering blokes, who say they can make anything we need from mecho scrap. Wish they'd hurry up."

At that point, Zainal joined them in the hall but he didn't need Leon's diagnosis to know how serious the Deskis' condition was.

THEY MADE A GOOD MEAL THAT EVENING, THE HIGHLIGHT BE-ing a fermented beer that was being brewed in Camp Rock. It had a kick to it, all right, but the taste was weird.

"We'll get it right. We'll get it right," said Worry, who had joined them at the table with his cup and the pottery pitcher that held his ration of beer. "Castlemaine XXXX or Foster's it ain't, but we'll have a respect-able pint by the time winter comes. We'll need it then."

"We will?"

"Hmmm, meteorologist bloke says he thinks winters are bad here. Sees signs on the trees and stuff. We'll do a good business in rocksquat furs."

"Business?" Kris asked. She seemed to be asking a lot of questions.

"Sure, worker's worth his hire—in privileges. Mitford won't allow gold used as barter or we'd never keep people at their chores. They'd be out gold-digging. Working on some wine, too, out of those green berries. Right tasty. And a cordial for them who don't like the taste of beer."

"There are such people?" Kris said, her expression bland. "How do you like it?" she asked Zainal, who was cautiously sipping his beer. "Is there anything like this on Barevi or Catten?"

"Yes! Not as good as this," Zainal said, a comment which did his credit no harm.

The beer might taste odd, but it had the same effect as anything brewed on ol' Terra. Two cups and Kris was ready to sack out. Zainal remained behind with Joe and Oskar who was, perhaps unwisely, getting his cup refilled too often.

EARLY THE NEXT MORNING, IT WAS CLEAR THAT HE HAD, AND Astrid, with Joe and Zainal's assistance, took him down to the lake for a remedial swim. Having nothing better to do, Sarah and Kris tagged along. They had the lake to themselves at that hour, it was still full dark outside. So they were all together when Kris' comunit bleeped.

"Sentries report something big coming in," Worry said. "Get out here."

"But it's still dark. They won't *see* the glyphs," Kris said in a wail, once again feeling the muscle-aching labor of making those marks in the hillside.

"I stay with Oskar," Astrid said, taking his limp arm from Zainal's grasp.

The five of them ran back up the steps, glad of the light from the glass-covered lamps that made a fall less likely. They ran along the corridors and through Cheddar Cave, where the bakers greeted them cheerfully, then they erupted out, onto the ledge.

Listening intently, they could indeed hear the distant rumble of an airborne vehicle.

"Riding lights passing over," said a voice just beyond them on the ledge and Kris recognized it as Worry's. "I've notified Mitford. He's alerting the local sentries. Is that Zainal there?" Worry swung a lantern. "Could you possibly tell . . ."

"It slows for landing," Zainal said.

"I suppose there's no way of knowing where it *will* land?"

"No," and Zainal shook his head. "A guess would be where it landed before," and he pointed in that direction.

"Cor! We can't make that before it lands."

"We make it before they depart," Zainal said, and pivoting on his heel, passed Joe and Sarah as he made for the steps.

Kris followed, beckoning for the others to come, too. She made a quick detour into Cheddar. Grinning at the bakers, she held her hand over the loaves just out of the oven.

"We gotta run but can we take some bread?"

"Sure . . ."

And she tossed a loaf each to Joe and Sarah, who had paused to see what she was about. Then they went after Zainal. The rumble was getting louder, like a swarm of very angry, very large insects.

Once they were off the Rock, Zainal set a bruising pace. When they stopped for a breather, the ship was passing overhead.

"Transport," Zainal said, peering up at the dark mass, outlined in blinking running lights.

Kris begged the stitch in her side to stop but when Zainal took off again, she was right on his heels and the others behind her. Despite the darkness, they managed to get over the rough ground with few stumbles and no falls. Something in the sound of the alien airship seemed to rev them up to the effort. Pictures of the wounds scavengers made on unresisting bodies plagued her when the stitch in her side returned and she ignored it again. If only she could keep from stumbling. . . .

Zainal vaulted the first hedge, for once not considerate of those behind him. But he wasn't showing off his physical superiority so Kris suppressed the surge of resentment as she trailed farther and farther behind him. She stood at the hedge that was too high for her to vault, Joe and Sarah coming to a halt beside her.

"Well, let's borrow an army trick," Joe said, observing the problem, and threw himself on the vegetation, making a way through the branches. Kris and Sarah carefully crawled over his body, then helped him through, and they were away after Zainal, who had reached the other side of the field.

"Damned Cat," Kris muttered under her breath but put her best effort into shortening his lead.

By now, the ship was well ahead of them but she could make out by the running lights that its stern end was swinging round. Did it land on its tail? How did it disgorge its unconscious passengers? The mass of it disappeared below the hill down which they were pelting, faster than was wise in the light and the conditions underfoot. In the growing light of day, they could see Zainal plunging through a gap in the hedging and they altered their hellbent pace in that direction and through to the next field.

Was this the one on which they'd been spread out, all unwitting of the dangers that lurking underneath them? Kris wondered but all the big fields looked similar. The main concern was that, even if the ship landed several fields onward, they would be close enough to prevent loss of life and injury. The skies were brightening. But, dammitalltohell 'n' gone, the Cats weren't at the right angle to have seen the glyphs in the dark—even with the sparkling stones to outline the figures.

And—she nearly lost her balance at the thought—what if Zainal left with them? She whimpered, once, twice, but hadn't breath for more as she pumped her tired legs harder to keep up with the man.

Underfoot she felt from one pace to another the big ship's mass settle to the ground. *Its mighty engines roaring,* she thought irreverently. Oh, god, what if the Cats captured them again? She was halfway to halting while she briefly considered that aspect of rushing to rescue unknown folks. The thought of Coo wasting away, of those of his species who had already died, and the baby that should be born, spurred her on. *Aren't you the altruist!* But such considerations lent the requisite energy to her legs.

Joe and Sarah nearly ran into her when she stopped at the next hedgerow, stunned by the mass of the landed vehicle. No wonder they'd had to use the larger Botany fields.

The ship had put down in the uppermost third of the space available. Suddenly lights came up, illuminating the field with beams so bright she had to shield her eyes.

"They don't . . . do things . . . by halves . . . do they?" Sarah said, panting, as she looked out through spread fingers at the scene, but she sounded cheerfully impressed.

Kris was quite willing to catch her breath until she saw Zainal, clearly outlined in the spotlights, running uphill, toward the ship. That alarmed her so much that she found herself holding her breath and getting funny bright lights on her peripheral vision. So she made herself breathe long and deep. Now a wide ramp was emerging from an expanding hold aperture.

"Damn him," she muttered and pushed her way through the hedge, ignoring scratches on face and hands and wrenching her coverall free from a snag.

Just then Catteni started to unload their cargo, three and four obviously unconscious bodies at a time, two limply draped on broad shoulders and two, equally flaccid, hauled out by the fabric of their coveralls. The fact that the Catteni then lined them neatly up in rows seemed oddly incongruous. Lots of Catteni and, despite her urgent need to be near Zainal, Kris felt her pace slowing.

"Oh, god, do I . . . know . . . what . . . I'm doing?"

"If . . . you do . . . let us . . . know," Joe said, coming up beside her: his stride faltered and his breath was labored. He bent over, hands on knees, to restore himself.

Two Catteni paused in the unloading as Zainal approached: both covering him with hand weapons. With the ship still wheezing steam and interior parts of it clanking, she couldn't hear what was said, even if she understood Catten, but Zainal was plainly acting authoritatively and both Catteni seemed to recoil. They hurried back into the ship but, now that the hold was wide open, Kris saw that one veered forward while the other merely resumed his labors.

The Catteni worked so swiftly that there were two full rows of unconscious bodies already spread out. Two cartons, presumably the usual knives, hatchets, and blankets, were in place at the side of the field.

Not quite brave enough for a closer confrontation with Catteni soldiers, Kris, Joe, and Sarah, struggling to get their breath back, halted of one accord, just beyond the first two cartons, half-hidden in the shadows beyond the bright spotlights. Zainal swiveled slightly to his left, nodded at them, and then turned back. The other Catteni ignored him as they continued to unload.

Suddenly, those going back in the ship snapped to an attentive halt and three Catteni strutted into view. Two stopped at the edge of the ramp while the third continued on to Zainal. They were of a height but Kris loyally thought Zainal was just a shade taller, and broader, and prouder.

She heard bits and pieces of the staccato language the Catteni spoke: the newcomer began to gesture impatiently, she thought. Then, with less vigor, he turned his head from side to side. Body language was not all that different, Kris thought. He didn't like what he heard or he didn't know if he could comply. Zainal seemed to stand even taller then and crossed his arms on his chest as if he had delivered an ultimatum.

That the other man was indecisive was now obvious to Kris. Suddenly, he gave an abrupt nod and, doing a snappy pivot on one heel, marched back up the ramp, his two guards falling behind as an escort. Zainal just waited, arms crossed, allowing the stevedores to make their way to either side of him.

"Why didn't he go aboard?" Joe asked.

"He didn't seem to receive an invitation to do so," Kris remarked. "Then, too," and she recalled what Zainal had mentioned once, "he said that what was dropped is never picked up."

"Did he mean himself? I mean," and Sarah was surprised, "he acted like he outranked the captain or whoever that was. And whatever it was he asked for, I think he's going to get it. They didn't seem surprised to have another Catteni come out of the dark just like—" and Sarah snapped her fingers—"that either."

"Not that I've ever seen Catteni soldiers," and Kris paused to make it plain she didn't consider Zainal in that category, "display surprise or any other emotion."

"Just doin' my job, man," Joe murmured.

"They said Zainal was an Emassi," Sarah said, "so he wouldn't fraternize with the likes of those stevedores anyhow."

"He was a spacer, any road," Joe added, "not ground force."

"You've been hearing things about Zainal?"

"Don't get antsy, Kris," Sarah said, patting her shoulder placatorily and grinning in the darkness. "We *like* Zainal. He's good stuff."

"Us Aussies appreciate a chap like Zainal," Joe put in. "Hell's fire, we're all in this together. Operation Fresh Start, m'girl."

The unloading continued inexorably and the skies lightened.

"Should we, ah . . ." and Joe nodded his head toward the hedge-row.

"No way. I'm not hiding from the likes of them."

"Atta girl," Sarah said, chortling. "You tell 'im."

" 'Sides, they can't do any more *to* me than they've already done, dropping me here," Kris said firmly. She wet her lips and tried to suck some moisture out of her cheeks to ease her dry throat. There'd be a stream nearby somewhere . . . when the Catteni had lifted off again. She wasn't moving until they did. They *could* just decide to cart Zainal off with them.

The three watching were startled to hear low mutterings and swearing behind them. Swinging around, they saw dark figures pushing through the hedge and the next thing Kris knew, a somewhat breathless Mitford came to a jarring stop to her left. He'd brought quite a mob with him to judge by the numbers of white faces in the gloom, straggling onto the field. Though what men and women, armed with the primitive weapons they had, could do against the Catteni, she didn't know. A show of resistance might bring out the forcewhips, and the skin on her back crawled at the very thought of that deterrent.

"What's happened? What's Zainal doing?" Mitford asked in measured gasps.

"I think he's asked for stuff for the Deskis. That's what we need, isn't it?" Kris replied.

"He been inside yet?" someone asked from the anonymous crowd.

"No, and I don't think he got asked."

Someone snorted in disbelief.

"Look at the way they're unloading those poor slobs," another man said. Kris thought it was one of the Doyles from the rueful lilt in the voice. "Poor bastards."

"Well, they'll be made welcome," Mitford said emphatically. "Won't they?"

"Sure, sarge, sure."

Now Mitford snorted, having set matters straight on that score.

More cartons were placed and the Catteni, seeing the observers, grinned and exchanged comments with each other.

"Not flattering, I'm sure," and that was Lenny's amused voice. "The same to you, m'bhoy!" he said in a louder tone, although he was instantly hissed silent up by those around him.

The Catteni looked back and one made a long forward step as if to see the reaction. No one moved a step, but Kris saw bows come up with notched arrows and spears readied to throw. The Catteni seemed surprised, but a shout from the ship had him speeding up his return.

It seemed they had to wait forever. But the sun was up and the urgency that had prompted their arrival was now irrelevant. But, and that thought sent a surge of pure panic through Kris, the Catteni made several drops in a trip, didn't they? Had they landed beyond Camp Rock? No, Zainal had said that they were coming in at a landing angle. This was their first drop? *Couldn't Zainal have them drop the whole load here and save us from running all over the planet, picking up survivors?* Kris thought irritably. She tried to moisten her throat again and then felt Mitford press something against her: his water bottle. Well, he hadn't run off at the drop of a hat as she had but kept his cool long enough to bring necessary supplies.

She swilled the first sip around in her mouth and then finally swallowed it, taking a larger drink before she passed the bottle to Sarah beside her.

And they waited: Zainal had not visibly moved a muscle since the captain, or whoever, had left him. He was like a statue, bathed in the very white white of the glaring spots, making the in-and-out traffic go around him. At length, Kris decided that was funny and began to chuckle to herself.

"I'd like a laugh myself," Mitford muttered.

"He's like a traffic island. He's making them go around him but he's not moving an inch. See," and she pointed out a pair who were forced to divert, "and wouldn't you think, being Catteni, they'd push him out of the way? If they could? If they dared?"

"Yeah, you're right," Mitford answered in a pensive tone. He raised his voice a little louder so the others would hear. "Yeah, our Zainal's showing them, that's for sure."

Kris thought how clever of the Sergeant to broadcast his observation. And if Zainal really did . . .

Two Catteni came out with a largish carton which they placed to one side of Zainal. Four more came with smaller packages. At that point Zainal raised his left arm, gesturing broadly for them to approach.

"All right, let's pick our parcels up," Mitford said and called out five names.

"I'm coming, too," Kris said, stepping forward beside Mitford, and found Joe and Sarah in step with her. When the Sergeant gave her a frowning look, she added. "We're *his* patrol."

Mitford grunted. Then, as a phalanx, they approached the ship, Mitford in front. Kris could feel herself trembling at being so close to a Catteni vessel, much less the creatures themselves. Two passed them, with their loads of human bodies. She'd already noticed that this drop was a very mixed bag indeed. She'd noticed Deskis, Rugarians, more Turs, and some odd-looking troglodytes she hadn't ever seen on Barevi.

As they neared the hold opening, she became aware of the stench emanating from the cargo: sweat, excrement, the stale odor of bodies long enclosed in an inadequate space, and the acrid tang of whatever was used to keep people in stasis for the length of the journey.

"What a pong!" Sarah said, fanning the air in front of her.

So they did not dally as they collected the crates. It took four men to manage the big one, and the Catteni laughed to see their struggles with the mass and the weight, so it was as well that Zainal's patrol elected to come along. Even the smaller crates were heavy, and Kris felt her back muscles strain as she picked up hers.

"You coming?" she murmured to Zainal, who had resumed his crossarm pose.

"Soon. I have not all I want."

"You'll stay with us?" It was extremely important to Kris that he did. She was in a panic that somehow she'd lose him, now when she had suddenly realized how much he meant to her.

"I stay."

On the way back to the sidelines, she held herself to even slow steps, determined that she would not give the Catteni any chance to laugh at her.

"Janiemac, what did they put in this?" Lenny Doyle exclaimed as he helped ease the crate to the ground. "Careful now, it might be breakable."

"Naw, Lenny, but we sure are," Ninety said, groaning, and he made a big display of rubbing the small of his back.

"Is he coming?" Lenny asked Kris, gesturing to Zainal.

"Says he is. They haven't given him all he asked for."

"Let's hope they give him more than he should get," and, with a sudden spurt of fury, Kris recognized Dick Aarens' nasty voice.

"Why 'n' hell bring him along?" Kris demanded of the Doyles.

"Only way to be sure he does his share," Lenny said. Then he added. "He's getting far too cocky, showing off to everyone that he was the only one who could figure out how the mechos work and what parts'll work for us. You don't suppose the Catteni would take him back?"

"Fat chance of that . . . My God, look at the piles of folks," Kris said, for the original, fairly neat order of the rows had altered and bodies were being crammed close together.

"That's more than were in our drop," Mitford said, obviously doing a body count. "Many more. Maybe they're doing us a favor after all, putting the whole nine yards down in the one spot."

"Yeah, but sarge, where'll *we* put 'em when they're awake?"

"We'll make room. A lot of 'em are ours!" the Sergeant said in a determined growl.

"Yeah, but enough's enough. We've just got comfortable and now . . ."

"So we share. We remember, don't we, what it was like. So we dammitall *share!*" There was no further argument as the unloading continued. "I'd rather have them with us, where we can see 'em, than turning wild and causing our camps no end of trouble."

Fatigue from the tearing run to get here, as well as from hefting that heavy carton, began to take its toll of Kris' energy. Wearily, she sat herself down on the carton.

"I've a loaf of bread to share," she announced, suddenly remembering that she had, and reached into the map case. She broke off a piece and passed the loaf to Mitford.

"Good idea," Mitford said. "At ease, men . . . and women. Let's watch the big fat smelly Cats at work."

So everyone assumed lounging positions, on the grass, seated on the line of supply cartons or just hunkered down. Joe and Sarah shared their loaves and many in Mitford's group had thought to bring food, which they distributed.

" 'Lift that bale, tote that barge,' " sang Lenny's tenor voice softly.

"I could sure stand getting a little drunk and landing in jail," another male voice said and sang the final word down to the bottom of his voice range.

Everyone laughed and the Cattenis heard.

"They're twitching."

"Let's not lay it on too thick."

"Ah, sarge!"

"Easy does it. You do remember forcewhips, don't you?"

"They're not carrying any."

"Only because everyone's unconscious."

"Are you counting, Tesco?" Mitford added.

"I would if you . . . eight hundred twenty, one, two, and three . . . don't interrupt me allatime."

"Let's not make them too mad, blokes," Joe Marley said. "They're taking it out on 'em."

Everyone shut up, now that Joe had pointed out the rough—rougher—way the Catteni were depositing the unconscious bodies. Almost slamming them into the ground.

"Zainal, can you tell them not to mash the cargo?" Mitford said, raising his voice to parade-ground level.

Zainal swiveled at the hips and, seeing one Catteni doing exactly what Mitford protested, snapped a savage bark. The erring Catteni made a big show of placing his burden down more carefully. The others, under Zainal's watchful gaze, behaved more circumspectly.

"Is Zainal going to stay there until they finish?" Lenny asked, leaning down to Kris, his expression anxious.

"I think so. At least he can curb their boyish bad habits."

"How does he get away with it?" Lenny asked.

"Because he knows how to give orders," Mitford said almost admiringly.

Idle conversation continued among the watchers gang, but no more bursts of laughter to annoy the Catteni. Tesco had got up to a thousand when Mitford gestured for Dowdall to take over. Then more cartons were brought out which the Catteni stacked on the other side of the field, in a sort of farewell gesture of bad feelings. Still Zainal waited.

All the soldiers had disappeared within the ship and the silence was broken only by noises from the vessel itself, metallic complaints and emissions of liquid and steam. Suddenly the watchers could all hear the sound of boots on metal and a second delegation, five Catteni this time, appeared in the opening. Two stayed inside, three came down, and two stopped partway. The remaining Catteni, dressed in a more elaborate uniform and shorter by a full head than Zainal, came right up to him and presented first a sheaf of what Kris thought had to be printout, and then another folder. These were presented most punctiliously. Kris thought for a moment that the officer was going to click his heels together and bestow a Teutonic military bow on Zainal.

Zainal accepted the offerings, almost diffidently, said a few words in a low voice, and casually sauntered away from the ship. The blinding blue-white lights went out, the ramp was retracted, and they could hear warm-up engine sounds from the ship.

For a moment Kris feared that the exhaust from its engines would fry the nearest bodies. But, whining at a pitch that made everyone cover their ears defensively, the big transport lifted vertically in a slow ascent, then edged forward. When it was several fields beyond its landing site, the rear engines glowed from yellow to white to a blue actinic light that made Kris and the others cover their eyes.

The wind of its passage was enough to knock several off their feet: the bodies of the latest victims fortunately were low enough to be under the blast path.

Kris could no longer contain herself but rushed out to Zainal, who had begun to walk more briskly, undisturbed by the takeoff wind.

"Did you get what you wanted? What *did* you want that took so long?" she cried as she neared him.

"I got the explore report," and he held up the folder, "and medicals on Deskis." He held up the sheaf. "Treatment for Deskis . . ." and he pointed to the carton Kris had lugged over. "Medicals for humans and Rugarians," and he indicated the others. "And testers."

"How come they snapped to for you, Zainal?" Joe asked.

Zainal grinned. "I may be down but not out."

Kris giggled nervously at his casual use of the slang. *Go to the head of the class,* she thought.

"I am still Emassi and they *know* it," he added, snapping out the "know."

"So what's 'Emassi' when you're at home?" Joe demanded, cocking his head to one side.

"A . . . born rank." Zainal shrugged it off.

"Birth rank," Kris corrected automatically. She wanted Zainal to speak English properly.

"I understood him," Joe said in tacit reprimand.

Kris firmly closed her lips to a smart retort. Now was not the time to bicker.

"Look at it this way, folks, we've almost doubled our population— the easy way," Mitford announced when he jumped to the top of the crate.

"Back at the old stand, huh, sarge?" someone shouted.

"Yeah, and we'll follow the same routine. Only this time we're ahead of the game. We know the drill. Dowdall, get back to Camp Narrow and organize beds and food. Send me at least twenty more people. Bring some buckets and pitchers so we can water 'em. We'll start sending folks back as soon as they're able to walk. It's not that far and that's a blessing. You, you, you and you, start moving among 'em and pick out the injured— those Cats really banged some of 'em down hard—and any d.o.a.'s. Lenny, Ninety, break open these cartons. Su, Jay, start distribution. Then, Jay, you lead the first group of fifty back to Camp Narrow." Mitford jumped down again and stood by Zainal. "It looks to me like they emptied their entire load on this one field. That right, Zainal?"

Zainal nodded.

"Is that report readable?" Mitford peered at the glyphs, which resembled those that Kris had helped carve in the hillside.

"Yes. I also told them that this planet is occupied by others of high-tech skill."

"Did they believe you?"

"No." Zainal's grin was bleakly amused. "But they will tell to those who need to know."

Mitford gave him a sharp stare. "Why didn't they believe you? Did they think you were lying er something, to get off planet?"

Zainal shook his head. "I told them, first, that I am dropped and I stay." He did not look in Kris' direction but she knew, definitely, that he was saying that for her benefit and her heart did a little painful jump. *Stupid!* But she was so glad that he hadn't gone. "They believe report says this planet . . . empty."

"Lord," Joe Marley said in a groan, "how'd they miss the garages?"

"Garages do not show warm-blood life forms," Zainal said and grinned.

A nearby groan from one of the bodies interrupted the conversation and they sprang into action. Actually, Kris thought as she took Mitford's own canteen to the nearby stream to fill it, Zainal, she, and the others needn't have run so fast or risked broken bones to get here. It had taken the Catteni several hours, at least, to unload. They could've walked, or waited for breakfast, but she was damned glad they hadn't. She'd have missed Zainal standing there like a Gibraltar Rock. Would he have continued to stand there all day, if they hadn't been willing to accede to his requests? Or demands? Being an Emassi certainly granted him privileges, even if he had been dropped.

Chapter Twelve

THEY WERE SO WELL ORGANIZED, AND Mitford harangued so effectively, that the "indigenous personnel," as he referred to them, were served hot, revitalizing drinks from a hastily erected camp kitchen before the sun was halfway up the sky, and later sandwiches for lunch. The newly awakened were kindly advised to stick to water at first and then slowly chew down a third of a ration bar: gorging on empty stomachs led to unpleasant reactions.

Mitford had immediately sent the medical crates—all but one tester kit—on to Camp Rock with news of this new drop and a request to Worry to send Leon and other medical assistance. The Catteni had broken a few bones for those they had slammed down so hard. Some of the new lot would have to be accommodated at the Rock, as people were beginning to call the cavern camp, almost affectionately. Kris felt considerable gratification at the thought that Leon would now be able to treat Coo, Pess, and the pregnant female and to keep the newly arrived Deskis healthy.

By the time the first batch of fifty moved slowly out on their way to Camp Narrow, Mitford had taken Kris off wake-up duty and put her onto debriefing: getting names, occupations, origins, and lastly but just as importantly, what they might know of recent events—recent to them—on Earth. The mere fact that people were resisting the Catteni continued to boost morale. Today's encounter on the field also ranked as a major plus.

"Getting something out of the Cats without having to pay for it," was the happy summation.

When she took a few moments to eat her lunch, Mitford approached her for a synopsis of her findings.

"So far the humans I've got originated from North America, Canadians as well. Then there seems to be a whole raft of English, French, and German. Resistance," and she grinned, "is increasing and the Catteni have had to call in reinforcements to deal with stoppages and sit-downs and all kinds of passive movements. There's also active sabotage, too, blowing up Catteni supplies or shipments destined for Catten or Barevi."

"Shipments? Arty things?"

"Not that I heard. Somehow, sarge, I don't think our artistic tastes would parallel Catteni."

"Hmmm. Possibly. Any useful professionals?"

"Two Canadian dentists, nineteen teachers—it seems the Catteni emptied a private school for one reprisal. They took . . . all the girls away," and the words came reluctantly out of her. "Some of the teachers are nuns. They resisted the kidnapping. One said she had had her arm broken. It looks a bit crooked, and I can feel the excess calcium where the break was, but basically it's completely knitted."

"A long time coming here, then. What *do* they use for this stasis junk?"

Kris shrugged as she flipped over her sheets to pick out the more interesting occupations. "Five hairdressers, two masseurs, a reflexologist . . ."

"A what?"

"Makes your feet happy."

"Argh."

"You should try it, sarge, it can really relax you!"

"I said *useful occupations!*"

"How about two chemists, five pharmacists, a structural engineer, nineteen housewives, three with kids still attached, and . . . you know, there's not a single person over fifty among those I've talked to."

"Don't give me nightmares," Mitford said.

"Two jewelers, three ex-soldiers, and a detective-inspector." She came to the end of her report on the morning's interviews.

It took the rest of the long Botany day to process everyone. Zainal talked to the new Deskis and sent several up to watch for fliers, but Mitford felt that, having disassembled the garages, whatever mecho summoned the fliers had been disabled, but he was quite willing to post sentinels, "just in case."

Three hundred and two dead were left on the field. Some could be identified by others who had been captured with them at the same time, so their names were recorded. Kris had to look away from the small bodies of the children. Those under five could not endure the stasis. Their deaths, so needless, so terrible, distressed her.

"You never know them," Zainal murmured to her when he saw the tears in her eyes.

"No, and no one will now."

She turned away, fighting with the fact that Zainal was Catteni, too, and a member of the species who had caused the deaths. She told herself firmly that Catteni or not, Zainal had done all he could to help and certainly he had been able to reduce unloading injuries. They should also give thanks that he'd been able to ensure just one drop site. Even Mitford's talents as an organizer would have been stretched to mount multiple rescue operations and get everyone under cover before the scavengers emerged from the night ground.

Zainal touched her arm gently. "We go now. Night falls."

"Yes, it does," she said, heaving a sigh against the stresses of the very long day in which she had been going all-out most of the time.

THE RESCUE TEAMS WERE SOMEWHAT CHEERED BY THE HOT meal awaiting them at Camp Narrow. Having so many barns available for housing—since the resident population of the camp was only a few hundred—made the difference between total chaos and mere confusion. Many of the newly arrived did their best to help, either settling their injured comrades or lending a hand with the chore of feeding the multitude. Leon and his medics had set up an infirmary for the injured and the weak. Kris saw Zainal and Leon examining the contents of the tester kits, Zainal carefully translating the properties of the various vials to the doctor.

Since there were a number of totally frightened aliens in that category, Leon had Zainal stay on to translate. Slav could at least reassure members of his own species who, Kris noticed as she ate, seemed quite cheerful. They were certainly inspecting Slav's weapons and even trying to pull his bow, hissing in the Rugarian equivalent to laughter. Several of them were females, which might account for Slav preening as much as he did. She hadn't really thought about how the other species would manage, either in relationships or propagation. If what was dropped on a planet stayed down, at least mating would be possible for all five species. But not Zainal. She put that exclusion to the back of her mind.

Mitford was everywhere, encouraging, detailing jobs, trying—it seemed to Kris, watching him from the corner of the kitchen barn where she had wearily slumped—to make himself known to all the Terrans. To her surprise, she even heard him speaking a few words of German and French to representatives of those nationalities. She knew French well enough to tell that his usage was rudimentary, but he was trying. And the folks responded with a little more hope in their manner. Then she saw Aarens, hunkering down by a very pretty girl and chatting her up in what sounded like extremely fluent French. She was clearly flattered and, as clearly, recovering from the shock of the journey. Aarens, who wore a vest of many pockets and a belt of tools, including an assortment of screwdrivers of all sizes, was making her laugh.

"Come," and Zainal held out a hand to her. "You sleep. Tomorrow is another day."

Grinning at his unwitting use of the famous Scarlett O'Hara phrase, she extended her hand and let him haul her to her feet. She couldn't help but notice that many eyes followed them out of the barn. Maybe she should paint "one of the good guys" on his forehead. Then she flinched, remembering her own recent and less than charitable thoughts. But she'd been tired and upset when she'd thought them. And she'd had the grace not to voice them. She was even more tired now and where on earth was Zainal taking her? Halfway to the Rock? He turned her in at the last barn which, she noted, was relatively empty. Others were already sacked out— or would that be strawed out? She giggled.

"Soft bed," Zainal said when he had gently herded her to the far corner, where a huge mound had been carefully prepared.

"Oh, thank you thankyou thankyou," and turning, she just let herself fall backwards into it. She was faintly aware that Zainal was tucking her against his body and then she was out for the count.

SHE AND ZAINAL BOTH DREW DEBRIEFING DUTY THE NEXT DAY, she with humans and he with the various aliens. As they were in the same barn for that job, she saw how he handled the different species: the forty Deskis with dignity, the twenty-nine Ilginish with a cool, diffident manner, and the thirty-eight Turs with a sharp, very Cattenish delivery. Slav had been handling contact with his own species, of whom there were sixty. Since there were over eight hundred humans, there were five other debriefers beside Kris, three of whom could speak other languages: German, French, and Italian.

Late that afternoon, Mitford called a meeting of his aides in the garage of the Welcome Committee to organize the dispersal of the huge addition to Botany's population. Worry and Esker had made the trip over from the Rock: Tesco and the Doyles, who were in charge of Camp Narrow, were on hand: Aarens was conspicuous by his absence. She'd last seen him breakfasting with a half-dozen girls.

Kris was amused to see that pieces of mechos were doubling as stools while the carcasses, in various stages of dismantlement, had been pushed back to allow enough space for the meeting. She noted the veritable snow of sketches, diagrams, and drawings that were tacked up on the walls and hung over different worktops, which were littered with components being reused.

Mitford made a point of having Zainal sit on his right while Slav was on his left.

"First off, folks, I'd like to say that we owe a lot more to Zainal here than we can ever repay. He got us nutrients that'll keep our Deskis alive and tester kits so we won't have to risk poisoning to find out what is edible. He got," and now Mitford held up the folder that the Catteni captain had passed to Zainal, "the 'official' "—and he paused for a sardonic grin—"survey report on this planet. You will be glad to know that we're on the biggest of Botany's four continents, the temperate one. Zainal's translated the report and, frankly, I don't think much of the exploratory team that landed on this world. Neither does Zainal."

"Nice to know the Cats aren't as great as they think they are," someone said. "No offense, Zainal!"

"None taken," Zainal said with a cheery wave and a bland expression on his face.

"Zainal will summarize the report to us. Floor's yours," and Mitford sat down, gesturing for Zainal to stand.

"The report says that the planet has good air to breathe, good water to drink, and the . . . green plants . . . grow so plants for other worlds can . . . grow well, too. True. The report says two . . . Cats . . ." and Zainal's use of that nickname in a pejorative tone of voice elicited grins from his audience, "disappeared one night. Guard saw movement but did not go see. He thought men go to leak." Zainal might not be obviously trying to ingratiate himself, but he was couching his comments very cleverly indeed. "Not found anywhere. Guard tells of strange movement. This planet has dangers. Two more are not seen so all sleep inside."

"Ah, c'mon, Zainal, how'd they miss the garages and these barns and all?" Esker wanted to know.

"Sensors look for live flesh and ship lands in cold season." Zainal shrugged. "Sensors register metal but not much for . . ." he turned to Kris, "those who work in ground . . ."

"Miners."

"Miners and no special metals needed by Catteni."

"Some of those mecho alloys are very special indeed," Lenny Doyle said, "very special."

"I agree," Zainal said, "but the stupids on survey do not know. Take dirt, water, stone samples, and flesh of rocksquats, avians, loo-cows, and critters they find on other lands but . . . they do not see trees for forest."

Ninety laughed aloud at that. "Attaboy, Zainal,"

Kris had been watching reactions and, of all there, only Dowdall and Tesco didn't seem to respond in any way to Zainal: they just sat there, eyes on the Catteni. Kris wondered from their attitude if they even believed what he was saying.

"What about winters here, Zainal?" Lenny asked.

"Report of . . ." he frowned and turned to Kris, "what falls from skies, wet, cold, solid but . . . runs like water from sun . . ."

"Snow."

"Ah, snow."

"Deep snow?" Lenny asked.

"Not when here. Oh, hand wide," and Zainal held his big thick hand flat, thumb down, to indicate the depth.

"That's deep enough."

"Longer day than Catten, longer year."

"How long?"

"Report says," and now he held up four fingers, then all five, and finally two.

"Oh, lordee, that's longer by three more months. How're we going to feed twenty-five-hundred-plus all winter long?"

"Find more silos and start breeding rocksquats in captivity," Mitford said. "Anyone volunteer to farm rocksquats?"

"Hell, sarge, don't take the fun out of it for us hunter types," Worry said plaintively.

"Say, Zainal, how long did this team of surveyors stay on Botany?"

Zainal looked down at the report. "Twenty days."

"Hell's fire, we've surveyed better than they did, haven't we?" Ninety said, laughing.

Zainal tapped the sheets. "This has tests done which Leon and Joe Marley need. Useful. Some plants deadly."

"Tell us something we didn't find out the hard way," Tesco muttered.

"That'll help even at this date," Mitford said. "Now, would you mind telling us about your conversation with Catteni ship captain?"

Zainal's wide lips twisted briefly in mild contempt. "Not captain. Below captain. One step."

"His exec?" Mitford suggested.

Zainal shrugged. "Emassi may command, even Emassi who is drop. They obey. Good habit. They do not believe mechs. Do not *wish* to believe what is not in report." He gave an amused snort. "They will. They also debrief." He shot a glance at Mitford. "We will see."

"Yeah, but they won't see any mechos if they do a fly-by now, will they, since we've disabled them all," Ninety said, almost querulously.

"So?" Zainal asked. "We *are* here. We can use mechos. Next time Catteni drop, different story. I do not stand," and he imitated his cross-armed stance at the bottom of the ramp, "and wait."

"You'd attack one of your own ships?" Ninety asked, surprised.

"Why not?" And Zainal regarded Ninety with amused condescension. "A ship useful when mechos return next year to collect."

"You mean you'd mount an expedition to follow them to their home system?" Kris asked, amazed by his intention.

Zainal nodded. "Be very good to see who farms whole planet."

"Hell, I'd be scared out of my wig," Dowdall said, regarding Zainal with interest. "Wouldn't they be a bit much for you by yourself?"

"You come with me?"

"Me?" Dowdall was surprised and then he grinned, rather nervously, back at the Catteni. "Man, if you're willing to go, I guess I would be, too."

"We have six airline pilots now plus two retired NASA mission specialists," Kris said brightly. "Maybe we could . . . Boy, I'd just give my eyeteeth to be in a first contact group."

"No eyeteeth left," Zainal told her with a big grin.

A rather odd silence followed that remark which made Kris blush though no one was actually looking at her.

"A lot of us here would, not just those NASA blokes," Worry said, breaking in. "But I think that's down the road awhile. You didn't happen to find out if they're going to dump more people on us, did you?" he asked wistfully.

Zainal shook his head. "Not the question to ask. Captain takes orders. Low captain. Not smart," and he held up one big hand, rocking it as he had seen Ninety do. "You Terrans make trouble, get put here. Simple." He grinned in what Kris took as approval. "Terrans make big trouble for Catteni." His grin broadened.

"And you *like* that?" Tesco asked, an edge to a voice that was louder than it need be.

"Yes, I do," and he jerked one thumb at his own chest, "other Catteni do not!" And he shook his head. "Good on you," he added, "to make big trouble. Makes Catteni think."

Worrell guffawed out loud. "Good on you, Zainal, too. Couldn't be cast off with a nicer bloke."

"So we can expect more?" Mitford said, not entirely pleased with that prospect.

"Believe so. But . . ." and Zainal held up his hand, "maybe report changes minds. Maybe . . ."

"But don't count on it, huh?"

"And the Cats would let us take the rap from the creatures who own this planet?" someone at the front of the garage asked in a sharp voice.

"Possession is nine-tenths of the law," Kris said emphatically, having caught the hostile tone in the murmured comments around the garage. "We're here and we're obviously going to stay."

"Catteni are not the highest. We take orders, too," Zainal surprised everyone by saying.

"From those Eosi you were telling me about?" Mitford demanded, scowling, his body tense.

"We work for the Eosi, who own most planets good for humans, Catteni, and others. You do not want to meet them," Zainal said, shaking his head.

"Oh, yes I would if they're the ones responsible for this whole schtick," Mitford said, his scowl black.

"That's what we heard back on Earth at any rate," Worrell said.

"Not that we saw any Eosi on Earth. Just their mercenaries." He grinned. "We'd made the planet a little too unsafe even for the occupying forces."

"And all this time I thought the Catteni were our enemies," Dowdall said, trying to digest the information. "While they're just hired hands."

"Now you know," Mitford said, scowling.

"How come we're only finding out about these Eosi now?" asked Dowdall, shooting an accusing glance in Zainal's direction. He wasn't a man who liked surprises.

Zainal grinned. "First I have no words. Second you do not ask. Do not debrief *me*."

The Doyles and Worrell laughed and Dowdall, now no longer quite as hostile toward Zainal, managed a weak grin.

"Eosi make good use of all peoples," Zainal said. "Ve–ry clever species."

"Then let's take all the heat off Zainal," Kris said. "Let's make the bad guys the Eosi and spread the word." A second thought struck her and she hurried on. "Do you speak Eosi, if they came to investigate this place again?"

Zainal considered that question. "If report goes high enough, I think they send but not Eosi. High Emassi. But I do speak with Eosi."

He didn't much like to, either, Kris decided from his expression.

"So do we wait until some high muckymuck reads a report sometime this century or what?" demanded Tesco.

Zainal looked briefly at Mitford, who nodded and took over the reply to Tesco.

"We do as we have been, what we can with what we have. If a mecho ship comes to look Botany over, we grab it if we can."

"And go where with it?" Tesco asked sardonically. "Not even NASA got beyond Jupiter."

"I take ship. I am space captain," Zainal said, "but will need crew."

"Well, that's a great idea but how'll you do it? If you Cats don't know about the species which farms this planet, how would you know how to pilot one of its spaceships?"

"If ship has living pilot, we make pilot take us back," Zainal replied, not at all confounded by the snide query. "If mecho, it will return to base: that is what it is made to do. We ride on it."

"And then what?" Tesco demanded surlily.

Zainal shrugged. "First, ship has to come here. Where there is much . . . Yankee in-gen-oo-it-tee."

Kris let out a laughing cheer, seconded by some of the other Americans present.

"Those of us from Oz aren't that bad in the make-do line either," Worry said staunchly.

"Which ship comes first, *then* we make plans. Right?" Zainal said and turned to Mitford, who stood up again.

"That's it, Zainal, right on the nose. So, listen up, folks. We gotta get the latest recruits settled in and let 'em know the score. Worry, you call a meeting at the Rock as soon as you get back and tell 'em what happened. All patrols are to make housing their priority so hunt out some more garages. We'll need to get ready for the next group. I'll get on the blower to Shutdown and BellaVista," and he glanced fondly down at the comunit attached to his belt. "We might even claim Botany as *ours!* And the hell with Eosi or whatever."

"Long live King Mitford . . ." Lenny Doyle said facetiously.

Mitford's expression turned sour instantly and he waved an angry finger at Lenny.

"Can that sort of crap, Doyle. I'm no king nor want to be. Anyone else wants to carry the can on this planet, they're welcome to it!" He glared around him and no one doubted the sincerity of his wish to step down, but no one offered to take over either.

"Ah, I was kidding, sarge," Lenny said contritely. "You're doing great."

"I'll second that," Worry spoke up, lifting his hand to raise a cheer. Which was unanimous.

"Well," and Mitford was only partially mollified, "I didn't ask for it, but someone had to organize you sorry collection of individuals."

"Which you have done admirably," Kris said. "No one else could have! So relax, sarge."

"Ahhhh," and he made a mock swipe at her and then his expression cleared. "Is there any of that beer left?"

The moment beer was mentioned, Kris noticed that the tension oozed out of the air. She was willing for a few pints herself until she saw Zainal edging toward the door. With the general movement and shifting in the room, she slipped after him.

It was full dark out, no moons up yet. She could see Zainal moving across the light shining out of the next barn door, left partly ajar.

"Zainal," she called softly, knowing he could hear an even softer whisper. She saw him pause, saw him stride out a few steps, and then she ran to catch up with him, catching him by the arm. "Don't you dare run out on me, buddy!"

He strode on, making her half run to keep up. "Do they still not understand? We Catteni are not our own masters . . . either!"

"No, I don't think they did understand. I certainly didn't."

"We do Eosi . . . dirty work. Explore for Eosi, fight for Eosi, police for Eosi, *kill* . . ." and that word came out violently, in great repugnance, "when killing needed. People hate Catteni. They better hate Eosi!"

The pent-up outrage within him had carried them well past the barns now and into the openness where the meat crates had been stacked.

"I didn't know that, Zainal. I think it will be easier for you when everyone else does."

"I do not ask easy," he said, angrily whirling toward her, a dark shape, his gray skin making him more invisible in the shadows.

"Yeah, but you don't need hate. And there are, I have to say, a couple of people . . ."

"Couple? More than couple. Couple only two, yes?"

"Yes, perhaps, but they are stupid people who don't like any one not just like they are. So let's make them hate the real villains, the Eosi. Catteni have to take orders, though it never occurred to me you guys were taking orders from anyone." She paused, trying to sense if she was saying the right things. "So what are these Eosi like that they can command tough, big, brave Catteni?"

"They . . ." and there was more to Zainal's pause than a search for an appropriate word. For the first time she sensed fear from him. "They are brains," and he tapped his forehead, "who know . . . everything."

"Brainy know-it-alls," she began, with laughing irreverence, and he caught her hands.

"Do not laugh at Eosi until you have met one."

She caught the tremor in his hands and heard it in his voice.

"You have?"

"Yes, as a child, I go with father to be . . . examined by Eosi." He inadvertently squeezed her hands so hard, it took a great effort not to cry out. The examination must have been a painful process if his response to the memory of it was this fierce.

"You passed?" she asked, more curious than flippant.

At that, Zainal straightened his shoulders and stood more erect. He probably hadn't even noticed that he had been unconsciously contracting in on himself.

"I am Emassi. We speak to Eosi." Then she could see his teeth, whiter than his skin, even in the shadows he stood in. And he was not smiling.

Kris thought of the Cabots and Lodges of the old Boston proverb. Well, it was one way of shaking off the aura that Zainal's fearfulness of the Eosi had put into the atmosphere around them. But that chain of command did explain why the transport captain didn't dare ignore Zainal.

"Maybe no one will come to Botany and we won't have to worry about Catteni or Eosi or even the mechos' makers," she said soothingly.

Zainal snorted. "No, they will come. The Eosi will send high Catteni." He paused a moment, evidently considering what he had just said.

"And the mechos will send their representative and they'll come together in a head-on collision and leave us to get on with our lives." She spread her hands wide and then banged both fists together, knuckles to knuckles. "Poof! They all disappear in a cloud of smoke and that's that!"

He had her in his strong hands then, and she was being lifted up a few inches off the ground so that they were eye to eye. He was smiling now.

"Is that how you wish it?"

"Sure, why not? The wheels of the universe turn in mysterious ways," she said, airily bending several aphorisms to her purpose. "Terrans will make so much trouble that the Eosi will have to give up on our planet. Or better yet, the Catteni will get a dose of the smarts and start collaborating with the irresistible Terran forces and go out against the Eosi domination and free the entire galaxy! You do come from this galaxy, don't you?"

"We do." He sounded cheerful again. Then his expression altered as he looked down at her. "You like this Catteni?" he asked. "This Emassi, this Eosi-speaker?"

She swallowed for she picked up on his sudden uncertainty.

"Yes," she said, trying not to sound as eager as she was. *Catteni wouldn't scare off easily, or would they?* One kiss, a few hair touslings.

"I go slowly, like Jay," and he grinned. "You are not like Patti Sue . . ."

"I should hope the hell I'm not."

"But you will have heard things about Catteni . . ."

"I know you, Catteni Emassis Zainal," and she jabbed a finger at his chest so hard she nearly bruised the tip. "You're the one I worry about."

"You worry about me?" and if the notion pleased him, it also amused.

"Why, they could have shot you where you stood yesterday morning. My heart was in my mouth the whole time."

"You worry about me?" He caught her by the arms, picking her up as if she weighed no more than . . . than a Deski, her legs dangling.

"Yes, you great lummock. And with me you don't need to go slow. I've been hoping you'd make some sort of a move on me for the . . ."

He kissed her then, and the mere touch of his lips to hers was the catalyst for a storm of emotions within her, emotions and sensations that coursed up her veins and bones so that she had to fling her arms about his neck to be sure she wasn't reeling.

But Catteni don't kiss, she thought irrationally along with some other more sensual observations. His lips were firm and he seemed to know exactly how to kiss with great effectiveness. Oh, lordee, but of course he'd seen Joe and Sarah exchanging affectionate kisses in the evenings. *Oh, lordee, but he'd learned fast.*

With one arm pinning her to him, his other hand made short and devastatingly accurate examinations of her body. But he'd said, back in the flitter—oh, ages ago—that he hadn't tried a Terran before. That was when she'd had to deck him. She wanted to deck *with* him.

"Catteni are good lovers," someone else had told her more recently.

Well, she was going to find out, like real soon. She wriggled a bit to get some space and shoved her hand into his coverall, to feel the sexily smooth skin she had admired during his illness.

He murmured against her lips and then began to move off, taking great eager strides wherever he was hauling her. Wherever could he be taking her? There was so little privacy to be had in any camp, and Kris wouldn't have thought they could find a secluded spot in a place currently jam-packed with bodies, but Zainal seemed to know exactly where he was going. Had he planned any of this? Then he altered his stride, grunted as he climbed up and over and into something metallic.

By the smell she knew it had to be one of the reconverted mechos she'd heard about and she was now being laid down in the load bed. On piles of blankets. Oh, they were in one of the reconstructed air-cushion vehicles that had collected the stores from the drop field.

She didn't think about much after that because Zainal's hands, gentle for all the size and strength of them, were peeling off her coverall and she was trying to do the same with his, only their hands were get entangling.

"Always you must help . . ." he said on a laughing note.

She threw her arms over her head. "So you do it."

Nor did he waste time. He had hauled off her boots and shucked her out of the coverall in seconds. Then she saw him, a gray blur above her, as his hands pushed back her hair and his fingers outlined her face, in such a gentle, tender, loverly fashion that her senses were overwhelmed. Who'd've thought a Catteni could behave like this?

She felt him lean into her, carefully, as if afraid to crush her with his mass. One other fact about Cattenis sprang to mind: they were big! She could feel that he was, too. And she had a pang of fright.

"I do not hurt you," and his voice was no more than a hoarse whisper. "Not you, Kris. Do you believe? I go slow, slow, slow . . ." and she could feel the pressure that was slow . . . oh, much too slow. She squirmed, trying to force herself down and him in.

She heard his gasp but he would not accede to her whispers but kept up the slow penetration until she was moaning for completion.

Never in her albeit brief experience at this sort of dalliance had she been so eager to accept all a man could give her. Not even with Brace Tennemann, and she'd thought he was the best-looking man on the football team in her sophomore year.

"You go too slow, Zainal," she cried, again trying to pull him as close as his firmly propped arms would let her, kissing whatever part of him was in reach, sensuously caressing the marvelous skin of his body.

"Slow makes it better," he said, his tone rippling with laughter, possibly with delight at her urgency. "Slow is better for me, too."

And slowly he continued his seduction of her willing self, until she was so strung out with the incredible sensations he was producing she wondered how she could survive the climax. Then it came over her, and him at the same instant, for they cried aloud in the same instant: cries of joy and immeasurable elation.

Just when she felt she could stand no more of the exquisite relief, it began to ease, and she was able to feel the shudders still rippling through him. They were both gasping for breath and he fell to one side of her, limp with such a massive release.

"You go that slow the next time, Zainal, and I'll kill you," she murmured.

"Slow is better for you and very, very good for me," he said, almost smugly but his hand, running softly down her body, expressed his tender concern for her.

"This is going to be an equal opportunity partnership, buddy," she said. "I get to call the pace now and then."

"Oh, do you?" To her total astonishment, he moved to cover her again.

"My god!" Where did he find the energy so quickly?

He chuckled in her ear. "Like the thorns of Barevi, it doesn't take a Catteni long to rearm."

"Oh, my god!"

"No, oh boy oh boy oh boy?" he asked teasingly.

"No, man oh man oh man!" She paused, taking a deep gulp of breath. "I think we . . . do . . . it your way again. Please!"

Emassi Zainal was only too happy to oblige.

———

SOMETIME, DURING THE NIGHT, ZAINAL MOVED HER BACK TO their assigned sleeping places, clothes and all. She grinned when she woke up and found herself discreetly clothed, her boots at the side of the straw mound she was occupying. Zainal was, it was true, on the other side of her, but beyond him were Joe and Sarah, much as they had bedded down all together during the patrol. It was very considerate of him to think of her reputation: if, indeed, he had given it a moment's thought in the midst of last night's ardor. She was, when she stretched, quite sore, despite his go-slow policy, and understood precisely why most human females would have felt terribly violated by their treatment in Catteni hands. *But it does indeed depend on the man!* Catteni or human!

Someone was moving outside in the aisle, rattling each barn door in turn to rouse the residents. Another Botanical day was starting.

This one was filled with sending people on to BellaVista, Shutdown, or the Rock. The word was that Camp Narrow would concentrate its efforts on recycling the mechos so those with mechanical skills or technical training would be based there. Now that they had the two vehicles, they could collect what they needed from the other garages, including "body" parts to make more useful vehicles. More comunits were being assembled and more mobile carriers made out of existing chassis.

"Not speedy, but they sure do maneuver the obstacles," Lenny told her at noontime. "Some of these lads are really clever," he went on enthusiastically. "They figured out how to short-circuit, or whatever it is you do with programming chits . . ."

"Chips."

"Chips, then, how to keep the versatility but give control to the driver. Clev . . . er!"

"Indeed."

"They don't have much speed, which the lads are still trying to improve."

"Personally, I'd rather not ride over this landscape at speed," Kris said.

Lenny just grinned. "You've never done it."

Kris went back to debriefing, but was called over to help Mitford and his aides figure out where best to place the remaining recruits.

"How long does it take a person to become the 'indigenous personnel'?" she asked Mitford at one point. She was finding it necessary to shift position a lot to ease her soreness. But it was worth it. Zainal smiled a lot today as he went from one group of aliens to another.

"Huh? Oh," and Mitford grinned, leaning back to stretch his arms and ease his shoulder muscles. "Here, let's just say until they have to help a new batch in-flow. Say, tell me about this seaside building your patrol found?"

"There's not much to tell. It was closed up tight even though Zainal tried every which way to get inside. Maybe the fish aren't running."

"I do like seafood. Like clam chowder, too," and Mitford for once sounded a little wistful. Kris was rather pleased that she was audience to that mood.

"With one of those air cushions, we could start at dawn and be back by nightfall with a sack of clams," Kris suggested.

"You could at that."

If Dowdall hadn't interrupted just then, Kris was sure they might have been given a go-ahead on such a luxury run. But the vehicles were more urgently needed for other tasks.

On the third day, she, Zainal, Joe, and Sarah escorted an air-cushion car, carrying some of the less able recruits on their way to BellaVista via the Rock. Worry greeted Zainal and the others effusively from his "office."

"Your patrol needs to hunt for us," he told them, "and you're to break in some of a mixed bag of the new blokes and sheilas. The Rock's going to be Supply Depot for meats and green groceries."

"Mixed bag?" Kris asked.

"Too right, since you've got Zainal and he can speak Deski, Rugarian, and Turs."

"Oh, that kind of mixed bag," Kris said. If they had Turs to train, Zainal was the right teacher.

"We also need you on short day trips," Worry said more confidentially to Kris. "In case of . . . you know what?" And he tilted his chin skyward.

"Oh, in case we get surveyed again," Kris said, looking at Zainal, who now sported a comunit.

Mitford expected to be back in the Rock the next day but he'd had a private word with Kris.

"Keep pretty close to Zainal, will you, Kris?"

"Why?" she'd asked, glaring at Mitford.

"I don't want to lose our most valuable alien asset."

"You won't lose him."

"Not by his choice, I don't think," and Mitford gave Kris a searching look which she returned without a blush. He nodded, as if he knew more than he would commit to words. "He's Emassi and can deal with Eosi . . . I guess they permit Emassi Catteni to speak to them. We might need him badly to deal, for us, with these Eosi. That is, if one of them ever does see a report on this planet."

"Zainal is sure they'll send some sort of Emassi, higher in rank than he is. Eventually," and then Kris realized she'd reassured the Sergeant on the very point that concerned him.

"There's a lot more going on, on Earth, on Barevi and Catten, than any of us knew," he went on.

"That's for damn sure," Kris said.

"Just so's you know I'm counting on you, Bjornsen."

She gave the Sergeant a level look, noticing the new lines around his eyes, the muddy look in the pupils from the many problems he was dealing with.

"You can count on me, sergeant," she said, and this time she did give him a formal salute.

He grinned as he returned it.

THEY WERE STILL BUNKED IN THE MITCHELSTOWN CAVE AND the possessions they had left behind were untouched. Fresh coveralls and pairs of boots had been added to each shelf. Seeing these, Kris and Sarah voted on a dip in the lake so they could wash themselves and their coveralls since they now had fresh ones to wear. Not that the coveralls showed any of the hard usage they'd been given over the past five weeks.

A youngster, not one of the rookies, caught them before they left their quarters.

"Kris Bjornsen?" he asked, looking from Kris to Sarah.

"Yes," Kris said.

"Dr. Dane wants you to come speak to him. When you can. It's not urgent, he said."

"Tell him we got his message and will see him shortly. And what's your name?"

"I'm Buzz," and the boy grinned to show two missing front teeth, "because I buzz about the place like a hornet. Mom says I'm too noisy to be a bee and there aren't bees on Botany anyway. My real name's Parker but I don't like it at all."

"Buzz is a grand name for an active boy like you," Kris said and smiled back at him. "See you around."

"You will," he answered cheerfully over one shoulder, already "buzzing" off.

LEON WANTED TO REPORT ON SOME OF THE FINDINGS NOW HE had test kits. The information would be invaluable to any hunting parties since Leon and his assistants had been able to identify other nutritionally rich plants, berries, and nuts.

"We've put some of the younger members of the Rock out looking for these," and he tapped the nutlike shells. "I've seen them in quantities around here. And these berries are rich in C and A." He pointed to some of the green globes that Joe had thought might be digestible. "We're trying to dry them for storage. I know you hunter types would prefer to go for the meat but these can be just as important to a properly balanced diet."

"Can we see Coo?" asked Kris.

"If you can catch him," Leon said dryly. "That stuff was magical on all the Deskis. I'm keeping a real close watch on Murn, the female. Even Pess is back on duty. Thanks, Zainal." And Leon gave him a comradely clap on the arm. "You saved their lives, you know."

Zainal merely flicked his eyebrows up but Kris had a sense that he was not as diffident as he appeared. Leon was obviously of the same mind.

The Rock was full again. That seemed as it should be to Kris. Further, many more of the "indigenous" personnel waved or smiled at Zainal when they met him.

They hunted the next day, returning home laden with rocksquats and another loo-cow since Bart and Pete in the Cheddar wanted to roast one whole to show the rookies that it could be done and the meat was tasty.

They hunted the next two days, in different directions, and spent part of the day picking the nuts and stripping the branches of every berry shrub they located.

"We'd've had more," Sarah said with a jaundiced glare at Joe Marley, "if more had actually landed up in the sack!"

Joe merely raised his eyes in innocent surprise. Oskar guffawed aloud as he handed over a heavier sack than Joe had.

They did not hunt the next day, although that was the plan. Just past third moonrise a sentry excitedly stamped into Mitchelstown cave and called out Zainal's name.

"Yes?"

"You gotta come. Something's about to land. Not as big as the others but big enough," and with that, the man ran out.

"Wake Worrell," Zainal called after him.

"That's where I'm going," the man cried over his shoulder and was told to keep his bloody voice down as he proceeded down the corridor to Worry's quarters.

"All come," Zainal said, pushing his large feet into his boots.

The sentry's arrival had awakened everyone, but they hadn't moved to dress. Now they did. In a hurry. But when Joe and Oskar reached for their spears, Zainal stopped them.

"No use against Catteni hand weapons and shows bad faith," he said.

"Who do you think it is, Zainal?" Joe asked before Kris could.

"Catten. And early even for them."

It was two-moon time, so the night was bright with them, and clear. When they went up to the height with Worrell in tow, they could see the approach of the ship, its running lights twinkling.

"Small, fast ship," Zainal said. "It is heading for that field, I think," and he pointed to what was the nearest expanse, a twenty-minute hike from the Rock.

"They know where we are?" Worry sounded upset.

"Life-form readings," Zainal said succinctly. "They know where transport landed. The Rock shows many people."

"Not dumb. Well, *these* Catteni at least," Worry said and started down from the heights. "No offense intended, Zainal."

"None taken," was the easy answer.

"Maybe we should let them wait long enough to discover the scavengers?" Joe suggested slyly.

Zainal only grunted but Kris thought the notion held a certain charm for him as well. So it wasn't surprising when Zainal neatly slingshot a rocksquat fast asleep on a boulder and hauled it along with them as they traversed the rocky hillside.

The craft had landed long before they reached it. A open portal spilled light onto the stubble of the field. Light didn't attract scavengers: it repelled them. Just outside the illuminated area, Zainal casually dropped the rocksquat.

"How long does it usually take?" Joe muttered.

"Longer near light," Zainal said and continued on his way to the ship.

It was a sleek one, Kris saw, and looked like it was meant for speed and maneuverability with its swept-back wings and tapered nose. But it was a large affair, not as big as the *Challenger* had been nor the *Enterprise,* but a fair size—three, four times the height of Zainal and about as long as a Boeing 727 but much wider.

Zainal halted right in front of the door and cracked out sharp Catteni words.

Instantly three Catteni filled the doorway, one of them striding down the ramp toward Zainal. Watching his face, Kris saw his eyes widen for an instant, in surprise, she thought, and his right hand, which she could see, briefly clenched into a fist. Then he seemed to make an effort to relax completely as he listened to what was said.

"My report cause trouble," he said to the others in a brief aside before spitting out more Catteni phrases.

Kris decided one Catteni was an officer, and of high rank, to judge by the excellent fit of his tunic and the complexity of insignia on his collar and cuff. Zainal didn't seem in awe of him, or even respectful, unless Cattenis always snapped at each other: sort of like the English, who are scrupulously polite to people they do not like and continuously insult their intimate friends. The Catteni language sounded as if it was composed of growls, grunts, gutturals and fricatives, without a single mellowing vowel. However, it might only *sound* vicious. You'd think the Chinese were cursing each other until they smiled and bowed so politely.

"There is other trouble," Zainal said after a spate of raw staccato noise. "With Terrans and with Eosi." Now he grinned malevolently . . . at least his mouth looked malevolent in profile.

"And . . ." Worry prompted.

"I am drop. I stay drop. He say it is duty to come. I say I drop, I stay. His loss, your gain." Then he turned his grin on Worry, and Kris thought his look was as mischievous as if he was holding some kind of a royal flush in his hand in a high-stakes poker game.

"Ughh," Sarah said suddenly, moving closer to Joe.

Zainal looked over his shoulder and so did Kris, so they both saw the first tentacular strands of a scavenger feeling its way out of the ground to encircle the dead rocksquat. Zainal said something and stepped aside for the captain to see. Although the tentacles seemed to avoid the lighted area of the body, they gleamed slimily in the shadows. Strips of the squat animal noticeably disappeared at an ever increasing rate as the scavenger decided its victim was tasty.

Then Zainal held out his comunit, pointing to various elements of it, patently displaying irrefutable evidence of alien artifacts that had been recycled. That elicited a surprised exclamation from the captain and the other two, who bent closer to see the device. For one moment, Kris was afraid Zainal would let them have it.

That was when Kris thought Zainal began his own demands, for the captain shook his head vehemently at first but, as Zainal became insistent, he seemed to relent and ask questions of his own to which Zainal replied with a quick shake of his head or an affirmative nod. Then the captain said something to one of the others who went off, down the blue-white-lit companionway to the bow of the ship.

The captain continued his interrogation. Some of his questions Zainal answered. Others he shrugged off, impatiently or irritably or with an amused, superior expression.

The messenger returned with a handful of printouts, some crumbled. The captain barked at him and, with a startled and penitent look, the man hastily reassembled them in good order before passing them over to the captain, who glanced down at the first sheet before he gave all to Zainal. Zainal immediately passed them to Worrell.

"Maps of this world from space," Zainal murmured. "Show mountains, metal deposits, other data. He does not want to give." Kris could see that only the sternest self-control kept Worrell from peering avidly at the material.

Zainal now stepped back from the open portal but the captain followed him a step or two, managing sharp and penetrating glances at the "indigenous personnel," as if determined to store their faces for future reference. Kris did not like that scrutiny though it gave her a chance to identify this Catteni as another Emassi like Zainal with his fine, almost patrician features. With his gaze still on Kris, the captain asked a short question. Zainal answered with a sort of supercilious expression on his face. Shock registered on the other man's face and he gave Kris a second startled look.

"I tell them you are very smart Terrans, all of you, and I am proud to be in your patrol, Kris."

"Thanks a peach skin, Zainal." If this fellow ever landed on Botany and started looking around for her, she'd make herself very scarce. He must blame *her* for Zainal's decision not to "take up his duty."

Then his look turned knowing and sly. He said two short words.

So fast that his movements blurred, Zainal shot out a fist and decked him, ignoring the weapons which the other two immediately aimed at him. He stood back, arms crossed on his chest—old Stoneface—while the captain, waving aside the guards, got to his feet, rubbing his jaw.

"Nice to know he gets a bit of his own back," Worry murmured to Kris. "What'd the bloke say?"

"How would I know?" Kris muttered out of the side of her mouth, but, from the look on the captain's face, she also decided to get into the act. Zainal had given her the clue—*he* was in *her* patrol. She gave Zainal a stern look as if he shouldn't have retaliated. "Now wasn't that a half-ass thing to do when all we have to defend ourselves with is slingshots?" she said to Zainal in as imperious a tone as she could muster, as if telling him off. Which she was since the drawn weapons had scared her badly. She'd seen them in action and the charge they propelled jerked every nerve in a body unless you were lucky enough to be knocked out first.

"Worth it," Zainal said but he made a subservient nod of his head at her and, stepping back slightly behind her, crossed his arms again.

The captain asked one more question, his tone almost plaintive as he rubbed his jaw.

Zainal gave a "that's impossible" sort of hitch of his shoulder.

The captain said something else, more briskly now, waving at his two subordinates, who moved off into the body of the ship. With a very respectful salute to Zainal, and a crisp but equally respectful bow to her, the captain stepped back into the ship and the portal slid shut, putting them in a darkness lit only by the one remaining moon in the sky.

"Hey, couldn't they leave the lights on until we got safely off this field?" Sarah cried.

"Stamp as you go," Zainal said, turning and trotting away from the ship, coming down hard every third step.

"You'll tell us what we couldn't understand?" Worry asked, trying to pace Zainal but his shorter legs were unequal to it.

"I will."

They were safely away from the ship when it raised vertically, as the transport had done, and then gathered speed in an ascent angle.

"VTOL! Wow!" Joe said. "Do all your ships have that capacity, Zainal?" He pantomimed the action.

"The ones that land, yes. Biggest, stay above," Zainal replied and continued on.

Stamping, even every third or fourth step, jarred her tired body, but every time Kris felt herself slacking off, she thought of the slimy look to the scavengers' tentacles or feelers and that reinforced her step. They reached stony footing and, as one, leaned against the safety of the nearest rock.

"That last bit he said, before you socked him," Kris asked firmly.

"Socked him?" Zainal asked.

He wasn't temporizing, because she realized "hitting" and its synonyms might not yet have come up in conversation. She demonstrated.

"In Catten women lead only other women," Zainal said. "But special . . . ah, rank of women do command even Emassi."

"Why did you hit him?"

Zainal's lips curled in a snarl before he answered. "He put a bad name on you. A wrong name."

"Thanks, but didn't you take a chance? They might have shot us because you hit their leader. That sort of thing got you in trouble before, you know."

Zainal grinned, pressing his thumb against his chest. "The trouble is mine. I do not 'sock' to kill so the others do not fire. They only . . . how do you say . . ." and he crouched, reacting with his hand standing for the weapon.

"Reflex action?" Joe suggested.

"Hmmm," Zainal said although he had not quite understood the term.

"Let's leave the subject of Kris' honor aside," Worry said. "Why did you want these?" He was unfolding the sheets. "Can't even see what they show in the dark."

"Maps of this planet from space to tell us where we are. Where to go. Where . . ." and now he paused, frowning, unable to find words to use, "where biggest garage is."

"Really? Had your blokes found it?"

He shook his head. "Show where metal is. A very . . . oh, funny? No, not funny." He struggled, turning to Kris to help him out.

"An anomaly?"

"How in hell would he understand 'anomaly'?" Worry asked.

"Oh, hush, I'll explain it. An anomaly is something that should not be where it is. A deviation from the normal. A queer difference."

"Ah, yes." Zainal became quite agitated. "That is it. More metal than good to be there. Many places. Lots of metal. Not right metal. Anomaly . . . hmmm," and he almost tasted the word. "Something that is different."

"They didn't *want* to give you these maps?" Sarah asked, also trying to discern details from the printout.

"No."

"They wanted you to go with them, didn't they?" Kris asked pointedly.

"Yes, they said all was okay," and his grin was broad with malice, "to come home. More than one day. Catteni drop me here. I stay here. They cannot make one rule for me, because I am useful to them, and one for other Catteni."

"Man's got a sense of honor, so he has," Joe said in mild surprise.

"Why not?" Kris snapped back.

"Why not indeed," Joe said in a placatory fashion.

"Why didn't you go when you could? What was the duty they want you for?"

"Emassi duty," and Zainal's voice turned inflexible. "Too late for that duty now. Once I wanted that duty. Not now. Much has happened. They drop me. I stay drop."

"Dropped," Kris said automatically.

"Dropped. Funny language, English."

"You're not the first to think so."

"Nor will I be last," and he grinned in the night at her.

"So," Worry said, "they wanted you for a duty you no longer feel you need do?"

"Right. No one believes what I told transport men about Mecho Makers."

"So that's why you showed him the comunit," Sarah carried on, "because he knows what supplies came with us and that certainly wasn't included."

"Right," Zainal said.

"So you showed him and now they will have to believe you," Sarah went on, "but why wouldn't they believe you?"

"I dropped," and he emphasized the final *d* of the past tense.

"So now what?" Kris asked, worried.

"We wait. We see."

"And if the Eosi come before the Mecho Makers?"

"Not Eosi but someone higher than . . ." Zainal jerked his thumb upward indicating the late captain. "We wait. We see."

"I don't like this," Worry said. Then the comunit he wore at his belt bleeped, a curious intrusion in the night. "Worrell here . . . Oh, Mitford. Yes, Zainal did make contact with the spacecraft. Here," and Worry handed the unit to Zainal. "He shoulda called on yours."

The conversation was one-sided but since everyone listening knew what had happened from Zainal's point of view, some of his responses were amusing. Possibly not on Mitford's end, but in the middle of a cold night—and Kris was beginning to feel the chill in the air—the responses held a humorous element. Finally Zainal gave a series of "okays" in response to Mitford's instructions, depressed the off button, and passed the device back to Worry.

"He knows. We know. We say nothing," Zainal informed them.

"Say nothing?" Worry exclaimed. "The whole camp got wakened by that damned sentry rousing you and then me. They'll *demand* to know."

Zainal shrugged and struck off up the next tier of rock.

"False alarm, that's what we'll tell them. It was a false alarm. Ship just flew over," Worry went on.

"Wrong time of night to overfly anything," Joe suggested, climbing behind Worry. "Moons went down early."

"Nonsense," Kris said firmly as she followed Joe, Worry, and Zainal. "We tell the truth, or how will they trust us?"

"Good point," Sarah said, starting up. "We want to build trust, not destroy it."

"Say nothing," Zainal called down to them. "Smile and say nothing. Sarge will tell them what they need to know."

"He's got a point there," Worry said.

"One thing puzzles me," Joe said, spacing out words as he climbed, "why your survey didn't tumble to the fact that this world—well, this continent at least—is all carved up into neat fields? Surely they must have seen the anomaly in that . . . a clear indication this planet was, had been, cultivated?"

Zainal answered. "Loo-cows and rocksquats not smart so planet is not occupied! They do not 'see' the machinery." He added a plainly derogatory phrase in the harsh Catteni.

Then they all had to save their breath for climbing. When they reached the Rock, only the sentries were awake, as they should be, and Worry brushed off their questions with a "Nothing to worry about. Tell you in the morning, I'm bushed."

Chapter Thirteen

MITFORD ARRIVED THE NEXT MORNING IN A refitted tractor which had been altered to carry six passengers. Mitford had with him the two NASA Mission Specialists, both of whom, he said, had had training in discerning planetary features from space. Kris, Zainal, and the others had breakfasted, well prepared for a Mitford debriefing. The MSS —a man and a woman with really nothing to distinguish them from anyone else except that they had been in space—took charge of the maps at one end of Mitford's desk which Worry had hastily surrendered to the Sergeant.

"Why'n't you take off with 'em?" was Mitford's first sharp question to Zainal.

He smiled. "I like it here better." Zainal didn't look at Kris but Mitford did and she mildly returned his stare in a "none of your business" attitude. "I dropped," and again he made much of the past tense, emphasizing the *t* sound. "I stay."

She really didn't think it was only her presence that had caused Zainal to stay: he had made it clear to the ship captain that he felt bound by some obscure point of honor, though he might have used that as an excuse, she thought. Still and all, they must have really wanted him back to send a special fast courier to collect him. Hadn't they known where Emassi Zainal had been taken, considering the circumstances of his capture *before* the grace period had expired? The captain had registered surprise, not a pleasant one, either, on seeing Zainal at his portal. Possibly the captain hadn't known who he was going to meet on this planet.

She found it hard to believe that Zainal liked her so much he couldn't live without her. Kris gave her head a little shake of denial but she couldn't help grinning slightly. Catteni and human were biologically sterile, even if they could enjoy sexual relations and "enjoy" was a pale word to apply to that tempestuous event. She was sort of hoping he'd ask for more: not that they'd had time for any further such . . . enjoyments. She didn't consider herself remarkably sexy—well, until Zainal had aroused her. Even without the sexual rapport, she liked Zainal. He was a complex man. *Man oh man, wasn't he just!* And he had conducted himself with tact and a respect for others during a very difficult few weeks. Back on Barevi, having a Catteni "interested" in you was not what you wanted. Zainal was, in all respects, different.

She had to wrench her thoughts back. The NASA pair were excited about some aspect of the symbols Zainal was translating from the map legend. Craning her head, she could see that not only were there overviews of each hemisphere of the planet but close-ups—if you wanted to call pictures of entire continents close-ups—showing contours, mountains, valleys. There were even seascapes of the ocean floors and their mounts and abysses. Complete! Then she gave full attention to what was being said.

"The position is perfect for a command post, sarge," the man— Bert Put—was saying, tapping an elevation point, almost dead center of this, the main continent. "Not easy to get to but that's only a sensible precaution and here," he pointed a blunt finger again, "is another concentration that matches the same symbol of the abattoir which we've already discovered. Possibly a garage, situated below the main facility. Every thing's on remote, so it doesn't matter how far above the garage the command point is."

"That location's not all that far . . ." Mitford said, pulling at his lower lip in a pensive fashion. "Hmmm." He walked his fingers the distance. "Well, a good week's march."

"Not now we have that vehicle," Worry said eagerly.

"We've only got the one big one in operation . . ." Mitford began, "but hell's bells, it'll get a patrol there and back faster 'n' safer than they could trot it. Okay, Zainal, Kris, Bert, Joe as medic, Sarah as hunter, and you'll need a good mechanic." Mitford winced. "He's a pain in the butt, I know, folks, but the best mechanic we've got is Dick Aarens."

"Aw, sarge," Kris began in protest.

"Now," and Mitford held up a placatory hand and stared her down, "he's not going to trouble you with Zainal along."

"He hates aliens' guts," Kris complained.

"He may, but he's proved that he can read the Mecho Makers' schematics and alter them as easily as you'd play with a Lego set. This is not an outing. This is a patrol! You gotta pass by Camp Narrow on your way so I'll go with you and give Aarens the business. You," and Mitford turned to Zainal, including Joe and Sarah in the same glance, "discipline as and when he needs it. As hard as need be. The trip may even do him good."

"We'll see that it does," Kris promised caustically, but she wasn't at all pleased at Aarens' inclusion in what should have been a great jaunt with good people she trusted. Even if she didn't know Bert Put well, she liked his frank, open face and enthusiasm and the avid way he had examined the alien charts, like a boy with a gizmo he had never expected to own.

Careful inspection of the terrain to be crossed suggested this would take three, possibly four days, at the speed the modified tractor could make.

"We run faster," Zainal said with a little grunt.

"Not over some of the ground, m'friend," Mitford said, pointing out several areas that appeared to be significant heights, also wide and rivers. "That thing hops barriers like a gazelle, saves you having to take the long way around. We tested its stability on every sort of terrain and it's better 'n' a tank. Can't tip because it just lifts on its air cushions. More comfortable than the tractors I remember as a kid."

"Sarge, you were never a kid!" Kris said teasingly.

"I begin to think you're right, Bjornsen," and he slipped the map over to Dowdall. "Dow'll make you a copy to take along. The originals aren't going out of my possession. Now, figure out the supplies you'll need and you're to take along some furs. You'll be at altitude and it's bound to be colder this time of year."

ZAINAL LOOKED EVEN LARGER IN THE FUR VEST THAT HAD been made for him. But he wore it with an air that made it seem regal ermine.

"Biggest damn rocksquat I ever saw," Sarah said, grinning from ear to ear.

"I am funny?" Zainal asked in mock indignation. He flexed his shoulders. "It fit well. Warm." He slid out of it and, folding it up with care, tied the bundle with a thong.

There were fur rugs as well as vests for each member of the expedition, including Dick Aarens. Kris was still struggling to accept the necessity of him joining the patrol.

"I know he's a horse's ass, Kris, but he helped put this vehicle together and he knows how to get the most out of it. You *will* need him on the team."

"I *will* not like it, sarge, and if he so much as . . ."

"Clobber him. Or better still, let Zainal do it. Only not too hard. You may need him undamaged." Mitford gripped her arm in a firm but friendly emphasis to his orders.

BERT PUT'S PRESENCE HELPED A GREAT DEAL, EVEN WHEN ALL he had to look at was the relevant section of map that Dowdall had competently produced. They let Mitford off at Camp Narrow, reluctantly collected a cockily grinning Dick Aarens, who was still festooned with his belt of tools and vest of pockets which bulged with unidentifiable lumps.

"Ready when you are," he said jauntily, climbing up to the seat Mitford had vacated between Joe Marley and Sarah McDouall.

"Just don't let it go to your head, buddy," Kris said, glaring at him because he was deliberately playing kneesies with her.

"Only trying to be friendly," Aarens said in an almost plaintive whine. "Maybe I should drive. I know this baby inside out."

"I drive," Zainal said and that was that. Mitford had tested his skill on the way to Narrow and this wasn't the first ground vehicle Zainal had ever driven.

Zainal turned the control handle and the Hopper moved forward. It had been so named on the trip down since it invariably "hopped" any terrain that exceeded its preprogrammed optimum angle. They had all learned to hang on to something to be secure against unexpected maneuvers. Generally the air-cushioned vehicle proceeded smoothly.

Aarens' attempts to chat up Sarah failed when she made it obvious —by linking one arm through Joe's—that she was uninterested. Aarens sulked until Bert Put's look of disbelief at such childish behavior shamed him into neutrality.

The Hopper might be faster than the average tank, but it was no McLaren on a Grand Prix circuit. It also "flew" neatly over a wide, meandering river and three narrower ravines they encountered the first day. When they camped for the night on a rock ledge, above a small cataract and pool, Zainal and Bert figured they had covered nearly seventy miles.

Rocksquats and some tasty little fish taken from the stream provided supper. After reporting in to Mitford, Zainal assigned watches and gave Aarens the dog watch. When Kris woke the next morning, she found Aarens asleep.

"What is there to watch for?" Aarens demanded in outrage when Zainal roughly shook him awake. "Hey, take it easy. Scavengers can't attack on rock and no one's even seen fliers out at night."

"There're renegades still unaccounted for," Kris said, "and you know damned good and well they'd want this Hopper."

"We haven't seen *any*one," he protested.

"Do you think they'd be stupid enough to expose themselves until they were ready to attack?" Kris went on, livid with rage at his stupid arrogance, clutching her hands at her sides because she was afraid she'd deck Aarens. Even as she thought of the joy she'd have in seeing him prostrate on the hard rock underfoot, she realized the unwisdom of such retaliation. They might indeed need Aarens if the machine failed.

"But no one did attack us," he replied in sullen self-defense.

That night he was made to gather firewood and rocksquat dung as punishment for dereliction. Nervously, Kris woke several times that night during Aarens' watch, to be sure he remained awake. Evidently Zainal did the same thing. The time they woke together, Zainal pulled her close to him and affectionately nuzzled her neck but that, unfortunately Kris thought, was as amorous as he got. She was glad of that much, though she ached for more.

It took them six days to make the designated point, and the garage they found was visible for miles above the barren wasteland that spread out before it.

"Strange place for a garage," Joe Marley said, trying to gauge the height of the doors.

"The command post is directly above this, isn't it?" Kris said, peering over Bert's shoulder to check the map.

"It would appear to be . . . up there," Bert replied, pointing and then sighing at the sheer façade of the cliff it topped. Only the solar panels, too regular in shape to be a natural formation, marked its location. "I wonder if we can get the Hopper up there from another approach . . ." and he looked eastward along the range.

"No, we have rope," and Zainal hefted the coil from the storage shelf of the Hopper.

"And pitons," Joe said gratefully, having watched Jay Greene include those recently manufactured items in their supplies.

"If you'll bring the Hopper alongside, I'll just start dismantling those solar panels," Aarens said, speaking for the first time that day. "I wouldn't want anything called down on you guys while you're climbing that cliff," he added with a sneer.

"Too right," Joe Marley said. "I'll help you. We don't all need to climb."

Zainal peered at the sun, already well down the sky.

"Not today. Tomorrow. Today we all help remove panels. Get inside, too." But he did not appear too sanguine about that possibility as he inspected the huge gray-metaled doors. "No crack."

When they reported in to Mitford, he was glad to hear they'd reached their destination but warned them to go slow if this appeared to be a totally different sort of installation. Since it might well be the control point for an entire planet, the Mech Makers might well have equipped it with safeguards.

Aarens took down the solar panels. "That's what I'm here for, isn't it?" he demanded nastily. "What I'm good at. You guys'll take forever and you . . ." and his hostile gaze settled accusingly on Zainal's heavy fingers, ". . . might damage the panels. Some were damaged beyond use, you know. You guys don't respect technology like you should."

Knowing how the patrol had had to struggle with the solar panels, Kris reluctantly had to admit that Aarens did it faster, and probably better than any one else could. The fact did not endear Aarens to anyone and he had to stand watch that night, too, though he complained about the duty.

"I have big hands," Zainal said, raising one big fist and examining it as if he'd never seen it before. He smiled and turned toward Aarens, his intent very clear. "Big hand, big damage."

"You wouldn't dare," and Aarens moved around the fire near Sarah, who promptly resettled herself, leaving him all alone again. "You need me as your mechanic. To tell you what's up there."

"Perhaps," Zainal said, "but I have pilot spaceship many years now. I know a thing or two about circuits and more about spaceships."

Aarens retreated into dour silence again, glaring across the campfire at them.

"Wake me for the dog watch," Joe said in a low voice to Zainal. "I don't trust him."

"Where he go?" Zainal asked, with a shrug.

"Not so much where would he go, but what would he do? Like disable the Hopper for spite or slip some of those poisonous leaves into our morning tea? Hell, I wouldn't trust him not to usher renegades in and laugh while they slit our throats."

Aarens said nothing the next morning when he was awakened at dawn with the others. But he had a smug sort of twist to his features as if he'd won a round by not having to stand a watch as the others did. Which he had, Kris thought, disgruntled.

Try as they could, and Aarens was doing his level best to solve the problem, they could not find out how the door opened, and there was only the one.

So, having spent a fruitless morning, Zainal decided to use the afternoon daylight to make the climb.

"Whyn't we start tomorrow, early, first thing?" Aarens demanded in a suddenly nervous twitch. "Get some rest today. Hunt."

"No, we climb," and Zainal slung one coil of rope to his shoulders, "I, Kris, Bert. Aarens, you go hunt greens by river. Joe, Sarah, watch. Kris, give Joe your comunit." When she had, Zainal approached the cliff beside the garage where there were some irregularities providing foot and hand-holds. At least in the first fifty or so feet.

It wasn't as hard a climb as it seemed looking up at it. Indeed, the rock face was most obliging even though it had an outward bulge that was a trifle awkward to maneuver. Then they came to the area of squared-off, dressed stone which must be the control post. A farther twenty feet, easily scaled, got them to the array of solar panels crowning the cliff top. But, once again, no discernible way into the facility they knew must be contained behind the rock. That is, until Kris, exasperated with the whole thing, climbed well above the panels and discovered the vents.

"Well, they had to have venting somewhere, didn't they?" she said when she had called Bert and Zainal to inspect her find. Then she saw both men regarding her, and she looked back at the vents and realized she was the slenderest one among them. "I knew we should have brought Lenny."

It took a good two hours to pry the grill off the vent with the use of the heaviest chisel of the ones Zainal "borrowed" from a protesting Aarens, who had showered imprecations on them if they nicked any of the blades. When Zainal had chipped enough space for his fingers, he gave one mighty pull and wrenched the vent cover off.

They slung a rope under Kris' arms and, not without scratching herself, she squeezed into the opening and was let down. A long way down into musty darkness.

Then, as soon as she touched the ground with her feet, lights came up: an orangey glow rather than the blue-white of the lighting the Catteni used. She could see the panels that lined the "front" of the facility and then the long boxy rectangles that ranged along the back. There was nothing that resembled seating, nothing that resembled anything she was familiar with, bar the sloping control panels with their regular indentations. There were six rectangles of an opaque material which looked like screens, placed high up on the walls, and one larger like a blank picture window in front.

"I think Bert better get down here or you, Zainal," she said. "I haven't a clue what to do next."

Bert's head appeared in the vent aperture. "Tell me what you have in front of you, Kris. Maybe I can talk you through it."

"Ha!" She ran her fingers lightly over the left-hand group of indentations and, in the next instant, everything lit up. "Oh, lord, I hit something. Hey, and there're sorts of pictograms that even I can read. And one of them looks like doors." She pressed her fingers together, ditheringly, and felt totally out of her depth to be confronted with such technology. She could now feel a humming through the soles of her boots, low and not menacing. She told them about it.

"We hear, too," Zainal said, his voice encouraging.

"How many door pictograms?" Bert asked.

"Five."

"Do they differ in any way?"

"You mean in size? Yes."

"Try the smallest and see what happens."

Reluctantly she put her finger in the depression beside the small door. She heard a whoosh and saw a door panel swing open behind her.

"I've got access to the inside."

"Take a look around, then."

She did and come on to a blind corridor, wide and tall, cut into the rock. She reported.

"Try the next door glyph."

She did and heard a roar from both of them, then Bert's raucous "Open sesame!" She felt the cool air before she realized that she had inadvertently opened the outer door. She was overwhelmingly relieved, however, when Bert and Zainal entered the room.

Bert's face was a study—the eager boy on Christmas morning with all the games he'd asked Santa for—as he pored over the control panel. Zainal was more interested in the rectangles on the inner wall, looking for the way in to their innards.

"Well, here goes on the Big Daddy Bear," Bert said in a tone of decision and pressed the last of the line of "doors."

Immediately Zainal's comunit bleeped.

"Hey, man," and Joe's triumphant tones were audible to all three, "you did it. The main portal's sliding back inside the cliff, smooth as a baby's ass. And, wow!"

"What's inside?"

"Some kind of aircraft: one, no, two of 'em, parked in tandem. Stubby wings, looks like air-cushion jobs as I can't find any wheels, but I'd say they were atmospheric planes. Maybe for the Inspector General to have a look around, see if all the mechos are doing their jobs right. Hey, now, wait just a sec, there, Aarens . . ." Abruptly the transmission cut off.

Zainal leaped for the outer door, Bert and Kris almost bumping into each other to follow.

Over the bulge of the cliff, they couldn't see what was happening at the base by the garage until Zainal's unit beeped again.

"S'all right here," Joe said. "Sorry to panic but that fool got himself inside one of the planes and I didn't know what would happen."

"We need that fool up here," Zainal said, scowling, and Kris just wished that Aarens could see that expression: he'd take less risks if he had Zainal to account to.

While they awaited Aarens' arrival, Bert studied the panel hieroglyphics, trying to figure out what did what. There were only a few identifying signs that made any sense, the doors being one. Another was a line of six depressions, marked with a blunt-nosed object, some sort of a projectile. One space did not light up.

"Could have fired one off," Bert said. "A probe? Some kind of a capsule?"

"Or a torpedo," was Kris' guess.

"Yeah, could be any of those."

"Zainal?"

The Catteni came in to study the line, shaking his head after a few moments. The comunit bleeped.

"He won't go," Joe said, thoroughly disgusted.

"He won't go?" Zainal repeated, blinking.

"He won't climb up. Seems he's afraid of heights."

"Afraid of heights?" Zainal echoed, as if he didn't believe his ears, or thought he had misunderstood the words.

"Wouldn't you know?" Kris said.

"He will climb," Zainal said flatly. The look on his face boded no good for Aarens.

"I'll help," Kris said happily, looking forward to Aarens' reaction when he realized he couldn't pull that sort of an act on a Catteni.

They rappelled down, Kris reveling in the maneuver, for she'd always liked the exercise in her survival course. Joe and Sarah now had Aarens cornered in the garage, behind the two stubby-winged planes, nose-to-tail in the long building. The garage was much higher than it needed to be to accommodate just the two planes. The garage was also lit, so all its functions were controlled from above. Kris wondered if the planes were also remote-control devices. Maybe that was what the screens beside the control panels were for: remote viewing. Zainal now confronted Aarens, picked him up by the fold of his coverall, and was carrying him, one-handed, to the front.

"No, no, I tell you I won't go. I can't handle heights. I'll faint. I'll be sick all over you. . . ." Aarens was protesting, batting vainly at the hand that carried him.

"You are needed up. You will go up!" Zainal told him and then gestured at Joe to bring the spare rope.

Without actually releasing the now violently struggling mechanic, Zainal created a harness that strapped his arms tight to his chest, with loops under his arms to lift him. Then Zainal fastened the loose ends of the harness to himself and started up the rock face, hauling Aarens, who was flailing hard with his legs to impede his upward progress.

"You'd better use to your legs to keep from bruising yourself against the rock," Sarah suggested with objective indifference.

"Ah, I can't. I can't stand heights. Oh, god, oh, god, oh god," and he kept up that litany as Zainal inexorably hoisted him, dangling and banging against the cliff face. "Oh, god, oh, god."

Kris followed behind, not that she could have rescued Aarens, or even wanted to, or would need to since Zainal had the exercise under complete control.

"Oh god oh god, oh god," Aarens' voice rose to an hysterical pitch.

"Keep your eyes shut then, you damn fool," Kris advised. "Don't look. Don't look down. . . ."

Aarens did not become sick but he did have an episode of incontinence. Kris was able to move out of the way of it, which was as well, as it left a wet streak down the cliff.

The "oh god oh gods" became piteous and hoarse but Zainal ignored them and then Bert helped haul the terrified man up on to the shallow ledge and through to the door into the control room.

"Pull yourself together," Bert said with disgust to the quivering mechanic as he untied the ropes. Zainal was shrugging out of his harness. "This complex goes deep into the mountain, Zainal. Care to have a look?"

"No, I stay here," Zainal said, looking down at the sorry sight Aarens presented. "He must do work."

Kris was as glad to leave the close confines of the control room because Aarens' accident was smelling the place up. She didn't know how Zainal could stand it, but the door was left open and perhaps the wind at this height would clean the air and dry Aarens off.

Bert led her out of the control room, through one door, and then down a short flight of very wide steps with low risers. Lights came up, brightening slowly, as if slow from disuse, to the same orange glow that shone in the control room. They entered the first room and it was empty of everything but a sort of long pedestal table but no chairs or stools or anything to sit or rest on. The table did look used, with some edges smoothed and some scratches marring its surface. Scratches from what? Bert urged her to the room on one side.

"I don't know if these are beds or what," he said, pointing to large square platforms, built up a foot off the floor surface. "Much less this?" and he showed her an equally large room beyond, which had a square depression in its center with what seemed to a drain in the middle. "I can't find any water outlets or hoses or anything."

They prowled here and there about the rooms and decided that those that had the same built-in equipment might be sleeping accommodations. The purpose of others was not immediately apparent. Some had large rectangular coffers which defied their attempts to open them. The wall shelving was all above her shoulder height.

"Big creatures? Appendages at this level?" Kris asked, pretending to remove something from a shelf.

"Not been used in yonks," Bert allowed, scuffing the dust on the floor.

"I don't know *what* this is," Aarens voice said, issuing from somewhere near the ceiling. "No reaction anywhere."

Bert and Kris grinned at each other.

"Maybe we better tell them that they're on intercom," Kris said.

Bert shrugged. "Why?"

"Why are you touching the bullets?" Zainal was saying, a note of concern in his deep voice.

"They're for those torpedo-type gizmos on a rack in the garage," Aarens was saying in a smooth sly tone. "Could be . . ."

"Don't!" Zainal's command crackled.

Just then they heard a rumbling that echoed up from below. With one accord they ran back to the control room.

Zainal was standing over the prone body of Dick Aarens, his right hand still clenched in a fist. In his left hand he held the comunit, its on light glowing.

"I decked him," Zainal said. Then he pointed to the panel where one of the bullet depressions shone red.

Was red always the color of alarm?

"He pressed it. It go off."

"Thanks, Zainal," Joe's voice could be faintly heard from the comunit. "We moved. The right way. Thing launched in a blaze and we'd've been all too close to its exhaust. Wait till I get a hold of that Aarens!"

"You'll have to stand in line," Kris said, pulling the comunit over to her so that she could register her priority. "When he comes to, that is." She toed the prone body. "What did he think he was doing, Zainal?"

"Make trouble," Zainal said.

"Oh!" That was from Bert Put because Kris was shocked into immobility by the very thought of deliberately summoning the Mecho Makers, and having to answer to whatever used solid rock as a bed and ate at a table without sitting and had shoulder-high storage units.

"Oh, my god!" she finally said, leaning weakly against Zainal.

"Maybe good idea after all," he said at length, nodding his head. "Then we know worst, or best."

"How could it be best?" Kris asked, very glad when Zainal put a supporting arm around her, his fingers tightening briefly on her shoulder encouragingly.

"First, best to know. Second, fun to find out who makes mechos." He grinned at her exclamation of protest.

"If the condition of this place is any evidence, no one or no thing has been here in a long time, Zainal," Bert said, shaking his head. "Wish I could have seen it go," he added sorrowfully.

"Ask Joe when we get down again."

"And what do we do with sleeping beauty?" Kris asked, prodding Aarens' shoulder again.

Zainal took a deep breath and then let it out.

"It'd be more fun to lower him down when he knows he's up high," Bert said with a malicious expression on his usually pleasant face.

"And listen to the oh-god-oh-god-oh-gods for hours?" Kris said.

"Well, if I promise not to touch anything, can I stay up here and see if I can figure out any more of what that panel controls?" Bert asked.

Zainal shrugged and looked at Kris. "I don't see why not, NASA-man," she said with a grin.

"First, we report to Mitford," Zainal said.

"He's not going to like this," Kris said, shaking her head. "Especially since I think we were probably supposed to prevent just such a thing happening."

To her surprise, Mitford took somewhat the same attitude Zainal had: he wouldn't have authorized sending a message, if that was indeed what Aarens had managed to do. But he was, in a way, relieved that it had gone off.

"And if your guys are watching this planet, Zainal, it's going to give them a shock."

"There is that," Zainal replied.

"Should we come back to the Rock, sarge?" Kris asked.

"Might as well, but on your way back, check out the other sites on the part of the map I gave Bert." Then Mitford signed off.

IN THE END, ZAINAL LOWERED THE UNCONSCIOUS AARENS down the rock face, with Kris guiding the strapped body's descent. It wasn't what she'd rather have done with Aarens, but that would have been playing the game on his level. Sarah and Joe loaded up a sack of food, water, and furs which Zainal then hauled, more carefully, up to Bert. He would leave his comunit with Bert so the MS could stay in contact.

"Tell Bert there's no real rush for him to come down," Joe said to Zainal on the com, winking at Sarah in a conspiratorial fashion.

They decided not to untie the unconscious Aarens but put him in the Hopper, between the seats. Sarah flung his fur over him.

"It may stink in the morning but that's his problem," she said. "There's stew for supper," she added. "Just the four of us." Then Sarah smiled, a different sort of knowing smile. It didn't take a moment for Kris to catch on and she grinned back, nodding her head. "We could stand our watches together tonight. Be sort of cozy, wouldn't it?"

"Great idea," Kris said, her eyes wandering over the area to see where she would place hers and Zainal's blankets and furs. Certainly far enough away from Aarens to be able to ignore any complaints from him when he finally came to, and far enough not to impinge on the privacy of Joe and Sarah.

"I hear Catteni make great lovers," Sarah went on conversationally.

"You have?"

"Yeah. Back on earth, I knew a couple of girls who took up with Catteni . . . on purpose, to find out what they could," Sarah hastened to add.

"Ah, line of duty," Kris said.

"Well, the word I got was that giving out was not the hard part of the job." Sarah winked at Kris, and waited a moment, evidently wanting some indication of how Kris accepted the information. "In fact, they used to come home smiling. Oh, I know there were plenty yelling rape, and I heard all about Patti Sue, and I know some of the rougher types were brutal. But Zainal's different. Oh my word, but he's different and if I hadn't met Joe . . ." Sarah's smile was enviously wistful. Then her expression changed to her useful forthright candidness. "What I'm trying to say is, don't worry about liking Zainal that way, Kris. And I think you do like him."

"Hmmm. I think I do, too, Sarah. And thanks."

Then, while Sarah went back to the fire to stir the stew, Kris watched Zainal rappelling down the façade, his movements deft and graceful. But then she was accustomed to his size and she certainly was no longer going to be worried about what other people thought. Still it was good of Sarah to speak up as she had. Especially since a lot of people now on Botany had mentally paired Zainal and herself off a long time ago. She watched while he untethered himself, neatly coiled the rope for future use, and then entered the garage. She watched him have a good look at the launch tube that had released the capsule: at the other four sitting in their tubes. Ventilators had come on when the missile had surged out of the garage so that the fumes had dispersed, but he sniffed, trying to decided what fuel had been used, she thought. Then he inspected the rest of the puzzling cabinets, panels, and equipment. He settled himself on the sloping stubby wing of the last plane and took some bark paper and his carbon pencil out of a thigh pocket. She joined him when he began to make accurate sketches of the interior.

"Is Bert doing the same upstairs?"

"Up stairs?" Zainal asked, puzzled. When she pointed upward, he grinned. "Yes. We get it all down for Sarge. For report."

Kris liked watching Zainal work, the deft way his fingers moved, big but not clumsy. She thought of how they would move on her, while they stood their double watches that night, and shivered with anticipation.

He had considerable skill as a draftsman because he only needed a quick glance before he sketched in a whole section accurately: frowning as he held the sketch up against the model to be sure he had done it with precision.

"You're a man of many talents, aren't you, Zainal?" she said when he had finished the job.

"Not so many," he said in an abstracted tone. Then he put pencil and paper to one side and, catching her arm, pulled her against him, all his attention on her.

"How about standing a double watch with me tonight?" she asked almost coyly. She disliked "coy" because girls who are five foot ten don't do "coy" well, but Zainal had changed many of her attitudes.

He ruffled her hair, which was growing long again and would soon have to be braided or get in the way.

"I can possibly do that," he replied amiably.

"Sometimes, Zainal," she began, tsck-tscking in surprise, "you sound more American than I do."

"That's good?"

"I mean, it's great you've learned English so well so quickly."

"I like to learn something else quickly and well," he said and nuzzled her neck, biting her ever so gently.

"Are love bites part of a Catteni wooing?"

"Wooing?" he asked against her neck.

"Making love."

"I think so. I have not loved a Catten."

His phrasing made her catch her breath. If he hadn't loved a Catten, did he love her? *Don't be stupid, Kris girl. He's an Emassi where he comes from and has met Eosi. He's too important for a girl like you from ol' backwater-of-the-galaxy Terra.* But her arm, of its own accord, tightened around his neck and she kissed his cheek. His smooth cheek.

"Don't you Catteni ever need to shave?"

She had no idea what possessed her to ask a question like that then, but that was her all over.

He laughed down at her. "Shave? Ah, take off face hair. No face hair on Catteni." Then he rubbed his cheek against hers.

"HEY, YOU HAIRY LOT," Sarah called from the campfire, unaware of the topic of their conversation. "DINNER!"

Zainal slipped his arm about her waist and pushed her off toward the fire and their dinner.

"When we stand watch tonight, I do not think we *stand* long," he said so only she could hear him, "though of course it can be done that way, too."

"Whatever," she managed to reply though the idea fascinated her.

Over the stew, Joe Marley was full of speculation about the prospect of a reaction to the homing capsule.

"Maybe it is not homing," Zainal suggested.

"What else could it be?" Joe replied. "Nothing's been blown up anywhere, if it was a torpedo, or Mitford would have told us. Besides, those mothers are big, complex affairs. It was fueled, too, judging by the stink it left behind. So possibly it could be a homer."

"True."

"And maybe now we've got into this place," and Joe jerked his finger at the maw of the garage, the orange light so dim they could not even see the tail of the first plane, "we might figure out how to get into the seaside facility."

"Not if we have to take Aarens along with us to get it to open," Kris said firmly.

"Bert comes," Zainal said.

"If we have time for it before the Mecho Makers come back at us," Joe said gloomily.

"It could take decades for the homer to reach its destination."

"Then what good is a homer?" Joe demanded. "No, to be efficient, and these Mecho Makers are damned efficient engineers, it would have to reach home in a relatively short period of time." He wasn't happy at the thought of what response would be made.

"Why borrow trouble, Joe?" Kris asked.

"Well, it's only smart to think ahead, to plan for contingencies."

"That's Mitford's job," Kris said easily. "And Worry's. Let him do that for all of us." Her stomach was full and it was great to be able to lounge around the fire, close to Zainal, and know he was close to her and would be closer once they got Joe and Sarah off to their own bed.

"Honest, Zainal, d'you think we'll get a response soon?"

"We get one sooner from Catteni is my say," he said, hands clasped behind his head, his eyes gleaming gold in the firelight. He looked both alien and wonderfully familiar to Kris.

"Why? Would they have put up a satellite er something?"

They had to explain what kind of satellite Joe meant and Zainal agreed that Catteni had such equipment.

"But they do not yet believe in the Mecho Makers. Though maybe since . . ." and he paused, a slight frown creasing his forehead.

"Since that captain came?" Kris said, prompting.

Zainal grinned at her. "He believed and is able to act without order."

"Was he under Eosi orders to come here, then?"

Zainal shook his head. "He came to get me."

"But you were dropped and you stay," Sarah said teasingly.

Kris, who was aware that that had been a far more significant encounter than anyone else could know, glanced quickly at Zainal to see how he reacted.

"I stay," he said and then grinned.

"But he might have activated a warning device?" Joe asked, getting the matter straight in his own mind.

"That is possible."

"So they would know something's been launched."

Zainal nodded.

"Maybe they won't drop any more unwilling pioneers on us then," Sarah said hopefully.

Zainal chuckled. "They had more Terrans to drop in safe place. Many more."

"Oh, lord, however will we manage?" Sarah cried.

"We've done very well so far," Kris said with some asperity. Sarah and Joe were late droppers-in and acting as if they'd been here all along. *Well, what's wrong with that?* Kris chided herself. *At least they want to be part of this crazy colony.*

"So we have," and Zainal unfolded himself from the ground. "We take first watch," he added casually.

"No, you'd fall asleep after all that lugging of bodies up and down that cliff face," Joe said as casually.

"We should do something about feeding Aarens," Sarah remarked with no enthusiasm for the task. "And changing him or that Hopper will sure stink tomorrow."

"He's not awake," Zainal said with a shrug.

"You didn't hit him too hard, did you, Zainal?" Kris asked wistfully.

"Naw," Joe answered. "I've been checking him. Zainal just decked him right proper, that's all. Something we've all wanted to do, I might add."

"Oh god oh god oh god, not you, too?" Kris said mischievously. That brought a laugh from the others.

The comunit beeped and Joe answered it. "Bert . . . checking in, are you? . . . Naw, we wouldn't go off and leave you to explain to the Mecho Makers. We're about ready to sack out now. Found nothing new, all right . . . Oh . . . Well, we have had a day full of surprises, at that. You'll stand first watch? Oh, that's good of you, mate. You got the place to watch from all right. Over and out." Then he grinned at Zainal. "He's first watch. He'll wake me. And I'll wake you. I'll check Aarens again now."

"Just give me a shout," Zainal said. He held out his hand to Kris, who let him pull her up and into his arms as Sarah disappeared into the dark after Joe. In the firelight, his eyes were golden. "I do not know your thought, Bjornsen," he said, "but I am lucky you were in the thornbushes of Barevi."

"You think you were lucky? After all that's happened since then?" She leaned back against his arms to catch the look in his eyes.

"You change my life. Not many change a Catteni."

"No, I don't think many do," she could agree wholeheartedly.

"Now, there is a long time before we *stand* our watch." There was devilment in his yellow eyes as he looked down at her. "What shall we do with all that time by ourselves?"

"Hmmm, oh, I think we can find something to do."

And, of course, they did.

L'envoi

SERGEANT CHUCK MITFORD KEPT TO HIM-
self the news that Aarens had sent off what appeared to be a homing projectile. Damn the man!
Just like him to act with malicious intent. Before
he'd heard who was leading the patrol, he'd been
eager for the expedition to the putative control
facility. Another chance to show off how clever
Dick Aarens was. And the man did have a genuine
mechanical bent. All the experts agreed. But that
didn't keep him from being a royal pain in the
butt! And he'd been equally eager to devolunteer
when he knew that he'd have to deal with Zainal.
And that the Bjornsen girl was part of the team.

"D'you know about *them?*" Aarens had ranted.
"D'you know she's *sleeping* with that Cat?"

"If she is, it's her own business, Aarens, and I
wouldn't put on that innocent look were I you,"
Mitford had replied. "You're quite the lover boy on
your own, aren't you? However, I'm warning you, I

get one more complaint of harassment and, not only will I put you in the stocks every night so we'll know where you are, I'll get Dane to castrate you. Get me?"

"You wouldn't dare?" That had shaken the mechanical genius because he knew all too well by now that Mitford did not make false promises.

So Aarens had taken the initiative the first chance he saw. But then, there would have been no message *in* the homing device, if that's what it was. Perhaps the Mecho Makers would ignore its return. False alarm.

Mitford sighed and linked his fingers behind his head. He'd hate for all he'd built out of sfa here on Botany to go down the tubes. He was rather proud of what the order he'd been able to achieve out of nothing. And it had been pure heaven to be without any smartass captains and lieutenants with their smartass West Point training to tell him half of what he did wasn't in the Book. Well, it wasn't because he was writing this book himself.

He hadn't wanted the job but he'd come to enjoy it. Starting off fresh and making one world the way it should be. Not many men get that chance.

Tomorrow morning, he'd start on contingency plans. One thing sure, they might be in for some serious trouble from the Mech Makers for messing up their machines. They'd probably have to leave the garages and barn facilities, so he'd better scout for more caves where they could hide and carry on in spite of owner occupation.

And then there were the Catteni. Would they maybe have dumped some sort of a satellite spy eye to orbit the planet? To see if there was any contact with a technically advanced species who had a prior claim on the planet? He'd have to check with Zainal. Mitford had a hunch that more went on in that early morning meeting with the Emassi ship than Zainal had reported. But he respected Zainal far too much to grill him. That guy was honorable and people were beginning to see him in that light. Which was another load off Mitford's shoulders. If the Emassi were up to something that would affect Botany, Mitford was pretty certain Zainal would level with him.

Mitford grunted and muttered to himself, "I drop, I stay." And chuckled. Glad he hadn't listened to those who'd wanted to waste the Catteni on that field.

He wasn't all that happy that the Bjornsen girl had taken up with him, though. He'd've fancied her himself. A leader had a few privileges. Damned few.

He suspected nothing was going to change the Catteni's plans for Botany. This was such a convenient dumping spot for all the troublesome dissidents the Catteni couldn't handle on Earth . . . and Barevi.

Well, possession is nine-tenths of the law. Only what law applied to Botany? He'd make it his if he could. He was getting pretty good at this governing business. Making a better show than either Democrats or Republicans ever had.

Or would they all be caught into between two master races . . . the mysterious Eosi and the even more unknown quantity of the Mech Makers? Could be interesting. Could be fatal. Well, he wouldn't worry about that. This was a large continent.

He must remember to get in more bark sheets or have someone start to manufacture paper. They'd need more copies of the maps, geographical and spatial. Surely there was someone among his lot of individuals who knew how to make decent paper! He fumbled at his breast pocket, got out the slip of bark he kept there and one of the newer, more streamlined pencils and jotted down a note. There! Tomorrow he'd start figuring out how to cope with invasions. Would he, as planetary leader, get a chance to confront representatives of either faction? Hmmm. Maybe he could get them to accept a compromise? They turn the planet over to him. Fat chance of that but Mitford chuckled at his presumption. ASS-U-ME, he thought, remembering the old axiom of assuming too much. Whatever!

He'd get his six hours' sleep first, get his mind rested for the duties of the morning. Operation Fresh Start, as he had facetiously called it on the morning he had "assumed" command of this mixed bag of individuals, was moving into a new phase and he'd better be ready for it. So he turned over, socked the fluff-filled pillow into proper order, and slept.

THE LAUNCH HAD BEEN OBSERVED. THE SPATIAL DIRECTION OF the torpedo noted, and the report forwarded to those concerned with such matters.